Praise for Anne Perry and

DEATH OF A STRANGER

"For sheer storytelling, you can never do better than Anne Perry. Rich in characters, period detail, and surprising plot twists, her latest proves that this author is yet at her most skillful."
—*Alfred Hitchcock's Mystery Magazine*

"Perry has written another compelling story of greed, cunning, and passion, featuring characters that readers have come to know and love."
—*Library Journal*

"[A] master of crime fiction who rarely fails to deliver a strong story and a colorful cast of characters."
—*The Baltimore Sun*

"[Perry] offers an ingenious and baffling plot, compelling characters, both major and minor, plus plenty of courtroom drama."
—*Publishers Weekly*

"[A] tour de force . . . The plot steams along to a heart-stopping climax."
—*Booklist* (boxed and starred review)

By Anne Perry
Published by Ballantine Books

DEATH OF A
STRANGER

ANNE PERRY

BALLANTINE BOOKS • NEW YORK

A Ballantine Book
Published by The Random House Publishing Group
Copyright © 2002 by Anne Perry
This book contains an excerpt from *No Graves As Yet* by Anne Perry, published by Ballantine Books. Copyright © 2003 by Anne Perry

www.ballantinebooks.com

ISBN 0-345-44006-4

Manufactured in the United States of America

First Hardcover Edition: October 2002
First Mass Market International Edition: January 2003
First Mass Market Domestic Edition: September 2003

OPM 10 9 8 7 6 5 4 3 2 1

To David Thompson,
for his friendship and his profound help

Author's Note

All characters are fictional except William Colman, who won the right to be mentioned as a character in the story, but of course his words and actions in this are invented by me. I hope they are acceptable to him.

DEATH OF A STRANGER

Prologue

Monk stood on the embankment staring at the lights reflected on the misty waters of the Thames as dusk settled over the city. He had solved his latest case to the satisfaction of his client, and twenty guineas were sitting comfortably in his pocket. Behind him, coaches and carriages moved through the spring evening and the sound of laughter punctuated the clip of hooves and jingle of harness.

It was too far from here to Fitzroy Street for Monk to walk home, and a hansom was an unnecessary expense. The omnibus would do very well. There was no hurry because Hester would not be there. This was one of the nights when she worked at the house in Coldbath Square which had been set up with Callandra Daviot's money in order to give medical help to women of the streets who had been injured or become ill, mostly in the course of their trade.

He was proud of the work Hester did, but he missed her company in the evenings. It startled him how deeply, since his marriage, he had been accustomed to sharing his thoughts with her, to her laughter, her ideas, or simply to looking across the room and seeing her there. There was a warmth in the house that was missing when she was gone.

How unlike his old self that was! In the past he would not have shared the core inside him with anyone, nor allowed someone to become important enough to him that her presence could make or mar his life. He was surprised how much he preferred the man he had become.

1

Thinking of medical help, and Callandra's assistance, turned his mind to the last murder he had dealt with, and to Kristian Beck, whose life had been torn apart by it. Beck had discovered things about himself and his wife which had overturned his beliefs, even the foundations of his own identity. His entire heritage had not been what he had assumed, nor his culture, his faith, or the core of who he was.

Monk understood in a unique way Beck's shock and the numbing confusion that had gripped him. A coaching accident nearly seven years before had robbed Monk of his own memory before that, and forced on him the need to re-create his identity. He had deduced much about himself from unarguable evidence, and while some things were admirable, there were too many that displeased him and lay shadowed across the yet unknown.

Even in his present happiness the vast spaces of ignorance troubled him from time to time. Kristian's shattering discoveries had woken new doubts in Monk, and a painful awareness that he knew almost nothing of his roots or the people and the beliefs that had cradled him.

He was Northumbrian, from a small seaboard town where his sister, Beth, still lived. He had lost touch with her, which was his own fault, partly out of fear of what she would tell him of himself, partly because he simply felt alienated from a past he could no longer recall. He felt no bond with that life or its cares.

Beth could have told him about his parents and probably his grandparents too. But he had not asked.

Should he try now, when it mattered more urgently, to build a bridge back to her so he could learn? Or might he find, like Kristian, that his heritage was nothing like his present self and he was cut off from his own people? He might find, as Kristian had, that their beliefs and their morality cut against the grain of his own.

For Kristian, the past he believed and that had given him identity had been wrenched out of his hands, shown to be a fabrication created out of the will to survive, easy to understand but not to admire, and bitterly hard to own.

If Monk were at last to know himself as most people do automatically—the religious ties, the allegiances, the family loves and hates—might he, too, discover a stranger inside his skin, and one he could not like?

He turned away from the river and walked along the footpath toward the nearest place where he could cross the street through the traffic and catch the omnibus home.

Perhaps he would write to Beth again, but not yet. He needed to know more. Kristian's experience weighed on him and would not let him rest. But he was also afraid, because the possibilities were too many, and too disturbing, and what he had created was too dear to risk.

1

THERE WAS A NOISE outside the women's clinic in Coldbath Square. Hester was on night duty. She turned from the stove as the street door opened, the wood still in her hand. Three women stood in the entrance, half supporting each other. Their cheap clothes were torn and splattered with blood, their faces streaked with it, skin yellow in the light from the gas lamp on the wall. One of them, her fair hair coming loose from an untidy knot, held her left hand as if she feared the wrist were broken.

The middle woman was taller, her dark hair loose, and she was gasping, finding it difficult to get her breath. There was blood on the torn front of her satin dress and smeared across her high cheekbones.

The third woman was older, well into her thirties, and there were bruises purpling on her arms, her neck, and her jaw.

"Hey, missus!" she said, urging the others inside, into the warmth of the long room with its scrubbed board floor and whitewashed walls. "Mrs. Monk, yer gotter give us an 'and again. Kitty 'ere's in a right mess. An' me, an' all. An' I think as Lizzie's broke 'er wrist."

Hester put down the wood and came forward, glancing only once behind her to make sure that Margaret was already getting hot water, cloths, bandages, and the herbs to steep, which would make cleaning the wounds easier and less painful. It was the purpose of this place to care for women of the streets who were injured or ill, but who could not pay a

4

doctor and would be turned away from more respectable charities. It had been the idea of her friend Callandra Daviot, and Callandra had provided the initial funds before events in her personal life had taken her out of London. It was through her also that Hester had met Margaret Ballinger, desperate to escape a respectable but uninteresting proposal of marriage. Her undertaking work like this had alarmed the gentleman in question so much he had at the last moment balked at making the offer, to Margaret's relief and her mother's chagrin.

Now Hester guided the first woman to one of the chairs in the center of the floor beside the table. "Come in, Nell," she urged. "Sit down." She shook her head. "Did Willie beat you again? Surely you could find a better man?" She looked at the bruises on Nell's arms, plainly made by a gripping hand.

"At my age?" Nell said bitterly, easing herself into the chair. "C'mon, Mrs. Monk! Yer mean well, I daresay, but yer feet in't on the ground. Not unless yer offerin' that nice-lookin' ol' man o' yours?" She leered ruefully. "Then I might take yer up one day. 'E's got an air about 'im as 'e could be summat real special. Kind o' mean but fun, if yer know wot I'm sayin'?" She gave a guffaw of laughter which turned into a racking cough, and she bent double over her knees as the paroxysm shook her.

Without being asked, Margaret poured a little whiskey out of a bottle, replaced the cork, and added hot water from the kettle. Wordlessly she held it until Nell had controlled herself sufficiently to take it, the tears still streaming down her face. She struggled for breath, sipped some of the whiskey, gagged, and then took a deeper gulp.

Hester turned to the woman called Kitty and found her staring with wide, horrified eyes, her body tense, muscles so tight her shoulders all but tore the thin fabric of her bodice.

"Mrs. Monk?" she whispered huskily. "Your husband . . ."

"He's not here," Hester assured her. "There's no one here who will hurt you. Where are you injured?"

Kitty did not reply. She was shuddering so violently her teeth chattered.

"Go on, yer silly cow!" Lizzie said impatiently. "She won't

'urt yer, an' she won't tell no one nuffin'. Nell's only goin' on
'cos she fancies 'er ol' man. Proper gent, 'e is. Smart as a whip.
Dresses like the tailor owed 'im, not t'other way 'round." She
nursed her broken wrist, wincing with pain. "Get on wiv it,
then. You may 'ave got all night—I in't."

Kitty looked once at the iron beds, five along each side of
the room, the stone sinks at the far end, and the buckets and
ewers of water drawn from the well at the corner of the
square. Then she faced Hester, making an intense effort to
control herself.

"I got in a fight," she said quietly. "It's not that bad. I daresay I was frightened as much as anything." Her voice was surprising: it was low and a trifle husky, and her diction was
clear. At one time she must have had some education. It
struck in Hester a note of pity so sharp that for a moment it
was all she could think of. She tried not to let it show in her
expression. The woman did not want the intrusion of pity. She
would be only too aware of her own fall from grace without
anyone else's notice of it.

"Those are bad bruises on your neck." Hester looked at
them more closely. It appeared as if someone had held her by
the throat, and there was a deep graze across the front of her
breastbone, as though a hard fingernail had scored it deliberately. "Is that blood yours?" Hester asked, indicating the
splatters across the front of Kitty's bodice.

Kitty gave a shuddering sigh. "No. No! I . . . I reckon I
caught his nose when I hit him back. It's not mine. I'll be all
right. Nell's bleeding. You should see to that. And Lizzie
broke her wrist, or somebody did." She spoke generously, but
she was still shivering, and Hester was certain she was far
from well enough to leave. She would have liked to know
what bruises were hidden under her clothes, or what beatings
she had endured in the past, but she did not ask questions. It
was one of the rules; they had all agreed that no one pressed
for personal information or repeated what they overheard or
deduced. The whole purpose of the house was simply to offer
such medical help as lay within their skill, or that of Mr.
Lockhart, who called by every so often and could be reached

easily enough in an emergency. He had failed his medical exams at the very end of his training through a weakness for drink rather than ignorance or inability. He was happy enough to help in return for company, a little kindness, and the feeling that he belonged somewhere.

He liked to talk, to share food he had been given rather than paid for, and when he was short of funds he slept on one of the beds.

Margaret offered Kitty a hot whiskey and water, and Hester turned to look at Nell's deep gash.

"That'll have to be stitched," she advised.

Nell winced. She had experienced Hester's needlework before.

"Otherwise it will take a long time to heal," Hester warned.

Nell pulled a face. "If yer stitchin's still like yer stitched me 'and, they'd throw yer out of a bleedin' sweatshop," she said good-humoredly. "All it wants is buttons on it!" She drew in her breath between her teeth as Hester pulled the cloth away from the wound and it started to bleed again. "Jeez!" Nell said, her face white. "Be careful, can't yer? Yer got 'ands like a damn navvy!"

Hester was accustomed to the mild abuse and knew it was only Nell's way of covering her fear and her pain. This was the fourth time she had been there in the month and a half since the house had been open.

"Yer'd think since yer'd looked arter soldiers in the Crimea wi' Florence Nightingale an' all, yer'd be a bit gentler, wouldn't yer?" Nell went on. "I bet yer snuffed as many o' our boys as the fightin' ever did. 'Oo paid yer then? The Russkies?" She looked at the needle Margaret had threaded with gut for Hester. Her face went gray and she swiveled her head to avoid seeing the point go through her flesh.

"Keep looking at the door," Hester advised. "I'll be as quick as I can."

"That supposed ter make me feel better?" Nell demanded. "Yer got that bleedin' fat leech comin' in 'ere again."

"I beg your pardon?"

"Jessop!" Nell said with stinging contempt as the street

door closed again and a large, portly man in a frock coat and brocade waistcoat stood just inside, stamping his feet as if to force water off them, although in fact it was a perfectly dry night.

"Good evening, Mrs. Monk," he said unctuously. "Miss Ballinger." His eyes flickered over the other three women, his lips slightly curled. He made no comment, but in his face was his superiority, his comfortable amusement, the ripple of interest in them which he resented, and would have denied hotly. He looked Hester up and down. "You are a very inconvenient woman to find, ma'am. I don't care for having to walk the streets at this time of night in order to meet with you. I can tell you that with total honesty."

Hester made a very careful stitch in Nell's arm. "I hope you tell me everything with total honesty, Mr. Jessop," she said coldly and without looking up at him.

Nell shifted slightly and sniggered, then turned it into a yell as she felt the thread of gut pulling through her flesh.

"For goodness sake be quiet, woman!" Jessop snapped, but his eyes followed the needle with fascination. "Be grateful that you are being assisted. It is more than most decent folk would do for you." He forced his attention away. "Now, Mrs. Monk, I dislike having to discuss my affairs in front of these unfortunates, but I cannot wait around for you to have time to spare." He put his thumbs in the pockets of his red brocade waistcoat.

"As I am sure you are aware, it is quarter to one in the morning and I have a home to go to. We need to reconsider our arrangements." He freed one hand and flicked it at the room in general. "This is not the best use of property, you know. I am doing you a considerable service in allowing you to rent these premises at such a low rate." He rocked very slightly back and forth on the balls of his feet. "As I say, we must reconsider our arrangement."

Hester held the needle motionless and looked at him. "No, Mr. Jessop, we must keep precisely to our arrangement. It was made and witnessed by the lawyers. It stands."

"I have my reputation to consider," he went on, his eyes

moving for a moment to each of the women, then back to Hester.

"A reputation for charity is good for anyone," she returned, beginning very carefully to stitch again. This time Nell made no sound at all.

"Ah, but there's charity . . . and charity." Jessop pursed his lips and resumed the very slight rocking, his thumbs back in his waistcoat pockets. "There's some as are more deserving than others, if you take my meaning?"

"I'm not concerned with deserving, Mr. Jessop," she replied. "I'm concerned with needing. And that woman"—she indicated Lizzie—"has broken bones which have to be set. We cannot pay you any more, nor should we." She tied the last stitch and looked up to meet his eyes. The thought passed through her mind that they resembled boiled sweets, to be specific, those usually known as humbugs. "A reputation for not keeping his word is bad for a man of business," she added. "In fact, any man at all. And it is good, especially in an area like this, to be trusted."

His face hardened until it was no longer even superficially benign. His lips were tight, his cheeks blotchy. "Are you threatening me, Mrs. Monk?" he said quietly. "That would be most unwise, I can assure you. You need friends, too." He mimicked her tone. "Especially in an area like this."

Before Hester could speak, Nell glared up at Jessop. "You watch yer lip, mister. You might knock around tarts like us." She used the word viciously, as he might have said it. "But Mrs. Monk's a lady, an' wot's more, 'er 'usband used ter be a rozzer, an' now 'e does it private, like, fer anyone as wants it. But that don't mean 'e in't got friends in places wot counts." Admiration gleamed in her eyes, and a harsh satisfaction. "An' 'e's as 'ard as they come w'en 'e needs ter be. If 'e took ter yer nasty, yer'd wish as yer'd never bin born! Ask some o' yer thievin' friends if they'd like ter cross William Monk. Garn, I dare yer! Wet yerself at the thought, yer would!"

The dull color washed up Jessop's face, but he did not reply to her. He glared at Hester. "You wait till renewal time, Mrs.

Monk! You'll be looking for something else, and I'll be warning other propertied men just what sort of a tenant you are. As to Mr. Monk . . ." He spat the words this time. "He can speak to all the police he likes! I've got friends, too, and not all of them are so nice!"

"Garn!" Nell said in mock amazement. "An' 'ere was us thinkin' as yer meant 'Er Majesty, an' all!"

Jessop turned, and after giving Hester one more icy stare he opened the door and let the cold air in off the cobbled square, damp in the early-spring night. The dew was slick on the stones, shining under the gaslight twenty yards away, showing the corner of the end house—grimy, eaves dark and dripping, guttering crooked.

He left the door open behind him and walked smartly down Bath Street toward the Farringdon Road.

"Bastard!" Nell said in disgust, then looked down at her arm. "Yer improvin'," she said grudgingly.

"Thank you," Hester acknowledged with a smile.

Nell suddenly grinned back. "Yer all right, you are! If that fat sod gives yer any trouble, like, let us know. Willie might knock me around a bit, wot's out o' place, but 'e'd be good fer beatin' that slimy pig, an' all."

"Thank you," Hester said seriously. "I'll keep it in mind. Would you like more tea?"

"Yeah! An' a drop o' life in it, too." Nell held out the cup.

"Rather less life this time," Hester directed as Margaret, hiding a smile, obeyed.

Hester moved her attention to Lizzie, who was looking increasingly anxious as her turn approached. Setting her broken bone was going to be very painful. Anesthetic had been available for more serious operations for several years. It made all sorts of deep incisions possible, such as those needed to remove stones from the bladder, or a diseased appendix. But for injuries like this, and for people unable or unwilling to go to a hospital, there was still no help but a stiff dose of alcohol and such herbs as dulled the awareness of pain.

Hester talked all the time, about anything and nothing—the weather, local peddlers and what they were selling—in order to distract Lizzie's attention as much as possible. She worked quickly. She was accustomed to the terrible wounds of the battlefield, where there was no anesthetic and not always brandy, except to clean a blade. Speed was the only mercy available. This time there was no broken skin, nothing to see but the crooked angle and the pain in Lizzie's face. Hester touched the wrist lightly, and heard the gasp, then the retching as the raw ends of bone grated. With one swift, decisive movement, she brought the ends together and held them while Margaret, gritting her teeth, bound the wrist as firmly as she could without stopping the blood to the hand.

Lizzie retched again. Hester handed her the whiskey and hot water, this time with an infusion of herbs added. It was bitter, but the alcohol and the heat would ease her, and in time the herbs would settle her stomach and give her a little sleep.

"Stay here tonight," Hester said gently, standing up and putting her arm around Lizzie as she rose unsteadily to her feet. "We need to see that bandage stays all right. If your hand swells up a lot we'll have to loosen it," she added, slowly guiding her over to the closest bed while Margaret pulled back the covers for her.

Lizzie looked at Hester in horror, her face bloodless.

"The bone will be fine," Hester assured her. "Just take care not to knock it." As she spoke, she eased Lizzie onto the bed, bent and took her shoes off, then lifted her legs and feet up until she was lying back against the pillows. Margaret pulled the covers over her.

"Lie there for a bit," Hester advised. "Then if you want to get into bed properly, I'll come and give you a nightshirt."

Lizzie nodded. "Thank you, miss," she said with profound sincerity. She struggled for a moment to find words to add, and then merely smiled.

Hester went back to where Kitty was sitting, waiting patiently for her turn. She had an interesting face: strong features and a wide, passionate mouth, not pretty in the usual sense, but well proportioned. She had not been on the streets long enough for her skin to be marred, or sallow from poor food and too much alcohol. Hester wondered briefly what domestic tragedies had brought her there.

She looked at her injuries. They were mostly rapidly darkening bruises, as if she had been in a struggle with someone but it had not lasted long enough to do her the damage that Nell and Lizzie had suffered. The deep graze on her breastbone needed cleaning, but no stitches would help. It was not bleeding much, and a little ointment to aid healing would be sufficient. The bruises would hurt for some time to come, but arnica would ease that.

Margaret brought more hot water and clean cloths, and Hester began to work as gently as she could. Kitty barely winced when Hester touched the graze, cleaning away the blood, which was now dried, and exposing the raw, torn edges of the skin. As always, Hester did not ask how it happened. Pimps quite often disciplined their women if they thought they were not working hard enough, or were keeping back too big a part of their earnings. Vicious fights between one woman and another happened now and again, mostly over territory. It was best not to appear inquisitive, and anyway, the knowledge would be of no use to her. All the wounded were treated much the same, however their hurts were incurred.

When Hester had done all she could for Kitty, and given her a cup of strong, sweet tea laced with a very small drop of whiskey, Kitty thanked her and went back out into the night, pulling her shawl tighter around her. They saw her go across the square, head high, and disappear into the black shadow of the prison to the north.

"I dunno." Nell shook her head. "She shouldn't be out on the street. In't fer 'er sort, poor bitch!"

There was nothing useful to say. A hundred different circumstances took women into prostitution, often only to supplement a too-meager income from something else. But it all stemmed from the eternal struggle for money.

Nell looked at her. "You keep a still tongue, don't yer! Ta, missus. I'll be seein' yer again, I 'spec'." She squinted a little at Hester, regarding her with wry kindness. "If I can 'elp yer sometime . . ." She left the sentence unfinished, shrugging very slightly. Nodding to Margaret, she went out as well, closing the door quietly behind her.

Hester caught Margaret's eye and saw the flash of humor and pity in her expression. There was no need for words; they had already said all there was to say. They were there to heal, not to preach to women whose lives they only partially understood. At first Margaret had wanted to change things, to speak what she saw as truth, guided by her own beliefs. Gradually she had begun to realize how little she knew of her own hungers, except that to be tied in a convenient marriage where the emotion was no more than a mutual respect and courtesy would be a denial of everything inside her. It might seem comfortable to begin with, but as time passed and she stifled the dreams within her, she would come to feel her husband was her jailer, and then despise herself for her own dishonesty. The choice was hers; no one else was to blame.

She made it, and stepped into the unknown, aware that she was closing doors she might later regret, and which after that could never be opened again. She did not often wonder what she had given away, but there had been long nights with few patients when she and Hester talked frankly, and even touched on the prices of different kinds of loneliness, those that were perceived by others and those that were masked in marriage and family. All choice was risk, but for Margaret, as for Hester, accommodation to half-truths was impossible.

"For his sake, I can't do that!" Margaret had said with a self-conscious laugh. "Poor man deserves better than that. I'd despise myself for it, and him for letting me." Then she had gone for a bucket and water to scrub the floor, as she did now, and together they cleared up and put away the unused bandages and ointments, then took turns in snatching a little sleep.

Two other women came in before morning. The first needed two stitches in her leg, which Hester did quickly and efficiently. The second was cold and angry and badly bruised. A mug of hot tea, again mildly laced with whiskey and a little tincture of arnica, and she felt ready to return to her room and face the coming day, probably most of it asleep.

Dawn came clear and quite mild, and by eight o'clock Hester was eating toast and drinking a cup of fresh tea when the street door opened and a constable was silhouetted against the sunlight. Without asking, he came in.

"Mrs. Monk?" His tone was heavy and a little sharp. The police hardly ever came to the house. They were not welcome, and had been told so in unmistakable terms. Largely they respected what was done there, and were happy enough, if they wished to speak to any of the women, to wait and do it in some other place. What could have brought him there this morning, and at eight o'clock?

Hester put down her mug and stood. "Yes?" She had seen him several times on the street. "What is it, Constable Hart?"

He closed the door behind him and took off his helmet. In the light his face looked tired, not merely from a sleepless night on duty, but from an indefinable weariness within. Something had bruised him, disturbed him.

"You 'ad any women in 'ere last night that were knocked about, cut mebbe, or beat bad?" he asked. He glanced at the teapot on the table, swallowed, and looked back at Hester.

"We do most nights," she replied. "Stabs, broken bones, bruises, disease. In bad weather the women are sometimes just cold. You know that!"

He took a deep breath and sighed, pushing his hand through his receding hair. "Someone in a real fight, Mrs. Monk. I wouldn't ask if I didn't 'ave to. Jus' tell me, eh?"

"Would you like a cup of tea?" She evaded the answer for a moment. "Or toast?"

He hesitated. His exhaustion was plain in his face. "Yeah . . . ta," he accepted, sitting down opposite her.

Hester reached for the teapot and poured a second mug. "Toast?"

He nodded.

"Jam?" she offered.

His eyes went to the table. His face relaxed in a rueful smile. "You got black currant!" he noticed, his voice soft.

"You'd like some?" It was a rhetorical question. The answer was obvious. Margaret was still asleep, and making the toast would give Hester a little more time to think, so she was happy to do it.

She came back to the table with two slices, and buttered one for herself and one for him, then pushed the jam over to him. He took a liberal spoonful, put it on the toast and ate it with evident appreciation.

"You 'ad someone," he said after several moments, looking at her almost with apology.

"I had three," she replied. "At about a quarter to one, or about then. One later, three o'clock or so, and another an hour after that."

"All in fights?"

"Looked like it. I didn't ask. I never do. Why?"

Hester waited, watching him. There were hollows under his eyes as if he had lost too many nights' sleep, and there was dust and what looked like blood on his sleeves. When she looked further, there was more on the legs of his trousers. His hand, holding the mug, was scratched, and one fingernail was torn. It should have been painful, but he seemed unaware of it. She was touched by both pity and a cold air of fear. "Why did you come?" she asked aloud.

He put down the mug. "There's been a murder," he replied. "In Abel Smith's brothel over in Leather Lane."

"I'm sorry," she said automatically. Whoever it was, such a thing was sad, the waste of two lives, a grief to even more. But murders were not unheard of in an area like this, or dozens of others in London much the same. Narrow alleys and squares lay a few yards behind teeming streets, but it was a different world of pawnbrokers, brothels, sweatshops, and crowded tenements smelling of middens and rotting timber. Prostitution was a dangerous occupation, primarily because of the risk of disease and, if you lived long enough, starvation when you became too old to practice—at thirty-five or forty.

"Why did you come here?" Hester asked. "Was somebody else attacked as well?"

He looked at her, his eyes narrow, his lips pulled tight. It was an expression of understanding and misery, not contempt.

"Dead person wasn't a woman," he explained. "Wouldn't expect you to be able to 'elp me if it was. Although sometimes they fight each other, but not to kill, far as I know. Never seen it, anyway."

"A man?" She was surprised. "You think a pimp killed him? What happened? Someone drunk, do you suppose?"

He sipped his tea again, letting the hot liquid ease his throat. "Don't know. Abel swears it in't anything to do with 'is girls. . . ."

"Well, he would, wouldn't he?" She dismissed the idea without even weighing it.

Hart would not let it go so quickly. "Thing is, Mrs. Monk, the dead man was a toff . . . I mean a real toff. You should 'ave seen 'is clothes. I know quality. An' clean. 'Is 'ands were clean too, nails an' all. An' smooth."

"Do you know who he was?"

He shook his head. "No. Someone pinched 'is money an' calling cards, if 'e 'ad any. But someone'll miss 'im. We'll find out."

"Even men like that have been known to use prostitutes," she said reasonably.

"Yeh, but not Abel Smith's sort," he replied. "Not that that's what matters," he added quickly. "Thing is, a man like that gets murdered an' we'll be expected to get whoever did it in double quick time, an' there'll still be a lot o' shouting an' wailing to clean up the area, get rid o' prostitution and make the streets safe for decent people, like." He said this with ineffable contempt—not a sneer of the lips or raising of his voice, just a soft, immeasurable disgust.

"Presumably if he'd stayed at home with his wife, he'd still be alive," Hester responded sourly. "But I can't help you. Why do you think a woman was hurt and could know something about it? Or that she'd dare tell you if she did?"

"You thinking 'er pimp did it?" He raised his eyebrows.

"Aren't you?" she countered. "Why would a woman kill him? And how? Was he stabbed? I don't know any women who carry knives or who attack their clients. Fingernails or teeth are about the worst I've heard of."

" 'Eard of?" he questioned.

She smiled with a slight downward curl of her lips. "Men don't come here."

"Just women, eh?"

"For medical reasons," she explained. "Anyway, if a man's been bitten or scratched by a prostitute, what are we going to do for him?"

"Beyond have a good laugh—nothing," he agreed. Then his expression became grave again. "But this man's dead, Mrs. Monk, an' from the look of the body, 'e got 'imself in a fight with a woman, an' then somehow or other 'e came off worst. 'E's got cuts an' gashes in 'is back, an' so many broken bones it's hard to know where to begin."

She was startled. She had imagined a fight between two men ending in tragedy, perhaps the larger or heavier one striking an unlucky blow, or possibly the smaller one resorting to a weapon, probably a knife.

"But you said he was robbed," she pointed out, thinking now of an attack by several men. "Was he set on by a gang?"

"That don't 'appen 'round these streets." Hart dismissed it. "That's what pimps are for. They make their money out of willing trade. It's in their interest to keep the customers safe."

"So why is this one dead?" she said quietly, beginning to understand now why Hart had come there. "Why would one of the women kill him? And how, if he was beaten the way you describe?"

Hart bit his lip. "Actually, more like 'e fell," he answered.

"Fell?" She did not immediately understand.

"From an 'eight," he explained. "Like down stairs, mebbe."

Suddenly it was much clearer. If a man had been caught off balance, not expecting it, a woman could easily have pushed him.

"But what about the cuts and gashes you spoke of?" she asked. "You don't get those falling down stairs."

"There was a lot o' broken glass around," he replied. "An' blood—lots of it. Could 'ave smashed a glass, dropped it an' then fallen on it, I suppose." He looked miserable as he said it, almost as if it were a personal tragedy. He pushed his hand back through his hair again, a gesture of infinite weariness. "But Abel swears 'e was never at 'is place, an' knowing the state of it, I believe 'im. But 'e went somewhere often enough."

"Why would one of Abel Smith's women kill him?" she asked, pouring more tea for both of them. "Could it have been an accident? Could he have tripped and fallen down the stairs?"

" 'E wasn't found at the bottom, an' they deny it." He shook his head and picked up his mug of fresh tea. " 'E was on the floor in one o' the back bedrooms."

"Where was the broken glass?" she asked.

"On the floor in the passage an' at the bottom o' the stairs."

"Maybe they moved him before they realized he was beyond help?" she suggested. "Then they denied it out of fear. Sometimes people tell the stupidest lies when they panic."

He stared at the distance, the potbellied stove halfway along the wall, his eyes unseeing, his voice still too quiet to carry beyond the table where they sat. " 'E'd been in a fight. Scratch marks on 'is face that never came from any fall. Look like a woman's fingernails. An' he were dead after 'e hit the ground, all them broken bones an' a bash on the head. Wouldn't 'ave moved after that. An' there's blood on 'is 'ands, but they wasn't injured. It weren't no accident, Mrs. Monk. At least not entirely."

"I see."

He sighed. "It's going to cause a terrible row. The family's going to raise 'ell! They'll 'ave us all out patrolling the streets and 'arassing any women we see. They're going to 'ate it . . . an' then customers is going to 'ate it even more. An' the pimps'll 'ate it worst of all. Everybody'll be in a filthy temper until we find whoever did it, an' probably 'ang the poor little cow." He was too wretched to be aware of having used a disparaging term in front of her, or to think of apologizing.

"I can't help you," Hester said softly, remembering the women who had come to the house the previous night, all of them injured more or less. "Five women came, but they all went again and I have no idea where to. I don't ask."

"Their names?" he said without expectation.

"I don't ask that either, only something to call them by."

"That'll do, for a start." He put down his mug and fished in his pocket for his notebook and pencil.

"A Nell, a Lizzie and a Kitty," she answered. "Later a Mariah and a Gertie."

He thought for a moment, then put the pencil away again. " 'Ardly worth it," he said dismally. "Everybody's a Mary, a Lizzie, or a Kate. God knows what they were christened—if they were, poor souls."

She looked at him in the sharp morning light. There was a dark shadow of stubble on his cheeks and his eyes were pink-rimmed. He had far more pity for the women of the streets than he had for their clients. She thought he did not particularly want to catch whoever had pushed the man down the stairs. The murderer would no doubt be hanged for something which could have been at least in part an accident. The death may not have been intentional, but who would believe that when the woman in the dock was a prostitute and the dead man was rich and respected? What judge or juror could afford to accept that such a man could be at least in part responsible for his own death?

"I'm sorry," she said again. "I can't help."

He sighed. "An' you wouldn't if you could . . . I know that." He rose to his feet slowly, shifting his weight a little as if his boots pinched. "Just 'ad ter ask."

It was nearly ten o'clock in the morning when the hansom pulled up at her house in Fitzroy Street.

Monk was sitting in the front room he used to receive those who came to seek his services as a private agent of enquiry. He had papers spread in front of him and was reading them.

She was surprised to see him and filled with a sudden upsurge of pleasure. She had known him for nearly seven years, but had been married to him for less than three, and the joy of it was still sharp. She found herself smiling for no other reason.

He put the papers aside and stood up, his face softening in response.

There was a question in his eyes. "You're late," he said, not in criticism but in sympathy. "Have you eaten anything?"

"Toast," she replied with a little shrug. She was untidy and she knew she smelled of vinegar and carbolic, but she wanted him to kiss her anyway. She stood in front of him, hoping she was not obvious. She was sufficiently in love that it would have embarrassed her to be too easily read.

He undid her bonnet and tossed it casually onto the chair, then he put his arms around her and kissed her rather more warmly than she had expected. She responded with a whole heart, then, remembering the lonely and rejected women she had treated during the night, she kept her arms around him and held him more closely.

"What is it?" he asked, his voice demanding, knowing the difference in her.

"Just the women," she replied. "There was a murder last night. That's why I'm late. The police came to the house this morning."

"Why? What would you know about it?" He was puzzled.

She knew what he was imagining: a prostitute beaten and bleeding coming to the house, then returning to her brothel and being beaten again, this time to death. "No. At least not the way you mean," she answered. "It was a man who was killed, a client, if you can call him that. They think he fought with one of the women and somehow or other she pushed him downstairs. They wanted to know about women who came in cut and bruised as if they had been in a struggle."

"And you had seen some?" he said.

"Of course. Every night! It's mostly that and disease. I couldn't help because I don't know how they got hurt, or where to find them again."

He pushed her back a little, looking more closely at her face. "And would you help the police if you could?"

"I don't think so," she admitted. "I don't know. . . ."

He smiled very slightly, but his eyes read her perfectly.

"All right . . ." she agreed. "I'm glad I can't help. It relieves me of having to decide if I would or not. Apparently he was, in Constable Hart's words, 'a toff,' so the police are going to make everyone suffer, because the family will make sure they do." She grimaced with disgust. "They'll probably tell us he was a philanthropist walking the back streets and alleys trying to save the souls of fallen women!"

He lifted his head and very gently pushed back the hair that had fallen across her brow. "Unlikely . . . but I suppose it's possible. We believe what we need to . . . at least for as long as we can."

She rested her head against his chin. "I know. But I can't excuse persecuting a lot of women who are wretched enough anyway, or the pimps who will only take it out on them. It won't change anything."

"Someone killed him," he said reasonably. "They can't ignore that."

"I know!" She took a deep breath. "I know."

2

Hester had foreseen that the area around Cold-bath Square would suffer an added diligence from police harrying women who were either prostitutes or who could not prove their legitimate occupations, but when it happened she was still taken aback by the reality. The very next evening in the house she saw immediate evidence of it. Margaret was not in; she was mixing with her more natural society, endeavoring to elicit further donations of money toward the rent of the house and the cost of bandages and medicines necessary to treat those who came to it. There were also other expenses to be met, such as fuel for the stove, and carbolic and vinegar for cleaning, and, of course, food.

The first woman to come to the house was not injured but ill. She had an intermittent fever which Hester judged to be a symptom of venereal disease, but there was little she could do for her beyond offering comfort and an infusion of herbs to lower her temperature and give her some sense of relief.

"Are you hungry?" Hester asked, passing her the steaming mug. "I have bread and a little cheese, if you like."

The woman shook her head. "No, ta. I'll just 'ave the medicine."

Hester looked at her wan face and hunched shoulders. She was probably not more than twenty-five or twenty-six, but she was weary, and sleeplessness, poor food, and disease had robbed her of all energy.

"Would you like to stay here for the night?" Hester offered. It was not really what the house was for, but in the absence of those in greater need, why should this woman not use one of the beds?

A spark flared for a moment in the woman's eyes. "Wot'll it cost?" she said suspiciously.

"Nothing."

"Can I go in the morning, then?"

"You can go any time you wish, but morning would be good."

"Yeah, ta. That'd be fine." She still did not quite believe it. Her mouth pulled tight. "In't no point out there," she said grimly. "No trade. Rozzers all over the bleedin' place—like flies on a dead rat, they are. In't nothin' fer no one, even them wot's still clean." She meant free from disease, not like herself.

There was nothing for Hester to say. The truth would be a condescension this woman did not need. It would not give hope, only separate her from any sense of being understood.

"It's that bleedin' toff wot was snuffed last night," the woman went on miserably. "Stupid cow! W'y anyone'd want ter go an' do a thing like that fer, I dunno!" She took a sip of the herbs and twisted her mouth at the bitter taste.

"Sugar'll probably make it worse," Hester said. "But you can have some if you'd like."

"Nah, ta." She shook her head. "I'll get used ter it."

"Maybe they'll find out who it was, and things will get back to normal," Hester suggested. "What are you called?" It was not quite the same thing as asking her name. A name was a matter of identity; this was merely something to use in making her personal.

"Betty," was the reply, after a longer draft of the herbal infusion.

"Are you sure you wouldn't like a piece of bread and cheese? Or toast?"

"Yeah . . . toast'd be good. Ta."

Hester made two pieces and put them on a plate with cheese. Betty waited while Hester took one piece herself, then she took the other. Her hand closed around it with satisfaction, almost urgency.

"Reckon 'is family's real put out," she went on after a moment or two. " 'Em rozzers is buzzin' around like the devil's arter 'em. Poor bastards. They in't bad, most o' the time. Knows we gotter make a livin', an' the men wot comes 'ere does it 'cos they wanter. In't nobody else's business, really." She ate over half the toast before speaking again. "S'pose they come arter summink wot their wives don' give 'em. Never could work that out, but thank God fer it, I say."

Hester stood up and made more toast, skewering the bread on a fork and holding it to the open door of the stove till the heat of the coals scorched it crisp and brown. She returned with another good slice of cheese and gave it to Betty, who took it in wordless gratitude.

Hester was half curious. She had been involved in too many cases with Monk not to try reasoning as second nature, but she was also concerned for the disruption to the neighborhood. "Why would any woman kill a client?" she asked. "Surely she would realize it had to end like this?"

Betty shrugged. " 'Oo knows? Even soused out of 'er mind, yer'd think she'd 'ave 'ad more sense, wouldn't yer?" She bit into the toast and cheese and spoke with her mouth full. "Bring the wrath o' God down on all of us, stupid bitch." But there was more resignation in her voice than anger, and she turned her full attention to the food and said no more.

Hester did not raise the subject again until close to morning. She had slept in one of the beds herself, and was roused by Constable Hart knocking on the door.

She got up and let him in. He looked mithered and unhappy. He glanced around the room and saw only the one bed occupied.

"Quiet?" he said without surprise. Perhaps involuntarily his eyes went to the stove and the kettle.

"I'm going to have a cup of tea," Hester remarked. "Would you like one?"

He smiled at her tact, and accepted.

When the tea and toast were made and they were sitting at either side of the table, he began to talk. It was light in the street outside but there was hardly any traffic yet. The huge mass of the Coldbath prison stood silent and forbidding to the north, the sun softening its walls only slightly, the cobbles of the road still damp in the crevices. Light glinted on a pile of refuse in the gutter.

"So I don't suppose you've 'eard anything?" he said hopefully.

"Only that there are police all over the streets, and none of the women are doing much trade," she replied, sipping her tea. "I imagine that'll go for a lot of other occupations as well."

He laughed without humor. "Oh, yeah! Burglaries are down—and robberies! It's so bleedin' safe to walk around now you could wear a gold Albert in your waistcoat an' go from Coldbath to Pentonville, an' still find it there! The reg'lars like us almost as much as a dose o' the pox."

"Then maybe they'll help," she suggested. "Get things back to normal. Do you know who he was yet?"

He looked up at her, his eyes solemn and troubled. "Yeah. 'Is son got worried 'cos 'e were supposed to be at a big business meeting, an' 'e never come 'ome that night. Seems 'e weren't the kind o' man to miss something like that, so everyone got upset. Asked the local station about accidents an' so on." He spread black currant jam liberally on his toast. "He lived up Royal Square, opposite St. Peter's Church, but the station put the word about, an' we was askin' around too, knowin' as 'e wasn't from our patch. Son came over and looked at 'im in the morgue last evening." He bit into the toast. "Knew 'im, right enough," he said with his mouth full. " 'Ell of a stink 'e kicked up. Streets not safe for decent men, what's the world coming to, and all that. 'E'll write to his Member of Parliament, 'e said." He shook his head wonderingly.

"I think for his family's sake he would be wiser to say as little as possible, at least for the moment," she replied. "If my father were found dead in Abel Smith's place, I would tell as few people as I could. Or found alive either, for that matter," she added.

He smiled at her for an instant, then was grave again. " 'E were called Nolan Baltimore," he told her. "Rich man, 'ead of a company in railways. It was 'is son Jarvis Baltimore who came to the morgue. 'E's 'ead o' the company now, an' going to make sure 'e raises Cain if we don't find who killed 'is father an' see 'em 'anged."

Hester could imagine the reaction of shock, pain, outrage, but she thought young Mr. Jarvis Baltimore would live to regret his actions today. Whatever his father had been doing in Leather Lane, it was extremely unlikely to be anything his family would wish their friends to know about. Because it was murder, the police would have to do all they could to establish the facts, and if possible bring someone to court, but it might have been better for the Baltimore family if it could simply have remained a mystery, a disappearance tragic and unexplained.

But that choice was no longer open to them. It was only a passing thought, a moment's pity for the disillusion and then the public humiliation, the laughter suddenly hushed when they entered a room, the whispered words, the invitations that stopped, the friends who were unaccountably too busy to receive, or to call. All the money in the world would not buy back what they might be about to lose.

"What if it were nothing to do with any of the women in Abel Smith's place?" she suggested. "Maybe someone followed him to Leather Lane and took a good opportunity when they saw it?"

He stared at her, hope and incredulity struggling in his face. "God 'elp us if that's true!" he said in a whisper. "Then we'll never find 'im. Could be anyone!"

Hester could see that she had not necessarily been helpful. "Have you any witnesses at all?"

He shrugged very slightly. "Dunno who to believe. 'Is son says 'e was an upright, decent man in a big way o' business, respected in the community an' got a lot o' powerful friends who'll want to see justice done, an' the streets o' London cleaned up so 'onest folk can walk in 'em."

"Of course." She nodded. "He can hardly say anything else. He has to, to protect his mother."

"An' 'is sister," Hart added. "Who in't married yet, 'cos

she's a Miss Baltimore. 'Ardly do 'er chances any good if 'er father was known to frequent places like Leather Lane for their usual trade." He frowned. "Curious that, in't it? I mean, a man that'll go to places like that 'isself, turning down a young woman 'cos 'er father does the same thing. I can't work folk out . . . not gentry, leastways."

"It won't be his father, Constable, it'll be his mother," she explained.

"Oh?" He put his empty mug down on the table. "Yeah, o' course. I see. Still, it don't help us. Don't really know where to begin, 'cept with Abel Smith, an' 'e swears blind Baltimore weren't killed in 'is place."

"What does the police surgeon say?"

"Dunno yet. Died o' broken bones an' bleedin' inside, but dunno whether 'e died at the bottom of Abel's stairs or somewhere else altogether. Could'a bin anyone as pushed 'im, if it were the stairs."

"Or maybe he was drunk and just fell?" she said hopefully.

"Give me three wishes, an' right now all of 'em'd be that," he said with intense feeling. "The whole place is like a wasps' nest all the way from Coldbath up to Pentonville, an' down as far as Smithfield. An' it'll get worse! We just got the women an' the pimps on our backs now." He sighed. "Give it a day or two an' we'll have ever so discreet bellyachin' from the toffs whose pleasure it is to come 'ere an' have a bit o' fun, 'cos now they can't do it without falling over the police at every street corner. There's goin' to be a lot o' red faces around if they do! An' a lot o' short tempers if they don't. We can't win, whatever."

She sympathized with him silently, getting him more tea, and then fresh toast with black currant jam, which he ate with relish before thanking her and going disconsolately out into the ever-broadening daylight and resuming his thankless task.

The following day the newspapers carried headlines on the shocking death of well-respected railway owner Nolan Baltimore, found in extraordinary circumstances in Leather Lane, off the Farringdon Road. His family was desolated with grief, and all society was outraged that a decent man of spotless reputation should be attacked in the street and left to die in such circumstances. It was a national scandal, and his son, Jarvis Baltimore, had sworn that it would be his crusade to clear away the crime and prostitution that stained the capital city's honor and made such foul murders possible. The metropolitan police had failed in their duty to the citizens of the nation, and it was every caring man's responsibility to make sure that it was not allowed to remain so.

Of far more concern to Hester was the fact that the night after Constable Hart's second visit to her, a young woman was brought into the house by her friends so seriously beaten that she had to be carried. The three frightened and angry women waited huddled in the corner, staring.

The injured woman lay on the table curled over, holding her abdomen, her body shaking, blood oozing between her fingers.

White-faced, Margaret looked at Hester.

"Yes," Hester agreed quietly. "Send one of the women for Mr. Lockhart. Tell him to come as quickly as he may."

Margaret nodded and turned away. She gave directions to one of the waiting women where to start looking for the doctor, and not to stop until she had found him. Then she went over to the stove for water, vinegar, brandy, and clean cloths. She worked blindly, reaching for things because she was too shaken and too horrified to see clearly what she was doing.

Hester must staunch the bleeding and overcome her horror at such a wound, telling herself to remember the battlefields, the shattered men she had helped lift off the wagons after the charge of the Light Brigade at Sebastopol, or after the Battle of the Alma, blood-soaked, dead and dying, limbs torn, hacked by swords or splintered by shot.

She had been able to help them. Why was this woman any different? Hester was there to do a job, not indulge her own emotions, however deep or compassionate. The woman needed help, not pity.

"Let go of it," she said very gently. "I'll stop the bleeding." Please God she could. She took the woman's hands in hers, feeling the clenched muscles, the fear transmitting itself as if for a moment she were part of the same flesh. She was aware of the sweat breaking out on her skin and running cold over her body.

"Can you 'elp 'er?" one of the women asked from behind. She had come over silently, unable to keep away in spite of her fear.

"I think so," Hester replied. "What is her name?"

"Fanny," the woman said hoarsely.

Hester bent over the woman. "Fanny, let me look at it," she said firmly. "Let me see." With more strength she pulled the woman's hands away and saw the scarlet-soaked cloth of her dress. She prayed they would find Lockhart and he would come quickly. She needed help with this.

Margaret handed her scissors and she took them, cutting the fabric to expose the flesh. "Bandages," she said without looking up. "Rolled," she added. She lifted the dress away from the wound and saw raw flesh still running blood but not pumping. Relief washed over her, breaking out in prickling sweat again. It might be only a surface wound after all. It was not the gushing, arterial blood she had dreaded. But still she could not afford to wait and see if Lockhart turned up. Choking for a moment on her words, she asked for cloths, brandy and a needle threaded with gut.

Behind her, one of the women started to cry.

Hester talked all the time she worked. Most of it was probably nonsense; her mind was on the bloody flesh, trying to stitch it together evenly, without cobbling, without missing a vessel where the blood was still oozing, without causing more pain than was absolutely unavoidable.

Silently, Margaret handed her more and more cloths, and took away those that were soaked and useless.

Where was Lockhart? Why did he not come? Was he drunk again, lying in someone else's bed, under a table, or worse, in a gutter where no one would ever recognize him, much less find him and sober him up? She cursed him under her breath.

She lost track of how long it was since Margaret had sent

the woman out. All that mattered was the wound and the pain. She did not even notice the street door opening and closing.

Then suddenly there was another pair of hands, delicate and strong, and above all clean. Her back was so locked in position that when she straightened up it hurt, and it took her a moment to refocus her eyes on the young man beside her. His shirtsleeves were rolled up above his elbows, his fair hair was damp around his brow as if he had splashed his face with water. He looked down at the wound.

"Good job," he said approvingly. "Looks as if you've got it."

"Where have you been?" she replied between her teeth, overwhelmed with relief that he was there, and furious that he had not come sooner.

He grinned ruefully and shrugged, then turned his attention back to the wound. He explored it with sensitive, expert touch, all the while looking every few moments at the patient's face to make sure she was no worse.

Hester considered apologizing to him for her implied criticism and decided it did not matter now. It would not help, and she did not pay him, so perhaps he owed her nothing. She caught Margaret looking at her, and saw the relief in her eyes also.

It seemed as if the bleeding was stopped. She handed Lockhart the final bandages soaked in balm and he bound them in place, then stood back.

"Not bad," he said gravely. "We'll need to watch her for infection." He did not bother to ask what had happened. He knew no one would tell him. "A little beef tea, or sherry if you have it. Not yet, but in a while. You know what else." He lifted his shoulders in a slight shrug and smiled. "Probably better than I do."

Hester nodded. Now that the immediate crisis was over she was overwhelmed with weariness. Her mouth was dry and she was trembling a little. Margaret had gone to the stove for hot water so they could wash the worst of the blood away, and to make tea for them.

Hester turned to the waiting women, and the question in all

their faces. "Give it time," she said quietly. "We can't tell yet. It's too soon."

"Can she stay 'ere?" one of them asked. "Please, missus! 'E'll only do it again if she goes back."

"What's the matter with him?" Hester let her fury out at last. "He could have killed her. He's got to be a madman— you should get rid of him. Don't you have some kind of—"

"It weren't Bert!" another of the women said quickly. "I know that 'cos 'e were out cold drunk in the gutter w'en it 'appened. I know that fer sure, 'cos I seed 'im meself. Great useless, bleedin' oaf!"

"A customer?" Hester said in surprise and increasing anger.

"Nah!" The woman shuddered.

"Yer dunno that," the third woman said grimly. "Fanny in't sayin' 'oo it were, missus. She's that scared she won't say nuffin', but we reckon as it's some bastard as she knows, but it in't 'er reg'lar pimp, 'cos like Jenny said, 'e were blind drunk an' not fit ter beat a rice puddin', never mind do that ter anyone." She grimaced. "Besides, wot sense does it make ter put yer own women out o' work? Gawd! There's little enough around now without cuttin' anyone open. Even a bleedin' eejut can see that!"

"Then who would do it?" Hester asked as Margaret poured hot water into a bowl on the other table, then added cold to it to make it bearable to wash in. The carbolic was already to hand.

Lockhart rolled his sleeves farther up, ignoring the blood on them, and began to wash. Hester followed straight after him and he handed her the towel.

Margaret made tea for all of them, including herself, and brought it over, hot and very strong. Hester was glad to sit down at last and made no demur when Lockhart carried the bowl away to empty it down the drain.

Fanny was lying on the main table, her head on a pillow, her face ashen white. It was too soon to think of moving her, even to a bed.

"Who would do it?" Hester repeated, looking at the woman.

"Dunno," the first one replied. "Ta." She accepted a mug of tea from Margaret. "That's wot's got us frit. Fanny's a good girl. She don' take nothin' wot don' belong to 'er. She does wot she's told, poor little cow! P'rhaps she was once quite decent." She lowered her voice. "Parlor maid or summink like that. Got inter trouble, an' afore yer can say 'knife,' 'ere she is in the street. Don' talk much, but she 'ad it rough, I'd say."

Lockhart came back with the empty bowl and accepted his tea.

"If I could get me 'ands on the sod wot did that to 'er," the middle woman said. "I'd slit 'is ... sorry, miss, but so I would."

"You shut yer mouth, Ada!" her companion warned. "There's rozzers all over the place. Comin' outa the bleedin' woodwork, they are. Don' wanna be, but they're gettin' leant on every which way, poor sods. Someone's tellin' 'em ter clear us up. Others is tellin' 'em ter leave us alone, so they can 'ave their fun. Poor rozzers is runnin' around like blue-arsed flies, fallin' over each other."

"Yeh! An' poor little cows like Fanny is gettin' cut up by some bleedin' lunatic!" Ada retorted, her face pinched, her voice rising with barely controlled hysteria.

Hester did not argue. She sat quietly and thought about it, but she did not ask any more questions. The three women thanked them, and after saying good-bye to Fanny and promising to return, they went out into the night.

After an hour Lockhart looked closely at Fanny, who seemed to be quite a lot easier, at least in her fear. He helped Hester and Margaret carry her over to the nearest bed and laid her on it. Then, promising to come back the following day, he took his leave.

Hester suggested Margaret take a turn to sleep, and she would watch. Later they would change places. In the morning Bessie Wellington would come to take care of the house for the day and keep it clean. She had once been a prostitute herself, then kept a bawdy house until fiercer competition had driven her out of business. Now she was glad to find a warm room to spend the day, and was gentle enough with such patients as remained in the beds. She asked for no payment, and her knowledge of the area was worth almost as much as her labor.

When Hester returned the next evening, she was met by Bessie at the door, her face red, her black hair pulled back into a screwed knot and poking out at all angles. She was bursting with indignation.

"That slimy toad Jessop was 'ere arter money again!" she said in a whisper which carried halfway across Coldbath Square. "Offered 'im a cup o' tea, an' 'e wouldn't take it! Suspicious sod!"

"What did you put in it, Bessie?" Hester asked, concealing a wry smile. She came in and closed the door behind her. The familiarity of the room engulfed her, the scrubbed boards still smelling of lye and carbolic, the faint echo of vinegar, the heat of the stove, and over near the tables the pungency of whiskey and the sharper clean tang of herbs. Automatically her eye went to the bed where she had left Fanny. She saw the dark tangle of her hair and the mound of her body under the blankets.

"She's all right, poor little bitch," Bessie said with anger rumbling in her voice. "Can't get a word out of 'er 'oo done that to 'er, mind. Don' understand that. If it were me, I'd be cursin' 'im up an' down ter everyone wot'd listen—an' them wot wouldn't!" She shook her head.

"Only a bit o' licorice," she said in answer to Hester's original question. "An' a spot o' whiskey ter 'ide the taste, like. Pity that. Waste o' good whiskey. Not that there's any other sort, mind!" She grinned, showing gap teeth.

"Did you throw it away?" Hester asked anxiously.

Bessie gave her a sideways look. " 'Course I did, bless yer! Wouldn't wanna give anyone cold tea, would I?" She stared back with mock innocence, and Hester could not help at least half wishing Jessop had drunk it. Surely, Bessie would not cause him anything worse than an acute discomfort and possibly embarrassment. Would she?

She went over and looked at Fanny, who was still frightened and in considerable pain. It took half an hour to take off the bandages and look at the wound to make sure it was not infected, rebandage it, then persuade her to take a little broth. She was barely finished when the street door opened with a gush of chilly, damp air, and she turned to see a woman of uncertain age standing only just inside. She was plainly dressed, like a good lady's maid, and her face was pinched hard with disapproval. Even her nose was wrinkled, though it was impossible to tell if it was the odor of lye and carbolic or fierce disgust that consumed her.

"Yes?" Hester said enquiringly. "Can I help you?"

"Is this a . . . a place where you take in injured women who are . . . are . . ." She stopped, apparently unable to say the word in her mind.

"Prostitutes," Hester said for her, with a touch of asperity. "Yes, it is. Are you injured?"

The woman blushed scarlet with mortification, then the blood drained out, leaving her face gray. She swiveled on her heel and went out of the still-open door.

Bessie stifled a laugh.

The next moment another young woman stood in the entrance, very different in appearance. Her complexion was extremely fair, her yellow hair thick. She had pale lashes and brows, but a healthy color in her face, which was too bland of feature to be pretty but had an openness and a balance about it which was immediately pleasing. She appeared nervous and was obviously controlling deep emotions, but there was no sign of injury or physical pain in her. The quality of her clothes, which, even though they were of unrelieved black, made it quite obvious she spent a considerable amount of money on them, and her bearing—head high, eyes direct—said that she was not a woman of the streets, however successful. It occurred to Hester with a jolt of embarrassment that probably the first woman had indeed been her maid, and there very much against her will. Perhaps she should not have made the remark she made.

She put down the dish and spoon with which she had been

feeding Fanny, and went toward the visitor. "Good evening. Can I help you?"

"Are you in charge here?" the young woman asked. Her voice was low and a trifle hoarse, as if her feelings were held in so tightly the effort had half closed her throat, but her diction was perfect.

"Yes," Hester replied. "My name is Hester Monk. What can I do for you?"

"I am Livia Baltimore." She took a deep breath. "I understand this place . . ." Studiously, she avoided looking around her. "This is a refuge where women of the streets come if they are injured? I beg your pardon if I am mistaken. I do not mean to insult you, but my maid informed me that this is the correct place." Her fists were clenched by her sides, her body rigid.

"It is not an insult, Miss Baltimore," Hester replied steadily. "I do this because I wish to. Medicine deals with those who need, it does not make social judgments." She hesitated, uncertain whether to say anything about Nolan Baltimore's death or not, then instinct broke through regardless. "I am sorry for your bereavement, Miss Baltimore. Please come in."

"Thank you." She glanced once behind her, then closed the door. "Perhaps you can also help me . . ."

"If I knew anything about it, I would already have told the police," Hester replied, turning and moving back toward the table. She knew what Livia Baltimore had come seeking. It was natural enough, and showed a great deal of courage, even if little wisdom. She was touched with pity for the pain this young woman would experience as she realized more fully the reality of the places her father had frequented, whatever his purpose. She would have kept her emotions, her dreams, her grief, far safer had she stayed at home. But perhaps she would not only gain information but be able to give it as well. Even if vast areas of her father's life were unknown to her, she would still have some sense of his personality.

"Please sit down," Hester offered. "Would you like tea? It's a miserable night."

Livia accepted. Apparently the maid had been dismissed to

wait for her in the carriage, or whatever other form of transport she had used. Either Livia wished this conversation to be private or the maid had declined to remain in such a place. Possibly it was both.

Breathing heavily, Bessie filled up the kettle again from a ewer on the floor and set it on the stove. "It'll be a few minutes," she warned grudgingly. She sensed condescension and resented it.

"Of course," Hester agreed, then turned to Livia. "I really have no idea what happened to Mr. Baltimore," she said gently. "I deal only with injury and illness here. I don't ask questions."

"But you must hear things!" Livia urged. "The police won't tell me anything. They speak to my brother, but they say there was a woman involved, and she may have been hurt."

Her black-gloved hands clenched and unclenched on her reticule. "Perhaps he saw a woman being attacked, and he tried to help her, and they set upon him?" Her eyes were eager, desperate. "If that were so, she might have come here, surely?"

"Yes," Hester agreed, knowing the word was true but the thought was not.

"Then you would have seen her, or your woman would?" Livia half nodded toward Bessie, standing with her arms folded beside the stove.

"I would have seen her," Hester conceded. "But several women come here every night, and they are all injured . . . or ill."

"But that night . . . the night he was . . . killed?" Livia leaned forward a little across the table, in her eagerness forgetting her distaste. "Who was here then? Who was hurt, and might have seen his . . . murder?" Her eyes filled with tears and she ignored them. "Don't you care about justice, Mrs. Monk? My father was a good and decent man, and generous. He worked so hard for what he had, and he loved his family! Doesn't it matter to you that someone killed him?"

"Yes, of course it matters," Hester responded, wondering how to answer the woman, little more than a girl, without overwhelming her with facts she could neither understand nor believe. "It matters when anyone is killed."

"Then help us!" Livia pleaded. "You know these women. Tell me something!"

"No, I don't know them," Hester cut across her. "I do what I can for their injuries . . . that's all."

Livia's eyes were wide, uncomprehending. "But . . ."

"They come in through that door." Hester nodded to the street entrance. "Sometimes I have seen them before, sometimes I haven't. They are either injured with cuts, bruises, or broken bones, or they are in a critical state of disease, most often syphilis or tuberculosis, but other things as well. I don't ask more than their first names, merely for something to call them. I do what I can, and often that is not much. When they are well enough, they go away again."

"But don't you know how they were injured?" Livia pressed, her voice rising. "You must know what happened!"

Hester looked down at the tabletop. "I don't need to ask. Either a customer lost his temper, or they kept a bit of the money for themselves and their pimps beat them," she replied. "And now and again they took a bit of trade in someone else's patch and got into a fight that way. The competition is pretty rough. Whatever it is, it really doesn't make any difference to what I need to do."

Livia obviously did not understand. It was a world, even a language, beyond her experience or imagination. "What is a . . . pimp?"

"The man who looks after them," Hester replied. "And takes most of what they earn."

"But why?" There was no comprehension in Livia's eyes.

"Because it's dangerous for a woman on her own," Hester explained. "Most of them have no choice. The pimps own the buildings, in a way they almost own the streets. They keep other people from hurting the women, but if they think they're lazy, or cheating them, then they beat the women themselves, usually not badly enough to scar their faces or make them unfit to work. Only a fool damages his own property."

Livia shook her head as if to get rid of the idea. "Then who hurts them when they come here to you?"

"Customers, perhaps, who are drunk and don't know their own strength, or just lose their tempers," Hester said. "Other women sometimes. Quite often they come because of disease."

"Lots of people get tuberculosis," Livia pointed out. "All sorts of people. I had a cousin who died of it. She was only twenty-eight. They call it the White Death, don't they." That was a statement. "And the other is . . ." She would not speak the words. Her own embarrassment at the subject was too deep to allow such candor. At last she let herself look around the room at the whitewashed walls and the cupboards, some of them locked.

Hester saw her glance. "Carbolic, lye, potash, vinegar," she said. "It's good for cleaning. And tobacco. We keep that locked."

Livia's eyes widened. "Tobacco? You let people use tobacco? Even women?"

"For burning," Hester explained. "It's a good fumigant, especially if we have lice or ticks, or things like that."

Livia's face twisted as if she could smell the reek of it already. "I just want to know what they saw," she begged. "What happened to my father?"

Hester studied her, the youth in the soft curves of her cheek and throat, the unlined skin, the earnest gaze. But already the shadow of grief had touched her; there was a hollowness, a papery quality around her eyes and a tightness to her mouth. The world was a different place from the one it had been three days before, and that innocence could not be found again.

Hester struggled for something to say that would stop this girl, for that is all she was in spite of her years, and send her back to her own life to believe whatever she wanted to. Unless there were a trial, she would never have to know what her father had been doing in Leather Lane. "Let the police find out, if they can," she said aloud.

"They're finding nothing!" Livia answered indignantly. "These women won't talk to them! Why should they? It's someone they know who killed him. They're probably afraid to tell."

"What was your father like?" Hester asked, then instantly regretted it. It was a stupid question. What does any woman say her dead father was like? Everything she wanted him to be, reality blurred by loss, loyalty, the sense of decency that says you speak no ill of the dead. "I mean, why might he have come to Leather Lane at night?" she amended.

Livia looked slightly embarrassed and defensive. "I don't know. It must have been business of some kind."

"What does your mother say?"

"We don't discuss it," Livia responded, as if it were the most usual thing to say. "Mama is an invalid. We try to keep anything troublesome or distressing from her. Jarvis . . . my brother . . . says he must have been going to meet someone, possibly to do with navvies, or something like that. My father owned a railway company. They have a new track which is almost completed. It will go all the way from the dockside here in London up to Derby. And we have a factory near Liverpool as well, for making railway wagons. Perhaps he was seeing someone about laborers, or steel, or that kind of thing?"

Hester could not meet her eyes and answer. That was not the sort of business people conducted in Leather Lane at night, but what use was there in pointing that out to Baltimore's daughter? "These women wouldn't know about that," she said instead. "They scrape the best living they can by selling their bodies, and they pay a heavy price for it. . . ." She saw the incomprehension again. "You think they should be in factory labor? Sweatshops? Do you know what that pays?"

Livia hesitated. "No . . ."

"Or the hours?"

"No . . . but . . ."

"It's honest, right?" There was an edge of scorn in her voice she had not intended, and she saw the sting of it in Livia's face. "They can't afford to be honest at one and sixpence a day for fourteen or fifteen hours' work," she said more gently, but still with the underlying anger—not for Livia but for the facts. She saw Livia's eyes widen and her throat constrict. "Especially if they've got children to keep, or debts to pay," she added. "They can make a pound or two every night on the streets, even after giving their pimp his cut."

"But . . ." Livia started again, looking toward the curled-up outline of Fanny in the nearest bed.

"The risks? Injuries, disease, the unpleasantness of it?" Hester asked. "Go into a sweatshop sometime, see if you think it's any better. They're cramped, ill-lit, dirty, over-crowded. There's just as much disease there. A different kind, maybe, but I'm not sure it's any better. Dead is dead, whatever the cause."

"Can't you help me at all?" Livia said softly, shock and something like humility in her face. "At least ask them?"

"I can ask," Hester promised, overwhelmed with pity again. "But please, don't hope for much. I don't think anyone knows. And of course, if it was business of some sort, it would be well away from any of these women. The police say he was found in Abel Smith's . . . house . . . in Leather Lane, but Abel swears it wasn't any of his women who killed him. Perhaps they are telling the truth, and he was killed by who-ever he went to see?" She hated telling what she thought was almost certainly a lie. But very possibly no one would ever know who had killed Baltimore, let alone why, so perhaps his daughter would be able to cling to her illusions.

"That would be it," Livia said, grasping hope as if it were a lifeline. "Thank you for your logic, your good sense, Mrs. Monk."

Hester pressed her advantage, and it was at least in part for Livia as well. "Perhaps your brother would stop asking the po-lice so hard to drive the women off the streets?" she suggested. "It may have nothing to do with any of them, and harrying them will make them even less likely to tell you anything."

"But if they don't know anything . . ." Livia started.

"They may have seen nothing," Hester conceded. "But they will get to hear. Word passes quickly in places like this."

"I don't know. Jarvis doesn't listen to—"

Before she could finish the train of her thought the street

door swung open wide and a young man shouted for help, panic harsh in his voice. His face was white, his hair streaked across his brow in the rain, and his thin clothes were sodden and sticking to his narrow chest.

Livia swung around, and Hester rose to her feet just as a far larger man came staggering in holding a woman in his arms. She was so pale her skin looked waxy in the gaslight, and her eyes were closed, her head lolling as if she were completely insensible.

"Put her there." Hester pointed to the larger, empty table.

" 'Aven't yer got a bed?" The large man stifled a sob. His face was twisted with emotion; anger was so much less painful than the terror which obviously engulfed him.

Hester was accustomed to all kinds of feelings pouring out beyond control, and she made no judgment of them, no response to those that were unfair.

"I need to see what is wrong," she explained. "I have to have a firm surface, and the light. Put her there."

He obeyed, his eyes imploring her to help, to find some answer beyond his imagining.

Hester looked at the girl lying in front of her. The man had put her down as gently as he could, but it was still clear that her bones were broken. Her arms and legs lay awkwardly; the flesh was swelling and the bruises were darkening even as Hester watched. The veins in the girl's neck and shoulders were blue, her skin gray-white. She was breathing but her eyelids did not flutter at all.

"Can yer 'elp 'er?" the man demanded, the youth now beside him.

"I'll try," Hester promised. "What happened? Do you know?"

"Someone beat the 'ell out of 'er!" he exploded. "Can't yer see that? Yer blind or summink?"

"Yes, I can see that," Hester said, looking at the woman, not at him. "I wanted to know how long ago, how you found her, if she's been stabbed or cut. If you can tell me that without my moving her, so much better. I can see how her arms and legs are. What about her body? Did you see where she was punched or kicked?"

"Gawd, lady! D'yer think I'd'a let it 'appen if I 'ad? I'd'a killed the b-bastard if I'd b-bin there!" he stuttered in a futile effort to find a word bad enough for the rage that ate him. "If yer can't 'elp 'er, at least don' 'urt 'er any more, yer 'ear me?"

Hester put her hands very gently on the woman's arms, feeling for the grating edges of bone where the flesh was already misshapen and damaged. She found one break in the left arm, two in the right. The left knee was swollen and at least two small bones were broken in the right foot. The collarbone was broken on one side, but there was little she could do about that. Cutting the cloth of the girl's bodice, she exposed a purple bruise at least six inches wide across the ribs and stretching down below the waist. This was what she feared—it meant internal bleeding she could do nothing to help. She had a fair knowledge of anatomy, mostly learned in the battlefield while looking at the actuality of torn-open bodies, not the neater, more leisurely education of medical school, or dissections of the dead. Still, she knew where the major arteries were and what could happen to them when damaged.

"Do something! Damn yer!" the man said desperately, shifting his immense weight from one foot to the other and back again in his fever of anxiety.

Without answering, Hester continued to learn as much as she could without moving the broken body of the woman. She wished Margaret were there to help. Bessie was kind, but she had not the inner calm, the steady hands that Margaret had. She identified too much with the women, having lived all her life among them. She saw the pain and the fear from the inside, and it robbed her of the dispassion needed for practical help in such critical injuries as these.

"Go and find Mr. Lockhart," she ordered, and saw Bessie's face flood with relief that she could do something useful and at the same time escape the pain. She was out of the door without even grasping for her hat.

Hester turned to Livia, ignoring the man.

"Miss Baltimore!" she said firmly. "Would you be good enough to pass me that roll of bandage on the table? And then fetch a splint from the cupboard over there." She pointed with her other hand. "In fact, fetch three."

Very slowly, Livia stood up. She looked pale enough to faint.

"If you would do it quickly, please," Hester instructed, holding out her hand.

Livia obliged, still moving as if in a dream, fumbling with the bandage, rolling in the ends, then going to the cupboard. She returned after a moment with three splints and passed one across.

Hester took it from her. "Now, would you hold the girl's shoulders, please? Lean on them. I need them to remain still."

"What?"

"Just do it! Lean your weight on her shoulders. Be firm, but gentle." She looked up. "Go on! I'm going to set these bones so they heal as straight as possible. I need someone to hold her still. It's far kinder to do it while she is insensible anyway. Can you imagine how it will hurt if we leave it until she regains herself?"

Livia stood frozen to the spot.

"You don't catch diseases that way. Just do it!" Hester snapped. "I can't set it by myself. You came here to find out who killed your father. If you can't even bring yourself to look at this world, how are you going to learn anything about it? You want these people to help you? You'd better give a little help yourself."

Slowly, still looking as if she were going to pass out, Livia put her hands on the young woman's shoulders and leaned forward, resting her own body's weight on them.

"Thank you," Hester acknowledged. Then she carefully took the lower arm and, feeling the sickening grating of bone, pulled the limb straight. The youth handed her the splint and the bandages, his hands gentle as he laid them by the limb, and she bound them together as firmly as she dared. Fortunately there was no broken skin, so there was no possibility of infection from dirt, but she knew very well that there might be considerable internal bleeding which she could not reach or stop.

With Livia's shocked and reluctant help she set the other bones as well. The large man stoked the fire and fetched more water. Hester made poultices for the broken ribs and collar-bone, and placed them gently on the injuries.

"Now all we can do is wait," she said at last.

"She gonna be all right?" the big man asked.

"I don't know," she said honestly. "We'll do all we can."

"I . . ." He swallowed. "I'm sorry if I were a bit short wif yer first off. I'm s'posed ter keep an eye after 'er, but she don' belong 'round 'ere. Dunno wot 'it 'er, 'alf the time." He passed a huge hand over his face, as if he could wipe away his emotions. "Strewth! Why'd the stupid little cow go moufin' off ter someone? Times I've told 'er ter keep 'er mouf shut! But they in't got the wits they was born wif, some o' them! Fink 'cos a man pays 'em money 'e's gonna treat 'em nice? Some o' them swine fink 'alf a crown buys yer soul. Bas-tards!" He made a low growl in his throat as if he were going to hawk and spit, then changed his mind.

"You can't do anything more for her now," Hester said gen-tly. "You might as well go home." She turned to Livia Balti-more. "And you should go home, too. I suppose your carriage is still somewhere close by?"

"Yes," Livia agreed very quietly. Hester wondered what re-ception she would get from the maid. Probably icy with dis-approval she dared not voice, but she might very well be handing in her notice in the morning—and shattering the in-valid Mrs. Baltimore with outraged accounts of the whole episode. Livia would need all her courage and her patience to deal with that.

"Thank you for your help," Hester said with a very slight smile. "If I learn anything that might be of use to you, I shall tell the police."

Livia took a card out of her reticule and handed it across.

"Please do. Either write or call."

"I will," Hester promised, knowing Livia hesitated.

"I'll walk yer to yer carriage," the big man offered.

Livia looked startled, then relieved. A flash of light crossed her face which could even have been humor. "Thank you," she said, then went out of the door into Coldbath Square, followed by the man.

It was ten minutes later that Bessie returned with Lockhart, tired and disheveled as always, but perfectly willing to help.

"You don't eat proper!" Bessie chided him, as she had apparently been doing ever since she had found him. "Steak and kidney pudding, you need!" She went over to the stove. "I'll get you some 'ot tea. Best I can do. But it's yer own fault!" She did not explain what she meant by that, and Lockhart shot a wry look at Hester, but there was affection in it. He understood Bessie better than she understood herself.

Hester explained what they had done for the girl and took him over to her.

He looked at her carefully, for a long time, but he could not tell Hester the one thing she needed to know, whether there was internal bleeding or not.

"I'm sorry," he said, shaking his head and looking at the girl with pity. "I just don't know. But if she's still no worse by morning, she might survive it. I'll come back midday or so. Until then, you can do as much for her as I can. You've made a good job of the bones."

It was a little after seven, and full daylight, when Hester awoke to find Bessie standing over her, her eyes bright, her hair struggling out of its fierce knot, her dress even more rumpled than usual.

"She's come 'round!" she said in her penetrating whisper. "Don' look too good, poor creature. Yer'd better see to 'er. Kettle's on. Yer look like summit out o' the morgue yerself, an' all."

"Thank you," Hester said a trifle dryly, sitting up and wincing. Her head throbbed and she was so tired she felt worse than when she had lain down. She swung her legs to the floor and stood up, aware now of the girl on the other bed only yards away from her, eyes open, face so white it seemed hardly warmer than the pillow.

"Don't move," Hester said gently. "You're safe here."

"I'm all broken inside." The girl breathed the words rather than spoke them. "Heavens, I hurt!" Her voice was soft, her diction clear, not that of the streets.

"I know, but in time it will ease," Hester promised, hoping it was true.

"No, it won't," the girl said with resignation. "I'm dying. That's my punishment, I suppose." She did not look at Hester but stared up at the ceiling with blank eyes.

Hester put her hand over the girl's, touching it very lightly. "Your bones will heal," she told her. "I know it hurts now, but it will get better. What shall I call you?"

"Alice." Suddenly her eyes filled with tears, but she was too weak and too tired to sob. She was also too broken to be held in anyone's arms.

"Just rest," Hester said, aching to be able to do more for her. "You're safe here. We won't leave you alone. Is there anyone you would like me to tell?"

"No!" She turned to look at Hester, her eyes frightened. "Please!"

"I won't if you don't wish it," Hester promised. "Don't worry!"

"I don't want them to know," Alice went on. "Let me just die here and be buried . . . wherever they put people no one knows." She said it without self-pity. She was asking for an end, privacy, not help.

Hester had no idea whether the girl would recover or not. She was uncertain how to help, or if she could. Perhaps the best thing would be to leave her, but she could not do that. She was compelled by her own inner will for life not to allow someone else to give up. To be beaten was another thing, but she was not there yet.

"Who did this to you?" she asked. "Don't you want to stop them? Before they do it to someone else?"

Alice turned her head a little. "You can't stop him. No one can."

"Anyone can be stopped, if you know how, and if enough of us try," Hester said decisively. "If you help. Who is he?"

Alice looked away again. "You can't. It's legal. I owe him money. I borrowed too much, then I couldn't pay it back."

"Who? Your pimp?"

Alice stared up at the ceiling. "You might as well know. There's nothing more he can do to me now. But I don't know his name, not his real name. I was respectable then, a governess! Can you imagine that? I used to teach gentlemen's children. In Kensington. I fell in love." There was immeasurable bitterness in her voice and it was so little above a whisper that Hester had to strain to hear her. "We got married. We had six months of happiness . . . then I realized he gambled. Couldn't help it, he said. Maybe he was right. Anyway, he didn't stop . . . he began to lose." She took a deep breath and gasped with pain. It was a moment or two before she could continue.

Hester waited.

"I borrowed to get him out of debt . . . then he left me," Alice said. "Only I still had to pay back the money. It was then that the moneylender told me he could get me looked after on the streets . . . especially . . . if I went into this brothel. It caters to men who like clean girls . . . ones who speak nicely and carry themselves like quality. Pay a lot more for it. That way I could pay off my debt and be free."

"And you went . . ." Hester said slowly. It was so easy to understand—the fear, the promises, the escape from despair. The price might not seem any worse than the alternative.

"Not at first," Alice replied. "Not for another three months. By then the debt was twice as high. That was two years ago." She fell silent.

Bessie came over with a cup of beef tea, her eyes questioning.

Hester looked at Alice. "Try a little," she offered.

Alice did not bother to answer. Her thoughts were inward,

remembering pain, defeat, perhaps humiliation more than she would ever forget.

Hester put her arm around Alice's shoulders and eased her up a few inches. The girl gasped with pain, but she did not resist. She lay as leaden weight against Hester, her splintered arms stiff, her body rigid.

Bessie held the cup to her lips, her own face crumpled with concern, her hands so gentle her touch could hardly be felt as more than a warmth.

It was a quarter of an hour before the tea was finished, and Hester had no idea whether it had helped or not, but she knew of nothing else to try.

Alice sank into a restless sleep, and when Margaret came in at nearly nine o'clock her optimism over raising more funds vanished the moment Hester told her of the night's happenings.

"That's monstrous!" she said furiously. "You mean someone out there is lending money to respectable women in financial trouble, and then demanding they pay it back by working in a brothel that caters to men who like to use women they think are decent . . . to . . . God knows what!"

"And now with police all over the place they can't get the trade to pay off, so they are getting beaten," Hester finished for her. "Yes, that's exactly what I mean. Fanny is probably another of them, only she's too frightened to tell us." She remembered Kitty, who had also spoken well and carried herself with pride. "Heaven knows how many more there are."

"What are we going to do?" Margaret demanded. There was no doubt in her that they would do something. She expected no less from Hester; it was written plainly in her face and in her brave, candid stare.

Hester did not want to let her down, or any of these women who trusted her to be able to do what they could not. But those reasons were trivial. Above them all was the evil Hester so easily imagined could have happened to hundreds of women she knew—or to herself, had chance been only a little different.

"I don't know," she admitted. "Not yet. But I will." She would ask Monk. He was clever, imaginative, and he never gave up. A very slight warmth opened up inside her at the certainty of his help. He would hate this with exactly the same passion as she did. "I will," she repeated.

3

BEFORE HESTER RETURNED from Coldbath Square on the morning after Alice's attack, Monk received a new client in Fitzroy Street. She came into the room with the air of tension and tightly controlled nervousness that almost all his clients showed. He estimated her to be about twenty-three, and not beautiful, although her bearing was so filled with grace and vitality it was a moment or two before he realized it. She was dressed in a dark skirt and matching jacket fitted to her waist, and the cloth of it was obviously discreetly expensive, it sat so perfectly. She was carrying a bag much larger than a reticule, about a foot or more square.

"Mr. Monk?" she asked, but only as a formality. There was an air of purpose about her which made it plain she was there because she knew who he was. "My name is Katrina Harcus. I believe you undertake enquiries for people, privately. Is that correct?"

"How do you do, Miss Harcus," he replied, gesturing to one of the two large, comfortable chairs on either side of the fireplace. There was a fire burning today. It was spring, but still chilly early in the morning and in the evening, particularly for anyone sitting still, and who might be in a state of some distress. "You are quite correct. Please sit down and tell me what I may do to help you."

She accepted, setting the bag at her feet. From its shape he guessed it might contain documents of some sort, which already marked her as unusual. Most women who came to him did so about personal matters rather than business: jewelry lost, a servant who had occasioned their suspicion, a prospective son—or daughter-in-law—about whom they wished to know more, but without betraying themselves by asking any of their own acquaintances.

He sat down opposite her.

She cleared her throat as if to dispel her nervousness, then began to speak in a low, clear voice. "I am about to become engaged to marry a Mr. Michael Dalgarno." She could not help smiling as she said his name, and there was a brightness in her eyes which made her feelings obvious. However, she hurried on without waiting for Monk's acknowledgment or congratulations. "He is a partner in a large company building railways." Here her face tightened and Monk was aware of increased anxiety in her. He was accustomed to watching people minutely, the angle of the head, the hands knotted together or at ease, the shadows in a face, anything that told him what emotions people were concealing behind their words.

He did not interrupt her.

She took a deep breath and let it out silently. "This is very difficult, Mr. Monk. I need to speak in confidence, as I would were you my legal adviser." She looked at him steadily. She had very fine eyes, golden brown rather than dark.

"I cannot conceal a crime, Miss Harcus, if I have evidence of it," he warned. "But other than that, all you say to me is in confidence."

"That is what I had been told. Forgive me for having to as certain it for myself, but I need to tell you things that I would be most distressed were they repeated."

"Unless it is to conceal a crime, they will not be."

"And if there is a crime involved?" She spoke quite steadily and her eyes did not flinch from his, but her voice had sunk to a whisper.

"If it is a crime planned, then I must seek to prevent it by any means I can, including informing the police," he answered. "If it is one that has already happened, then I must share with them any knowledge I may come by, if I am certain it is true. Otherwise I would be complicit in the act myself."

His curiosity was piqued. What kind of help did this very composed young woman want from him? Her manner was unusual; it seemed as if her request was going to be even more so. He realized how disappointed he would be if it proved to be a case he could not accept.

"I understand." She nodded. "I do fear a crime, but I wish you to prevent it, if that is possible. If I had the skill to do so myself, then I would. However my greatest concern is to protect Michael—Mr. Dalgarno. I may be mistaken, of course, but whether I am or not, word of my suspicions must never come out."

"Of course not," he agreed, desiring to spare her the explanation she obviously found painful. "If they are innocent it would be embarrassing and perhaps worse; if they are guilty they must not be warned." He saw the relief in her face at his quickness of understanding. "Tell me what you fear, and why, Miss Harcus."

She hesitated, reluctant to take the final step of commitment. It was not difficult to understand, and he waited in silence.

"This is gathered from things Mr. Dalgarno has told me in the course of conversation," she began, her eyes steady on his face, watching and judging his reaction. "Little pieces of information I have overheard . . . and now actual papers which I have brought with me for you to read and consider. I . . ." She looked away for the first time. "I took them . . . stole them, if you like."

He was careful not to express shock. "I see. From where?"

She raised her eyes. "From Mr. Dalgarno's rooms. I am worried for him, Mr. Monk. I think there is fraud being practiced in the building of the new track for the railway, and I am very afraid he may be implicated, although I am certain he is innocent . . . at least . . . at least I am almost certain. Sometimes even good people yield to the temptation to turn the other way when their friends are involved in something wrong. Loyalties can be . . . misplaced, especially when you owe much that is good in your life to someone else's generosity, and trust in you." She looked at him intently, as if to judge how much he understood.

Some far memory stabbed him at the thought, but he kept his face blank. He could not tell her how acute was his feeling for just that kind of obligation, and the pain of failure.

"Is it a fraud from which Mr. Dalgarno might profit?" he asked levelly.

"Certainly. He is a junior partner in the company, so if the company made more money then he would also." She leaned forward a fraction, just a tiny movement, but the earnestness in her face was intense. "I would give everything I have to prove his innocence and protect him from future blame, should there be any."

"What is it exactly that you have overheard, Miss Harcus, and from whom?" There was something in the mention of railways that stirred an old memory within him—light and shadows, unease, a knowledge of pain from before the accident. He had rebuilt his life since then, created something new and good, recognizing and piecing together the facts of himself he had discovered, and the shards of memory that had returned. But the vast mass of it was lost like a dream, somewhere in the mind but inaccessible, frightening because it was unknown. What detection had shown him was not always pleasant: a man driven by ambition—ruthless, clever, brave, feared more than liked.

She was watching him with those intense, golden-brown eyes. But she was consumed by her own discomfort.

"Talk of great profit which must be kept secret," she answered him. "The new line is due to be completed very soon. They are working on the last link now, and then it will be ready to open."

He was struggling to make sense of it, to understand why she should imagine dishonesty. "Is it not usual to make a large profit from such an undertaking?"

"Of course. But not one that must be kept secret, and . . . and there is something else which I have not yet told you."

"Yes?"

Her eyes searched his face minutely, as if every inflection, no matter how tiny, were of importance to her. It seemed she cared for Dalgarno so profoundly that her concern over his involvement was more important to her than anything else. A misjudgment of Monk could be a disaster.

She made her decision. "If there has been fraud, and it is to do with the purchase of land, then that would be morally very wrong," she said. "But if it concerns the actual building of the track, the cutting through hills, which is sometimes necessary, or the building of bridges and viaducts, and something is done which is not right, a matter of design or materials, do you not see, Mr. Monk, that the consequences could be far more serious . . . even terrible?"

A memory stirred in him so briefly he was not even sure if he imagined it, like a darkness at the edge of the mind. "What sort of consequence are you thinking of, Miss Harcus?"

She let her breath out in a sigh, then gulped. "The worst I can imagine, Mr. Monk, would be if a train were to come off the rails and crash. It could kill dozens of people . . . even hundreds . . ." She stopped. The idea of it was too dreadful to allow her to continue.

Train crash. The words moved something inside Monk like a bright, vicious dagger in his mind. He had no idea why. Certainly a train crash was a fearful thing, but was it any worse than loss at sea, or any other of a dozen disasters, natural or man-made?

"You understand?" Her voice came to him as if from far away.

"Yes!" he said sharply. "Of course I do." He forced his attention back to the woman in front of him, and her problem. "You are afraid that some fraud in the construction of the railway, whether in the land used or the materials, may cause an accident in which many people could lose their lives. You think it possible Mr. Dalgarno may share the blame for this, even though you believe it extremely unlikely that he would be morally guilty. You would like me to find out the truth of the matter before any of this happens, and thereby prevent it."

"I am sorry," she said softly, but she did not lower her gaze. "I should not have questioned your understanding. That is exactly what I would like. Please . . . before you say anything else, look at the papers I have with me. I dare not leave them in case they are missed, but I believe they matter." She reached for the bag at her feet and picked it up. She opened it and took out fifteen or twenty sheets of paper and leaned across, offering them to him.

He accepted them almost automatically. The first one was folded over, and he opened it. It was a survey map of a large area of countryside, most of it with many hills and valleys, and a line of railway track marked clearly through it. It took him a moment or two to recognize the names. It was in Derbyshire, on a line running roughly between London and Liverpool.

"This is the new line Mr. Dalgarno's company is building?" he asked.

She nodded. "Yes. It goes through some very beautiful land between mining districts and the big cities. It will be used a great deal for both goods and passengers."

He did not repeat his comment about quite normal profit. He had said it once. He looked at the next paper, which was a map of a much smaller section of the same area, and therefore in greater detail. This time the grid references were on the corners, the scale below, and every rise and fall of the land was written in, and in most places the actual composition of the soil and rock beneath the surface. As he stared at it he had an odd sense of familiarity, as if he had seen it before. And yet as far as he knew he had never been to any part of Derbyshire. The names of the towns and villages were unknown to him. One or two of the higher peaks were identified, and they were equally unknown.

Katrina Harcus waited without comment.

He looked at the next sheet, and the next. They were deeds to purchase stretches of land. He had seen such things often before. There would be many of them necessary in the construction of a railway. Land always belonged to someone. Railways had to stop at towns if they were to be any use, and the way in and out lay through areas that were bound to be built upon. It was sometimes a long and difficult matter to acquire a passage through.

Some enthusiasts believed the rights of progress overruled everything else. All structures across the path of the railway should be demolished, even ancient churches and abbeys, monuments to history, great works of architecture, private homes. Others took the opposite view and hated the noise and destruction with a violence that did not stop short of action.

He flicked back to the first map again. Then he realized what it was that had jolted his memory, not the land at all, but the fact that it was a surveyor's map. He had seen such maps before, with a proposed railway line penciled through them. It had to do with Arrol Dundas, the man who had been his friend and mentor when he had left Northumberland as a young man and come south, the man to whom he had owed just that kind of loyalty of which Katrina Harcus had spoken, the debt of honor. Monk had been a banker then, determined to make his fortune in finance. Dundas had taught him how to look and behave like a gentleman, how to use charm and skill and his facility with figures to advise in investment and always earn himself a profit at the same time.

He had deduced much of this from fragmentary facts that came to him in other cases—a snatch of recollection, a momentary picture in the mind—rather than remembered it in any sequence. And with it always came the memory of helplessness and pain. He had failed terribly, overwhelmingly. As he looked at the map now, the grief engulfed him again. Arrol Dundas was dead. Monk knew that. Dundas had died in prison, disgraced for something he did not do. Monk had been there, and unable to save him, knowing the truth, trying repeatedly to make anyone else believe him, and always failing.

But he did not know where, nor exactly when. Somewhere in England, before Monk had joined the police. It was his inability then to effect any kind of justice which had driven him to become part of the law. He had not learned more than that. Perhaps he had not wanted to. It was part of the man he used to be, and so much of that was not what he admired or wanted anymore. His youth belonged to that same hard, ambitious man who hungered for success, who despised the weak, and who all too often disregarded the vulnerable. And nothing he could do now would help Dundas or retrieve his innocence. He had failed then, when he knew everything. What was to be gained now?

Nothing! It was just that the survey map, with its proposed railway, and the purchase order for land had brought back a past of which he had no knowledge, almost as if he had broken from a dream to step into it, and it was the reality, and everything since only imagination.

Then it was gone again, and he was sitting in the present, in his own home in Fitzroy Street, holding a sheaf of papers and looking at a troubled young woman who wanted him to prove to the world, and perhaps most of all to her, that the man she was going to marry was not guilty of fraud.

"May I make notes of some of this, Miss Harcus?" he asked.

"Of course," she agreed quickly. "I wish I could allow you to keep them, but they would be missed."

"Naturally." He admired her courage and the fact that she had taken them at all. He rose to his feet and fetched pen and paper from his desk, bringing the inkwell back with him and sitting at a small table by his chair. He copied rapidly from the first map, then the second, taking the grid references, the names of the principal towns and the main features of the route.

From the other papers he took the areas, prices, and names of the previous owners of the land purchased. Then he looked at the rest that she had handed him. There were purchase orders and receipts for an enormous amount of materials, including wood, steel, and dynamite; for tools, wagons, horses, food for men and animals; and endless wages for the navvies who cut the land, built bridges and viaducts, laid the track itself—but also for ostlers, blacksmiths, wheelwrights, carpenters, surveyors and a dozen other minor tradesmen and artisans.

It was a vast undertaking. The sums involved amounted to a fortune. But building railways had always been about speculation and venture capital, about winning or losing everything. That is why men like Arrol Dundas were drawn to it, and it needed their skill and willingness to take risks.

Arrol Dundas in the past, Dalgarno now, and Monk as he had been however many years ago.

He must read the papers closely, he told himself. Notes were not enough. If there were anything fraudulent it would not be in the open for a casual observer to see. Had it been, then Katrina Harcus herself would have read it, and in all probability understood. Unless, of course, she had understood but could not bring herself to face Dalgarno with it, and she wanted Monk to stop him before he was committed beyond retreat?

He read the bills and receipts carefully. The expenses seemed reasonable. Two of them were signed by Michael Dalgarno, the others by a Jarvis Baltimore. The figures were added correctly and there was nothing unaccounted for. Certainly some of the land purchased was expensive, but it was the stretches previously occupied by houses, workers' cottages, tenant farmers. The payment did not seem to be more than the land was worth.

He looked at the last two orders for navvies' wages. They were what a hardworking and skilled man might expect. He flicked down the list. Masons received twenty-four shillings a week. Bricklayers were paid the same, also carpenters and blacksmiths. The navvies who used picks were paid nineteen shillings, the shovelers seventeen. The last two seemed a trifle high. He looked at the signature at the bottom—Michael Dalgarno. Was that really fraud—a shilling or two on the price of pickmen?

He looked at the last one. The pickmen were twenty-four shillings, the shovelers twenty-two shillings and sixpence. The signature was . . . he felt the blood pounding in his head. He blinked, but his vision did not clear. It was there in front of him—William Monk!

He heard Katrina Harcus say something, but it was no more than a jumble of sound in his ears.

This made no sense. His name on the order! And his hand! There was no arguing it. He had lost the past up to 1856, but since then he remembered everything as well as anyone else. Date? When was it? He could prove he had nothing to do with it.

Date! There it was at the top, just under the company name. Baltimore and Sons, August 27, 1846. Seventeen years ago. Why was this receipt in with the present-day ones? He looked up at Katrina Harcus. She was watching him, her eyes bright, eager.

"Have you found something?" she said breathlessly.

Should he tell her? Everything in him shrank from the thought. It was his fear, to be kept secret until he understood it. All she cared about was Dalgarno. Someone had accidentally picked up an extra piece of paper and an old receipt had been mixed in with the current ones. It was coincidence that it was the same company. But then why not the same? There were only so many large manufacturers and builders in the business. It was the same area, London to the northwest. Not really such a coincidence.

"Not yet." His mouth was dry; his voice came with an effort. "The figures seem correct, but I shall make notes of all the facts and investigate them. From what you have here, though, there does not seem to be any irregularity."

"I heard them speak of an enormous profit, far above and beyond what is usual," she said anxiously, her brow furrowed. "If it were there openly"—she gestured to the papers—"I could have found it myself. But I am deeply afraid, Mr. Monk, firstly for Michael, his reputation and his honor, even his freedom. Men can go to prison for fraud. . . ."

Monk was cold inside. He, of all people, knew that! As if it were only days ago, hours even, he could see Dundas's white face in the dock as he was sentenced. He could remember their last parting. And he knew exactly where he had been when Mrs. Dundas had told him of her husband's death. He had gone to visit her. She was sitting in the dining room. He could recall exactly the sunlight through the windows shining bright and hard on the glass cabinets, almost obscuring the Staffordshire china dogs inside. The tea had been cold. She had been sitting there by herself, time sliding by, as if the world had stopped.

"Yes, I know," he said abruptly. "I will look into the land

purchases very carefully, and the quality of the materials and that the building is actually what is specified here. If there is anything that can cause or contribute to a rail crash I shall find it, I promise you, Miss Harcus." It was a rash thing to say, and he knew it the moment the words were out of his mouth, but the compulsion within him was greater than any whispered caution in his mind.

She relaxed, and for the first time since she had entered the room, she smiled. Her smile was dazzling, intensely alive, making her face almost beautiful. She rose to her feet.

"Thank you, Mr. Monk. There is nothing you could say that would make me happier. I feel confident that you will do everything I hope. Indeed, you are all I had believed of you."

She was waiting for the papers. Could he keep the one with his own name on it? No. She was watching him. There was no possibility.

She took them from his hand and replaced them in her bag, then from her purse she carefully took out five sovereigns and offered them to him. "Will this suffice as a retainer for your services?"

His lips were dry. "Certainly. Where may I reach you to report anything I find, Miss Harcus?"

The gravity returned to her face. "I have to practice the utmost discretion. It is important that Mr. Dalgarno, and indeed the Baltimore family, have no idea whatsoever of my concern, as I am sure you will appreciate."

"Of course."

"I do not know whom I may trust, or who among my friends would feel a divided loyalty if they were aware of my fears. Therefore I think it would be prudent of me to place no one at all under that burden. I will be in the Royal Botanic Society Gardens in the afternoon at two o'clock, from the day after tomorrow until I see you." She smiled very slightly. "It is no inconvenience to me. I have always had a fondness for plants and my presence will not cause any surprise. Thank you, Mr. Monk. Good day."

"Good day, Miss Harcus. I will be there as soon as I have anything to tell you."

He sat for a little while after she had gone, reading and rereading his notes. Apart from the order signed by himself, the others made excellent sense. It was all exactly what he would have expected. Obviously they were only samples of a very much larger quantity which would stretch over years of activity. But would anyone be blatant enough to alter or corrupt receipts so that someone looking at them could see a discrepancy? Surely the differences would lie between the paper and the reality. For that he would have to go to Derbyshire and look at the track itself.

If, on the other hand, as seemed far more likely, the fraud lay in the purchase of land, if he went to the appropriate offices in Derbyshire, he would be able to find the original copies of the survey and begin to trace the ownership, the transfer of money, and anything else that was relevant.

When Hester came home at nearly eleven, exhausted and frightened by the events of the night, he was relieved to see her. She was later than usual and he had become anxious. He made an effort to put everything to do with railways out of his mind, even the fact that his own name had been on one of the orders. She had been up all night, and obviously wished to speak to him about something so urgently she barely waited until she had sat down.

"No, thank you," she replied to his offer of tea. "William, there is most despicable business going on in Coldbath." And she proceeded to tell him about the young women who had been lent money and required to pay it back at extortionate rates of interest by prostituting themselves for the particular tastes of men who liked women of good family. "It is their pleasure to humiliate them in a way that using an ordinary woman of the streets could never do," she said furiously. "How can we fight it?" She stared at him with anger burning in her eyes and her cheeks flushing.

"I don't know," he replied honestly, feeling guilty as he said it. "Hester, women have been exploited like that for as long as anyone knows. I don't know how to help it, except now and then in individual cases."

She would not accept defeat. She sat on the edge of her seat, her back rigid, her body stiff. "There has to be something!"

"No . . . there doesn't have to be," he corrected her. "Not this side of God's justice. But if there is, and you can find it, I'll help you all I can. In the meantime I have a new case, possibly to do with fraud in the building of railways . . ." He saw the look of impatience in her face. "No, it's not just money!" he said quickly. "If a railway track is built on land that is fraudulently obtained, or there is an unjust profit, that is illegal and immoral, but what if it is built on land that is wrongly surveyed, that subsides under the weight of a coal train? Or if the bridges or viaducts are constructed with cheap or substandard materials or labor? Then you risk having a crash. Have you thought how many people are killed or injured in a rail crash? How many people does a passenger train carry?"

Her impatience vanished. She let out her breath in a slow sigh. "There might be land fraud; I don't know anything about that. But navvies know materials. They wouldn't build with anything that wasn't good enough, and they wouldn't build in a substandard way." She spoke with complete certainty, not as if it were an opinion but a fact.

"How on earth would you know that?" he asked, not patronizingly but as if she might have an answer, not because he thought she could, but because she was tired and had seen too much pain, and he did not want to hurt her anymore.

"I know navvies," she replied, stifling a yawn.

"What?" He must have misheard. "How do you know navvies?"

"In the Crimea," she said, pushing her hair back off her brow. "When we were stuck in the siege of Sebastopol in the winter of '54 to '55, nine miles from the port of Balaclava and with the only road washed out so not even a cart could get through. The army was freezing to death, or dying of cholera." She shook her head a little, as if the memory still hurt. "We had no food, no clothes, no medicine. They sent hundreds of navvies out from England to build us a railway . . . and they did. Without any help, and all through the Russian winter, they worked, and swore, and fought each other, and it was all finished by March. A double track, with tributary lines as well. And it was perfect." She looked at him with a spark of pride and defiance, as if they were her own men, and perhaps she had nursed a few of them if there had been accidents or fever.

He tried to picture it, the gangs of men laboring to cut a track through the mountains in the middle of the bitter snow, thousands of miles from home, to relieve the armies who had no other way out. He dared not think of the soldiers, or of the incompetence which had brought about such a thing.

"You didn't mention that before," he said to her.

"Nothing brought it to mind," she replied, stifling another yawn. "They were all volunteers, but I don't think you'll find it any different here. But look into it. See if there has ever been an accident caused by bad excavation or bad building of track. See if you can find a tunnel that caved in or a viaduct that collapsed or rails that were built on bad ground, or at the wrong incline, or anything else that was the navvies' doing."

"I will," he agreed. "Now go to bed. You've done all you can." He reached out and put his hand over hers. "Don't think about the usurer and the women. There's always going to be violence. You can't stop it; all you can do is try to help the victims."

"That seems pretty pathetic!" she said angrily.

"It's like the police," he said with a half-smile. "We never prevented crime from happening, we only caught people afterwards."

"You took them to the courts!" she argued.

"Sometimes, not always. Do the best you can; don't cripple yourself by agonizing over what you can't reach."

She conceded, giving him a quick, gentle kiss, and then all but stumbled her way to the bedroom.

Monk left the house and went into the city to begin searching for the information which would help him answer Katrina Harcus's questions. He tried to concentrate, but nagging like a constant, dull toothache was the sight of his own name on the receipt of Baltimore and Sons from seventeen years before. He did not even think of denying it was his. He had recognized it beyond doubt, the familiar, bold writing, more assertive than now, written by the man he used to be, before he looked more closely at himself and knew how others perceived him.

He went to see a merchant banker for whom he had solved a small domestic mystery to his great satisfaction.

"Baltimore and Sons?" John Wedgewood said, hiding his curiosity with difficulty. They were sitting in his oak-paneled office. A crystal tantalus was on the side table, but Monk had declined whiskey. "Well-respected company. Financially sound enough," Wedgewood went on. "A great tragedy, especially for the family. I take it that it is the family who has asked you to investigate? Don't trust the police." He pursed his lips. "Very wise. But you'll need to move very swiftly if you are to forestall scandal."

Monk had no idea what the man was talking about. It must have been clear from his face, because Wedgewood understood before Monk had time to frame a reply.

"Nolan Baltimore was found dead in a brothel in London," Wedgewood said, puckering his brow with distaste, and something which might or might not have been sympathy. "I apologize. I rather leaped to the conclusion that you had been asked to find the truth of the matter before the police, and if possible to persuade them into some sort of discretion."

"No," Monk answered, wondering for an instant why he had not read about the case in newspaper headlines, then realizing the answer before the question was on his tongue. It must be the murder Hester had referred to, and which had set the police buzzing around the Farringdon Street area in what was very probably a hopeless quest. No doubt the press would learn the reason for all the activity soon enough. They had only to ask one of the local inhabitants sufficiently inconvenienced, and sooner or later the story would emerge, suitably dramatized.

"No," he repeated. "I am interested in the reputation of the company, not Mr. Baltimore personally. How good is their work? What skill and honesty have their men?"

Wedgewood frowned. "In what regard?"

"All regards."

"Are you asking on behalf of someone interested in investment?"

"In a manner of speaking." It was true enough. Katrina Harcus was investing her life, her future, in Michael Dalgarno.

"Financially sound," Wedgewood said without hesitation. "Weren't always. Had a shaky spell fifteen or sixteen years ago, but weathered it. Don't know what theirs was about specifically, but a lot of people did then. Great age of expansion. People took risks."

"Their workmanship?" Monk asked.

Wedgewood looked a little surprised. "They use the traveling navvies, the same as everyone else. Platelayers, miners, masons, bricklayers, carpenters, and blacksmiths—all that sort of thing. And there are engine men and fitters, foremen, timekeepers, clerks, draftsmen and engineers." He shrugged slightly, looking at Monk with puzzlement.

"But they're all competent or they wouldn't last. The men themselves see to that. Their lives depend on every man doing what he should, and doing it right. Best workmen in the world, and the world knows it! British navvies have built railways all over Europe and America, Africa, Russia, and no doubt will go to India and China as well, and South America too. Why not? They all need railways. Everybody does."

Monk steeled himself to ask the question he dreaded. "What about accidents, crashes?"

"God knows how many men get killed in the construction." Wedgewood pursed his lips, a flicker of anger and sadness in his eyes. "But I never heard of one that was down to poor building."

"Substandard materials?" Monk asked.

Wedgewood shook his head. "They know their materials, Monk. No navvy is going to put in the wrong stone or wood, or anything else. They know what they're doing. They have to. Don't shore up a wall properly, or put in insufficient timber, and the whole lot will come down on top of you. It's my business to know, and I've never heard an instance of navvies getting it wrong."

"But there have been accidents!" Monk insisted. "Crashes, people killed!"

Wedgewood's eyes widened. "Of course there have, God help us. Terrible ones. But they were nothing to do with the track."

"What then?" Monk found himself holding his breath, not for Katrina Harcus but for himself. It was Arrol Dundas who filled his mind, and his own guilt in whatever had happened seventeen years ago.

"All sorts of things." Wedgewood was looking at him curiously. "Driver error, overloaded wagons, bad brakes, signals wrong." He leaned forward a little. "What are you after, Monk? If someone wants to invest in Baltimore and Sons all they have to do is ask in the financial community anywhere. They don't need a private agent of enquiry for that. Any merchant banker would do."

"I have a nervous client," Monk admitted. "What about unsuitable land?"

"No such thing," Wedgewood replied instantly. "Good navvies can build on anything, and they do. Sand. Swamps, even—it just costs more. They need to lay pontoons, or sink stilts until they come to bedrock. Are you sure you aren't after his personal life?"

Monk smiled. "Yes, I am sure. The Baltimore family is not my client, nor is anyone related to them. I have no concern in his death unless it has to do with his railway's honesty or safety."

"I doubt it has," Wedgewood said ruefully. "Just a very regrettable lapse of personal judgment."

Monk thanked him and left to pursue the other idea nagging more and more insistently in his mind. Perhaps no one would risk a fraud in which one sharp-eyed navvy might betray him. And the amounts of profit he made might be small. Far easier and less dangerous, and certainly with more money to be made from it, would be something to do with the purchase of the land for the track.

He did not mention this to Hester. It was far more real, closer to him and not to be laid so easily at some anonymous door, although he had no memory he could pin down. There was nothing but a nameless anxiety, something dark at the back of his mind.

The following day he started specific enquiries. Who decided where a railway line should run? What provisions were there for obtaining the land? Where did the money come from? Who surveyed it? Who bought it?

It was not until he had answered these questions, all ending back with the railway company, that it crossed his mind to wonder what happened to the dispossessed who had once lived in the houses knocked down to make room for progress, or to those who had worked the land now divided or gouged out for cuttings?

None of the answers surprised him, as if he had once known them as easily as did the small, neat clerk who sat across the office table from him. The clerk looked slightly baffled at the question.

"They move to live somewhere else, sir. They can hardly stay there!"

"Do they all agree to that?"

"No sir, not quietly," the clerk acceded. "An' sometimes if it's a big estate—aristocracy, or the like—then the railway just 'as ter go 'round it. No choice. 'Em as 'as got the power, in Parliament or that, can see their land don't get cut up. An' o' course there's gentry what object like mad to their 'unting being sliced in 'alf."

"Grouse and pheasants?" Monk asked with slight surprise. He had imagined farmland.

"Foxes, actually," the clerk corrected him. "Likes ter ride after 'em, an' can't get 'orses ter jump tracks like they do 'edges, an' all." The light in his eyes betrayed a certain satisfaction in this, but he did not elaborate. He had long ago

learned not to have personal opinions, as far as anyone else
would know.

"I see," Monk acknowledged.

"Yer bin abroad, sir?"

"Why?"

"I was jus' wonderin' 'ow yer missed knowin' all this kind
o' thing. Lot o' fuss about it in the papers, goin' back a bit,
like. Protests, an' all. Work o' the devil . . . railways. If the
good Lord 'ad meant us ter travel that way, an' at that speed,
'E'd 'ave made us with steel skins an' wheels on our feet."

"And if He hadn't meant us to think, He wouldn't have
given us brains," Monk countered immediately, and even as
the words were on his tongue, he heard an echo of them as if
he had said them before.

"Yer try tellin' that to some o' them ministers 'oo's
churches get knocked down an' moved!" The clerk's face was
eloquent of his awe, and an amusement he was trying hard to
suppress.

"Knocked down and moved?" Monk repeated the words as
if they were incredible, but he believed them—in fact, he
knew they were true. Again memory had jabbed at him and
then disappeared. For an instant he saw a lean face, dark with
outrage, above a clerical collar. Then it was gone. "Yes, of
course," he said quickly. He did not want the man to tell him
more about it. The memory was unpleasant, touched with
guilt.

"O' course they protest." The clerk shrugged his shoulders.
"All kinds of 'em out by the score. Talk about Mammon an'
the devil, an' ruin of the land, an' so on." He scratched his
head. " 'Ave ter say I wouldn't take kindly if it were me mam
an' dad 'oo's gravestones were took up, an' they was left ter
lie under the tracks o' the five forty-five from Paddington, or
whatever. I reckon I'd be out there wi' placards in me 'and an'
threatenin' 'ellfire on the profiteers as did it."

"Has anybody ever done more than threaten?" Monk had
to ask. If he did not, the question would remain in his mind,
written across everything else until he found the answer.
"Anyone ever sabotage a line?"

The clerk's eyebrows rose almost halfway up his forehead. "Yer mean blow up a train? Gawd! I 'ope not!" He bit his lip. "Come ter think on it, though, there've bin a few nasty crashes, one or two of 'em nobody knows for sure 'ow they 'appened. Usually blame the driver or the brakeman. There was a real bad one up Liverpool way about sixteen years ago, an' that was one as 'ad a church removed, an' the vicar was right cut up about it." He stared at Monk with increasing horror. "Terrible one, that was. I was still livin' at 'ome, an' I can remember me dad comin' inter the parlor, 'is face white as the tablecloth, an' no newspaper in 'is 'and. It was a Sunday dinnertime. We'd bin ter church so we 'adn't seen the early papers."

" 'W'ere's the papers, George?' me mam asked 'im.

" 'We in't gettin' no papers terday, Lizzie,' 'e answered 'er.

" 'Nor you neither, Robert,' 'e adds ter me.

" 'There's bin a terrible crash up Liverpool way. Near an 'undred people killed, an' only God in 'Is 'eaven knows 'ow many injured. I'm a 'tellin' yer because yer'll 'ear it any road, but don' go lookin' at no paper. There's things in there yer don' wanna know. Pictures they drawed yer don' wanna see.' That was ter protect me mam, o' course."

"But you looked?" Monk said, knowing the answer.

"O' course!" The clerk's face was pale at the memory. "An' I wished I 'adn't. Wot me dad never said, fer me mam's sake, was that a coal train 'ad 'it a load o' children on an 'oliday outing, one o' them excursion trains. They was all comin' 'ome from a day at the seaside, poor little beggars." His mouth was tight with grief and he blinked away the vision even now, as if he could see the artist's impressions back in front of him with all their horror and pain, the mangled bodies in the wreckage, rescuers trying desperately to reach them while there was still time, driven to try, and terrified of what they would find.

Was that what waited buried at the back of Monk's mind, like a plague pit, waiting to be opened? What kind of a man was he that he could have had any part—even any knowledge—of a thing like that and forgotten it? Why, if he'd had no part in it, did it not stay an innocent grief such as this man felt?

What had he done then? Who had he been before that night nearly seven years ago when in an instant he had been obliterated and re-created again, washed clean in his mind but in his body still the same person, still responsible?

Was there anything on earth as important as learning that? Or as terrible?

"What caused the crash?" He heard his own voice as if from far away, a stranger speaking in the silence.

"Dunno," the clerk said softly. "They never found out. Blamed the driver and the brakemen, like I said. That's the easiest, seein' as they were dead an' couldn't say nothin' diff'rent. Coulda' bin them. 'Oo knows?"

"Who laid the tracks?"

"Dunno, sir, but they was perfick. Bin used ever since, an' nothin' else's ever 'appened."

"Where was it exactly?"

"Can't remember, sir. It wasn't the only rail crash, o' course. I just remember 'cos it were the worst . . . it bein' children, like."

"Something caused it," Monk insisted. "Trains don't crash for no reason." He longed to be told it was human error for certain, nothing to do with the planning or building of the line, but without proof he could not believe it. Arrol Dundas had been tried and sent to prison. The jury had believed him guilty of fraud. Why? What fraud? Monk knew nothing about it now, but what had he known then? Could he have saved Dundas if he had been prepared to admit his own part? That was the fear that crowded in on him from all sides like the oncoming of night, threatening to snatch back from him all the warmth and the sweetness he had won in the present.

"I dunno," the clerk insisted. "Nobody knew that, sir. Or if they did, they weren't tellin'."

"No . . . of course not. I'm sorry," Monk apologized. "Where can I find out about land acquisition and surveying for railways?"

"Best go ter the nearest county town for the track in question," the clerk replied. "If yer want that old one, go ter Liverpool, I reckon, an' start from there."

"Derbyshire? Derby, I suppose." That was not really a question. He had supplied his own answer. "Thank you."

"Yer welcome, I'm sure. I 'ope it's some use to yer," the clerk said graciously.

"Yes. Yes, thank you." Monk left the office in something of a daze. Liverpool was what mattered, but if he found out whatever land purchase was concerned in the present Baltimore line, at least he would be familiar with the mechanics of it. Liverpool had waited sixteen years, and he had to report back to Katrina Harcus. If it had been fraud which had somehow caused the first crash, he was morally obliged more than any other man to prevent it from recurring. He could not go off to Liverpool chasing the demons of his memory and allow the whole nightmare to happen again because he was too preoccupied to attend to it.

He went back to Fitzroy Street to collect clean clothes and sufficient money, and to tell Hester where he was going and why. Then he took a hansom to Euston Station, and the next train to Derby.

The journey cost nineteen shillings and threepence and took nearly four hours, with a change at Rugby, which he was glad of. The second-class carriage was divided into three compartments, each less than five feet long and with twelve bare, narrow wooden seats in it. The compartments did not connect, and the partitions were covered with advertising posters. The whole was only five feet high, which meant that Monk had to duck to avoid hitting his head. First-class would have been higher, but also more expensive, and not necessarily any warmer or cleaner—although the louvered windows would have stopped vendors from sticking their heads in at the stations and breathing gin on the occupants!

It was a chilly day, alternate sun and rain, which was usual for late March, and of course there was no heating on the train. The metal foot warmers filled with hot water were restricted to first-class. Still, it was a lot better than the nicknamed "Parliamentary trains," required to fill Lord Palmerston's legislation that rail travel should be available to the ordinary people at a penny a mile.

Monk was delighted to get out at Rugby and stretch his legs, use the convenience, and buy a sandwich from one of the peddlers on the platform.

He also bought a newspaper to read on the next part of the journey. Having been in America at the very beginning of the civil war which was raging there, he was interested to see an article on the progress of the Union troops under a Major General Samuel R. Curtis, beginning a campaign in Missouri. According to the latest dispatches, the Confederates, outnumbered, had withdrawn to northwestern Arkansas.

He remembered with a shiver of grief the slaughter he had witnessed in the battle he had been caught up in during the previous summer, the uncontrollable horror he had felt, and Hester's courage in helping the wounded. His admiration for her had never been more intense, more based in the hideous reality of the broken bodies she tried to save. Everything he had ever thought or felt about her before was seen through different eyes, her anger, her impatience, the cutting edge of some of her words now passionately understood.

He looked at the peaceful countryside through the carriage windows with a sharper gratitude for it, and an upsurging will to protect it, preserve it from violence or indifference.

He was pleased when the train pulled into the station in Derby and he was able to begin his search.

He spent all day in the city records offices looking at every purchase along the entire track from one border of the county to the other until his eyes ached and the pages swam in front of him. But he found nothing illegal. Certainly there were profits made, advantage taken of ignorance, and hundreds of families dispossessed of their homes—although there was also some effort made to find them new houses—and an enormous amount of money had changed hands.

Monk tried to bring back the skills he must have had with figures in his banking days, in order to understand exactly what had happened and where the profit had gone. He pored over the pages, but if there had been any transgression it was too cleverly hidden for him to find. Perhaps he would have seen it sixteen or seventeen years ago, but if he had had that skill then, he had lost it since.

Railways were progress. In a country like England, with its mines and stockyards and shipbuilding, its cotton mills and factories, canals would inevitably have given way to faster, more adaptable railways that could cut through mountains, climb hills, and cross valleys without the time-consuming and expensive business of locks filling and emptying, and the moving of tons of water. The destruction along the way was merely a part of that progress that there was no art or skill to avoid. Farmers, landed gentry, vicars, or the tenants of villages or towns would not have liked canals any better.

He saw articles with drawings of protestors holding placards, cartoons in newspapers and periodicals calling the roaring, steam-belching iron engines the work of Satan, whereas in fact they were only the work of industry and time. Corruption, if there was any, was in the nature of man.

He sat until his head ached and his shoulders were stiff, searching every record he had determined to. There was gain and loss, but it was only the ordinary fortunes of commerce. There were stupid decisions, beside those that he could have foreseen as mistaken with the wisdom of some half-recollected experience. And of course there were those which were simply bad luck—but there was good luck as well. There were errors of judgment, but small, a matter of distance, a mismeasurement here or there.

As he pored over the pages the work became more and more familiar to him. Time stopped, like a wheel moving a cog, and he could have looked up from the lamplight on the papers to see Dundas smiling at him, not the empty inn bedroom, or the lonely tables of the records office or the library.

It was the second night that he awoke in the dark, lying rigid in the bed, startled by the silence and with no idea at all where he was. There were still shouting voices in his head—furious, accusing, people jostling each other, white faces twisted with grief.

He was breathless, as if he had been running. Without realizing it he had sat up in the bed. His body was stiff. What was the dream? He wanted to escape, run and run and leave it behind him forever!

And yet if he did, it would follow him. His mind knew that. If you fled your fears, they pursued you. He could remember that much from the coach crash which had taken his past, and from the nightmares that had followed it.

Nothing in him was willing to turn and look at those accusing faces. He felt almost bruised by them, as if they could physically have touched him, so real had they been. But there was no escape, because they were inside him, part of his mind, his identity.

Very slowly he lay down again, against sheets that were now cold. He was shivering. The fear was still there, some nameless horror that even when he found the courage to look, or could no longer help it, held no form. He could remember the anger, the loss, but the faces themselves were gone. What did they think he had done? Taken their land? Cut a farm in half, ruined an estate, demolished houses, even desecrated a burial ground? It was not personal; he had been acting for the railway!

But it was acutely personal to those who lost. What was more personal than your home? Or the land your fathers and their fathers had farmed for generations? Or the earth in which your family's bones were buried?

Was that what it was? The blind, terrified resistance to change? Then he was not guilty of anything but being the instrument of progress. So why did his body ache and why was he afraid to go back to sleep because of the demons in his mind which would return when he had no guard to keep them out?

Was it not land but the infinitely worse thing he dared not think of at all . . . the crash?

He had found nothing except the possibility that Baltimore and Sons had made too much profit from the land where the track had been diverted around the hill he had climbed with so much pleasure. Another, older survey had made it at least fifty feet less. With a skillful mixture of gradient and cutting, a tunnel would have been unnecessary. But the blasting would still have been expensive. Granite was hard and moving it was costly. Was the profit enough to justify calling it fraud? Only if he could prove foreknowledge and intent. And even then it was open to doubt.

4

THE FOLLOWING MORNING it took Monk an hour and a half after leaving the town to reach the workings of the new railway.

It was a fine day with a light wind rippling the grass, carrying the scents of earth and spring and the sound of sheep in the distance. From the height of the horse's back he could see the hawthorn hedges sweeping low, already with leaves bursting. Later he knew they would be heaped with white blossoms almost to the ground. He was following a track that climbed slowly up toward the summit over a mile away, beyond which lay the last curve of the railway line. The breeze was light and cool in his face, and sweet with the smell of earth and grass.

There was an acute pleasure in feeling the strength of a good animal beneath him. It was a long time since he had ridden, yet the moment he had swung up into the saddle, there was a familiarity to it and he was at ease. These great rolling spaces were at once a freedom and a resurrection of something quite different.

Far away to his right he could see the roofs of a village half hidden by trees, the church spire towering above them, and elms scattered over green parkland.

A rabbit shot out of the grass almost at the horse's feet, white tail flashing, and ran a dozen yards before disappearing again.

He half turned to speak, smiling, prepared to say how surprised he was to see it, and then realized with a jolt that there was no one else with him. Whom had he expected? He could see him as clearly as if he had been there, a tall man with white hair, a lean face, prominent nose and dark eyes. He would be smiling also, knowing exactly what Monk meant so there was no need to elaborate on it. It was a comfortable thought.

Arrol Dundas. Monk knew it as surely as if it had happened. They had ridden together on bright spring days like this, up hills in all kinds of country, towards rail tracks half finished where hundreds of navvies worked. He could hear the sounds of shouting, the thud of picks on earth, the ring as the iron hit stone, the rumble of wheels on boards as if they were only beyond the rise. He saw in his mind's eye the bent backs of men, bearded as navvies nearly all were, lifting shovels, pushing barrows of rock and earth, urging the horses on. He and Dundas would be going to see the progress, to estimate the time till completion, or to sort out some problem or other.

Here there was silence but for the wind carrying the distant sounds of cattle and sheep, the occasional bark of a dog. Half a mile away he could see a cart moving along a lane, but he could not hear the sound of the wheels in the muddy ruts; the cart was too far away.

What kind of problems? Protesters, angry villagers, farmers whose land was divided, saying their cows were giving no milk because of the disturbance and when the engines were roaring through, shattering the peace of the fields, it would only be worse.

It was different in towns. Houses were knocked down, and scores of people, hundreds, were dispossessed. He dimly remembered some plan to use the arches of viaducts to house the homeless. There were to be three classes of accommodation—different qualities, different prices. The lowest was to be on clean straw, and free. He could not remember if it had ever come about.

But there had been no moral or practical decision to make. It was progress and inevitable.

He tried to snatch back more detail of memory, not the emotional but the practical. What had they spoken of? What did he know of the land purchases in detail? What was the fraud involved? Wedgewood had said there was no such thing as land across which it was not possible to make a track. It was only a question of cost. And navvies knew how to set up rails on pontoons, if necessary, which could cross marshland, shifting streams, subsidence, anything you cared to think of. They tunneled through shale or clay, chalk, sandstone, anything at all. Again, it was only cost which made the difference. Back to money.

All land had to be purchased. Was it as simple as money passed back to the officer of the company who decided which route to take? A track diverted from one path to another, the officer bribed by the landowner in order to keep his property intact? Or otherwise worthless land sold at an inflated price, and the profits shared back with the officer, straight into his own pocket, defrauding the company and the investors?

That was obvious, but was it so much that it had been overlooked, at least for a while? What arrogance, to imagine they could escape forever.

Had Dundas been arrogant? Monk tried again to recapture a sense of the man he had once known so well, and the harder he looked the more any clear remembrance evaded him. It was as if he could see it only in the corner of his vision; focus on it and it vanished.

The wind was growing warmer across the grass, and far above him, piercingly sweet, he heard skylarks singing. It was timeless. It must have been like this when trains were only a thing of the imagination, when Wellington's armies gathered to cross the Channel, or Marlborough's, or Henry VIII's for that matter, bound for the Field of the Cloth of Gold. Why could he not turn in the saddle now and catch some clearer glimpse of Dundas?

The brightness of the sun on his face brought back a feeling of affection and well-being, but it was no more than that, a remembrance of being utterly comfortable with someone, laughing at the same jokes, a kind of happiness in the past that was gone, because Dundas was dead. He had died alone in a prison, disgraced, his life ruined, his wife isolated, no longer able to live in the city that had been her home.

Had he had children? Monk thought not. There were none he could recall. In a sense Monk himself had been son to him, the young man he had nurtured and taught, to whom he had passed on his knowledge, his love of fine things, of arts and pleasures, good books, good food, good wine, good clothes. Monk remembered something of a beautiful desk, wood like silk, shining, inlaid, a depth to the color like light through a goblet of brandy.

He had a sudden sharp vision of himself standing before the looking glass in a tailor's rooms, younger, thinner in the shoulders and chest, and Dundas behind him, his face so clear the tiny lines in the skin around his eyes were etched sharply, telling of years of squinting against the light, and quick laughter.

"For heaven's sake, stand up straight!" he had said. "And change that cravat! Tie it properly. You look like a popinjay!"

Monk had felt crushed. He had thought it rather stylish.

He knew later that Dundas was right. He was always right in matters of taste. Monk had absorbed it like blotting paper, taking a blurred but recognizable print of his mentor.

What had happened to Dundas's money? If he had been found guilty of fraud, there must have been a profit somewhere. Had he spent it, perhaps on fine clothes, pictures, wine? Or had it been confiscated? Monk had no idea.

He breasted the rise, and the panorama that spread out in front of him took his breath away. Fields and moorlands stretched to the farther hills five or six miles distant and around the curve of the escarpment on which he sat. The unfinished track snaked over farmland and open tussock toward the sudden dip of a stream and an adjoining marshy stretch across which spanned the incomplete arches of a viaduct. When it was finished it would be over a mile long. It was a thing of extraordinary beauty. The sheer engineering skill of it filled him with a sense of exhilaration, almost spiritual uplift at the possibilities of man and the certainty in his own mind of what it would be when the last tie was driven in. The great iron engines with more power than hundreds of horses would carry tons of goods or scores of people at breakneck speeds from city to city without resting. It was a marvelous, complicated beauty of strength, the force of nature harnessed by the genius of man to serve the future.

He remembered his own words: "It'll be on time!" He could see Dundas's face as clearly as if he had been there, hair a little windblown, skin burned, narrowing his eyes against the light. Monk was stung by loneliness that there was nothing but miles of empty grass rippling over the long curve toward the valley, broken by a few wildflowers, white and gold in the green.

He could remember the joy of it like a beat in the blood. It was not money, or gain of any natural things; it was the accomplishment, the moment when they heard the whistle in the distance and saw the white plume of steam and heard the roar of the train as it swept into view, a creation of immense, superb, totally disciplined power. It was a kind of perfection.

Dundas had felt exactly the same. Monk knew that with certainty. He could hear the vibrancy in his mentor's voice as if he had just spoken, see it in his face, his eyes. Time and again they had ridden until they were exhausted, just to see a great engine, boiler fired, belching steam, begin to move on some inaugural journey. He could see those engines, green paint gleaming, steel polished, great wheels silent on the track until the whistle blew. The excitement was at fever pitch, the railmen with faces beaming as at last the great beast stirred, like a giant waking. It would gather speed slowly—a puff, a gasp, a turn of the wheels, another, and another, the power as huge and inevitable as an avalanche, albeit man-made and man-controlled. It was one of the greatest achievements of the age. It would change the face of nations, eventually of the world. To have a part in it was to shape history.

Dundas had said that. They were not Monk's words. He could hear Dundas's voice in his head, deep, a little edge to it, a preciseness as if he had practiced to lose some accent he disliked. Just as he had taught Monk to lose his lilting country Northumbrian.

What had Monk really felt for Arrol Dundas? It had probably begun with ambition and, he hoped, gratitude. Surely later on affection had been the greater part? What he remembered now was the sense of loss, the absence of that warmth of friendship, and the certainty of having owed Dundas so much more than knowledge and advantage, but things of the inner self that could never be repaid.

He tried to put together more of the pieces, memories of laughter shared, simple fellowship in traveling. It was not only riding up hills like this on horseback, but sitting in public houses somewhere, the sun shining on a stretch of grass by a canal, bread and pickles and the smell of ale, voices he could not place. But the feeling was the same—comfortable, looking to both past and future without fear or darkness.

It should have been like that now. He had found the woman he truly loved, far better for him than the women he had wanted then, or thought he wanted. In spite of the fear at the front of his mind, he smiled at his own ignorance, not of them so much as of himself. He had thought he wanted softness, pliancy, someone to answer his physical hungers, be there to provide the home that was the background for his success, and at the same time not intrude into his ambitions.

Hester was always intruding; whether he intended her to be or not, she was part of all his life. Her courage and her intelligence made it impossible for him to exclude her. She demanded his emotions. She was a companion of his mind and his dreams as well as of his physical self. What he imagined women to be had been startlingly incomplete. At least he had not committed himself to someone else, and hurt both himself and whoever she had been.

He jerked himself back to the present and stared below him. There were laborers all over the place, hundreds of them, swarming, tiny and foreshortened in the distance. About half a mile before the viaduct there was a ridge, and they were cutting through it. He could see the pale scar of the rock face and the slope where men were "running" the barrow-loads of earth and stones up to the top, balancing with high skill on the narrow planks. It was one of the most dangerous jobs. He knew that. A slip could cause a fall, with the weight of the load crashing on top of him.

They were almost through. It was not quite high enough to require a tunnel. He could remember the brickwork, the digging, the shoring-up of tunnels. The smell of clay was in his nostrils as if he had left it minutes ago, and the steady sound of dripping from roofs, the wet splashes on the head and shoulders. He knew the labor was backbreaking. Men sometimes worked for thirty-six hours with no more than a few minutes for food, then were replaced by another shift, also working night and day.

He urged his horse forward and went carefully down the incline, following what track there was, until he was on the level and only a hundred yards from the rail. Now the noise was all around him, the thud of pick heads hitting rock and earth, the rattle of wheels on the wooden runs up the cutting, the ring of hammers on steel, voices.

The nearest man to him looked up, his shovel idle in his hands for a moment, his back straightening slowly. His skin was caked with dust and the sweat cut rivulets through it. He regarded Monk's casual clothes and well-cut boots, and the horse standing at his shoulder. "Yer one o' the surveyor's men?" he asked. " 'E in't 'ere yet. Yer a day soon." He half turned. "Eh, 'Edge'og!" he shouted at a short, heavy-shouldered man with a shock of gingery hair. "Yer sure yer in the right place, then?"

There was a guffaw of laughter from half a dozen men further away, and they all resumed their digging and shoveling.

Hedgehog screwed up his face. "No, Con, we'd better start all over an' dig through that damn great 'ill over there!" he replied.

"Three weeks, mebbe," Con said to Monk. "If that's wot yer want ter know. I in't see'd yer 'ere before. Yer come up from Lunnon?"

Apparently they assumed he was from Baltimore and Sons' main office.

"Where's your foreman?" Monk enquired.

"I'm the foreman, Contrairy York," the first man replied. "Like I said, three weeks. Can't do it no faster."

"I can see that." Monk squinted along the line of the rail. The last bit of the viaduct would take another two weeks at least, and then there were sleepers to lay, the rails themselves to lay and tie. It was double track most of the way, single through the cutting and as far as the other end of the viaduct. There must be a plan for timetables and trains passing. A length like this was far too expensive to use only one engine at a time on.

He had studied the survey map. The shortest route lay through the hill he had just crossed. "Couldn't you have cut through that?" he asked. "Then you would have avoided having to build a viaduct."

" 'Course, we could," Contrairy said dismissively. "Cost, though! Too 'igh fer a straight cuttin', an' tunnels are about the most expensive things there is. Look at yer map. See the 'eight on it! An' granite! Takes time, an' all."

Monk swung around and looked up at the hill. He pulled out the map from his pocket and read the height on it, then looked at the crest of the rise again. Something flashed in his memory and was gone before he caught it, but it was a moment of unease, nothing more, nothing he could explain. He should check the alternative routes, see who owned which land, where the vested interests lay, estimate the costs of cutting and tunneling the hill for a direct route compared with the small cutting there was here, and the viaduct, and the extra land, and length of rail. It would be a long, tedious task, but the answer, if there was one, lay in the figures. He had had the skill once. It had been where his business lay . . . his and Dundas's. That was a chill thought he would rather not have owned, but it would not go away.

He thanked the navvy, mounted his horse again and rode slowly back up the slope, thinking. He had studied the surveyor's maps and reports, and Baltimore and Sons' estimate of costs for rerouting. On paper it seemed reasonable. The investors had accepted it. Some of the new land necessary was expensive, but the land for the old route had been expensive also. It was the hidden costs that would make the difference: the bribes to do one thing or another, what to purchase, what to avoid. That could be where the fraud lay.

It was warm here, even with the very slight breeze ruffling the grass. A rabbit popped up, gazed around, then bolted twenty yards, its white tail flashing until it disappeared down a hole.

It was a moment before it meant anything to him. He searched his memory. It was the rabbit. It signified something. He was on another hillside in the sun, but colder, a wind out of the east, clouds scudding across the sky and a sense of darkness in spite of the bright light.

He remembered he had watched a rabbit sit in the sun, nose twitching, then take fright and run, going into a hole. He had seen it with a slow-dawning horror!

Why? What could be more ordinary than a rabbit in the grass, running away and diving down one of its own holes into a vast warren riddling a hillside? Doubtless it would emerge somewhere else, a hundred yards away.

Except that if a rabbit could dig through the hillside and build tunnels using nothing but its feet, then an army of navvies with explosives would have little trouble digging a tunnel for a train. The hill could not possibly be granite! The survey had lied!

He could remember it now, the shock of realization, the gaslight wavering on the paper as he opened it out on the table in his hotel bedroom and read the legend on the map. But he could not recall what else there had been, try as he might, sitting there now with the sun and wind on his face, and his eyes closed, attempting to re-create the past.

Of course there was profit in some land and not in other. But surely the investors had also checked? They must have representatives who were aware of that. It would have to have been cleverer, far subtler than simply a lie, whether the land were granite instead of clay, or chalk or conglomerate, or whatever the hill was actually composed of.

And always in the back of his mind there was the jumbled horror of something dark, unclear and violent, the rending of steel, the scream of tearing metal, sparks in the night, then flame, and through it all fear so dreadful it cramped the stomach and locked the muscles in pain.

But there seemed nothing to connect the two. Arrol Dundas had been convicted of fraud, guilty or not. There had been a crash which Monk seemed to remember, and shortly after Dundas's death he had left merchant banking and gone into the police force, driven by the passion to serve justice in future, which had to mean he had believed with a passion that there had been injustice then.

But he could do nothing more here to help Katrina Harcus or learn any greater truth about Michael Dalgarno. If there were fraud at Baltimore and Sons, then Dalgarno was almost certainly involved in it, but it was merely profiting unjustly from land purchase. There was nothing to cause injury to anyone, except the loss of possible profit to the investors. That was yet to be proved, and speculation was always as likely to end in loss as in gain. He could call for an official audit if any evidence warranted it.

It was time he stopped evading the old truth that lay at the core of his fear. Remembered pieces were little help. He must use the detective skills he had refined so well. If he wanted to know it for a client, where would he begin were it himself and not Dalgarno that he were investigating for Katrina Harcus?

Begin with the known, facts that could be checked and proven without the possibility of misinterpretation. He knew the date on the work order with his own name on it that Katrina had handed to him with the others. That was proof that he had once worked for Baltimore and Sons, but not where, and not that he had had anything to do with the fraud for which Dundas had been convicted.

Could there be more than one fraud? No, too much of a coincidence.

Nonsense—lies to comfort! Of course there could. A man who will defraud once will adopt it as a pattern if he gets away with it. The question then became: was Dundas caught on his first attempt, or on the second or third, or the twentieth?

With a jolt so sharp he startled his horse by the sudden

change in his hands on the reins, Monk realized he had actually admitted the possibility that Dundas had been guilty. In fact, he had assumed it. What a betrayal of the belief he had held without shadow all his life, until now!

He turned his horse to head up the track and around the long slope of the hill back toward the ostlers' where he had hired it, and the railway station back to London.

Where would he find the history of Dundas's bank and its dealings? He did not even know in which city they had been headquartered. It could be any of a dozen or more. Presumably, Dundas would have been imprisoned at the closest place to the court in which he was tried, and that in turn would be the nearest large city to the scene of the fraud itself.

Or could it be where the principal investors banked?

He was still considering where to begin when he rode into the ostlers' yard and dismounted reluctantly. It was a good animal and he had enjoyed riding, even though it brought the best memories, cutting sharp with loss.

He paid the ostler and walked out of the yard with its smells of leather, straw, and horses, and the sounds of hooves on stone and men's voices soft as they talked to animals. He did not look back, he did not want to see it, although it was clear in his mind.

The stationmaster was on the platform, standing almost at attention with his tall top hat shining in the sun and his Crimean medals on his chest. Monk did not know what each one meant, but Hester would have.

He spoke to the man briefly, then paced the platform waiting for the next train. His original intention had been to return to London with whatever further information he had for Katrina Harcus. The promise he had made her was still strong in his mind. At least he was one step further forward in that. Like the other, this present railway was also rerouted around a hill that had been falsely surveyed. It would have been perfectly possible, and cheaper, to have blasted through it, first by cuttings, then if necessary tunneling.

If necessary?

Something else tugged at his memory, something about

grid references for areas on the map, but he could not unravel it. Everything he caught hold of slipped meaninglessly out of his mind, taking him nowhere.

He heard the train before it came into sight around the curve in the track, shining, roaring, billowing steam, and drew to a halt with a hiss and clank of metal. The driver was grinning. The stoker, smut-stained, wiped a heavy hand across his brow, smearing coal dust on his skin.

There was a bang of opening and closing doors. Someone struggled with a wooden box. A porter ran forward.

Monk climbed into a second-class carriage again, and sat down on one of the hard wooden seats. A few minutes later the whistle blew and the train jolted forward and began to pick up speed.

The journey to London seemed endless, full of stops where he could get off, stretch his legs and get on again. They rattled over the rails, rhythmically jolted from side to side. He drifted into sleep filled with dreams, and woke stiff and aware of waiting for something terrible. He forced himself to stay awake, eyes wide open, watching the countryside slide past him.

Was Katrina right, and Nolan Baltimore had discovered the land fraud, and Dalgarno had murdered him to keep him silent? But the old receipt with Monk's name on it was from seventeen years ago, and the fraud that had ruined Arrol Dundas had happened shortly after that, long before Dalgarno could possibly have had any position with the company at all. He would barely have been out of school.

Had that first fraud been practiced on Baltimore and Sons at all? Or was Monk's connection with them coincidence? If Dundas's bank had made a business of financing railways, he might have been connected with many.

But the fraud was the same! Or it seemed the same. He could remember the rabbits, the rerouting on the longer track, the protestors, the anger, the questions as to which land was to be used, and the accusations of profiteering.

Was he transplanting all that from the past, and his own broken memory, into the present where it did not belong?

No. Katrina Harcus had come to him because she had over-heard Dalgarno and Jarvis Baltimore talking of large and dangerous profits that must be kept secret, and she feared fraud. That was fact, nothing to do with memory, true or false, and very much in the present. As was Nolan Balti-more's murder, whether it had anything to do with the railway or not.

The train pulled into Euston at last, and Monk got out and hurried along the platform, jostled by tired and impatient travelers.

The huge space beyond the platform, arched over by a magnificent roof, was filled with peddlers, people hurrying to catch outgoing trains, porters with boxes and cases, friends and relatives come to meet those arriving or to wish good-bye to those leaving. Coachmen looked for their masters or mistresses.

A paperboy was calling out the latest news. Hurrying past him, Monk heard something about the Union troops in America having captured Roanoke Island on the Kentucky border. The violence and tragedy of that war seemed very far away; the searing heat and dust and blood of the battle he and Hester had been caught up in were in another world now.

When at last he got home he found Hester asleep, curled over in the bed as if she had reached to touch him and found him not there. One arm was still outstretched.

He stood still for several moments, hesitating whether to waken her or not. The fact that she did not stir, unaware of him, told him how tired she must be. There were times when his own impulse would have woken her anyway. She would not have minded. She would have smiled and turned to him.

Now he resisted. What would he say to her? That he had found nothing in Derby except ghosts of familiarity that he could not place? That there was a crash in the past which was so terrible he could neither remember it nor forget it, and he dared not look at the reasons because he was afraid that they involved some kind of guilt, but he had no idea for what? And he had nothing yet that would help his client.

He turned away and went to wash, shave, and change into

clean clothes. Hester was still asleep when he left to go to the Royal Botanic Gardens to meet with Katrina Harcus.

It was a bright, windy, March afternoon and a score of people had chosen to spend it admiring the early flowers, the vivid green of the grass, and the giant trees, still bare, wind gusting noisily through the branches. In spite of the brilliant light, the ladies had abandoned parasols. As it was, now and again both hands were needed to keep hats in place and skirts from being whipped and lifted above petticoats.

He saw Katrina after a moment. There was a distinction about her bearing which marked her out. Apparently she recognized him just as quickly and came over without any pretense that it was a casual meeting.

Her face was flushed, but that might have been the wind and sun rather than any expectation so soon.

"Mr. Monk!" She stopped in front of him breathlessly. "What have you learned?"

An elderly gentleman out walking alone turned and smiled at them indulgently, no doubt mistaking it for a lovers' meeting. Another couple walking arm in arm nodded and moved even closer to each other.

"Very little, Miss Harcus," he replied quietly. This was not a conversation he wished overheard.

Her eyes dropped and disappointment filled her face, too acute to be concealed.

"I have made enquiries about workmanship and materials," he went on. "From what I have heard, the railway navvies are too skilled to use inadequate materials of any kind. Not only their reputations and future livelihood would depend on it, but their lives at the time. They have built railways all over the world, and there is no known example of a bad one anywhere."

She lifted her eyes quickly to gaze into his face. "Then where is the secret profit coming from?" she demanded. "This is not enough, Mr. Monk! If the materials are good, then perhaps there was dishonesty in acquiring them?" She was watching him intently, her face burning with emotion. He realized again how deeply she was in love with Dalgarno, and how terribly afraid that he would be driven into crime and then ruined by it, not only morally but in every other way, perhaps even to end in prison like Arrol Dundas. Monk knew the bitterness of that only too well. It was one thing of which even his shattered memory had not completely let go.

He offered her his arm, and after only a moment's hesitation she took it and they walked side by side between the flower beds.

"I haven't looked closely at the possibility of land fraud yet," he said, speaking quietly so passersby, strolling in the bright day, would not overhear him. He was aware of their curiosity, politely masked as courteous nods and smiles as they passed. He and Katrina must make a striking picture, both handsome people, elegantly dressed and obviously involved in a conversation of deep emotional content.

She kept her hand lightly on his arm, a delicate gesture, one of trust rather than familiarity. "Please look into it, Mr. Monk, I beg you," she said urgently. "I am desperately afraid of what may happen if no one learns the truth before it is too late. We may be able to prevent not only the tragedy of an innocent man's being implicated in a crime, but the loss of an untold number of people's lives in the kind of disaster that only something like a rail crash could bring."

"Why do you fear a crash, Miss Harcus?" he asked, frowning a little at her. "There is no reason whatever to think there is either faulty material or workmanship. If there is land fraud, then that is dishonest, certainly, but it does not cause accidents."

She lowered her eyes and turned away until he could no longer see her face except in profile, and her hand slipped off his arm. When she spoke it was barely audible.

"I have not told you everything, Mr. Monk. I had hoped not to have to speak of this. I feel ashamed of having stopped on the landing and overheard a conversation below me in the hall. I tread very lightly, and I am not always heard. It is not intentional, simply a habit from childhood which my mother instilled in me: 'Ladies should move silently and with grace.' " She took a deep breath, and he saw that she blinked rapidly, as if to control tears.

"What did you overhear, Miss Harcus?" he asked gently, wishing he could offer her more comfort, even reach the unnamed grief inside her which was easy to guess. "I am sorry to insist, but I need to know if I am to look in the right places for the dishonesty you fear."

She kept her eyes averted. "I overheard Jarvis Baltimore say to Michael that as long as no one discovered what they had done," she said quietly, "then they would both be rich men, and there would be no accident this time to mar the profits, or if there were, no one would make the connection." She swung back to face him, her skin white, her eyes brilliant, demanding. "Can it matter where an accident is? It is still human life, still people crushed beyond any kind of help. Please, Mr. Monk, if you have any skill or wit at all which can prevent this happening, do so, not just for my sake, or for Michael Dalgarno's, whom God knows I would save from harm, but for the sake of those people who might be riding the train when it happens!"

He was cold inside, imagination of mangled bodies too vivid in his mind.

"I don't see how land fraud could cause an accident, but I promise I will do everything I can to find out if there has been any theft or dishonesty of any kind in Baltimore and Sons," he promised. He would have to for his own sake as much as hers. The knowledge of the Liverpool crash and the memory of Arrol Dundas were too violent to ignore. No one knew the cause of that carnage. Perhaps if he learned more about surveying, land purchase, the movement of money, he would see the connection. "I will tell you all I know," he went on. "But do not expect an answer sooner than three or four days."

She smiled at him, relief flooding her expression like sunlight. "Thank you," she said with sudden gentleness, a warmth that seemed to reach out to him. "You are all I trusted you would be. I shall be here every afternoon from three days hence, awaiting your news." And with a slight touch of his arm again, she turned away and walked back along the path past two elderly ladies talking to each other, nodding graciously to them, and on out of the gate without looking back.

Monk turned on his heel and retraced his steps to the road, but he could not rid himself of the sense of oppression that haunted his mind. There were no specific images, just a heaviness, as if he had been forcing something out of his recollection for so long it had dimmed the sharp outlines to a blur, but its presence had never left him. What was it that he had refused to face in the past? Guilt. He already knew the sense of failure because he could not help Dundas, made the sharper by Dundas's subsequent death. But what about his part in the fraud in the first place? They had worked together, Dundas as mentor and Monk as pupil. Monk had believed Dundas innocent. That was one thing he was sure of. The emotion of admiration and respect was still perfectly clear.

But had that been knowledge or his own naïveté? Or far darker and uglier than that, had he known the truth but been unwilling to speak it or prove it at Dundas's trial because it implicated himself?

Could a rail crash between a coal train and a holiday excursion trip have anything to do with fraud? The clerk who had told him of the crash had said no one ever found the cause of it. Surely they must have looked. Experts on the whole subject would have examined every detail. If it were even possibly fraud, they would have torn apart everything to do with it until all the facts were known.

He should put it from his mind. His guilt was only that he had believed Dundas innocent and he had failed to get him acquitted, nothing to do with the crash. Dundas had gone to prison and died there, a good man who had been unquestioningly generous to Monk, sacrificed by a judicial system which made mistakes. People are fallible. Some are wicked, or at least they perform wicked acts.

What about Michael Dalgarno, with whom Katrina Harcus was so deeply in love? It was time Monk met him face-to-face and formed his own judgment.

He crossed the outer circle and walked briskly down York Gate to the Marylebone Road, where he took the next empty hansom south toward Dudley Street and the offices of Baltimore and Sons.

He went up the steps and in through the door of the building. He climbed the oak-paneled stairs, his imagination racing. By the time he was inside in front of the clerk who answered the bell on the reception desk, he had decided at least roughly what he was going to say. He already had the printed card in his waistcoat pocket.

"Good afternoon, sir. How can I help you?" the clerk enquired.

"Good afternoon," Monk replied confidently. "My name is Monk. I represent Findlay and Braithwaite, of Dundee, who have been asked to acquire certain rolling stock for railways in France, and if their venture there should be successful, in Switzerland also."

The clerk nodded.

"The reputation of Baltimore and Sons is very high," Monk continued. "I should be much obliged for the advice of whoever is available to give it to me regarding possible business of great value, which must be of the best. If whoever is in charge of land and material purchase has the time to spare me, it could be of great profit to all of us." He produced the card which gave his name, an address in Bloomsbury, and a very general occupation of adviser and agent. He had found it useful on many occasions.

"Certainly, Mr. Monk," the clerk said smoothly, pushing his spectacles a little further up his broad nose. "I shall ask Mr. Dalgarno if he can spare the time. If you would be good enough to wait there, sir." That was an instruction, not a question, and taking the card in his hand, he disappeared through the doorway, leaving Monk alone.

Monk glanced around the walls at a number of very striking paintings and etchings, several of them of dramatic railway works, towering cliffs on either side of gorges carved by swarming teams of navvies, tiny figures against the grandeur of the scenery. Ramps curved upwards from the lower levels to the higher, dotted with wagons piled with stone, horses straining against the weight. Men were swinging picks, lifting shovels, hauling, digging.

He moved to the next, which showed the exquisite arc of a

viaduct stretching halfway across a valley of marshland. Again there were teams of men and horses lifting, carrying, building for the railway to press on its relentless way, to take industry from one city to another over whatever lay between.

He walked over to the other wall, where paintings hung of specific engines—magnificent, shining machinery belching steam into the sky, wheels gleaming, paintwork bright. He felt a long-forgotten pride surge back, a shiver of excitement and fear, a sense of extraordinary exhilaration.

The door opened and he turned almost guiltily, as if he had been caught in some forbidden pleasure, and saw the clerk waiting for him.

"Beautiful, aren't they?" the clerk said with pride. "Mr. Dalgarno can see you now, if you'd like to come this way, sir."

"Thank you," Monk accepted quickly. "Yes, they are very fine." He was reluctant to leave the pictures, almost as though if he looked at them long enough they would tell him something more. But Dalgarno was waiting, so there was no time now. He followed the clerk through into a spacious but very modestly furnished office, as of a company that had yet to make any income beyond that which it plowed back into further projects rather than luxury for its employees.

But Michael Dalgarno dominated the room so that carved desks or newly upholstered chairs would seem superfluous. He was roughly Monk's height, and he stood with the relaxed grace of a man who knows his own elegance. His clothes not only fitted him perfectly but were in every way appropriate to his situation—stylish, discreet, and yet with the slight individual touch that marked a man who was not one of the crowd. In Dalgarno's case it was the unusual fold of his cravat. His hair was dark with a heavy wave, his features regular, but pleasingly not quite handsome. Perhaps his nose was a little long, his lower lip rather too wide. It was a strong face in which the emotions were unreadable.

"How do you do, Mr. Monk," he said courteously but not with the eagerness that betrays too much hunger for business. "How may I be of assistance to you?" He indicated one of the chairs for Monk to be seated, then returned and sat in the one behind the desk himself.

Monk accepted, feeling almost familiar in the office, as if it had been his own. The piles of paper, bills, and invoices were things he was used to. The books on the shelf behind Dalgarno were about the great railways of the world, and there were also atlases, gazetteers, ordnance survey maps, and references to steel manufacturers, lumber mills, and the dozen major and minor industries connected with the building of railways.

"I represent a company acting for a gentleman who prefers to remain unnamed at this point," he began, as if it were the most ordinary way to conduct business. "He has the opportunity to supply a foreign country with a very large amount of rolling stock, specifically both passenger carriages and goods wagons."

He saw Dalgarno's interest, but the intensity of it was concealed.

"Naturally, I am searching this area for the best stock at the best price," he continued. "One at which all parties will gain from the deal. Baltimore and Sons has been mentioned as a company that is rather more imaginative than most, and is of a size to give individual advice and attention to a good client." He saw Dalgarno's eyes flicker. It was only a slight widening, a greater stillness, but he was experienced in observing people and reading the unspoken word, and he allowed Dalgarno to perceive that. He leaned back a little and smiled, adding no more.

Dalgarno understood. "I see. What sort of quantities are we speaking of, Mr. Monk?"

From some untapped recess of memory, the answer came to his tongue. "Five hundred miles of track, to begin with," he answered. "If it is successful, going up to at least two thousand over the next ten years. Approximately half of it would be over easy terrain, the other half would involve a good deal of cutting and blasting, probably at least five miles of tunneling. The rolling stock would begin with a hundred goods wagons, and perhaps as many passenger carriages, but we have excellent manufacturers in mind for the latter. Of course, we could always entertain another offer if it proved to be better."

"Let me understand you, Mr. Monk." Dalgarno's expression was utterly relaxed, as if he were only mildly interested, but Monk could see the tension in the muscles beneath the eloquent lines of his jacket. Far more than anything he saw or heard betrayed in Dalgarno's voice, he knew exactly how Dalgarno felt. He had sat in such a chair at Dalgarno's age. He could feel it as if he were sitting there now. It was deeper than memory; it was an understanding almost in the bone. With no idea why, his mind could change places with Dalgarno's.

"You are going to ask me if better means cheaper," Monk said for him. "It means better value for the money, Mr. Dalgarno. It must be safe; accidents are expensive. And it must last. A thing that has to be replaced before its time is expensive, however little you pay for it. There is cost in purchase, in contracts, in haulage, in disposal of the old, and above all in idleness while you obtain the new."

Dalgarno smiled—a broad, instinctive gesture. He had excellent teeth. "Your points are well taken, Mr. Monk. I can assure you that any offer Baltimore and Sons might make would meet with all your criteria."

Monk smiled more widely himself. He had no intention of committing to anything, both because Dalgarno would have no respect for him if he did and because he wanted to remain in Dalgarno's company for as long as possible. It was his only opportunity to form a personal opinion of the man. Already he found it hard to believe Dalgarno was anybody's dupe. He would never meet Nolan Baltimore to know if he might have used and misled the younger members of his company, but if he had, Monk doubted it would have included this man opposite him. There was an alertness, a confidence in Dalgarno he could feel, as if he knew the man's thoughts and could sense his nature. He understood very well why Katrina Harcus was in love with him, but not why she was convinced of his innocence. Surely that was a blindness of the heart?

"If I submit all the particulars," Monk went on aloud,

"would you be able to give me times, costs, and specifications within a month, Mr. Dalgarno?"

"Yes," Dalgarno said without hesitation. "Delivery might take a little while, especially of rolling stock. We have a very large order in place already, to be shipped to India. That country is building at a great rate, as I am sure you are aware."

"Yes, of course. But I am impressed that you ship to India!" He was astounded, although he could not have said why.

Dalgarno relaxed, putting his fingers together in a steeple in front of him. "Not us, Mr. Monk. Unfortunately, we are not yet large enough for that. But we are supplying components to another company. But I assume you know this."

That was not really a question. He was taking it for granted that Monk was testing him, and he was allowing his candor to show.

Monk recovered himself rapidly. "Can you speak for your senior partner also?"

Dalgarno's face clouded. It was impossible to tell if his hesitation was genuine or a matter of propriety. "Tragically, our senior partner died recently," he answered. "But he is succeeded by his son, Mr. Jarvis Baltimore, who is more than able to take his place."

"I'm sorry," Monk said appropriately. "Please accept my condolences."

"Thank you," Dalgarno accepted. "You will appreciate that at this moment Mr. Jarvis Baltimore is somewhat occupied attending to family affairs, and endeavoring to be of comfort to his mother and sister. And that is where I should be this evening, Mr. Monk. Mr. Baltimore's death was sudden and totally unexpected. But of course that is not your concern, and railways wait for no man. I give you my word we shall not let personal tragedy keep us from our duty. Any promise given by Baltimore and Sons will be honored to the letter." He rose to his feet and held out his hand.

Monk took it, rising also. It was a firm, strong grip, unaffected. Dalgarno was extremely sure of himself, but with a sharp edge of hunger, an ambition in which Monk could see himself as he had once been . . . in fact, not so long ago. He had left merchant banking and financial venture far behind, but as a policeman that ambition had merely been redirected. Every case was still a battle, a personal challenge.

His charges from Katrina Harcus were to save Dalgarno and to prevent any possible disaster, and to do either of them he needed to have as much knowledge as he could of Jarvis Baltimore.

"One further question, Mr. Dalgarno," he said casually. "There are always risks of land purchase posing problems. The best deals can founder on that if a section of the proposed track runs into difficulties. Not everyone sees progress as a blessing."

Dalgarno's face was mute testimony of his understanding.

"Who deals with that subject in your company?" Monk enquired. "Yourself? Or Mr. Baltimore?"

Was there a slight hesitation in Dalgarno, or was it only that Monk wanted to see it there?

"We've all dealt with it at one time or another," Dalgarno replied. "As you say, it is a subject which can cause a great deal of concern."

Monk frowned. "All?"

"The late Mr. Nolan Baltimore was also concerned with land," Dalgarno explained.

"Indeed." Monk was about to continue when the door opened and a man he instantly assumed to be Jarvis Baltimore stood in the entrance, his face a little flushed, his expression impatient. "Michael, I . . ." He saw Monk and stopped abruptly. "I'm sorry. I didn't know you had a client." He held out his hand. "Jarvis Baltimore," he introduced himself.

Monk took Baltimore's hand and felt a grip a little too powerful, as of someone determined to exert his authority.

"Mr. Monk represents a client interested in a large purchase of rolling stock," Dalgarno explained.

Baltimore fixed his expression into one of ease and interest, although his body still carried a barely suppressed tension. "I'm sure we can help you, Mr. Monk. If you give us your client's requirements, we will quote for you on all goods."

"And services?" Monk raised his eyebrows. "Mr. Dalgarno said you also have some skill in negotiating the purchase of land and right-of-way."

Baltimore smiled. "Certainly. At a fee, of course!" He glanced quickly at Dalgarno, then back at Monk. "Now I'm afraid we must both leave the discussion for today. My family has very recently been bereaved, and Dalgarno is a close friend—one of us, almost. My mother and sister are expecting us both this evening. . . ."

Monk looked to Dalgarno and saw the quick response in his face, the immediacy of his answer. Was that ambition, affection, pity? He had no way of telling.

"I'm sure you understand," Baltimore went on.

"Of course," Monk agreed. "Again, please accept my condolences. This was only a preliminary discussion. I will report back to my principals, and they will instruct me further. Thank you very much for your time, Mr. Baltimore, Mr. Dalgarno."

He excused himself and took his leave, turning over impressions in his mind as he made his way home.

"What was Dalgarno like?" Hester asked him an hour later over a supper of grilled fish with mashed potato and onions. "Do you think he is involved in any kind of fraud?"

He hesitated before he replied, surprised by how decisive his answer was. She was watching him with interest, her fork poised in the air.

"I don't know whether there is any fraud or not," he replied steadily. "But if there is, I would find it hard to believe he was duped. He seemed knowledgeable, intelligent, and far too ambitious to leave anything to chance—or to anyone else's judgment. I would think him the last man to trust his welfare to another."

"Then Miss Harcus's opinion of him is formed more by being in love than the reality?" She smiled a trifle ruefully. "We all tend to see people we care about rather more as we wish them to be. Are you going to tell her he is very well able to care for his own reputation?"

"No," he said with his mouth full. "At least not until I know if there is any land fraud or not. I'm going to Derbyshire to-morrow to look at the survey reports, and then at the site."

She frowned. "Why is she so convinced that there is something wrong? If it is not Dalgarno, who is it she thinks is to blame?" She put her fork down, forgetting her meal altogether. "William, is it possible that it was Nolan Baltimore, the man who was killed in Leather Lane, and his death had to do with land fraud, and not prostitution at all? I know he probably wasn't there because of land," she went on quickly. "I do know what Abel Smith does for a living!" Her mouth twisted in a tight little smile. "And I assume he went there for that purpose. But it would make sense, wouldn't it, if whoever killed him followed him there and chose that place in order to disguise his real motive?"

This time she ignored the quickening of his interest.

"And left Baltimore there so anyone would assume exactly what they do," she went on. "Except his family, of course. Did I tell you his daughter came to me in Coldbath Square to ask if I knew anything that could help clear his name?"

"What?" He jerked forward. "You didn't tell me that!"

"Oh . . . well, I meant to," she apologized. "Not that it makes any difference. I can't, of course. Tell her anything, I mean. But the family would want to believe it was nothing to do with prostitution, wouldn't they?"

"They wouldn't be keen to think it was land fraud either," he said with a smile. But the thought took fire in his mind. It fitted with what he had seen of the two younger men in Baltimore's offices, what Katrina Harcus believed of Dalgarno, and it made more sense of Nolan Baltimore's death than a prostitute's or a pimp's having killed him.

Hester was looking at him, waiting for his response.

"Yes," he agreed, taking more fish and potato. "But I still don't know if there is any fraud—or, if you're right, I suppose I should say was! I must go to Derbyshire tomorrow and see the site. I need all the maps, in large detail, and I need to look at exactly what they are doing."

She frowned. "Will you know from that? I mean, just looking at the maps and the land?"

This was the time to tell her of his jolting memory, his sense of familiarity with the whole process of surveying for railways, and the land purchase with its difficulties. He had told her long ago of the snatches he had remembered of Arrol Dundas and his helplessness to prove the truth at the time. She would understand why he was compelled now to learn the truth about Baltimore and Sons, whether Katrina Harcus needed it or not. If he explained his fears it would make it easier if he had to admit later on that he had been at least partly implicated in the fraud—and the disaster afterwards which it may have caused.

He thought of her work with the women in Coldbath Square. She would be going back there tonight. She was dressed for it already, a long night's hard and thankless labor. He might not see her again until after he came back from Derbyshire. It should wait until another time, when he would have the opportunity to be with her, to assure her of . . . what? That whatever he had been in the past, he was no longer that man anymore?

"I don't know," he said. That was in essence true, even if not all of it. "I don't know what better to try."

She picked up her knife and fork and started to eat again. "If I hear anything more about Nolan Baltimore, I'll tell you," she promised.

5

HESTER HAD SPENT a strange, unhappy evening after Monk's return, aware that there was something powerful in him that she could not reach. He was either unwilling or unable to share it. She had missed him while he was away, and taken the opportunity to put in as much work as possible at the house on Coldbath Square, and she would have been happy to go there far later, or even not at all, had he said only once that he wished her to stay.

But he did not. He was brittle, absorbed in thought, and he seemed almost relieved when she said good-bye just before ten o'clock and went out into the lamp-lit darkness and took the first passing hansom to Coldbath Square.

The night was chill and she was glad of the warmth that enveloped her when she pushed the door of the clinic open and went inside. Bessie was sitting at the table stitching buttons onto a white blouse, and she looked up, her face filling with pleasure when she saw Hester.

"Yer look pinched," she said with concern. "Nice 'ot cup o' tea'll do yer good." She put the sewing down and rose to her feet. "Like a drop o' the 'ard stuff with it?" She did not even reach for it, knowing Hester would refuse. She always did, but Bessie always offered. It was a sort of ritual.

"No, thank you," Hester replied with a smile, hanging her damp coat on the hook on the wall. "But don't let me stop you."

That was ritual also. "Now that you mention it," Bessie

agreed, "don't mind if I do." She went to the stove to make sure the kettle was on the boil, and Hester went to look at the patients.

Fanny, the girl who had been stabbed, was feverish and in a great deal of pain, but she appeared to be no worse than Hester had expected. Wounds like that did not heal easily. Her fever seemed to be down.

"Have you eaten anything?" Hester asked her.

Fanny nodded. "Nearly," she whispered. "I had some beef broth. Thank you."

Bessie was coming toward them, a wide, benign shadow between the beds, away from the light of the far end of the room.

"Mr. Lockhart was right pleased with 'er," she said with pleasure. " 'E come about midday. Sober as a judge." She added that last bit with pride, as if it were partially her achievement. Perhaps it was.

"Did you give him luncheon?" Hester asked without looking up at Bessie.

"What if I did?" Bessie demanded. "We can spare 'im a bit o' bubble an' squeak, an' a sausage or two!"

Hester smiled, knowing Bessie had brought it out of her own meager pantry. "Of course we can," she agreed, pretending she did not know. "Small enough reward for all he does."

"Yer right!" Bessie said vehemently, darting a slightly suspicious look at Hester, and then away again. "An' 'e looked at Alice, an' all, poor thing. Said as she's doin' as well as yer could expect. Spent a fair time talkin' to 'er. 'E an' Miss Margaret put arnica poultices on 'er, jus' like me an' yer did, an' it seemed ter 'elp 'er some." There was fear in Bessie's voice. Hester knew she wanted to ask if Alice was going to live, and yet she was too afraid of the answer to do it.

The fact that Alice had already survived three days since her injuries was the most hopeful sign. Had there been the internal bleeding they feared, she would have been dead by now.

Hester went to her and saw that she was half asleep, dozing fitfully, muttering under her breath as if troubled by dreams. There was nothing to do to help her. Either her body would heal in time, or she would develop fever or gangrene and die.

In a while, when she was more wakeful, they would give her a little more to drink, then sponge her down with cool water and give her a fresh nightgown.

Hester returned to the table at the far end of the room where Bessie was allowing the tea to brew and putting a generous dash of whiskey into her own mug.

There were still police on every street in the Coldbath area, harassing people, asking questions. Hester had noticed them, looking profoundly unhappy but unable to escape the necessity. Most of them were locally based and knew the women—and the men who regularly came to take their pleasures, although in the current climate there were fewer and fewer of them. Business was poor in other trades as well; all those on the edge of the law were nervous and tempers were short. There was no money to be spared for small treats like peppermint water, flowers, ham sandwiches, a new hat, a toy for a child. Sellers of matches and bootlaces were about the only ones doing well.

A little before midnight Jessop called again, pressing for higher rent. He stood in the middle of the floor with his thumbs hooked into the armholes of his red brocade waistcoat, trying to add restrictions and generally making a nuisance of himself. The few women who were hurt or ill had already complained of his presence, and would do so again if he kept on coming. He made them wary; he represented authority, no matter how distantly. Hester pointed that out to him and asked him to leave. He smiled with satisfaction and remained the longer, until Bessie lost her temper and filled the bucket with hot water, lye, and vinegar. She started to scrub the floor, splashing the bucket's contents all over his boots deliberately, and he left in umbrage. Bessie then made a very slapdash effort at cleaning a couple of yards of the floor, then threw the good water away. She and Hester curled up on two of the empty beds and slept on and off, undisturbed by patients for most of the night, only getting up twice to help Alice.

"I put a weapon into his hand, didn't I!" Margaret said with chagrin when Hester told her about Jessop's visit early on the following morning when she arrived just after nine o'clock, and Bessie had gone for some shopping.

Margaret was too honest for Hester to patronize her with an excuse. Today of all days she felt a burning need for candor.

"I'm afraid so," she agreed, but with a rueful smile to rob it of offense. They were busy seeing what bandages could be saved from those used and washed. They were not in a position to afford any unnecessary supplies. "But I don't think it will make any difference in a while. We'll have to find a new place as soon as we can. He'll put us out at the first opportunity. He was always going to do that."

Margaret did not reply. Her fingers moved nimbly over the rolls of cloth, sorting some out and throwing them away, keeping the others. "What are we going to do about the usurer and the women who are being beaten?" she said at last.

Hester had been thinking about just that since she had first learned the truth from Alice, and had come to the conclusion that by themselves there was nothing they could do that did not risk making the situation worse. The usury was not a crime that the law could reach in the ordinary way. She had toyed with other ideas, but never formed any coherent plan they might be capable of carrying out.

This morning she felt even more helpless in the face of pain, because her own happiness was dimmed, her confidence in herself shadowed by the fact that Monk had placed a distance between them. Something hurt him, and he was not able to share it with her.

"We need help," she said aloud. Already her mind was made up. "Someone who knows the law far better than we do."

"Mr. Monk?" Margaret said quickly.

"No, I meant a lawyer." Hester refused to allow herself to be hurt by the thought that it was not Monk she would turn to. "Someone who knows about usury, and that kind of thing," she answered. "I think we should go as soon as legal offices will be open. Bessie will be back by then, and it is not very likely anyone will come in during the morning who can't wait for us to return."

"But who could we find who would be interested in cases

like Fanny or Alice?" Margaret asked. "And we have no spare money to pay with. Everything is already committed to rent and supplies." She said that firmly, just in case Hester should be inclined to be impractical and forget their priorities.

"I know at least where to begin," Hester replied soberly. "I won't spend our supply money, I promise." She did not yet want to tell Margaret that she was planning to see Sir Oliver Rathbone. He had been on the verge of asking Hester to marry him once. He had hesitated, and then not spoken the words. Perhaps he had seen in her face that she was not yet ready to make such a decision, or even that she would never love anyone else with the fierceness or the magic with which she loved Monk. She could not help that, whether Monk ever returned her feeling or not, and at that time she had not known. It was only after that that she had discovered Monk did return her feelings, passionately and profoundly, and he had accepted that to deny his own emotions would be to deny all the best in himself, as well as the most vulnerable.

They were friends, all three of them, in a fashion. Rathbone still felt a deep affection for her. She knew that, and Monk had to be aware of it also. But they were allies in a cause which overrode personal wounds and losses. Rathbone had never turned down a case he believed in, however difficult or against whatever odds, and certainly not because it was brought to him by Monk.

She and Margaret would go to Vere Street and tell Oliver all that they knew. At least it would be a burden shared. Suddenly she knew how good it would feel to see him, to be aware of the warmth of his regard for her, and his trust.

Actually, it was after eleven o'clock before Hester and Margaret were ushered into Rathbone's office with its beautiful leather inlaid desk and cabinets full of books, and the long windows overlooking the street.

Rathbone came forward toward Hester, smiling broadly. He was not much more than average height. His charm lay in the intelligence in his face, in his wry, delicate humor and the supreme confidence of his bearing. He was a gentleman, and he had the ease of privilege and education.

"Hester, what a pleasure to see you, even if it has to be a problem that brings you here," he said sincerely. "Who is wrongly accused of what? I imagine it is murder? It usually is, with you."

"Not yet," she replied, warmth engulfing her just to hear the gentleness in his voice. She turned to introduce Margaret, and as he turned also she saw a sudden interest spark in his dark eyes, as if already he recognized her, or something in her that he was happy to see. "This is Miss Margaret Ballinger," she said quickly. "Sir Oliver Rathbone."

Margaret drew in her breath to reply, a very faint flush in her cheeks.

"We have met already," Rathbone said before Margaret could speak. "At a ball, I forget where, but we danced. It was just before that miserable business with the architect. It is a pleasure to see you again, Miss Ballinger." The expression in his face suggested that he was speaking honestly, not simply as a matter of good manners.

Margaret took a deep breath, just a trifle shakily. "Thank you for seeing us with no notice at all, Sir Oliver. It is very gracious of you."

"Hester always brings me the most fascinating problems," he demurred, inviting them with a gesture to sit down, and when they had done so, taking the seat behind the desk himself. "You said no one has been murdered yet. Should I deduce from that that you expect someone will be?" There was no mockery in his tone; it was light, but perfectly serious.

"Two people have been very badly injured, and more will be," Hester said a fraction more quickly than she had meant to. She was aware that Rathbone was at least as conscious of Margaret as he was of her. She realized with a yawning hollow inside her how much of his life lay beyond her knowledge. The material facts of it did not matter, it was the wealth of people he knew, the emotions, the laughter and hurt, the dreams that were the man inside.

He was waiting for her to continue.

"Miss Ballinger and I have rented a house in Coldbath Square in which to offer medical treatment to women of the street who are injured or ill," she said, ignoring the look in his eyes, the strange mixture of tenderness, admiration, and horror. "Lately at least two women have come in very seriously beaten," she went on. "One of them has said that she used to be a governess, then married, and her husband led her into debt. She borrowed money, and then could not repay it." She was speaking too quickly. Deliberately, she slowed herself. "The usurer offered her a position as a prostitute, catering to men who like to humiliate and abuse women who were once respectable." She saw the disgust in his face. If he could have listened to her and felt nothing she would have despised him for it.

Rathbone glanced at Margaret, saw the anger in her, and something in him softened even further.

"Go on," he said, turning back to Hester.

"I daresay you are aware that a Mr. Nolan Baltimore was murdered in Leather Lane just over a week ago?" she asked.

He nodded. "I am."

"Since then the police have patrolled the area with more men than usual, with the result that there is far less trade possible for such women. They are earning little or no money, and cannot pay the usurer. They are being beaten for their delinquency in their debts." Memory of the two women momentarily obliterated any sense of her own loneliness. She leaned forward earnestly. "Please, Oliver, there must be something we can do to stop it. They are far too terrified and ashamed to fight back for themselves." She watched him struggle for something to say to let her down gently. She was asking too much. She would have liked to withdraw, be reasonable, but the reality of their pain burned too hotly inside her.

"Hester . . ." he began.

"I know the whole world of Coldbath Square and Leather Lane are outside the law," she said quickly, before he could dismiss her. "It shouldn't be! Do we always have to wait until people come to us before we can help them? Sometimes we have to see the problem and address it anyway." She was aware of Margaret's slight stiffening. Perhaps she was unaccustomed to such frankness from a woman to a man. It was unbecoming, not the way either to win or to keep a husband.

"You mean decide for them?" Rathbone said with a wry smile. "That doesn't sound like you, Hester."

"I'm a nurse, not a lawyer!" she said sharply. "Quite often I have to help people when they are beyond knowing anything for themselves. It is my skill to know what they need, and do it."

This time his smile was full of warmth, a genuine sweetness in it. "I know that. It is a kind of moral courage I have admired in you from the day we met. I find it a little overwhelming, because I don't possess it myself."

She found tears prickling her eyes for an instant. She knew he meant it, and it was more precious to her than she had expected. But she still wished to argue. That was no help to women like Alice and Fanny. "Oliver . . ."

Margaret leaned forward. "Sir Oliver," she said urgently, her cheeks flushed but her eyes steady, "if you had seen that poor woman's body with its broken arms and legs, if you could see her pain, her fear, and the shame she feels because she has taken to the streets to pay her husband's debts, you would feel as we do, that to nurse her through the daily distress of at least partial recovery, only to set her out into Coldbath for it to happen again, because her debt is ever falling behind . . ."

"Miss Ballinger . . ."

"Then—" She stopped abruptly, the color deepening in her face as she became conscious of how forward she was being. "I am sorry," she said contritely. "It is not your sort of case. And it is not as if we had any money to pay you." She rose to her feet, her eyes downcast with embarrassment. "It was an act of desperation. . . ."

"Miss Ballinger!" He rose also, stepping around the desk towards her. "Please," he said gently. "I do not mean that I am unwilling, simply that I do not know what I can do! But I promise you that I will put my attention to it, and if there is anything that may be done within and through the law, I will tell you, and take your instructions. Money need not be a consideration. I hesitate only because I do not wish to promise what it is outside my power to give."

Margaret looked up at him quickly, her eyes candid and direct, her face filled with gratitude. "Thank you . . ."

Hester realized with a shock of amazement that Rathbone was acceding to a request entirely against his interests and outside his nature in order not to refuse Margaret. It was not Hester he was pleasing, as it had always been in the past. She was glad he agreed, of course, and grateful, but it was an odd sense of rebuff that it was not for her. It was not obvious—in no way had he been less than friendly to her, but the quality of his attention was different. She knew it as certainly as a change of temperature in the air. She should have been happy for both of them. She was happy! She did not wish Rathbone to spend the rest of his life in love with her when she would only ever love Monk. But just today, this was as if a door had closed in front of her, and something in it hurt.

Rathbone had turned towards her. She must smile, it was imperative.

"Thank you," she added to Margaret's words. "I think we have told you everything that we know. It is the principle rather than individual women so far, but if we learn anything further we will inform you, of course."

There was nothing else for any of them to say, and they were conscious of the courtesy of his having seen them at all at the expense of other clients waiting. They excused themselves, thanking him again, and five minutes later were in a hansom riding back toward Coldbath Square. They did not speak, each lost in her own thoughts. Margaret was still flushed, her eyes wide, turned away from Hester and staring out of the window at the passing streets. No words could have been more eloquent of the fact that very plainly she had not forgotten her first meeting with Rathbone, nor had its emotional mark on her been worn away in the time between. But it was something too delicate to share. Had their roles been reversed, Hester would not have spoken either, and she did not think of intruding now. She and Margaret had been honest and natural friends. Part of such friendship was respect, and the understanding of when not to speak.

She did not wish to share her own thoughts, except the superficial ones of the mind, the difficulty of knowing where to find the women who owed money to the usurer, of persuading them that help was possible . . . if indeed it was, and the effort needed to convince them that the exercise of courage would win them anything but further pain. Above all there was the necessity of being absolutely certain that that was true.

But Margaret had been in Coldbath Square long enough to know that for herself, so Hester also watched the streets pass by and thought of practical things.

In the afternoon another woman was brought in beaten for debt. She was not seriously injured, but she was very frightened, and it was that which marked her apart from the usual anger and misery of those hurt. She was almost silent as Hester and Margaret tended to her shallow, painful knife cuts. She would not say who had inflicted them on her, no lies and no truth, but they were very obviously intentionally made. No imaginable accident could have caused such vicious and repeated slicing of the flesh.

She stayed a few hours, until they were certain the bleeding was stopped and the woman had at least partially recovered from shock. Margaret wished her to stay longer, but shaking her head, she picked up her torn shawl, once a pretty thing with flowers and fringes, and went out into the square toward the Farringdon Road.

Margaret stood in the middle of the room and looked around at the tidy cupboards, the scrubbed tabletops and the floor.

Hester shrugged. "I suppose we should be glad there's nobody else hurt," she said with an attempt at a smile. "Do you want to go home? There really isn't anything to do, and Bessie'll be in later, if anything should happen."

Margaret grimaced. "And trail around behind Mama, calling on nice ladies who look at me with kindly despair and wonder why I haven't accepted a reasonable offer of marriage?" she said wryly. "Then they'll assume that there is something terribly wrong with me . . . too indiscreet to mention, and they will think I have lost my virtue!" She gave a little grunt of frustration. "Why is it that young women are presumed to have only two possible virtues—chastity and obedience?" she demanded with sudden fierceness. "What about courage, or honesty of opinion, not just a matter of not taking what does not belong to you?"

"Because they make people uncomfortable," Hester replied without hesitation, but giving Margaret a crooked, sympathetic smile.

"Can you imagine anything lonelier than being married to someone who always says what he thinks you want to hear, regardless of whatever it is that he thinks?" Margaret asked, her brows puckered in a frown. "It would be like living in a room full of mirrors, where every other face you saw was simply a reflection of your own."

"I think it would be a very particular kind of hell," Hester answered with a rush of wonder and pity that anyone could imagine they desired such a thing, and yet she knew many who thought they did. "You have a gift to put it into such vivid words," she added with admiration. "Perhaps you should try to convey it visually sometime?"

"That would be something really worth drawing," Margaret responded. "I am so bored with doing the predictable, just reproducing what I see in front of me, with no greater meaning."

"I can barely draw a straight line," Hester admitted.

Margaret flashed her a sudden smile. "There are no straight lines in art—except perhaps the horizons at sea. Would you like me to go out and see if I can find us some hot pies for luncheon? There is a good peddler on the corner of Mount Pleasant and Warner Street."

"What an excellent idea," Hester said enthusiastically. "One with flaky pastry—and lots of onions . . . please?"

In the late afternoon Bessie came in carrying a basket with herbs, tea, a bottle of brandy, and a loaf of bread. She set it down on the table and looked around the room before taking off her hat and cape.

"Nobody!" she said with disgust, hanging the cape and bonnet on the hooks near the door. " 'Ardly a bleedin' soul out in the streets neither, 'ceptin' damn bluebottles! An' bin like that all night too, they say." She looked at Hester reproachfully, as if somehow she had failed to do anything about it.

"I know!" Hester replied tartly. "The pressure is still on them to find whoever killed Nolan Baltimore."

"Some pimp 'e crossed up!" Bessie retorted. "What else? Der they think as someone's goin' ter tell 'em that if they asks often enough? Don't s'pose nob'dy knows, 'ceptin' 'im wot done it. An' 'e in't gonna tell. 'E'd be dancin' at the end of a rope 'fore 'e can say 'knife.' " She walked over to the cupboard and started to rearrange the things inside it so she could put the new groceries away. "Funny, innit? Some bleedin' usurer can beat a girl 'alf ter death, an' nob'dy gives a toss! But kill some toff wot's refused ter pay 'is debts an' 'alf the rozzers in Lunnon's out in the streets wastin' their time askin' questions they know nob'dy's gonna answer. Sometimes I think they're sittin' on their brains an' thinkin' wi' their backsides!" She glared at the basket. "Couldn't get no butter. Yer'll 'ave ter do wi' bread an' jam."

Margaret stopped riddling the stove and moved the kettle over onto the hob.

"Nob'dy's workin'!" Bessie went on relentlessly. "Them as brings the money in are frit o' bein' done by the rozzers . . . all this 'keep the streets decent' thing. An' them as is livin' 'ere in't got no trade 'cos no one's got no money! It's wicked— that's wot it is."

There was no answer to make. There was not even any purpose in either Hester's or Margaret's remaining for the rest of the afternoon. Hester said as much, and Bessie agreed with her.

"Yer get orff." She nodded. "There's nothin' much gonna 'appen 'ere. If that fat slug Jessop comes 'round lookin' fer yer, I'll give 'im a nice 'ot cup o' tea!" She grinned demonically.

"Bessie!" Hester warned.

"Wot?" She opened her eyes wide. "If it don't agree wif 'im, I know 'ow ter give summink ter make 'im sick it up! I won' let the bastard die, I gi' me word." She spat and made an elaborate gesture of crossing her heart.

Hester glanced at Margaret, and they both half hid smiles.

But all the way home and for the rest of the evening until Monk returned late and tired, Hester thought about the women, the police around the Farringdon Road and the Cold-bath area. It was no moral answer to the evil to get the police presence removed, but it was a practical answer to the lack of trade which was crippling everyone and turning tempers so ugly.

She had tried to avoid coming to the conclusion, but it was inevitable: the only thing that would make them leave would be to solve the murder of Nolan Baltimore. If the police were going to succeed, they would almost certainly have done so by now. The community had closed against them, which was to be expected. No one would tell them anything of meaning in case it would implicate himself, in prostitution if nothing else. And most of the inhabitants of the Leather Lane area were involved, at least peripherally, in fencing stolen goods, a little forgery, of documents if not of money, in pickpocketing, burglary, cardsharping and a dozen other illegal pursuits.

She could ask Monk, at least for advice, if not practical help. He knew and understood murder and its investigation. And perhaps it was in the interest of his own case to learn everything he could of the man who, until a week or two ago, had been the head of Baltimore and Sons. If there had been fraud, he might have known of it; he might even have been the man who perpetrated it. Surely it was reasonable to suppose his death was connected?

In fact, the jarringly ugly thought was irrefutable that Michael Dalgarno could have followed him to Leather Lane and killed him, precisely because he knew of the fraud and would have exposed it.

Why had Monk not thought of that?

Because he was so caught up in investigating the exact nature of the fraud, and whether it could provoke a disaster, that he had ignored Nolan Baltimore's murder.

She waited for him, barely thinking of what else she was doing. She found herself listening for the sound of horses in the street from six o'clock onwards, for the opening and closing of the door and his footsteps. When they finally came at nearly quarter to eight she was caught by surprise, and almost ran into the hall.

He saw her face, the expectation in it, and gave her a quick smile and then looked away. The weariness and anxiety in him were so easy to read she hesitated for a moment, uncertain whether to say anything more than a few words of welcome. Should she ask him if he were hungry or had eaten, or make some enquiry after his success that could be answered on the surface—or honestly, as he chose? She could not let it slide by. If he were not going to break the barrier, then she must.

"Did you find anything more about the fraud?" she asked, not casually, but as if she were waiting for and required an answer.

"Nothing helpful," he replied, taking his jacket off and hanging it up on the hook. "There's dubious profit in land sales, but nothing more than I imagine most companies make. There are some losses as well."

She felt as if he had closed a door. There seemed little more that she could ask, but she refused to let go. She watched him, but he moved around the room restlessly, without looking directly at her, touching things, straightening, putting away. Was she mithering him just at the time when he needed the silent understanding of a friend? Was she being selfish, expecting him to give her his attention, listen to her, think of her problems when he was exhausted?

Or was she breaking a barrier while it was still thin enough to be penetrated easily, before it became habit?

"We need to find out who killed Nolan Baltimore," she said very clearly.

"Do we?" There was doubt in his voice. He was standing near the mantelshelf staring down at the embers of the fire. It was a sharp evening, and she had lit the fire for company as well as warmth. "I don't see that his personal weaknesses have anything to do with railway fraud, if there is any."

"If he defrauded somebody of money, then Leather Lane seems an excellent place to kill him," she retorted, wishing he would look at her. "A perfect situation to blame someone else, and exact a rather painful revenge on his reputation as well."

This time he did look up and smile, but it was without pleasure. There was an openness that flickered for an instant in his eyes, as if there had been no shadow, then it was gone again. The anxiety was back, and with it the distance between them.

"Actually, when I said 'we,' " she corrected herself, "I meant Margaret Ballinger and me. Or perhaps I meant everybody in Coldbath. More women are getting beaten because they can't pay their debts. The police are all over the place so nobody's doing any trade."

"You wish to find who killed Baltimore so the police will leave and the prostitutes can get back into business?" he said with an edge of mockery she could not miss. "You have strange moral convictions, Hester."

Was that pain in his voice now? Did he feel she had let him down, that she should have taken a higher, more puritan stand? He was disappointed, and she felt rebuked.

"If I could change the world so no women ever went into prostitution, I would!" she said angrily. "Perhaps you can tell me where I should begin? Get every woman a decent living at something more respectable, perhaps? Or stop every man from wanting . . . or needing . . . to buy his pleasures outside his own home?" She saw his expression of surprise and ignored it. "Perhaps every man should be married, and every wife comply with her husband's wishes? Or better still, no man should have wishes he can't satisfy honorably . . . that would solve at least half of it! Then all we would have to do is change the economy . . . after that changing human nature should be relatively easy!"

"You have rather escalated your demands," he said quietly. "I thought all you wanted was for me to solve Nolan Baltimore's murder."

Her anger vanished. She did not want to quarrel with him. She wanted intensely, fiercely, to hold him in her arms and share whatever it was that hurt him so much, to take at least half of it, if not all, to fight it with him, beside him.

It was better to try, and be rebuffed, than not to try at all. Even rejection would not hurt more than this distance, which was a kind of little death. She walked over to him and stopped just in front of him, forcing him either to meet her eyes or deliberately look away.

"All I want is for you to advise me," she said. "What should I do? What questions should I ask? Some of the women will trust me, where they won't trust the police."

"Leave it alone, Hester." He lifted one hand as if to touch her cheek, then let it fall again. "It's too dangerous. You think they trust you, and they do, to take care of their injuries. But you aren't one of them and you never will be."

"But that's just the point, William!" She caught hold of his hand, gripping it hard. "I could have been! These women who owe money were perfectly respectable only a short while ago. They were governesses, parlor maids, married women who were abandoned, or whose husbands got into debt. They could have been nurses! I earned my own living in other people's houses before I married you. One mistake, one misfortune, and I could have borrowed money, and found myself on the streets to pay it back." She pulled a self-mocking face. "At least if I were a trifle younger."

"No, you wouldn't," he said very softly, but with absolute certainty. "You would never have lent yourself to that, at any age. You'd have led a rebellion, or taken ship to America, or even stuck a knife between his ribs, but you wouldn't have gone meekly to the slaughter."

"Sometimes you rate my courage too high," she replied, but with a rush of warmth inside her at the strength of his admiration. "I don't know what I would have done. Thank God I was never put to the test."

He stood silently for a moment, then bent and kissed her

long and with a tenderness so complete, so achingly profound, the emotion welled up inside her, bringing tears to her eyes.

Then he let go, and went into the room he used as a study, and closed the door.

She was asleep in exhaustion when he came to bed. She woke in the night and he was beside her, but he did not move or touch her, even when she turned closer to him.

In the morning he was gone. There was a note on the dresser:

Hester,

I am going to investigate more into land purchase for the railway, partly because it is the only fraud I can see in the Baltimore case, but mostly because I know that Arrol Dundas was convicted of land fraud in what seems to have been almost identical circumstances. It may even have been the same company, Baltimore and Sons. I don't know that beyond question, but I am fairly certain. I hope you will understand why I need to know absolutely.

If there is anything at all I can do to make sure Dalgarno does not end up in prison as Dundas did, for something of which he is innocent, then I must do so. I will not fail him in the same way. I may have to return to the railway itself, in Derbyshire.

Please, Hester, be careful! It is enough that you work in the Coldbath area, helping people who are troubled and are incapable of repaying you, even by telling you the truth. Certainly they cannot protect you if you attract the interest of the kind of men who so abuse them.

If you won't look after yourself for your own sake, or for mine, at least do it for theirs. If you are injured, or worse, to whom could they turn?

You have in the past eloquently criticized the Crimean generals who wasted their troops in quixotic gestures. And rightly. You have often said a woman would have been more practical and less glory seeking—now prove it!

I hope to see you minding your business—and not mine—when I return, when, if I can, I shall help you to find who-

ever killed Nolan Baltimore—if the police have not already
done so.

Even if it does not always seem as if I do, I love you profoundly, and I admire you far more than you realize.

William

She held the paper in her hands as if it could bring her
some part of him, or he would know the emotions inside her,
the love and the need, the loneliness for him, the longing to be
able to help with whatever private battle he was fighting.

Why could he write so much, and yet not tell her face-to-
face? She knew the answer even as the question formed. It
was obvious—because she could hold a letter in her hands,
read it and reread it, carry it with her, but she could not demand any further answers of it. Monk himself was gone . . .
alone.

And she was here . . . equally alone. He loved her, certainly. But why was it he could not trust her also—her loyalty,
her understanding, her courage? What was it in her she feared
might fail him?

It hurt too much to think of. She would go back to Coldbath Square and work. There would be something to do, even if
it were only to seek more ideas for raising money. Perhaps they
should start to look for other premises? Margaret's friendship
was valuable, although it no longer had quite the uncompli-
cated ease she had thought it did before they had gone to
Rathbone's office.

She must not show jealousy. That would be small-minded
and unbelievably ugly! She would despise herself for that.

And of course she must try to learn all she could about
Nolan Baltimore's death, taking reasonable care not to antago-
nize anyone.

Margaret was late in to Coldbath, but that was of no importance at the moment. Tempers were short throughout the area
so there were many quarrels and several people lashed out in
frustration and fear, but it was more often men who were the
victims, and the injuries were of the nature that heal with time

and very little care—mostly bruises, shallow cuts, and sore heads. Pimps were getting more careful about scarring or bruising their women, their only asset in a shrinking market.

Of course everyone knew it would not go on indefinitely, but it had already been long enough to blow a chill of bitter reality into the lives of all manner of people. The end of it still lay in some unknown time in the future. They lived from day to day.

"How is Fanny?" Hester asked as she came in out of the fine rain, taking off her cloak and hat. "And Alice?"

"Fair enough," Bessie answered, looking at her balefully from where she was sitting by the empty table, apart from her half-drunk cup of tea. "Quiet, it is. Like a bleedin' graveyard. 'Ad two girls come in wi' disease, that's all. Can't do much fer 'em, poor cows. Miss Ballinger in't in yet. Out showin' 'erself off 'round the swell 'ouses, I shouldn't wonder. Never seen such a change in anyone in me life!" She said it with fierce satisfaction and not the shadow of a smile. "Wouldn't say boo to yer w'en she first come 'ere. Now she's as bold as brass. Ask anyone fer money, she would. Wager yer sixpence she'll come waltzin' in 'ere wi' a grin all over 'er face an' tell us she's got a few pound more fer us."

Hester did smile, in spite of the gloom of the morning. It was true, Margaret had found a confidence, even a happiness, in work. That in itself was an accomplishment, whoever else they were able to heal, and whether or not their patients would slip back to exactly the same debt and abuse afterwards.

Bessie was right; half an hour later Margaret did come in carrying satisfaction with her like a burst of sunlight.

"I have another twenty guineas!" she said proudly. "And promise of more!" She held it out for Hester, her eyes bright, her face glowing.

Hester forced herself to warm to the success, even though she felt all she could taste in her own mouth was failure. "That's excellent," she said appreciatively. "It will keep Jessop at bay for a while, and that gives us time. Thank you very much."

Margaret looked pained. "You're not going to give him more than our agreement, are you?"

Hester relaxed a little; she almost laughed. "No, I am most certainly not!"

Margaret smiled back and started to take off her jacket and hat. "What can we do today? How are Fanny and Alice?" She glanced towards the beds as she spoke.

"Asleep," Bessie answered for Hester. "Nowt ter do fer 'em now, 'ceptin keep the roof over their 'eads, an' feed 'em now an' then." She frowned at the rain spattering the window. "I s'pose I'd best be doin' some marketin'."

"Stay inside and keep dry for a while." Hester made her decision. "Margaret and I have an errand in half an hour or so. It's important."

Bessie was suspicious. "Oh, yeh?" She did not trust Hester to look after herself, but she was not quite bold enough to say so in so many words. "Wot yer gonna do that I can't do fer yer, then?"

Hester had not been going to confide in Bessie, simply as a precaution, and also at least in part because she was not sure if her plan had any chance of success. Now, suddenly, she thought better of secrecy and decided to be frank.

"If we are to solve this problem of police all over the place, and therefore no trade for the women," she said briskly, before she should lose her nerve, "we have to find out what happened to Nolan Baltimore." She ignored Margaret's look of incredulity and Bessie's sucking her breath in between the gap in her teeth. "I intend to start asking a few questions, at least. People may speak to me who would not speak to the police," she finished.

" 'Ow yer gonna do that?" Bessie said with dismissal in her voice. " 'Oo's gonna tell yer anythin' about it? Come ter think, 'oo'd yer even ask?"

"The people in Leather Lane, of course," Hester replied, spreading out her cape so it would dry. "We need to know if Baltimore went there regularly or if it was his first visit. If he went there often, then someone will know something about him, who else he knew, what kind of a man he was away from his home and family. I would like to know whether he went there simply to use the women or if he could have had some other business. Maybe somebody from his life at home followed him there? His death might have nothing to do with the people who live in the Coldbath area."

Bessie's face brightened. "Cor! That'd be summink, eh?"

"But the people of Leather Lane might not know his name," Margaret pointed out. "I don't suppose he used it."

"I shouldn't think so," Hester agreed, realizing her point. "What we need is a picture to show people."

Margaret's eyes widened. "A picture! How on earth could we get a picture? Only the family would have one, and they're hardly likely to give it to us."

Hester took a deep breath and plunged in. "Actually . . . I have an idea for that. I am not very good at drawing, but you are."

"Oh!" Margaret's voice shot up in denial, and she started shaking her head, but her eyes did not leave Hester's. "Oh, no!"

"Do you have an idea which would serve better?" Hester asked with an attempt at innocence.

Bessie understood with dawning horror. "You never are!" she said to Hester. "The morgue! Yer gonna draw a dead body?"

"Not I," Hester corrected her. "Nobody would recognize their own mother from anything I drew, but Margaret is very good. She can really catch a likeness, even if she is too modest to say so herself."

"It's not that . . ." Margaret began, then tailed off, staring at Hester as disbelief slowly turned into understanding. "Really?" she whispered. "Do you think . . . I mean . . . would they allow us to . . ."

"Well, we may require one or two embellishments of fact," Hester admitted wryly. "But I intend to try as hard as possible." She became very grave. "It really does matter."

"As long as you do the embellishments," Margaret said, making a last attempt at reason.

"Of course," Hester agreed, not yet with any very clear idea of what she would say. There would be plenty of time to think about it as they walked the mile or so to the closest morgue, where Baltimore would have been taken.

"I don't have a pencil or paper," Margaret said. "But I've got a couple of shillings of my own . . . I mean, not supposed to be for the house . . ."

"Excellent," Hester approved. "We'll get what you need at Mrs. Clark's shop on the corner of the Farringdon Road. And I daresay an eraser as well. We may not have time to start over and over again."

Margaret shrugged, then gave a nervous laugh, almost a giggle. Hester heard a note of hysteria in it.

"It's all right!" Margaret said quickly. "I was just thinking what my drawing master would say if he knew. He was such an old woman it would be worth it just to see his face. He used to like me to draw demure young ladies. He made my sisters and me draw each other. He wasn't even sure if we should draw gentlemen. The idea of that would be bad enough—he'd have a seizure if he knew I was going to draw a corpse! I do hope he'll be wearing a sheet, or something?"

"If not, you have my express instruction to draw one in," Hester promised with an answering bubble of laughter, not because she found any pleasure in it, but because to think of the absurd was the only way to make it all bearable.

They put on their outdoor clothes again and set off, walking briskly in the rain. They purchased a block of paper, pencils and an eraser, and hurried on to the morgue, an ugly, slab-sided building set a little back from the street.

"What do you want me to say?" Margaret asked as they went up the steps side by side.

"Agree with me," Hester replied under her breath. As soon as they were through the door they were faced almost immediately by an elderly man with white whiskers and an alarmingly high voice, almost falsetto.

"Good mornin' to you, ladies. 'Ow can I be of 'elp?" He bowed very slightly, blocking their way as completely as if he had held out his arms. He fixed his eyes on Hester's face, unblinking, waiting for her to explain herself.

Hester stared back at him without flinching. "Good morning, sir. I am hoping you will accommodate our request, out of delicacy to Miss Ballinger's feelings." She indicated Margaret, a look of sorrow in her face. "She has just returned from abroad, visiting her mother, who has gone to a warmer climate—for her health, you understand." She bit her lip. "Only to hear of her uncle's most terrible and tragic death." She waited to see if he showed any sign of sympathy, but she waited in vain. She did not dare to look at Margaret in case she drew attention to her startled expression.

The morgue attendant cleared his throat. "Yes?"

"I have accompanied her so she can pay her last respects to her uncle, Mr. Nolan Baltimore," Hester continued. "She is not able to remain until the funeral. Heaven knows when that will be."

"Yer want ter see one o' our bodies?" He shook his head. "I'd advise agin' it, ladies. Won't be nice. Best remember 'im as 'e was, if I were you."

"My mother will ask me," Margaret spoke at last, her voice husky.

"Tell 'er 'e were restin' peaceful," the attendant said almost expressionlessly. "She won't know different."

Margaret managed to look shocked. "Oh, I couldn't do that!" she said hastily. "Besides . . . she might ask me to describe him, and it is so long since I saw him I might make a mistake. Then I should feel dreadful. I . . . I would be most grateful if you would simply allow me to have a few moments. You may be with us at all times, of course, if you feel that is the correct thing to do."

Hester gritted her teeth and swore under her breath. A verbal description of Nolan Baltimore would be of no use. They needed sketches to show people! How could Margaret not have understood that? She tried to catch Margaret's eye, but Margaret would not look back at her; she was concentrating totally on the attendant, and perhaps on controlling her awareness of the damp, faintly sickly smell in the air.

"Well . . ." he said thoughtfully. "I suppose it'd make no odds ter me, nor to 'im, fer that matter. But don't 'old me to account if yer pass out, mind!" He looked at Hester. "Yer'd better come an' stand beside 'er. If she falls over, or yer do either, I'm not fetchin' a quack fer yer. Yer pick yerself up again, understand?"

"Certainly," Hester said with considerable asperity. Then she remembered the role she had cast herself in and changed her attitude. "Certainly," she repeated, with considerably more respect. "You are quite right. We shall conduct ourselves appropriately."

"Right y'are." He turned around and led the way through the door and along the passage to the ice room, where corpses were stored if required to be kept for any extended period.

"Why did you ask him to stay?" Hester said in an almost stifled whisper.

The attendant stopped and turned around. "Beg pardon?"

Hester felt herself flush hot. "I . . . I said it was nice of you to say you would stay," she lied.

"Gotter," he said grudgingly. "The cadavers 'ere are in my charge. Some people don't think as it matters very much, but yer'd be surprised wot some folks get up ter wif bodies. There's mad people around, an' that's a fact!" He snorted. "An' people will steal bodies ter cut up, Gawd 'elp us!"

Margaret gulped, her face pale, but she kept her composure admirably. "All I wish to do is look at Uncle Nolan," she said huskily. "I would be obliged if I might do so without hearing more of such . . . atrocities. I quite appreciate why your care . . . and . . . and diligence are necessary. I am grateful for them."

"Jus' doin' me duty," he said stiffly, and opened the next door, ushering them into a small, very cold room with bare, whitewashed walls. "You said Nolan Baltimore? Last one over there." He walked across the damp stone floor to the fourth table, where a figure lay supine, covered by a large unbleached cotton sheet. The attendant looked at Margaret skeptically, as if to assess the likelihood of her fainting or otherwise making a nuisance of herself. He gave up the struggle and with a sigh of resignation pulled the sheet off the head and shoulders of the corpse.

Margaret made a little hissing sound of breath between her teeth, and swayed as if the floor beneath her were the deck of a ship.

Hester moved forward quickly and put her arms tightly around her, holding her hard enough to cause pain.

Margaret gave a little yelp, but the sharpness of Hester's grip seemed to steady her.

They both looked down at the mottled gray-white flesh of the face. It was coarse-featured, with fleshy cheeks and jaw. The large eyes were now closed, but the sockets suggested their shape. His hair was receding, wavy, a dark gingery gold. He was obviously a large man, heavy-chested, thick-armed. It was difficult to judge his height, but probably close to six feet.

The hardest thing was to imagine life and color in the features, to think what they would have been like animated by intelligence. And yet presumably to have built a company like Baltimore and Sons he must have had skill, imagination and immense drive.

"Thank you," Margaret whispered. "He . . . he looks so peaceful. How did he die?"

"We do our best," the attendant said, as if she had passed him a compliment.

"How?" she repeated, her voice rasping in her throat.

"Dunno. P'lice say as 'e likely fell down stairs. Yer can't see 'ere 'ow broke up 'e is inside. An' o' course we clean 'em up."

"Thank you," Margaret repeated, struggling to get her breath. The cold and the smell of carbolic were almost overcoming her.

Hester stared at the form on the table. She had seen so many dead men, although most of them not as neatly and clinically laid out as this one. But even without touching him or moving anything, she noticed a certain crookedness in the way he was positioned. Cleaned up or not, she guessed many of his bones had been broken or joints dislocated. It must have been a very hard fall. And staring at his head she noticed fine scratches on the neck stretching under the left ear down to the front of the throat, then starting up again on the front of the breastbone. Fingernails? They were scratches, not cuts, and the edges were new and raw, bloodless of course now, but the skin had a ragged look as if it had had no chance to heal.

"Yer seen enough?" the attendant asked, looking at Margaret and beginning to frown.

"Yes . . . yes, thank you," Margaret replied. "I . . . I should like to leave now. I have done my duty. Poor Uncle Nolan. Thank you so much for your . . ." She tailed off, unable to keep her composure and finish.

Hester realized that Margaret was at the end of her strength. This was probably the first time she had seen a dead man, although one woman had died in the house in Coldbath, but that was different, full of emotion, pity, and in the end some kind of peace. This was simply freezing cold and smelling of stone and carbolic. And it was old death, days old.

She put her arm around Margaret's shoulders and walked with her out into the passage again, crushing down her disappointment. At least she had a picture in her mind to try to put into words.

At the entrance they thanked the attendant again, then went as quickly as was even remotely decent out into the street and the gently falling rain.

"Tea!" Margaret gasped. "And somewhere to sit down, somewhere dry!"

"Wouldn't you rather get back to Coldbath?" Hester said in concern. "I'm not sure what sort of a place around here would offer— "

"I want to draw him before I forget!" Margaret hissed at her. "I can't do that standing up in the rain!"

Hester was taken completely aback. "Can you . . . I mean, could . . ."

"Of course I can! If I do it while he's still sharp in my mind! Which right now I feel will be forever, but common sense and profound hope say it will not." Margaret stared around and started to walk more briskly in an effort to reach just such a place, and Hester had to skip a couple of steps to catch up with her, and then seize her by the arm to stop her from bumping into a peddler who was hoping for a sale of bootlaces.

Eventually they found a tavern where they settled for a table in the corner, two half pints of cider and two hot pies. As soon as they were served, Margaret took out the paper and pencil and began to draw. Every now and then she sipped from her glass, but she ignored the pie. Perhaps the thought of eating while she saw the face of a dead man was too much for her.

Hester was suddenly profoundly hungry. In her case, relief outweighed more delicate feelings, and all she could think of was how clever Margaret was to bring character and life into a representation created out of lines on paper. In front of her, Nolan Baltimore's face took shape until she felt as if she must have known him.

"That's marvelous!" she said with deep respect, wiping her fingers on her handkerchief, then drinking the last of her cider. "If we show people that, they will certainly know whether they have seen him or not."

Margaret looked up at her, her eyes bright with pleasure for the praise. "I had better do another," she said gravely. "If we were to lose it we should be in difficulty." And immediately she set about depicting Baltimore from a slightly different angle, more three-quarter face.

Hester fetched her another glass of cider, and one more for herself, and watched patiently while Margaret did a third drawing as well, in remarkable detail, and shaded to show an almost three-dimensional likeness.

Then, before they ran even greater risk of attracting anyone's attention, they put the drawings away and left, going out into the damp streets, but with a clear sky above and a mild breeze promising to keep it so.

They had a very quiet afternoon at Coldbath. Hester deliberately took a short sleep in preparation for her plans, which might involve much of the night. She knew Monk would not be at home, and therefore needed no explanation as to why she was not either. She had no intention of taking Margaret with her. Margaret had already done magnificent work today. Also, of course, it was necessary to have two people here, just in case there should be some need for help from Mr. Lockhart. Someone had to go for him, and that was almost always Bessie. She seemed to have a great ability to find him at any time. Perhaps his friends sensed her affection for him, and her own past had taught her neither to question nor to judge.

Margaret argued a little, but Hester could see in her eyes a certain relief when it was pointed out that Bessie could not manage alone should someone seriously injured come in.

"Yes, I suppose so," she said with genuine reluctance. "But what about you? You shouldn't go alone either! Anything could happen to you, and we wouldn't even know. Why don't you—" She stopped.

Hester smiled. "Why don't I what? You can't think of a better idea anymore than I can. I shall be very careful indeed, I promise you. I look pretty much like the women who live in the area, and they go around by themselves. There are police all over the streets just now. We know that as well as anyone. As long as I don't look as if I am soliciting for trade, which I shall take care not to, I shall be as safe as anyone." And without waiting for further argument from Margaret, Bessie, or a voice of caution inside her own head, she took an old shawl from the cupboard of spare clothes and went out into the street. The evening was fine now, and quite warm. Looking straight ahead of her, she walked quickly in the direction of Leather Lane.

She intended to begin with the place where Nolan Baltimore's body had been found, but she must be careful. She did not wish to draw the attention of any police patrolling the streets and alleys, and particularly not of Constable Hart, who would recognize her in an instant, and probably have a very good idea of her purpose.

She slowed her step to something more like that of the middle-aged woman in front of her, keeping about twenty feet between them, and trying to appear to a casual eye to be much the same sort of person. She reached the angle where Bath Street becomes Lower Bath Street, then crosses the wide thoroughfare of Theobald's Road and becomes Leather Lane.

There was a constable on the corner, looking tired and dispirited. How was she going to show anyone a picture without drawing his attention? It would have to be done under one of the few street lamps. One could hardly be expected to recognize anybody in the dusk and shadows closer to the walls, or in a doorway or alley.

The constable watched her without speaking and without apparent interest. Good. That meant he took her for an ordinary resident. That was not flattering, but it was what she needed at the moment. With a tight little smile to herself, she walked on down Leather Lane.

There was a girl standing close to the next lamppost. The light shone on her bare head, making a bright mass of her hair. She was probably well under twenty, not particularly pretty, but there was still a certain freshness to her. She was not someone Hester knew, and she found herself suddenly very nervous about asking a complete stranger the questions she needed to.

But the answers might be known only by strangers, and she was not going back to Coldbath to tell them that she had been too cowardly to try! That would be worse than anything this girl could say to her.

"Excuse me," she began tentatively.

The girl looked at her, hostility already in her eyes. "Don't stop 'ere, luv," she said in a low, steady voice. "This is my patch, an' me man'll mark yer face if yer try it 'ere. Find yer own patch." She regarded Hester with more care. "Yer looks are nothin', but yer walk with yer 'ead 'igh. There's some as likes that. Try up that way." She pointed back up toward the huge mass of the brewery on Portpool Lane.

Hester swallowed her temper with difficulty. The insult stung, which was ridiculous. She knew her own passion well enough, there were too many remembered nights not to, but she still did not like to be told her looks were nothing. But this was no time to give back as good as she received.

"I don't want your patch," she said levelly. Her better sense knew the girl was only fighting for survival. She probably had to fight for everything she got, and then fight again to keep it.

"I just want to know if you have seen a particular man in the area."

"Look, luv," the girl answered pityingly, "if yer ol' man comes 'ere fer 'is pleasures, just look the other way an' 'ang on t' yer 'ouse an' yer kids. If yer got a roof over yer 'ead an' food in yer belly, don' go 'owlin' fer the moon. Yer won't get nothin' but a sore froat—an' if yer go upsettin' other folk, a bucket o' cold water thrown at yer, or worse."

Hester hesitated. What story could she make up that this girl would believe and still give her the information she needed? The girl was turning away already. Perhaps the only answer was the truth.

"It's the man who was murdered," she said abruptly, feeling the heat run through her body, and then the cold as she committed herself irrevocably. "I want the police out of the area so everything can get back to normal." She saw the look of disbelief on the girl's face. There was nothing for it but to go on now. "They aren't finding out who did it!" she said abruptly. "The only way to see the back of them is if somebody else does." She fished in her pocket and brought out the picture of Nolan Baltimore.

The girl squinted at it. "Is that 'im?" she said curiously. "I in't never seen 'im. Sorry."

Hester studied the girl's face, trying to judge whether to believe her or not.

The girl smiled mirthlessly. "I in't. I know as 'e were found at Abel Smith's place, but I in't never seen 'im 'ere."

"Thank you." She wondered whether to go on and ask this very self-possessed girl where the brothel was that might use women like herself, who walked with their heads high. That might be the one that belonged to the usurer. She drew in her breath.

The girl glared at her, the warning back in her eyes.

"Thank you," Hester repeated, and put the picture back into her pocket and walked on, almost as far as High Holborn, asking people, showing them the drawing, then back up the Farringdon Road and across Hatton Wall back to Leather

Lane again. She found no one who would admit to having seen Nolan Baltimore.

It was fully dark now, and definitely colder. There were very few people around. A man in a coat too big for him hurried along the footpath, dragging one foot a little, his shadow crooked on the stones as he passed under the street lamp.

A woman paraded along the opposite side casually, keeping her head high as if she were full of confidence. As she rounded the corner into Hatton Wall a hansom slowed. Hester did not see whether she was picked up or not.

A beggar reached an arched doorway and subsided into the brief shelter of it, as if for the night.

Hester had accomplished nothing. She was not even sure if people were lying out of fear or perversity, or if indeed no one had seen Baltimore.

If the latter, did that mean he had not been here? Or simply that he had been extremely careful? Would a man like Nolan Baltimore not automatically be careful not to be recognized? What had he come here for? A secret business meeting to do with land fraud? Or, far more likely, to indulge a taste for a bit of rough pleasure, and practices he could not indulge in at home.

At least she knew where Abel Smith's establishment was, and she decided as a last resort to go there and confront him. She retraced her steps along Leather Lane and finally went into a short alley off the street and up a rickety stair. All around her she could hear the faint drip of moisture, the creak of wood, and now and then the scurry of clawed feet. That last noise reminded her of the rats in the hospital at Scutari, and she clenched her teeth and moved a little faster.

The door opened as she reached it, startling her, and a bald man with a smiling face stood looking at her. The light behind him made a halo out of the few white hairs on his scalp.

"Are yer lost, then?" he asked, his voice sibilant as if he had a broken tooth. It was only when she reached the top step that she realized he was several inches shorter than she was.

"That depends on whether this is Abel Smith's house or

not," she replied, glad she was not out of breath as well as reasons. "If it is, then I am where I mean to be."

He shook his head. "I'm willin' ter try most things, luv, but yer in't right fer 'ere." He looked her up and down. "If yer desperate, I'll give yer a bed for the night, but find yerself somew'ere else fer tomorrer. Yer in't my trade."

"No, I'm not," she agreed. "But I know a few girls who are. I have the house in Coldbath that takes care of some of your sick and injured."

His eyes narrowed, and he whistled his breath out between the gaps in his teeth. "I in't got no one sick 'ere, an' I din't ask fer no 'ouse calls!"

"I'm not here about illness," she replied. Now she decided to stretch the truth a little. "I'm here about getting the police to move out of the area so we can all get back to business as usual."

"Oh, yeah? An' 'ow d'yer reckon on doin' that, then?" He eyed her slim, straight body and direct eyes with heavy skepticism. "They're sayin' as that toff wot got done was 'ere in me 'ouse . . . which 'e never were, 'ceptin' w'en 'e were dead!" He sniffed. "I never topped a customer in me life! Bloody stupid thing ter do, all ways 'round. But d'yer think them stupid sods believe me?"

"Where is the staircase he is supposed to have fallen down?" she asked.

"W'y? Wot diff'rence does it make ter you?" he demanded.

"Why do you want to hide it?" she countered.

"Go on! Git outa 'ere!" He flapped his hands at her. "Yer jus' trouble. Go on!"

Somewhere behind her a rat overbalanced an empty crate and it fell with a damp thud.

She stood still. "I'm trying to help, you fool!" she said fiercely. "If he didn't die here, then he died somewhere else! It didn't have anything to do with women at all, and if I can prove that, then the police will stop harassing us and we can all get back to the way it used to be! Do you want that, or not?"

His eyes were little more than slits in his pink face.

"W'y?" he said carefully. "I thought as yer was just a do-gooder wot tries ter save souls o' fallen women. Yer got summink else goin' on—in't yer?" He nodded several times. "Wot is it, then? Wot yer doin' in that 'ouse up Coldbath?"

"That is none of your business!" she snapped, seizing the chance. "Do we have to do this standing on the steps for anyone to hear?"

Reluctantly, he moved back and swung the door open for her to follow. She went in after him and found herself on a narrow landing with half a dozen doors leading off it. He walked ahead of her with a curious, rolling gait, as if he had been long at sea. He stopped at the fourth door along, opened it and led the way in. She went after him and found herself in a sitting room whose furnishings had once been green and red but were now faded and soiled to shades of brown, like old leaves. A desk against the back wall was covered with papers. There was a soft chair ahead of her, and a very small fireplace, presently filled with dead ash. The odor of stale air was oppressive. Warmth would only have made it worse.

"I would like to speak to some of your girls," she asked.

"They don't know nothin'," he said flatly.

"I don't care about your miserable trade!" She knew her voice was rising but she could not help it. "They may have seen this man in the street. Somebody brought him here. You say he didn't walk in . . . then who brought him? Haven't you even wondered who did this to you?"

"Yer bleedin' right I 'ave!" he spat, his face suddenly losing its pink, innocent look and burning instead like that of a malevolent baby, curiously evil because it was so ludicrous. He suddenly raised his voice. "Ada!" he yelled with startling volume.

There was a slight sound downstairs, but no one appeared.

"Ada!" he screamed.

The door flew open and a fat woman almost his own height burst into the room, her black ringlets clustered around her red face, her eyes blazing with indignation. She looked at him, then at Hester.

"No good," she said without being asked. "Too thin. Wot

yer call me fer, yer daft a'porth? Don't yer know nothin'?
Sorry for 'er, are yer?" She jabbed a short, fat finger toward
Hester. "Well, not in this 'ouse, yer great soft 'eap o' . . ." She
stopped, sensing his lack of self-justification. She realized
her error and swung around to face Hester. "Well, wot are yer
'ere fer then? Cat got yer tongue?'"

Hester pulled out the drawing of Nolan Baltimore and
showed it to her.

Ada barely glanced at it. " 'E's dead," she said flatly.
"Some 'eap o' dung left 'ere on our floor, but 'e in't nuffin' ter
do wi' us. Never see'd 'im afore, an' no one can prove we
'ave!"

"It's your word against theirs," Hester said reasonably.

Ada was hugely practical. She was too much of a survivor
to quarrel for the sake of it. "So wot der yer want, then? W'y'd
yer care 'oo put 'im 'ere?"

"Because I wish to find out who killed him so the police
will go away and leave us alone. And I wish to find out who is
lending money to women and making them pay it back by going on the streets," Hester replied. She took a wild chance,
feeling her flesh prickle at the risk.

Ada's black eyes opened even more widely. "Do yer, then?
W'y?" Her question was shot out like a missile.

"Because as long as there are police all over the place
there's no trade," Hester replied. "And people can't pay their
debts. Tempers are getting ugly and more and more women
will get hurt."

Ada was still suspicious. "And since when did women 'oo
speak like you care if women like us got trade or not?" she
said, her eyes narrow. "Thought you was all fired up ter clean
the streets and put decency back inter life." She said this last
with sarcasm like an open razor.

"If you think putting constables on every corner is going to
do that, you're a fool!" Hester retorted. "There's no 'like me'
and 'like you.' All kinds of women can find themselves in
debt and take to the streets to pay it. They might have to cater
to specialist tastes, but they take what they can get. It's better
than being beaten half to death."

"We don't do that ter nob'dy," Ada said indignantly, but beside the self-righteousness there was a ring of honesty in her voice as well, and Hester heard it.

"Do you cater to special tastes?" Hester asked.

"Not wi' girls wot are 'ere 'cos o' debts wot we know anythin' abaht," Ada replied. "They're jus' orn'ry girls wot wants ter make a livin', an' they don' get enough ter pay more'n their way."

Hester glanced at the room. What Ada said was easy enough to believe, although it was quite possible they had a second establishment, or even a third, which could be different from his. But for all she could tell, no one had seen Nolan Baltimore in the area. If he had been killed in one of Abel Smith's other houses, were there any, Smith would hardly have had the body dumped here. She was inclined to believe them.

Her silence unnerved Ada. "We don't do nothin' like that!" Ada reiterated. "Jus' straight bus'ness. An' we in't never beat no one." She sniffed fiercely. "Less they got uppity an' looked fer it. Gotta 'ave some discipline or yer in't got nothin'. People in't got no respect fer a great soft 'eap like 'im!" She glanced witheringly at Abel.

"May I speak to some of your girls, to ask if anyone saw Mr. Baltimore around the streets here, or knows where he could have gone?" Hester requested.

Ada considered for a few moments. "I s'pose," she said at last. Apparently she had weighed what Hester had told her and decided a degree of trust might get her what she wanted. "But don' take all night! Times is 'ard. We in't got opportunities ter waste!"

Hester did not bother to answer.

She spent nearly an hour speaking with one bored or frightened woman after another, but none of them were marked as far as she could see. Certainly none of them were prepared to admit having seen Nolan Baltimore in Leather Lane, only at the bottom of the stairs here on the night of his death.

"Daft question, if yer ask me!" one woman called Polly said with total disdain. " 'E were a toff. Money comin' outer 'is ears, an' all." Her laugh changed into a snarl, more disgust than anger. "Look at us, lady! D'yer think someone like that's gonna come 'ere ter the likes o' us? 'E wants summink special, an' 'e can pay fer it." She shrugged, and yanked the sliding shoulder of her dress back up again. " 'E prob'ly goes up Squeaky Robinson's way. 'E could pay 'is prices, an' no trouble."

"Squeaky Robinson?" Hester repeated, almost afraid to believe. "Who is he?"

"Dunno," Polly said immediately. "Nearer Coldbath, an' the brewery. 'Atton Wall, or Portpool Lane, mebbe. Don' wanner know. Neither d' you, if yer knows wot's good fer yer."

"Thank you." Hester stood up. "You've been very helpful. I appreciate it."

"In't told yer nothin'," Polly denied bluntly, jerking the dress back into position again and swearing under her breath.

"No," Hester agreed. "Except that Baltimore didn't die here. In fact, he didn't do business here at all."

"Yer right," Polly said with feeling. " 'E din't!"

Hester believed her. All the way back to Coldbath Square she turned it over in her mind and was sure that Nolan Baltimore had met his death somewhere else and been carried to Abel Smith's house in order to move the blame.

But she was a little closer to finding out where he had been killed, or why, though she would not forget the name of Squeaky Robinson, or the fact that, according to Polly, he catered to men with expensive and different tastes.

6

MONK HAD CONSIDERED very carefully all the information he possessed regarding the Baltimore and Sons railway, and he could see no obvious fraud in the purchase of land or any other part of the project. But even if there had been illegitimate profit made in either the buying or not buying of certain stretches of the track, he could think of no way in which it could be connected with a risk of accident. And that was what exercised his mind in ways Katrina Harcus could not imagine. Of course a present danger mattered, and he was acutely aware that if such existed he had a moral duty as well as a desire to do everything in his power to avoid it. But what hurt with a massive, drowning pain—because it was irretrievable—was the fear that in the past the fraud for which Arrol Dundas had died was in some way responsible for the crash Monk remembered with such awful guilt.

He strode across the grass of Regent's Park toward the Royal Botanic Society Gardens, barely noticing the other people strolling by. His mind was torn between past and present. Each held the key to the other, and he might find both in the few snatches of information Katrina held, locked in and obscured by her emotions. They had at least that in common. She was terrified for Dalgarno and what she did not know about him, and dreaded could be true. Monk was terrified in exactly the same way, but for himself.

It was bright sunshine with all the aching silver-and-gold clarity of spring, and the gardens were busy with people.

Having nerved himself to meet her, he felt a sharp disappointment that he looked for her for several minutes in vain. There were dozens of women of all ages. He could see colored silk and lace, embroidered muslin, hats with flowers, parasols in a jungle of points above the spread domes of cloth. They walked in twos and threes, laughing together, or on the arms of admirers, heads high, a flounce of skirts.

He stood in the gateway with a sense of acute disappointment. He had steeled himself for the meeting, and now he would have to do it again tomorrow. He had no idea where she lived or how to find her, and no other avenue of investigation to pursue to fill in the time until she might be here again.

"Mr. Monk!"

He swung around. She was there behind him. He was so pleased to see her he did not notice what she was wearing, except that it was pale and faintly patterned. It was her face he watched, her amazing, dark-fringed eyes, and he knew he was smiling. It probably misled her, as if he had good news to tell, and even though that was a lie, he could not alter it. The sheer relief bubbled up inside him.

"Miss Harcus! I . . . I was afraid you would not come," he said hastily. It was not really what he meant, but he could think of nothing more exact.

She searched his face. "Have you news?" she said almost breathlessly. He noticed only now how pale she was. He could feel the emotion in her as he could in himself, tight, curled like a spring ready to break.

"No." He said the word more brusquely than he had intended to, because he was annoyed with himself for misleading her. "Except that I have found nothing out of order in Mr. Dalgarno's conduct." He stopped. There was no relief in her eyes, and he had expected it. It was as if she could not believe him. If anything, the tension in her increased. Under the fine fabric of her dress her shoulders were rigid, her breathing so intensely controlled that merely watching her he could feel it himself. She started to shake her head very slowly from side to side. "No . . . no . . ."

"I have searched everything!" he insisted. "There may be irregularity in the purchase of land . . ."

"Irregularity?" she said sharply. "What does that mean? Is it honest or not? I am not completely ignorant, Mr. Monk. People have gone to prison for 'irregularities,' as you call them, if they were intentional and they have profited from them. Sometimes even if they were not intended but they were unable to prove that."

An elderly gentleman hesitated in his step and glanced at Katrina as if uncertain what the tone of her voice might mean. Was it anger or distress? Should he intervene? He decided not, and walked on with considerable relief.

Two ladies smiled at each other and passed by a few feet away.

"Yes, I know," Monk said very quietly, old, sickening memories coming back to him as he stood in the sunlit gardens. "But fraud has to be proved, and I can find nothing." Katrina drew in her breath as if to interrupt again, but he hurried on. "The sort of thing I am thinking of is routing a railway line through one piece of land rather than another to oblige a farmer or the owner of an estate so as not to divide his land. There might have been bribery, but I would be very surprised if it is traceable. People are naturally discreet about such things." He offered her his arm, aware that by standing in one place they were making themselves more noticeable.

She grasped at it till he could feel her fingers through the fabric of his jacket.

"But the crash!" she said with panic rising in her voice. "What about the dangers? That is not just a matter of "—she gulped—"of making personal profit that is questionable. It's . . ." She whispered the word. "Murder! At least morally." She pulled him to a stop again, glaring with a depth of horror in her eyes that frightened him.

"Yes, I know," he agreed gently, turning to face her. "But I have walked the track myself, Miss Harcus, and I know about railways. There is nothing in land acquisition, even bad land, that endangers the lives of people on the train."

"Isn't there?" She allowed him to move on slowly and

blend in with the others strolling between the flower beds. "Are you certain?"

"If land costs more than it should have done, or less," he explained, "and the company owners put the difference in their own pockets instead of those of the shareholders, that is theft, but it does not affect the safety of the railway itself."

She looked up at him earnestly. He could see the hurt and confusion in her face, the desperation mounting inside her. Why? What did she know about Dalgarno that she was still not telling him?

"What amounts of money could be involved?" she interrupted his thoughts. "A great deal, surely? Enough to keep an ordinary man in comfort for the rest of his life?"

Monk had a sudden start of memory of Arrol Dundas, so vivid he could see the lines in Dundas's skin, the curve of his nose, and a gentleness in his eyes as he looked across at Monk. He was back at the trial again, seeing people's faces drop in amazement as amounts of money were mentioned, sums that seemed unimaginable wealth to them but in railway terms were everyday. He could see the open mouths, hear the gasps of indrawn breath and the rustle of movement around the room, the scrape of fabric, the creak of whalebone stays.

What had happened to that money? Did Dundas's widow have it? No, that was impossible. People did not keep the profit of crime. Had it disappeared? There must have been proof that he had had it at some time in order to convict him.

Monk refused even to consider the other possibility, that somehow he himself had had it. He knew enough of his own life in the police force to know such wealth would have been exposed.

Katrina was waiting for him to respond.

He jerked himself back to the present. "Yes, it would be a great deal of money," he conceded.

Her mouth was a thin line, lips tight. "Enough to tempt men to great crime," she said hoarsely. "For people to believe the worst of anyone . . . quite easily. Mr. Monk, this answer is not sufficient." She looked down, away from his eyes and what they might read in hers. When she spoke again her voice was little more than a whisper. "I am so afraid for Michael I hardly know how to keep my head at all. Because I am afraid, I have taken risks I would never take in other circumstances. I have listened at doors, I have overheard conversations, I have even read papers on other people's desks. I am ashamed to confess it." She looked up suddenly. "But I am seeking with all my strength to prevent disaster to those I love, and to ordinary innocent men and women who only wish to travel from one town to another and who trust the railway to carry them safely."

"What is it that you have not told me?" he demanded, now a little roughly.

Again passersby were staring at them, perhaps because they were standing rather than walking, more likely because they saw the passion and the urgency in Katrina's face, and that she was still gripping Monk's arm.

"I know that Jarvis Baltimore is planning to spend over two thousand pounds on an estate for himself," she said breathlessly. "I saw the plans of it. He spoke of having the money in almost two months' time, from the profits they expect out of the scheme he and Michael spoke of." She was watching him intently, struggling to guess his judgment. "But both he and Michael have said it must be kept a most deadly secret or it will ruin them instead."

"Are you quite certain you have not misunderstood?" he questioned. "Was this since Nolan Baltimore's death?"

"No . . ." The word was hardly more than a breathing out.

So it was not an inheritance.

"The sale of railway stock to foreign railway companies?"

"Why should that be secret?" she asked. "Would someone not speak of it quite openly? Do not companies do it all the time?"

"Yes." He said that with certainty.

"There is some secret you have not yet discovered, Mr. Monk," she said huskily. "Something which is terrible and dangerous, and will drag Michael down to prison, if not death, if we do not find it before it is too late!"

Fear ran through him like a burning wave, but it was nameless and without sense. He reached for the only thing he knew which matched the violence and the enormity of what she was suggesting.

"Miss Harcus! Nolan Baltimore was murdered a short while ago. Most people assumed it was because he was frequenting a brothel in Leather Lane. But perhaps that is what they were intended to think."

She jerked up her head, staring at him with terrified eyes, her face white. She was totally oblivious of the people around her, of their curiosity or alarm. "You think it was to do with the railway?" She breathed out the words in horror, putting her hand up to cover her mouth, as if that could stifle the truth.

He knew the worst fear that had to be in her mind, and he hurt for her pain, but it was senseless to evade it now. It would not drive it away.

"Yes," he answered gently. "If you are correct, and there really is such a great deal of money involved, then if he knew of this scheme, he may have been murdered to assure his silence."

Now she was so white he was afraid she was going to faint. Instinctively, he reached for her arms to stop her from falling.

She allowed him to hold her for no more than seconds, then she pulled away with a jerk so sharp he all but tore the fine muslin of her sleeves.

"No!" There was horror in her face, and she spoke with such pent-up, choking emotion that several people nearby actually turned and looked at them both, then in embarrassment at being caught staring, turned away again.

"Miss Harcus!" he urged. "Please!"

"No," she repeated, but less fiercely. "I . . . I can't think that . . ." She did not finish.

They both knew what it was that tormented her. The possibility was too clear. If the fraud were as great as she feared, the profit as high, then Nolan Baltimore could easily have been murdered to silence him. It could have been because he knew and he and his murderer quarreled. He wanted too large a share, or he threatened the plans in any other way, or because he had not known but had discovered, and had to be silenced before he betrayed them. Michael Dalgarno was the obvious man to suspect. As far as Katrina knew, only Dalgarno and Jarvis Baltimore were involved.

Monk ached for her. He knew with hideous familiarity what it was like to live with the dread of learning the truth, and yet be compelled to seek it. All the denial in the world changed nothing, and yet the knowledge, final and irrefutable, would destroy all that mattered most.

For her it would mean that the man she loved in a sense had never really existed. Even before he had gone to Leather Lane that night, before anything was irrevocable, he had had the seed of it within him, the cruelty and the greed, the arrogance that placed his own gain before another man's life. He had betrayed himself long before he had betrayed Katrina, or his mentor and employer.

And if Monk had betrayed Arrol Dundas, and had even the slightest knowing or willing hand in the rail crash in the past, then he had never been the man Hester believed him to be, and everything he had so carefully built, with such difficult letting go of his pride, would come shattering down like a house of cards.

Suddenly this woman he barely knew was closer to him than anyone else, because they shared a fear which dominated their lives to the exclusion of everything else.

She was still staring at him in terrified silence.

"Miss Harcus," he said with a tenderness that startled him, and this time he did not hesitate to touch her. It was only a small gesture, but of extraordinary understanding. "I will find out the truth," he promised. "If there is a fraud, I'll uncover it and prevent any further accidents. And I will do what I can to discover who murdered Nolan Baltimore." He watched her gravely. "But unless there is fraud, and Michael Dalgarno is implicated, he would have no motive to have done such a thing. Baltimore was probably killed in some fight over money to do with prostitution, not a fortune but a few pounds some drunken pimp thought he owed. They may well have had no idea who he was. Had he a hot temper?"

The faintest shadow of a smile touched her lips, and her

whole body eased its stiffness. "Yes," she whispered. "Yes, he was quick-tempered. Thank you more than I can say, Mr. Monk. You have at least given me hope. I shall cling onto that until you bring me news." Her eyes flickered down, then up again. "I must owe you further, and you have expenses from all the traveling you have done on my behalf. Would another fifteen pounds be sufficient for the moment? It . . . it is all I can manage." There was a faint flush of embarrassment on her cheeks now.

"It would be quite sufficient," he answered, taking it from her hand and putting it into his inside pocket as discreetly as possible, pulling out a handkerchief as if that were what he had reached for. He saw her flash of understanding and acknowledgment and was sufficiently thanked in that.

It was time that Monk considered more seriously the possibility that Baltimore's death was not the prostitution scandal that the police, and everyone else, assumed, but a very personal murder simply carried out in or near the brothel in Leather Lane. If Dalgarno, or even Jarvis Baltimore, had wished to kill the older man, to do it behind the mask of his private vices was the perfect crime.

There was nothing to be gained by asking the superintendent in charge of the investigation, who would resent Monk's interference. The poor man was being pressured more than enough by the authorities and the outraged citizens who felt morally obliged to protest. No matter what he did he would not please them. The only solution they wanted was for the whole matter to disappear without trace, and that was not a possibility. If they did not complain, they appeared to condone prostitution and the murder of a prominent citizen; if they did, then they drew even more attention to practices they all wished to be free to indulge in and deny at the same time.

Nor was there much purpose in his speaking to the constables on the beat, who were being dragooned into protecting the Farringdon Road area against everybody's interests. If they knew who had killed Nolan Baltimore, whoever it was would have been charged already and the matter put to rest.

What Monk wanted to know was the movements of Nolan Baltimore on the night of his death, and exactly what Michael Dalgarno had known of them, and where he had been. How had they parted? What was Jarvis Baltimore's role?

Who could know these things? The Baltimore household, family and servants; possibly the constables on the beat near the house or the offices, if either man had not gone home that evening; or street peddlers, cabdrivers, people whose daily passage took them through that area.

He began with the easiest, and possibly the most likely to tell him something of worth. She sat on a rickety box propped up near the corner of the street, a shawl around her head and a clay pipe stuck firmly between her remaining teeth. An array of cough drops and brandy balls sat in bowls and tin dishes around her, and a heap of small squares of paper was held down by a stone.

"Arternoon, sir," she said in a soft Irish accent. "Now what can I be gettin' yer?"

He cleared his throat. "Cough drops, if you please," he said with a smile. "Threepence worth, I think." He fished a three-penny piece out of his pocket and offered it to her.

She took it and ladled out a portion of sticky sweets with a tin spoon. She dropped them onto one of the pieces of paper and twisted it into a screw, then handed it up to him. She drew deeply on the pipe, but it appeared to have gone out. She fished in her pocket, but he was there before her, a packet of matches in his hand. He held it out for her.

"It's a gentleman ye are," she said, taking it from him, picking out a match and striking it, holding the flame to the bowl of her pipe and drawing deeply. It caught and she inhaled with profound satisfaction. She offered the matches back to him.

"Keep them," he replied generously.

She did not argue, but her bright eyes, half hidden by wrinkles of weathered skin, were sharp with amusement. "So what are ye wantin' then?" she said bluntly.

He smiled widely at her. He had charm when he wanted it. "You'll be knowing that Mr. Baltimore was murdered in

Leather Lane a few days ago," he said candidly. He knew the folly of insulting her wits. Anyone who served in the street to her age was nobody's fool.

"Sure an' doesn't all London know it?" she replied. Her expression betrayed her contempt of him, probably not for his morals but for his hypocrisy.

"You'll have seen him coming and going," he went on, nodding his head toward the Baltimore house, thirty yards away.

"Of course I have, bad cess to him," she responded. "Not a halfpenny on a cold day, that one!" Perhaps it was a warning to him that she had no interest in helping to find his killer. An honest expression or a ploy to be paid now for help, it did not matter; either way if she told him anything he was happy to reward her for it.

"I am interested in the possibility that he was killed by someone who knew him," he admitted. "Did you see him that evening? Any idea what time he left home, and if he was alone or with anyone?"

She looked at him steadily, weighing him up.

He looked back, wondering whether she wanted money, or if poorly handled it would offend her pride.

"It would be very agreeable to find it was nothing to do with the women in Leather Lane," he remarked.

Real interest flashed in her eyes. "It would an' all," she agreed. "But even if I saw him leave, an' others follow after him, that doesn't mean to say they went further than the end o' the street, now does it?"

"No, it doesn't," he said, trying to keep the emotion out of his voice. He did not even know if he was excited or afraid. He did not want Dalgarno guilty! It was only the keenness of a scent which caught his eagerness, a thread of truth at last among all the knots and ends. "But if I knew which way they went then I might be able to find the cabbie who picked them up."

"Josiah Wardrup," she said without a flicker. "Saw him myself, I did. Almost like he was expectin' the old bastard."

"How very interesting," Monk said sincerely. "Perhaps he was? In fact, perhaps Mr. Baltimore went that way, at that time, quite regularly?"

She made a low sound of appreciation in the back of her throat. "It's clever you are, now isn't it?"

"Oh, now and then," he agreed. He fished in his pocket and brought out two shillings. "I think I'll reward myself with a few pence worth of brandy balls."

"Sure an' how many pence worth would that be, now?" she asked, taking the two shillings from him.

"Four," he said unhesitatingly.

She grinned and poured him a generous four pence worth.

"Thank you. Keep the change. I'm most obliged."

She put the clay pipe back in her mouth and drew on it with profound satisfaction. She had had a pleasant conversation, gained one and eight pence for nothing, and perhaps helped the cause of justice to get the rozzers off the backs of the poor cows who worked down the Farringdon Road way. Not bad for less than half an hour's work.

Monk took until the next day to find Josiah Wardrup, but with only a moderate amount of pressure the cabbie admitted that he had picked up Nolan Baltimore on that corner at least once a week for the last two or three years and taken him to the corner of Theobald's Road and Gray's Inn Road, which was a mere stone's throw from Leather Lane.

Monk was not sure if it was what he wanted to hear. It looked extraordinarily like a regular indulgence, but then insofar as it was regular, it would have been simple enough for anyone wishing him harm to have learned his pattern and followed him.

But if Wardrup had seen anyone else he was not saying so. He looked at Monk with blank innocence and demanded his suitable appreciation. And no, he had no idea where Mr. Baltimore went from the corner. He always stood there and waited until Wardrup had left, which caused him some wry amusement. What did anyone imagine a gentleman did in such an area?

The only fact Monk would glean of any interest was that on every occasion it had been the same corner. The times varied, the nights of the week, but never the place.

And yet the brothel in Leather Lane where his body was

found denied all knowledge of him. They said that not only had he not been there for business that night, he had never been.

Monk was alternately cajoling and threatening, but not one woman changed her words, and in spite of general opinion of their honesty, and the fact that Baltimore had undoubtedly been found there, he found to his surprise that he believed them. Of course he was also aware that he was far from the first person to have asked, and they had had more than enough time to compare stories with each other and determine a united front.

Still, Abel Smith's dubious and far from attractive establishment was not the sort of place one expected a man of Baltimore's wealth to frequent. But tastes were individual; some men liked dirt, others danger. Yet he knew of none who liked disease—except of course those already infected.

At the end of two days he was little wiser.

He turned his attention to Dalgarno, surprised how much he dreaded what he would find. And the search itself was not easy. Dalgarno was a man who seemed to do a great many things alone. It was not difficult to establish what time he had left the offices of Baltimore and Sons. A few enquiries of the desk elicited that information, but it was of little use. Dalgarno had left at six o'clock, five hours before Baltimore had been picked up by a hansom and taken to the corner of the Gray's Inn Road.

A newsboy had seen someone who was almost certainly Dalgarno go into the Baltimore house, and half an hour later Jarvis Baltimore go in also, but he had left the street before eight, and no one that Monk could question knew anything further. The Baltimore servants would know, but he had no authority to speak to them and could think of no excuse. Even if he could have, Baltimore could have been killed at any time after midnight and before dawn. No enquiry showed one way or the other whether Dalgarno had been in his rooms all night. Exit and entry were easy, and there was no postman or other servant to see.

He spoke to the gingerbread seller on the corner fifty yards away, a small, spare man who looked as if he could profit from a thick slice of his own wares and a hot cup of tea. He had seen Dalgarno returning home at about half past nine in the evening of Baltimore's death. Dalgarno had been walking rapidly, his face set in a mask of fury, his hat jammed hard on his head, and he had passed without a word. However, the gingerbread seller had packed up shortly after that and gone home, so he had no idea whether Dalgarno had gone out again or not.

The constable on night duty might know. He patrolled this way now and then. But he gave Monk a lopsided grin and half a wink. He did have a certain acquaintance who frequented these streets on less-open business; give him a few days and he would make enquiries.

Monk gave him half a crown, and promised him another seven to make up a sovereign, if he would do as he suggested. Only Monk would need more than a word secondhand; if there were anything, he must speak to the witness himself. What anybody else's business was in the street would remain unknown, and unquestioned.

The constable thought for a moment or two, then agreed. Monk thanked him, said he would be back in three or four days, and took his leave.

It was about three in the afternoon, cold and gusty, gray with coming rain. He could do no more about Dalgarno and Baltimore's death for now. It was probably exactly what it looked to be, and everyone assumed. He could no longer put off the search he had known from the beginning he would have to make. He must go back to Arrol Dundas's trial and see if the details would shake loose his memory at last, and he could remember what he had known then, the fraud, how it was discovered, and above all his own part in it.

He did not know where the trial had been, but all deaths were recorded and the files held here in London. He knew sufficient details to find the file, and it would tell him the place. He would go back there tonight and face his own past, pry open the lid of his nightmares and let them loose.

First he must go home, wash, eat, change his clothes, and pack a case, ready to go wherever it proved to be.

He had expected Hester to be out, either working at the house in Coldbath Square or raising more money to pay the rent and keep it supplied with food and medicines. He presumed it because he wished it so, to avoid the confrontation of his own emotions. He was aware that it was a kind of cowardice, and was ashamed of it, but he imagined what her feelings would be if she were forced to face the truth that he was so much less than she believed, and that was a pain he was not ready for. It would be so violent as to disable the concentration and intelligence he must bring to bear if he was to keep his promise to Katrina Harcus and prevent any new rail disaster.

Even that was an evasion. It was for himself that he would do it. It was his own compulsion never to allow such a thing to happen again. He must do that before he could bear to face the original which lay somewhere in his memory, fragmented, imperfect, but undeniable.

He opened the door and went inside, ready to do no more than change clothing, pack, have a cup of tea and a slice of bread with whatever cold meat he could find. He would leave a note for her to explain his absence. Instead he almost ran into her as she came out of the kitchen, smiling, ready to walk into his arms. But he saw the uncertainty in her eyes that told of her sensitivity to his aloneness, the withdrawal of the old honesty between them. She was hurt, and hiding it for his sake.

He hesitated, hating the lie and fearing the truth. It must only be seconds, less than that, or it was too long. He had to make the decision now! It was instinctive. He went forward and put his arms around her, holding her too closely, feeling her body yield and cling onto him in return. This at least was honest. He had never loved her more, all that she was, the courage, the generosity of spirit, the fierceness to protect, and her own vulnerability which she thought so hidden, and which was in reality so obvious.

He pressed his cheek into the softness of her hair, moving his lips gently, but he did not speak. At least without words he had not deliberately misled her. In a moment or two he would tell her he was going away again, and perhaps even why, but for a while let it simply be the truth of touch, without complication. He would remember that afterwards, keep it in his mind, and deeper than that—in the unspoken memory of the body.

It was late when he reached the public records office. All he knew was the year of Dundas's death, not the date. It could take him some time to find the record, since he was not certain of the place either. But at least it was an uncommon name. If he had still been with the police he would have demanded that the office remain open for him to search for as long as he required. As a private person he could ask nothing.

He simply requested the records section he wanted, and when he was conducted to it, sat on a high stool, straining his eyes to read the pages and pages of spidery writing.

The attendant was at his elbow to tell him they were closing when he saw the name Dundas, and then the rest of it: He had died of pneumonia in prison in Liverpool, April 1846.

He closed the book and turned to the man. "Thank you," he said hoarsely. "That's all I need. I'm obliged to you." Irrational how seeing it in cold writing like that made it so much more real. It took it out of imagination and memory and into the world of indelible fact that the world knew as well as he.

He strode out of the door, down the steps and along the street back to the station, where he bought a ham sandwich and a cup of tea while he waited for the last train north.

When the night train pulled into Liverpool Lime Street just before dawn, Monk got off shivering cold, his body stiff, and went to buy himself a hot drink and something to eat, then to look for some sort of lodgings where he could wash and shave and put on a clean shirt before he began to look for the facts of the past.

It was still far too early to find any records office open, but he knew without asking where the prison was. By seven o'clock it was gray daylight with a stiff wind coming up off the Mersey. All around him people were hurrying to work, steps swift, heads down. He heard the flat, nasal Liverpool voices with the lift at the end of each sentence, the dry humor, the cheerful complaints about the weather, the government, the prices of everything, and found it all oddly familiar. Even the slang he understood. He took a hansom and simply directed the driver, street by street, until the dark walls towered over them and memories came surging back like the flood tide of the sea, the smell of the wet stones, the sound of rain in the gutter, the unevenness of the cobbles and the chill wind around the corners.

He told the driver to wait, climbed out, and stood staring at the locked gates. He had been here before so many times in Dundas's last days, even the pattern of light and shadow on the walls was familiar.

More powerful than the blackness of the stone around him, and the smell of ingrained dirt and misery, was the old feeling of helplessness come back with shattering force, as if the air were thin in his lungs, starving him of breath.

He stood motionless, fighting to grasp something tangible—words, facts, details of anything—but the harder he tried the more completely it all eluded him. There was only the suffocating emotion.

Behind him, the cab horse shifted its weight, iron shoes loud on the cobbles, harness creaking.

There was nothing to be gained here. Remembered pain did not help. He had not doubted the truth of it. He needed something he could follow.

He walked slowly back to the hansom and climbed in.

"I want to look at old newspapers," he told the driver. "Sixteen years ago. Take me wherever they are."

"Library," the driver replied. "Less yer want the law courts?"

"No, thank you. The library will do." If he had to ask for a transcript of the trial he would, but he was not ready for that yet. To see such a thing he would have to give his name and his reasons. The newspapers were an anonymous way of learning, and he despised himself even as the thought was in his mind. Still, he knew it was self-preservation to guard against all the hurt he could. Pain was disabling, and he had to keep his promise to Katrina Harcus.

There was no one else interested in old records so early in the day, and he had the newspaper files to himself. It took no more than fifteen minutes to locate the trial of Arrol Dundas. He already knew the date of Dundas's death, so he worked backwards. There was the headline: FINANCIER ARROL DUNDAS ON TRIAL FOR FRAUD.

He turned to the beginning and read.

It was exactly as he had feared. The print swam before his eyes, but he could have recited the words as if they were in inch-high capitals. There was even a pen-and-ink sketch of Dundas in the dock. It was brilliant. Monk did not have to hesitate for an instant to wonder if it portrayed the man as he had been. It was so vivid; the charm, the dignity, the inner grace were all there, caught in a few lines, and the fear and weariness in the face, fine features become gaunt, nose too prominent, hair a fraction too long, folds in the skin too deep, making him look ten years older than the sixty-two the words proclaimed.

Monk stared at it and was back in the courtroom again, feeling the press of bodies around him, the noise, the smell of anger in the air, the harsh Liverpool voices with their unique rhythm and accent, the innate humor turned vicious against what they saw as betrayal.

All the time he felt the frustration again, the striving to do something he was prevented from at every turn. Hope seeped away like water poured into dry sand.

There was a picture of the prosecutor, a large man with a bland, placid face belying his appetite for success. He had educated himself out of his local dialect, but the nasal sounds of it were still there when he was excited, scenting the kill. Now and then he forgot and used a piece of idiom, and the crowd loved him for it. Monk had not realized then how much he was playing to the gallery, but now, with hindsight and memories of the scores of other trials he had attended, he could see that the prosecutor had been like a bad actor.

Did it all rest on the skill of lawyers? What if Dundas had

had someone like Oliver Rathbone? Would it have made any real difference, in the end?

He read on through the account of witnesses: first of all other bankers, disclaiming all knowledge of improper dealings, busy washing their hands of it, talking loudly of their innocence. He could remember their well-cut jackets and tight-collared shirts, faces scrubbed and pink, voices correct. They had looked frightened, as if guilt were contagious. Monk could feel his own anger clenching inside him, still urgent and real, not something finished sixteen years ago.

Next had come the investors who had lost money, or at least were beginning to realize they were not going to profit as they had expected. They had swung from professed ignorance to open anger when they saw that their financial competence was undermined. They had been foremost in damning Dundas with their sly, pejorative words, their judgment of his character, wise after the event. Monk could remember his fury as he had been forced to listen to them, helpless to argue, to defend, to speak of their own greed or repeat the eagerness with which they had been persuaded from one route to another, one purchase more or less, any cheaper way.

He had wanted to testify. He could feel his anger as if it had been yesterday, and all the pressure he had put to bear on the defense lawyer to let him speak. And every time it had been refused.

"Prejudice the jury," he had been told. "Pillar of the community; can't attack Baltimore or you'll only make it worse. His family has money in every big undertaking in Lancashire. Make an enemy of him and you'll turn half the county against you." And so it had gone on, until his own evidence had been so anodyne as to be virtually useless. He entered the ring like a boxer with one arm behind him, bruised by blows he could not return.

The landowner had surprised him. He had expected outrage and self-interest from him, and instead he had heard bewilderment, careful recounting of haggling and sales, attempts at diversion so as to keep one estate or another whole. But there was no spite, no desperation to preserve a reputation.

Large sums of money had changed hands, but in spite of all the prosecutor's attempts to make them seem dishonest or exorbitant, by and large they were exactly what everyone expected.

However, when all the amounts were entered into evidence, Monk heard the death knell of the defense in those meticulous records. He knew now as if it were all clear in his fragmented mind just what the final verdict would be, not because it was true but because there were too many of the negotiations conducted by Dundas, agreements with his signature on them, money in his accounts. He could deny, but he could not disprove. He had acted for others. That was his business.

But there were no other names written. He had trusted. They claimed they had trusted also. Who had betrayed whom?

Of course Monk knew the verdict—guilty.

But he had to know more of the detail, exactly how the fraud had been managed so that it had remained hidden until the last moment. How had Dundas expected to get away with it?

There was a sketch of Nolan Baltimore giving evidence. Monk stared at the few lines with fascination. It was an ugly face, but there was immense vitality in it, a power in the heavy bones and appetite in the curve of the mouth. It was intelligent, but portraying no sensitivity and little subtlety or humor. Monk was repulsed, yet it was only a sketch, one man's view. He could not recall ever having seen the man alive. He was simply the owner of Dalgarno's company, and the man whose murder had so inconvenienced Hester and the women she cared for. He had died in Leather Lane, in all probability pushed down the stairs by a prostitute, whom presumably he had refused to pay.

Or else railway fraud had at last caught up with him after all, and he had been killed as Katrina feared, either to prevent it from happening again or to keep it secret and allow it to go ahead. Had he been going to expose this one too, this all-but-duplicate of the old fraud which would have worked if . . . if what?

Monk laid the paper down on the flat tabletop and stared at

the rows of folders and ledgers on the shelves in front of him. What had happened to expose Arrol Dundas? Why had the scheme not continued undetected? Had someone betrayed him, or had it been carelessness, a transfer not concealed well enough, an entry not followed through, something incomplete, a name mentioned that should not have been?

If anyone had ever told Monk he had known from a confidence or deduction, he could not bring it back now, however hard he tried.

His eyes ached from the endless writing and the lines jumped in front of him, but he went back to reading the account of evidence day by day. Fraud trials were always long; there was so much detail following the intricacies of land sale and purchase, surveying, negotiation of routes, consideration of methods, materials, alternatives.

He rubbed his eyes, blinking as if there were grit in them.

He had given evidence himself, but there was no sketch of him. He was not interesting enough to engage the reader, so whether the artist had drawn him or not, no likeness had been used. Was he disappointed? Had he really been so incidental then, so unimportant? It seemed so.

He read what was given of his own interrogation by the prosecutor. At first he was startled to see that from the tone of the questions he was obviously a suspect too. But then, as he looked at it more rationally, and without the instinctive self-defense, the man would have been derelict in his duty not to have taken very serious consideration of the possibility.

So if he had been suspected then, why was he later considered to be of insufficient interest to have his picture included? He must have been vindicated. By the time the newspaper went to press, he was effectively no longer involved. Why? Did it matter now? Probably not.

According to what was reported in the paper, Monk had conducted some of the negotiations for purchase. It seemed to have been pulled out of him with extraordinary reluctance that he had not hired the surveyor, which was the fact that exonerated him. He had been in the witness-box altogether less than half an hour. If he had said anything at all to help clear

Dundas, it was not reported. He had been regarded as a hostile witness by the prosecution, but most of what he was asked concerned documents, and could hardly be denied.

He could not remember what he had said, only the feeling of being trapped, stared at by the crowd, frowned on by the judge, weighed and assessed by the jurors, fought over by the opposing counsel, and looked to for help he could not give by Dundas himself. That was what remained with him even now, the guilt because he had not been clever enough to make any difference.

Then another face was sharp in his mind, one not drawn by the artist, for whatever reason, perhaps compassion—that of Dundas's wife. She had sat with a terrible calm throughout the trial. Her loyalty had been the one thing even the prosecution had felt obliged to praise. He had spoken of her with respect, certain that her faith in her husband was both honest and complete.

Monk recalled her afterwards, the totality of her silent grief when she had told him of Dundas's death. He could picture the room, the sunlight, her face pale, the tears on her cheeks, as if it were then too late for anything but the hidden, inmost pain which never leaves. It was she he thought of more than Dundas, she whose grief outweighed his own, and which tore still at the deep well of emotion within him, unhealed even now.

And there was something more, but he could not bring it back. He sat staring at the old papers, yellowed at the edges, and struggled to recapture what it was. Time and time again it was almost there, and then it splintered into fragments and meant nothing.

He gave up and went back to the next stage of the trial. More witnesses, this time for the defense. Clerks were called, people who had written entries in ledgers, kept books, filed orders for money, purchases of land, title deeds, surveys. But it was all too complicated, and half of them had become uncertain under cross-examination. The main thrust of the defense had been not that there was no fraud but that Nolan Baltimore could equally be suspected of it.

But Nolan Baltimore was in the witness-box. Arrol Dundas was in the dock—and that perception made all the difference. It depended upon whom you believed, and then in that light all the evidence fell one way or the other. Monk could see how it had been, and he could find no loose thread to unravel a greater truth.

There seemed no question that Dundas had purchased land in his own name, farmland of poor quality, which he had paid market value for, little enough when you need it for running sheep. But when the railway was diverted from its original track, around a hill and through that farmland, which it was obliged to buy at a considerably larger amount, then Dundas's very rapidly turned profit was huge.

That in itself would be regarded as no more than exceptionally fortunate speculation, to be envied but not blamed. One might well resent not having done the same oneself, but only a small-minded man hates another for such advantage.

It only looked fraudulent when it emerged that the rerouting of the track from its original passage was not only unnecessary but brought about at all only by forged papers and lies told by Dundas. The original route would have been used, in spite of the fact that a certain owner of a huge estate was actually campaigning against it because it spoiled the path of his local hunt and the magnificent landscaped view from his house. The hill that had been the pretext for the rerouting was real, and certainly lay across the proposed path of the track, but it was less high in reality than on the survey they had used, which was actually of another hill of remarkably similar outlines, but higher, and of granite. The grid references had been changed in an imaginative forgery. The actual hill across the track could probably have been blasted into a simple cutting with a manageable gradient. If not, even tunneling for a short distance would have been possible. The cost of that had been wildly overestimated in Dundas's calculations, too much to have been incompetence.

All Dundas's past plans were reviewed, and no errors were found of more than a foot here or there. This miscalculation was over a hundred feet. When it was put together with his profit on the sale of the land, the assumption of intentional fraud was inescapable.

A defense of incompetence, misjudgment and coincidental profit might have succeeded, but it was Dundas's name on the purchase and on the survey, and the money was in Dundas's bank, not Baltimore's.

In the face of the evidence, the jury returned the only verdict it could. Arrol Dundas was sentenced to ten years' imprisonment. He died within months.

Monk was cold where he sat, drenched with memory. He could feel again the overwhelming defeat. It hurt with a pain so intense it was physical. It was for Dundas, white-faced, crumpled as if age had caught up with him and shrunken him inside and in a day he had been struck by twenty years. It was for his wife as well. She had hoped until the very end, she had kept a strength that had sustained them all, but there was nothing left to hope for now. It was over.

And it was for himself also. It was the first bitter and terrible loneliness he could recall. It was a knowledge of loss, a real and personal sweetness gone from his life.

How much of the truth had he known at the time? He had been far younger then, a good banker, but naïve in the ways of crime. It was before he had become a policeman. He was accustomed to making judgments of men's character, but not with the view to dishonesty he had developed later, not with the knowledge of every kind of fraud, embezzlement, and theft—and the suspicion carved deep into every avenue of his mind.

He had wanted to believe Dundas. All his emotions and loyalty were vested in his honesty and his friendship. It was like being asked to accept that your own father had deliberately deceived you over the years, and everything you had learned from him was tainted with lies, not just to the world, but specifically to you.

Was that why he had believed Dundas? And the rest of the world had not? All the proof had been pieces of paper. Anyone can produce paper, whoever else had been in the company, even Baltimore himself. But Dundas had fought so little! He had seemed to at first, and then to crumple, as if he knew defeat even before he really attempted to struggle.

But Monk had felt so certain of Dundas's innocence!

Had he known something which he had not said in court, something which would have shown that there was no deceit, or if there had been, that it was Baltimore's? After all, there was no proof here that it had been Dundas's idea to divert the track. Neither had there been anything to prove that he had met the landowner or accepted any favor from him, financial or otherwise. The police had not examined the landowner's records to trace any exchange of monies. Nothing was found in Dundas's bank beyond the profit from the sale of his own land. The worst that could be said of that was that it had been sharp practice, but that happened all the time. It was what speculation was. Half the families in Europe had made their fortune in ways they would not care to acknowledge now.

What could he have known? Where more money was? Why had he kept silent? To conceal Dundas's act? To keep the money from being taken back? For whom—Mrs. Dundas or himself?

He moved in the seat and felt his locked muscles stab, he was so stiff. He winced, and rubbed his hands over his eyes.

He had to know his own part in it—it was the core of who he had been then.

Then? He even used the word as if it could separate him from who he was now and rid himself of responsibility for it.

At last he faced the thing that was woven into the story and that in pursuing the evidence of money he had ignored—the crash. It was not mentioned in reports about the trial, even obliquely. Obviously it was either irrelevant or it had not happened yet. There was only one way to find out.

He turned the pages, looking at headlines only. It would be in the heaviest, blackest print when it came.

And it was—nearly a month later, at the top of the front page: RAIL CRASH KILLS OVER FORTY CHILDREN AS COAL TRAIN PLOWS INTO EXCURSION TRIP FROM LIVERPOOL.

The words seemed unfamiliar, although he must have read this before. But he had to have known about it anyway. Seeing this would have meant nothing. It would have been only someone else's report of a horror beyond words to re-create. Now as he stared at it, it was everything, the reality he had been torn between finding and leaving buried, the compulsion to know and the dread of confirming it at last, making it no longer nightmare but reality, never again to be evaded or denied.

An excursion train carrying nearly two hundred children on a trip into the country was crashed and thrown off the rails last night as it returned to the city along the new line recently opened by Baltimore and Sons. The accident happened on the curve beyond the old St. Thomas's Church where the line goes into single track for a distance of just under a mile through two cuttings. A goods train heavily loaded with coal failed to stop as it was coming down the incline before the tracks joined. It crashed into the passenger cars, hurling them down the slope to the shallow valley below. Many carriages caught fire from the gas used to provide lights, and screaming children were trapped inside to be burned to death. Other children were thrown clear as the fabric of the carriages was torn and burst open, some to escape with shock and bruises, many to be crippled, maimed, trapped and crushed under the wreckage.

Both drivers were killed by the impact, as were the firemen, stokers and brakemen on both trains.

Monk skipped over the next paragraphs, which were accounts of the attempts at rescue and the transport of the injured and dead to the nearest places of help. After that there followed the grief and horror of relatives, and promises of the fullest possible investigation.

But even searching with stiff fingers and dazed mind through all the succeeding weeks, into months, he found no satisfactory explanation as to what had caused the crash. In the end it was attributed to human error on the part of the goods train driver. He was not alive to defend himself, and no one had discovered any other cause. Certainly the torn and twisted track appeared to have been damaged by the crash itself, and there was no suggestion by anyone that it had been at fault previously to that. The earlier goods train along it carrying timber had had no difficulty at all and arrived at its destination safely and on time.

As he had already heard from the clerk days ago, there was nothing wrong with the track—there was no connection whatever with the fraud, or with Arrol Dundas, or therefore with Monk.

With overwhelming relief he kept telling himself that over and over again. He would go back to London and assure Katrina Harcus that there was no reason whatever to fear a crash on the new line. Baltimore and Sons had never been implicated in the Liverpool crash, and Baltimore himself had been exonerated of fraud in the trial of Dundas.

Which did not mean he had been innocent.

But if land fraud was what was happening now, on the same scale as before, then it was not unreasonable to believe it was Nolan Baltimore who was involved this time as well, rather than Michael Dalgarno. Monk could at least tell that to Katrina.

Although even as he said that to himself, he knew she would want more than hope, she would need proof—just as he did.

He went back to the station and caught the evening train to London. Perhaps because he had been reading most of the day, and had slept little and poorly on the previous night, in spite of the wooden seats and the awkward, upright position, the rhythmic movement of the train and the sound of the wheels over the track lulled him to sleep. He drifted into a darkness in which he was even more conscious of the noise; it seemed to fill the air and to be all around him, growing louder. His body was tense, his face tingling as if cold air were streaming past him, and yet he could see sparks red in the night, like chips of fire.

There was something he needed to do: it mattered more than anything else, even the risk of his own life. It dominated everything, mind and body, obliterating all thought of his safety, of physical pain, exhaustion, and carrying him beyond even fear—and there was everything to be afraid of! It roared and surged around him in the darkness, buffeting him until he was bruised and aching, clinging on desperately, fighting to . . . what? He did not know! There was something he must do. The fate of everybody who mattered depended on it . . . but what was it?

He racked his brain . . . and found only the driving compulsion to succeed. The wind was streaming past him like liquid ice. He strained against a force, hurling his weight against it, but it was immovable.

There was indescribable noise, impact, and then he was running, scrambling, blind with terror. All around him the sound of screaming ripped through him like physical pain, and he could do nothing! He was closed in by confusion, thrashing around pointlessly, bumping into objects in the darkness one moment, blinded by flames the next, the heat in his face and the cold behind him. His feet were leaden, holding him back, while the rest of his body ran with sweat.

He saw the face again above the clerical collar, the same as before, this time gray with horror, scrambling in the wreckage, all the time calling out.

He woke with a violent start, his head throbbing, his lungs aching, starved of air, his mouth dry. As soon as he moved he realized the sweat was real, sticking his clothes to him, but the carriage was bitterly cold and his feet were numb.

He was alone in his compartment. The smell of smoke was in his imagination, but the fear was real, the guilt was real. Knowledge of failure weighed on him as if it were woven into every part of his life, staining everything, seeping into every corner and marring all other joy.

But what failure? He had not saved Dundas, but he had known that for years. And now he was no longer rationally sure that Dundas had been innocent. He felt it, but what were his feelings worth? They could have been simply born of the loyalty and ignorance of a young man who owed a great deal to someone who had been as a father to him. He had seen

Dundas as he wished him to be, like millions before him, and millions to come.

The dream was a crash—that was obvious. But was it from reality, or imagination read into the accounts of those who were there, or even a visit to the scene afterwards, as part of the enquiry into what had happened?

It was not the rail line which had caused it. It was not the land fraud, which could make no difference to anything but money.

So why did he feel this terrible responsibility, this guilt? What was there in himself so fearful he still could not bear to look at it? Was it Dundas—or himself?

Could he find out? Was he just like Katrina Harcus, driven to discover a truth which might destroy everything that mattered to him?

He sat hunched in the seat, rattling through the darkness towards London, shivering and icy cold, thoughts racing off the rails into tunnels—and another, different kind of crash.

7

THE HOUSE on Coldbath Square was almost empty of women injured in the usual way of trade, because there was hardly any trade. Many of the local populace had found ways around the constant police presence and now conducted what business they could elsewhere, but the Farringdon Road was outwardly much the same as always. It required a more practiced eye to see the stiffness of street corner peddlers, the way everyone was watching over their shoulders, not for pickpockets or other small-time thieves, but for the ubiquitous constables placed, in frustrated boredom, as prevention rather than solution.

"On our backs like a jockey floggin' a horse what won't run," Constable Hart said miserably, nursing a mug of hot tea in his hands as he sat opposite Hester at the smaller of the two tables. "We won't run 'cos we can't!" he went on. It was midafternoon and raining on and off. His wet cape hung on one of the hooks by the door. "We're just standin' 'round lookin' stupid, an' gettin' everyone angry at us," he complained. "It's all to make the Baltimore family an' their friends feel like we're cleanin' up London." His expression of disgust conveyed his feelings perfectly.

"I know," she agreed with some sympathy.

"Nobody ever done that, nor ever will," he added. "London don't wanter be cleaned up. Women on the street in't the problem. Problem is men what comes after 'em!"

"Of course," Hester conceded. "Would you like some toast?"

His face lit up. It was a completely unnecessary question, as she had known it would be.

He cleared his throat. "Got any black currant jam?" he asked hopefully.

"Of course." She smiled, and he colored very faintly. She stood up and spent the next few minutes cutting bread, toasting it on the fork in front of the stove, and then bringing it over, with butter and jam.

"Thanks," he said with his mouth already full.

She and Margaret had spent their days trying to drum up more funding, having further conversations with Jessop which varied from placatory to confrontational and back again depending upon tempers, and pledges of help. Hester had never disliked anyone more. "Are you any closer to finding whoever killed Baltimore?" she asked Hart.

He shrugged, an air of hopelessness filling him as he stared gloomily at the crumbs on his plate. "Not as I can see," he admitted. "Abel Smith's girls all swear blind they din't do it, an' speakin' purely for meself, I believe 'em. Not that the higher-ups are goin' to listen to what I say." He looked up at her with sudden anger, his face set hard.

"But I'm damned if I'm goin' to see some poor little cow topped for killin' 'im just to satisfy 'is family an' their like, an' get business back to normal. No matter whoever says, ever so soft, that they'd like it that way!"

Hester felt a chill. "Do you think anyone would try to do that?"

He caught the doubt in her voice. "You're a nice lady, brought up proper. You don't belong 'ere," he said gently. He glanced around the long room with its iron beds, the stone sinks at the far end and the jugs and pails of water. " 'Course they would, if it comes to it. Can't go on like this much longer. Right and wrong gets to look different when you've bin 'ungry for a while, or slept in a doorway. I've seen 'em. It changes folk, an' 'oo's to say it's their fault?"

She wondered whether to tell him anything about Squeaky Robinson and his very different establishment, apparently somewhere near Reid's Brewery on Portpool Lane, or close beside. She was only half listening to him as she weighed it up.

"Of course," she agreed absently. If she told Hart he would feel obliged in turn to tell his superiors, and they would go blundering in, and very possibly warn Robinson without learning anything about Baltimore. After all, Robinson would deny it, just as everyone else was doing. Almost certainly he already had done.

"Not as I'm sure we want to find the truth," Hart went on dismally. "Considering what it'll be, like as not."

Now she did pay attention. "Not find it?" she challenged. "You mean just go on with the appearance until they get tired of it and say they're giving up? They can't keep half the London police force in Coldbath forever."

"Another few weeks at the most," he agreed. "It would be easier, in the end."

"Easier for whom?" Without asking, she poured him more tea, and he thanked her with a nod.

" 'Em as uses the 'ouses 'round 'ere for their pleasures," he answered her question. "But mostly for 'em in charge o' the police." He grimaced, shaking his head a little. "Would you like to be the one what goes and tells the Baltimore family that Mr. Baltimore came 'ere to gratify 'isself, an' maybe refused to pay what 'e owed, an' got into a fight with some pimp in a back alley somewhere? But the pimp got the better of 'im, an' killed 'im. Maybe 'e didn't even mean to, but when it was done it were too late, an' so 'e settled some old score or other by dumpin' the body at Abel Smith's?"

She tightened her lips and frowned.

"We all know it's likely the truth," he went on. "But knowin' an' sayin' is two different things. Most of all, 'aving other people know is a third different thing, an' all! Some of which is best not said."

It made her decision for her. If the truth was what she feared it was—that in some way Baltimore's death was personal, incurred by his behavior, either as a user of prostitutes or something to do with the railway fraud, because he was the

instigator of it, or some other member of his family was—
then the police were not going to wish to find either of those
answers.

"You are right," she agreed. "Would you like another piece
of toast and jam?"

"That's very civil of you, miss," he accepted, leaning back
in the chair. "I don't mind if I do."

Hester knew she must find an excuse to call on Squeaky
Robinson. After Hart had gone and Margaret came in, they
spent some time caring for Fanny and Alice, who were both
making slow and halting recovery. Then, as the afternoon
waned and a decided chill settled in the air, Hester brought in
more coals for the fire and considered telling Margaret to go
home. The streets were quiet, and Bessie would be there all
night.

Margaret sat at the table staring disconsolately at the medicine cabinet she had recently restocked.

"I spoke to Jessop again," she said, her face tight, contempt
hardening the line of her mouth. "My governess used to tell
me when I was a child that a good woman can see the human
side in anyone, and perceive some virtue in them." She gave a
rueful little shrug. "I used to believe her, probably because I
actually liked her. Most girls rebel against their teachers, but
she was fun, and interesting. She taught me all sorts of things
that were certainly no practical use at all, simply interesting to
know. I can't imagine when I shall ever need to speak German.
And she let me climb trees and get apples and plums—as long
as I gave her some. She loved plums!"

Hester had a glimpse of a young Margaret, her hair in pig-
tails, her skirts tucked up, shinning up the apple trees in
someone else's orchard, forbidden by her parents, and encouraged by a young woman willing to risk her employment
to please a child and give her a little illicit but largely harm-
less fun. She found herself smiling. It was another life, another world from this one, where children stole to survive and
would not have known what a governess was. Few of them

ever attended even a ragged school, let alone had personal tuition or the luxury of abstract morality.

"But I don't think even Miss Walter would have found anything to redeem Mr. Jessop," Margaret finished. "I wish with a passion that we did not have to rent accommodation from him."

"So do I," Hester agreed. "I keep looking for something else so we can be rid of him, but I haven't found anything yet."

Margaret looked away from Hester, and there was a very faint pinkness in her cheeks. "Do you think Sir Oliver will be able to help us with the women like Alice who are in debt to the usurer?" she asked tentatively.

Hester felt the odd sinking feeling of change again, a very slight loneliness that Rathbone no longer cared for her quite as he had. Their friendship was still the same, and unless she behaved unworthily, it always would be. And she had never offered him more than that. It was Monk she loved. If she were even remotely honest, it always had been. The love of friends was different, calmer, and immeasurably safer. The heat did not burn the flesh, or the heart, nor did it light the fires which dispelled all darkness.

And that was the core of it. If she cared for either Rathbone or Margaret, and she cared for them both, then she should be happy for them, full of hope that they were on the edge of discovering the kind of happiness that required all the strength and commitment there was to give.

Margaret was looking at her, waiting.

"I know he will do his best," Hester said aloud. "So if it can be done, then yes, he will do it." She breathed in deeply. "But before that, and apart from it, I want to make some more enquiries as to where Mr. Baltimore was killed, because I believe Abel Smith that it was not in his house."

Margaret looked at her quickly, a different kind of anxiety in her eyes now. "Hester, please be careful. Shall I come with you? You shouldn't go alone. If anything happened to you, no one would ever know—"

"You would know," Hester replied, cutting off her argument. "But if you come with me, then no one would, except perhaps Bessie. I think I would rather rely on you to rescue me." She smiled to rob the remark of sting. "But I promise I shall be careful. I have an idea which, even if I don't learn anything, could be of benefit to us. A little more in the way of funds, anyhow. And even a spoke in Mr. Jessop's wheel, which I would dearly like."

"So would I," Margaret agreed. "But not at the cost of danger to you."

"There's no more danger than coming here every night," Hester assured her, with something less than the truth. But she thought the risk was worth it, and it was slight, all things considered. She stood up. "Tell Bessie I should be back no later than midnight. If I'm not, then you can inform Constable Hart and send out a search party for me."

"I shall be here myself," Margaret retorted. "Tell me where you are going, so I shall know where to begin looking." She half smiled, but her eyes were perfectly serious.

"Portpool Lane," Hester replied. "I have an idea to see a Mr. Robinson who keeps an establishment there." She felt better for telling Margaret that, and as she put on her shawl and opened the door onto Coldbath Square, it was with more confidence than she had felt a few moments earlier. She turned in the doorway. "Thank you," she said gravely, then, before Margaret could argue, she walked quickly along the footpath in the rain and turned the corner into Bath Street.

She did not slacken her speed even when she was out of sight of the square because it was better for a woman alone to look as if she had a purpose, but also she did not want to allow herself time to reconsider what she was going to do, in case she lost her nerve. Margaret had an extraordinary admiration for her, especially her courage, and she was surprised now to realize how precious that was. It was worth conquering the fear that fluttered in the pit of her stomach to be able to return to Coldbath Square and say that she had gone through with her plan, whether she learned anything or not.

It was not entirely pride, although she was forced to admit that that did enter into it. It was also a gentler thing, the desire to live up to what Margaret believed of her and aspired to herself. Disillusion was a bitter thing, and she might already have brought about a little of that. She was aware of having been abrupt a few times, of a reluctance to praise even where it was due. The knowledge that Monk was keeping from her something that hurt him had driven her into an unusual sense of isolation, and it had touched her friendships as well.

She could at least live up to the mask of courage that was expected of her. She too needed to believe that she was equal to anything she set herself. Physical courage was easy, compared with the inner strength to endure the pain of the heart.

Anyway, Squeaky Robinson was probably a perfectly ordinary businessman who had no intention of hurting anybody unless they threatened him, and she would be careful not to do that. This was only an expedition to look and learn.

The huge mass of Reid's Brewery towered dark into the rain-drifted sky, and there was a sweet, rotten smell in the air.

She was obliged to stop where Portpool Lane ran close under the massive walls. She could no longer see where she was going. The eaves dripped steadily. There were shadows in the doorways, beggars settling for the night. Considering that she was in the immediate vicinity of exactly the kind of brothel she would have inhabited herself, had she been driven to the streets, the chances of her being misunderstood were very high. But she had passed a constable less than a hundred yards away. Certainly he was out of sight, but his presence was sufficient to deter the kind of customer who came here even more than most.

She leaned against the brewery wall, keeping away from the edge of the narrow curb, where the light from the street lamp shone pale on the wet cobbles. With her shawl covering her head and concealing most of her face, she did not look as if she were hoping to be noticed. The lane was a couple of hundred yards long, leading into the Gray's Inn Road, a busy thoroughfare, traffic running up and down it until midnight or more, and the odd hansom cab even after that. The town hall was just around the corner. Squeaky Robinson was more likely to have his house in the shadows up one of the alleys at this end, opposite the brewery. His clients would want to be as discreet as possible.

Did such men feel any shame at the exercise of their tastes? Certainly they would wish it secret from society in general, but what about each other? Would they come if their equals with similar tastes were aware? She had no idea, but perhaps it would be clever of the proprietor of such a place to have more than one entrance—more than two, even? If so, the alleys opposite would be perfect. This end, not the other, where there was a large, very respectable looking building and a hotel beyond.

Now that she had decided as much, there was no point in waiting. She straightened up, breathed in deeply, forgetting the sweet, decaying smell, and she wished she had not, as she coughed and gasped, drawing in more of it. She should never forget where she was, not even for an instant! Cursing her inattention, she crossed the road and walked smartly up the first alley right to the end, where any building would lie which opened onto both lanes, and onto the narrow streets at the farther side.

The alley was narrow, but freer of rubbish than she would have expected ordinarily, and there was a light on a wall bracket about halfway along, showing a clear path up the uneven stones. Was that coincidence, or was Squeaky Robinson taking care of the physical sensibilities of his clients by seeing they did not have to stumble over refuse on their way to their pleasures?

She reached the end of the alley, and on the outer edge of the light from the lamp she could see steps and a doorway. She already knew what she was going to say, and there was nothing to hesitate for. She went to the door and knocked.

It was opened immediately by a man in a dark suit, scuffed at the edges and too large for him, even though he was at least average in build. From the way he stood, he was ready for a fight any time one should seem necessary. He looked like a ruffian aping a down-at-heel butler. Perhaps it was part of the image of the establishment. He regarded her without interest. "Yes, miss?"

She met his eyes directly. She did not wish to be taken for a supplicant in distress, seeking to use the brothel to rescue herself from debt.

"Good evening," she replied stiffly. "I would like to speak with the proprietor. I believe he is a Mr. Robinson? We may have business interests in common where we could be of service to one another. Would you be good enough to tell him that Mrs. Monk, of Coldbath Square, is here to see him?" She made it an order, as she would have done in her old life, before her sojourn in the Crimea, when calling upon the daughter of a friend of her father whose servants would know her.

The man hesitated. He was used to obeying the clientele—it was part of their purchase—but women were stock-in-trade, and as such should do as they were told.

She did not lower her eyes.

"I'll see," he conceded ungraciously. "Yer'd better come in." He almost added something further, then at the last moment thought better of it and merely led her to a very small room off the passage, little more than a wide cupboard furnished with one wooden chair. "Wait there," he ordered, and went out, closing the door.

She did as he said. This was not the time to take risks. She would learn nothing by exploring, and she had no interest in the interior of a brothel yet, and hoped she never would have. It was easier to deal with the injured women if she knew less rather than more about their lives. She was concerned with medicine, nothing else. And if she was caught she would not be able to explain herself to Squeaky Robinson, and it was important he believe her. There would be enough stretching and bending of the truth as it was.

She had to wait for what seemed like a quarter of an hour before the door opened again and the would-be butler ushered her along the passage further into the warren of the building. It was narrow, cramped for width and height. The floors were uneven under the old red carpeting, but the boards did not creak, as she would have expected. Someone had taken great care to nail them all down so not one moved to betray a footstep. There was no sound in the silence except a random settling of the whole fabric of the building, a sigh of ancient timber slowly consumed by rot. The stairs were steep and ran both up and down within the one corridor, as if two or three rambling houses had been joined to give a dozen entrances and exits.

Finally the butler stopped and opened a door, indicating that Hester should go in. The room was a startling surprise, although only on entering it did Hester realize what she had expected. She had pictured dimness, vulgarity, and instead it was large, low-ceilinged, and the walls were almost obscured by shelves and cupboards. The floor was wood boards covered with rugs, and the main piece of furniture was an enormous desk with a multitude of drawers. On its cluttered surface was a brightly burning oil lamp shedding a yellow light in every direction. The room was also warm from a black stove on the far wall, and the whole place was untidy, but apparently clean.

The man sitting in the leather-upholstered chair was thin-faced, sharp-eyed, with straggling gray-brown hair and very slightly hunched shoulders. He regarded Hester with intelligent wariness, but none of the curiosity she would have expected had he no idea who she was. Presumably word of the Coldbath house had reached him, which she should have expected.

"Well, Mrs. Monk," he said smoothly. "And what business is it that could concern both you and me?" His voice was light and soft, a little nasal, but not sufficiently so to account for his nickname. She wondered what had given him that.

She sat down without being invited, in order to let him know she did not intend to be fobbed off but would stay until the matter was settled to her satisfaction.

"The business of keeping as many women as possible in a fit state to work, Mr. Robinson," she replied.

He moved his head a trifle to one side. "I thought you were a charitable woman, Mrs. Monk. Wouldn't you rather see all the women back in factories or sweatshops, earning a living the law and society would approve?"

"You don't earn a living at all with broken bones, Mr.

Robinson," she countered. She tried to sound as casual as possible, suppressing her emotions of anger and contempt. She was there to accomplish a purpose, not indulge herself. "And my interests are not your concern, except where they meet with your own, which I presume is to make as much profit as possible."

He nodded very slowly, and as the light flickered on his face she saw the lines of tension in it, the grayness of his skin in spite of being close-shaven, even at this time in the early evening. There was a tiny flicker of surprise in him, so small she might have been mistaken.

"And what kind of profit are you looking for?" he enquired. He picked up a paper knife and fiddled with it, his long, ink-stained fingers constantly moving.

"That is my concern," she said tartly, sitting up very straight, as if she were in a church pew.

He was taken aback, it was clear in his face. A trifle more masked was the fact that she had also woken his curiosity.

She smiled. "I have no intention of becoming your rival, Mr. Robinson," she said with some amusement. "I assume you are aware of my house in Coldbath Square?"

"I am," he conceded, watching her closely.

"I have treated some women who I think may have worked for you, but that is only a deduction," she continued. "They do not tell me, and I do not ask. I mention it only to indicate that we have interests that coincide."

"So you said." His fingers kept rolling the paper knife around and around. There were papers scattered on the desk which looked like balance sheets. There were lines ruled on them in both directions, and what seemed more like figures than words. The lack of trade must be affecting him more than most, as she had already thought. It added to her strength.

"Business is poor for everyone," she observed.

"I thought you did yours for nothing," he replied flatly. "So far you are wasting my time, Mrs. Monk."

"Then I'll come to the point." She could not afford to have him dismiss her. "What I do serves your interests." She made it a statement of fact and did not wait for him to agree or disagree. "In order to do it I have to have premises, and I am at the present time having a degree of difficulty with my landlord. He is obstructive and keeps threatening to increase the rent."

She saw his body tighten under the thin jacket, a distinct alteration in his position in the big chair. She wondered just how much the present situation had cost him. Was he short of money? Was he the usurer, or merely the manager of this place? Quite a lot might depend upon the answer to that.

"I practice business, not charity, Mrs. Monk," Robinson said sharply, his voice rising in pitch, his hand clutching the paper knife even more rigidly.

"Of course," she said without the slightest change in her expression. "I am expecting enlightened self-interest from you, not a donation. Tell me, Mr. Robinson, have you made a profit since the unfortunate death of . . . Mr. Baltimore, I believe his name was?"

His eyes narrowed. "You knew him?" he said suspiciously.

"Not at all," she answered. "I say unfortunate because it has interrupted what was a fairly satisfactory state of affairs in the area and has brought a police presence we would all prefer to be without."

He seemed to consider saying something and then changed his mind. She saw his breathing quicken a little, and again he shifted his position very slightly, as if easing aching bones.

"They apparently intend to remain until they find who killed him," she went on. "And I do not foresee any success for them. They appear to think he died in Abel Smith's house in Leather Lane." She did not move her eyes from his. "I think that is unlikely."

Robinson seemed scarcely to breathe. "Do you?" He was weighing everything he said, which made her wonder if he was frightened, and if so, of what, or of whom.

"There are several possibilities." She kept her voice light, as if they were discussing something of only moderate interest. "None of which anyone will assist them to find out," she added. "He will have been killed somewhere else, either intentionally or by accident. And whoever was responsible, very naturally, did not wish to be blamed or to attract the attention of the police, so equally naturally, they moved the body. Anyone would have done as much."

"That has nothing to do with me," Robinson replied, but she noticed the knuckles of his hand were white.

"Except that, like all of us, you would like to see the police leave and allow us to get back to our normal lives," she agreed.

Hope flashed for a moment in his eyes, briefly but quite unmistakably.

"And you have some way of doing that, Mrs. Monk?" he asked. Now his fingers were motionless, as if he could not divert even that much of his energy from her.

She wished she had! Any plan would be worth sharing now. If this was the place where Fanny and Alice had worked, she would give a very great deal to finish him legally, so he and anyone who was his partner would spend the rest of their lives in prison, preferably on the treadmill.

"I have certain ideas," she equivocated. "But my immediate concern is to acquire better terms for leasing premises. Since it will be in your interest that women who have . . . accidents . . . are treated quickly, freely and with total discretion, I thought you might be a good person to approach for . . . advice on the matter."

Robinson sat quite still, studying her while the seconds stretched into one minute, then two. She tried to judge him in return. She did not expect any assistance with accommodation; that was only an excuse to allow her to meet him and to see something of the place. Was this where Fanny and Alice, and others like them, had worked? If at least she could give Rathbone a name and address, then he would have something to pursue. Was this narrow-faced man with his stringy shoulders and carefully shaven face the intelligence behind the usury, the profit and the vicious punishment she had seen? Or simply another brothel owner with a rather-better-than-average establishment?

He was nervous about something. The way his long, thin fingers constantly moved, the pallor of his face, his rigid

body, all betrayed anxiety. Or was it simply that he was unwell, or preoccupied with something quite different? Perhaps
he never went out in daylight anyway, and his pallor was part
of the way of his life.

She had learned little. If she was to accomplish anything
she must take more risk. "You must be losing money," she
stated boldly.

Something in him changed. It was so subtle she could not
have described it, but it was as if some hidden fear had
clamped a tighter hold on him. Her heart sank. She must be in
the wrong place. Squeaky Robinson had not the nerve or the
intelligence to plan something as bold or complicated as the
scheme Alice had described. It would take planning with
long-term profit in view, a steady mind and a cool head to
carry out such a thing. Squeaky Robinson did not impress her
as having any of those qualities. The panic in him was too
close beneath the surface now as they sat staring at each
other.

But it could not be she whom he feared. She had posed no
threat at all, open or implicit. She had no power to hurt him,
and had not suggested that she wished to.

Was it his partner he was afraid of? The man who had set
this up, and relied on him to run it profitably and without attracting the law? Was that it?

"Perhaps you should consult your partner before you reach
any decision?" she said aloud.

Squeaky stiffened so violently he poked himself with the
paper knife and gave a sharp yelp. He started to say something, then abruptly changed his mind. "I don't have a partner!" He glared at the red mark on his hand, then resentfully
at her, as if it were her fault he had hurt himself.

She smiled disbelievingly.

"You looking for other premises?" he said guardedly.

"I could be," she replied. "But I would want very good
rates, and no chopping and changing them when it suited you
a proper business arrangement. If you have no one else to
consult, then consider what I have said and see if you can be
of assistance. It is in your interest."

Squeaky chewed his lip. He was only too obviously in a quandary, and the pressure of a decision was taking him ever closer to panic.

Hester leaned forward a little. "It is going to get worse, Mr. Robinson. The longer the police are here, the more likely it is that your clients will be obliged to find other places in which to entertain themselves, and then . . ."

"What can I do?" he burst out, and now his voice was high and sharp enough to have given him his nickname. "I don't know who killed him, do I?"

"I don't know," she answered. "Perhaps you do. I'm sure a man with the skill to run a house like this must have his ear to the ground. You could not succeed if you did not—" She stopped. He looked so acutely uncomfortable she was afraid he was actually in physical pain. There was a sheen of sweat over his skin and his knuckles were white.

". . . if you did not have an excellent knowledge of the area and everything that goes on in it," she finished. There was such a tension in the man a few feet from her that suddenly she wanted to escape. The emotion in his face, the desperation, had a physical presence almost at odds with the sly knowledge of his mind. It was as if he had been robbed of a safety he had known for so long he was still only half aware of his new nakedness and had had no time to shield himself or deal with it.

"Yes!" he said sharply. "Of course I have!" He was defensive now, as if he needed to assure her. "I'll think about it, Mrs. Monk. We need to get back to business as usual. If I hear from anyone what happened to this Baltimore I'll see if we can't . . . arrange something." He spread his hands, indicating the piles of paper. "Now I've got things to see to. I can't spare any more time to . . . to talk . . . when there's nothing to say."

She rose to her feet. "Thank you, Mr. Robinson. And you will not forget to mention to your partner the matter of a property to rent . . . very reasonably, seeing as it is in all our interests?"

He jerked up again. "I don't have . . ." he began, then his face ironed out and he smiled. It was a ghastly gesture, all teeth and rigid muscles. "I'll tell him. Ha, ha!" He laughed violently. "See what he says!"

She left, conducted out through the corridors again by the man in the dark suit too big for him, and found herself in the alley leading back to Portpool Lane. It was now swirling with fog and she could see the solitary lamp on the wall through a shifting haze. For several moments she stood still, becoming accustomed to the chill air and the smell of the brewery massive against the sky, shedding its denser shadow till it obliterated all other outlines, just as the Coldbath Prison did on the house in the square. Then she set out walking, keeping close to the walls to avoid being noticed, and hoping she did not trip on anyone sleeping on the stones of the path or huddled in an unseen doorway.

After speaking with him and seeing his reactions, she was almost certain that Squeaky Robinson ran the brothel where young women like Fanny and Alice were put to work in order to pay off their debts to the usurer. But Squeaky was panicking over something! Was it just the lack of business at the moment? If he were the usurer, surely he could afford to wait until the police either found out who killed Baltimore or were forced to give up.

But what if he was not? What if he was only a partner, and the usurer was pressing him as well? Then who was the usurer, and why was Squeaky so frightened at the mere mention of his existence?

She crossed Portpool Lane and turned left toward Coldbath Square, still walking briskly. There were a few other people about. The lights of a public house shone out across the pavement as someone opened a door. There was a peddler on one corner, a constable on another, looking bored and cold, probably because he was standing still. He was getting in everyone's way, and he had long since given up hope of discovering anything useful.

Was Squeaky Robinson so frightened because he had somehow lost his partner, the intelligence and driving force behind the enterprise? How? To prison, illness—even death? Was he panicking because he was suddenly alone and he had not the skill to carry on without help? She was convinced, after talking to him, that he was not the usurer. He had not the polish, the confidence, to have ensnared the sort of young women he used. If he were, she could not have rattled him as she had.

What had happened to the usurer? A warm rush of hope surged up inside her, and she quickened her step. It hardly mattered why he had gone, or where, if it left Squeaky unable to continue. His fear might be why he had turned violent and either half killed Fanny and Alice himself, or more probably had someone like the would-be butler do it. But his rule would be short-lived. No more women would be ensnared, and if the usurer was gone then he could not enforce repayment, not in law, surely? Oliver Rathbone might be able to help after all!

She got back to Coldbath Square to find Margaret pacing the floor waiting for her. Her face lit the moment Hester was in through the door.

"I'm so relieved to see you!" she said, rushing forward. "Are you all right?"

Hester smiled with a pleasure that surprised her. She really did like Margaret very much. "Yes, thank you. Only cold," she answered frankly. "But I would love a cup of tea, to get the taste of that place out of my mouth." She took off her shawl and hung it up on one of the pegs as Margaret went to the stove.

"What did you learn?" Margaret asked even while she was checking that the kettle was full and moving it onto the hob. She kept glancing at Hester, and her face was eager, her eyes wide and bright.

"I think the woman at Abel Smith's told me correctly," Hester answered, fetching two mugs from the cupboard. "That is the place where they cater to more individual interests." She said it with heavy distaste at the euphemism, and saw her own feelings reflected in Margaret's expression. "I met Squeaky Robinson. . . ." ·

"What was he like?" Margaret stopped even pretending to watch the kettle. Her voice was sharp with anticipation.

"Very nervous indeed," Hester replied succinctly. "In fact,

I would say positively frightened." She put the mugs on the table.

Margaret was astonished. "Why? Was Baltimore killed there, do you suppose?"

Hester had been so occupied with the thought of Squeaky Robinson's partner, and the possibility of his being absent permanently, and therefore the usury business collapsing, that she had not seriously considered the thought that Squeaky's fear might be primarily of the police rather than of financial ruin. But the rope was an infinitely worse prospect than poverty, even to the greediest man alive.

"I suppose he could have been," she said a trifle reluctantly, explaining what her hope had been.

"Perhaps it was the usurer who killed him?" Margaret suggested, but there was more will than belief in her face. "Maybe he couldn't pay, and someone lost his temper. It could have been as much an accident as anything. After all, it isn't in their interest to kill a client, is it? It can't be good for business. It isn't as if anyone had to go there. There are plenty of other places, even if they would be in different parts of the city."

"And they left the body at Abel Smith's, just as he said," Hester agreed. "Yes, that sounds possible." She could not keep the slight disappointment out of her voice. Also, it might have helped Monk if Baltimore's death had had something to do with land fraud on the railway. It would have tied the present to the past and vindicated his belief that Arrol Dundas had been innocent. Except, of course, it would increase Monk's sense of guilt that he had been unable to prove it at the time.

"Should we tell Constable Hart?" Margaret asked hopefully. "That would solve the murder and get rid of the police." The kettle started to whistle behind her. "And get rid of the driving force behind the usury at the same time!" She turned to the kettle and scalded the teapot, then put in the leaves, then the boiling water.

"Not yet," Hester said cautiously. "I would like to know a little more about Mr. Baltimore first, wouldn't you?"

"Yes. But how?" Margaret carried the teapot over to the table and set it down beside the milk and the mugs. "Can I help? I might be able to scrape an acquaintance with someone of whom I could ask questions . . . or you could. I wouldn't know what to say." There was the very faintest color in her cheeks, and she did not quite meet Hester's eyes. "We might be able to take something useful to Sir Oliver if we could prove a connection." She spoke very casually, and Hester smiled, knowing exactly how she felt and why she was compelled to mask it, even from her closest friend, or perhaps especially from her.

"That would be a good idea," she agreed. "I'll write to Livia Baltimore and ask if I can call upon her tomorrow evening with further information about her father's death. If I send the letter with a messenger, I'll have a reply long before I need to go."

Margaret looked startled. "What are you going to tell her? Not that her father was at Portpool Lane, surely?"

"Well, not the reason, anyway." Hester smiled with a downward twist of her mouth and reached for the teapot.

Hester sent the letter early in the morning, paying a messenger to take it to the Baltimore house in Royal Square, and before lunch the answer was returned that Miss Baltimore would be delighted to receive her that afternoon, and awaited her call with pleasure.

Meanwhile, Margaret had made discreet enquiries and arranged for herself and Hester to visit with her brother-in-law, who was acquainted with business matters and could tell them what was publicly known of Baltimore and Sons, and perhaps a certain amount of that which was rather more privately believed. An appointment was made for the following evening.

In the middle of the afternoon Hester left Fitzroy Street wearing a pale blue skirt and jacket, and a hat—a piece of apparel she loathed—and carrying a parasol against the bright, fitful sun. She had been given the parasol as a gift and she had never even unrolled it. Nevertheless it lent an air of respectability, suggesting young ladies who had time and care to consider guarding their complexions from the sun.

She took an omnibus from the Tottenham Court Road, and was happy to walk the last few hundred yards to the front door in Royal Square. She was admitted immediately and conducted to a small sitting room clearly kept for the ladies of the house to receive their guests. It was furnished in a very feminine manner. The windows were draped with curtains in a clear, soft yellow, the chairs were well padded and pastel-shaded cushions made them look particularly inviting. There was a tapestry frame in one corner and a basket of colored silks and wools beside it. The screen in front of the fireplace was painted with flowers, and on the round table in the center of the room a huge china bowl of white and yellow tulips gave off a light, pleasing perfume.

Livia Baltimore was waiting for her expectantly. She was dressed in the obligatory black of mourning, and it made her fair skin look drained of all color. The moment Hester was in the room Livia stood up, coming forward from the chair where she had been sitting, her book put down with a marker to keep the place.

"How kind of you to come, Mrs. Monk. I was hoping that with all your work for the distressed you would not forget me. I am sure you would like tea?" Without waiting for an answer she nodded to the parlor maid to confirm the instructions.

"Please sit down." She indicated one of the chairs as the door closed and she resumed her own seat. "You look very well. I hope you are?"

It would probably be polite to talk about a variety of subjects, as was usually done. None of them mattered; it was simply a way of becoming acquainted. It was not what one said but the manner in which one said it that counted. But this was not a usual social friendship; they would probably never see each other after this. There was only one thing which brought them together, and regardless of what conventions were observed, it was the only thing either of them cared about.

"Yes, I am," Hester replied, relaxing into the chair. "Of

course the area is in some difficulty at the moment, and some of the women are being beaten, simply out of temper and frustration because there is no business." She was watching Livia's face as she spoke. She saw the young woman's struggle to hide her distaste at the "business" in question. It was something she knew very little about. Well-bred young ladies were barely aware of the existence of prostitution, never mind the details of the lives of those involved. If she had been asked before her father's death, she would have known even less, but unkind tongues had made sure she was acquainted with at least the rudiments now.

"There are police on every corner," Hester went on. "Nobody's pockets have been picked in a couple of weeks, but there is less and less in them that would be worth the trouble. People are going elsewhere when they can, which I suppose is natural. I don't know why, but police make even honest people nervous."

"I don't know why they should," Livia responded. "Surely innocence should fear nothing?"

"Perhaps too few of us are entirely innocent," Hester replied, but she said it gently. She had no desire whatever to hurt this young woman whose life had been so abruptly invaded by tragedy, and knowledge nothing had prepared her for and which in other circumstances she would never have known. "But I came to tell you that I have continued to listen, and to enquire where I could into the death of Mr. Baltimore."

Livia sat motionless. "Yes?" Her voice was little more than a whisper. She blinked, ignoring the tears brimming her eyes.

"I went to the house in Leather Lane where his body was found," Hester said gravely, pretending not to notice. She did not know Livia well enough to intrude. "I spoke to the people there, and they told me they had no part in what happened to him. He died elsewhere and was moved in order to implicate them, and I assume to remove suspicion from someone else."

"Did you believe them?" There was neither acceptance nor rejection in Livia's tone, as if she was deliberately not daring to hope too much.

"Yes, I did," Hester said unequivocally.

Livia relaxed, smiling in spite of herself.

Hester felt a stab of guilt so sharp she questioned whether she should be there at all, telling this young woman things which were true, and yet so much less than the whole truth. It would inevitably lead her to knowledge which would destroy forever the memories of happiness and innocence that had molded her youth.

"Then he could simply have been set upon in the street?" Livia was saying eagerly, the color returned to her cheeks. "Whoever killed my father then used his death to try to have some kind of revenge on Mr. Smith, and of course escape blame themselves. Have you told the police this?"

"Not yet," Hester said guardedly. "I would rather know more first, so that they believe me. Do you know why he would be in the Farringdon Road area? Did he go there often?"

"I have no idea." Livia blinked away sudden tears. "Papa went out many evenings, at least two or three every week. I am sure that sometimes he went to his club, but usually it would be to do with business. He was . . . I mean, we were . . ." She gulped as realization overwhelmed her again. She forced her voice to remain almost level. "We are on the brink of a great success. He worked so very hard; it hurts us all that he will not be here to see it."

"The new line opening in Derbyshire?" Hester asked.

Livia's eyes widened. "You know about that?"

Hester realized she had shown too much knowledge. "I must have heard someone speak of it," she explained. "After all, expansion of travel and new and better rail lines are of interest to everyone." The maid returned with tea, and Livia thanked and dismissed her, choosing to pour it herself.

"It is very exciting," she agreed, passing Hester her cup. For a moment her face betrayed very mixed emotions—there was exhilaration, the sense of being on the verge of change that was wonderful, and also a regret for the loss of the familiar.

Hester was uncertain if it could have any bearing at all upon Baltimore's death, or what Monk needed to know, but she was curious to learn more. "Will it mean changes for you? This house seems charming. It would be hard to imagine anything better." She picked up her cup and sipped the hot, fragrant liquid.

Livia smiled. It softened her face and made her look the young, slightly shy girl that she must have been only a month before. "I am glad you like it. I have always been happy here. But my brother assures me that when we move it will be even better."

"You are to move?" Hester said with surprise.

"We will keep this for the London season," Livia explained with a slight gesture of her hand. "But we are to have a large estate in the country for our home. The only thing that will cloud it at all is that my father will not be here. He wanted to build all this for us. It is so unfair that he should not be able to have the rewards of his life's labor, all the risks and the skill that went into it." She picked up her tea also, but did not drink.

"He must have been a remarkable man," Hester prompted, feeling that her hypocrisy must show in her face. She despised Baltimore.

"He was," Livia agreed, accepting the praise eagerly, as if somehow her father could still be warmed by it.

Hester wondered how well Livia had known him. Was her change in tone due to the fact that she was not remembering him so much as saying what she wished were true?

"He must have been very clever," Hester said aloud. "And very forceful. A weak man would never have been able to command others in the manner that must be necessary in order to build a railway. Any sign of indecision, or wavering from a principle, and he would have failed. One has to admire such . . . spirit."

"Yes, he was very strong," Livia agreed, her voice tense with emotion. "When Papa was around one always knew one would be safe. He was always quite certain. I suppose it is a quality men have . . . at least the best men, those who are leaders."

"I think the leaders are the ones who do not allow us to see their uncertainties," Hester replied. "After all, if someone does not feel confidence in where they are going, how can they expect others willingly to follow them?"

Livia thought for a moment. "You are quite right," she said with sudden understanding. "How perceptive you are. Yes, Papa was always . . . I think *brave* is the word. I know now that there were some more difficult times, when I was a child. We have waited many years for this great success that is coming now." A smile flickered across her face. "It is not just the new railway line, you know, it is a new invention to do with rolling stock—that means carriages and wagons and so on. I apologize if I tell you what you already know."

"Not at all," Hester assured her. "I know only what anyone may read about, or overhear. What kind of an invention?"

"I am afraid I am not certain. Papa said little of it at home. He and my brother, Jarvis, did not discuss business matters at the table. He always said it was not suitable to speak of in front of ladies." There was a shadow of uncertainty in her eyes, not quite as strong as doubt. "He believed family and business should be kept separate." Her voice dropped again. "It was something he cared about very much . . . keeping the home a place of peace and graciousness, where things such as money and the struggles of trade should not intrude. We spoke of the values that matter: beauty and intelligence, the exploration of the world, realms of the mind."

"It sounds excellent," Hester said, trying to sound as if she meant it sincerely. She did not want to hurt Livia's feelings, but she knew that the inclusion of the ugly, and some attempt at the understanding of pain, was necessary for the kind of truth that makes the greatest beauty possible. But this was not the time or place to say so. "You must have been very happy," she added.

"Yes," Livia agreed. "We were." She hesitated, sipping her tea.

"Mrs. Monk . . ."

"Yes?"

"Do you think it is likely that the police will ever find out who killed my father? Please be honest . . . I do not want a comfortable lie because you think it would be easier for me."

"It is possible," Hester said carefully. "I don't know about likely. It may depend whether there was a personal reason, or if it was simply mischance, that he passed along the wrong street at the wrong moment. Do you know if he went intending to keep an appointment with anyone?" It was the question to which she most wanted an answer, and yet she was aware that the solution to Baltimore's death might mean social ruin to his family, particularly to Livia, who was young and as yet unmarried.

Livia looked startled, then, on the brink of speech, she stopped and considered, setting her cup down again. "I don't know. Certainly he did not tell us, but then he never discussed business with Mama or me. My brother might know. I could ask him. Do you think it would make a difference?"

"It might." How honest should she be? Her whole reason for being there was dishonest to Livia. She was thinking of Monk and his need to know about fraud, and Fanny and Alice and all the other young women like them—in fact, all the women of the whole Coldbath area who were still living on the streets but were unable to earn anything because of the constant police presence. She was not trying to find the murderer of Nolan Baltimore because it would ease the grief of his family, or even in the impersonal cause of justice.

"I know what people presume," Livia said quietly, her cheeks very pink. "I simply cannot believe it is true. I won't."

No one could easily believe it of her own father. Hester would not have believed it of hers. It was not rational. The brain said that one's father was human like any other man, but all the heart and the will denied the very idea that he would lower himself to indulge carnal appetites with a woman paid from the streets. It awoke something inside oneself as to the origin of one's own existence, the nature of one's physical creation, and something unbearable about one's mother as well. It was a betrayal beyond acceptance.

"No," Hester said, not really as a reply, simply an understanding. "Of course not. Perhaps your brother may know if he intended to meet someone, or if not, at least what his destination might have been."

"I have already tried," Livia said with both embarrassment and anger. "He simply told me not to worry myself, that the police would find the answer, and not to listen to anyone."

"That might be good advice," Hester conceded. "At least the part about not listening to what people say."

There was a knock on the door, and almost before Livia had finished answering, it opened. A dark, lithe man in his thirties came in, hesitating when he saw Hester, but only momentarily. He had an air of confidence about him which was arrogant, even abrasive, and yet had a certain attraction. Perhaps it was the feeling of energy in him which appealed, almost like a fire, at once dangerous and alive. He moved with grace, and he wore his clothes as if elegance were natural to him. He reminded Hester fleetingly of Monk as he would have been in his early thirties. Then the impression was gone. This man lacked a depth of emotion. His fire was of the head, not the heart.

Livia looked over at him, and her face lit instantly. It was not something she did consciously, but it was impossible to mistake her pleasure.

"Michael! I was not expecting you." She turned to Hester. "I should like you to meet Mr. Michael Dalgarno, my brother's partner. Michael, this is Mrs. Monk, who has been kind enough to call upon me in connection with a charity in which I am interested." She barely blushed at her lie. She was perfectly used to the accommodation of social exchange.

"How do you do, Mrs. Monk." Dalgarno bowed very slightly. "I am delighted to meet you, and I apologize for intruding upon your tea. I had not realized Miss Baltimore had company, or I should not have been so forward." He turned to look at Livia and smiled; it was deliberate and devastatingly charming. There was a candor to it that was as intimate as a touch.

The color swept up Livia's face, and neither Hester nor Dalgarno himself could have doubted her feelings for him.

He placed his hand on the back of Livia's chair, gently, as if it were her shoulder. It was oddly possessive. Perhaps so soon after her father's death, and in such circumstances, the statement of anything further would be inappropriate, but the gesture was unmistakable.

Hester had a fleeting thought that as the daughter of a wealthy man, about to become vastly wealthier through the sale of the components, Livia Baltimore was a young woman who might expect a great number of suitors, many of them driven by the least noble of motives. She must have known Dalgarno for some time. Was it a genuine love, begun as friendship long before the promise of wealth, or was it a classic piece of opportunism by an ambitious young man? She would never know, nor did she need to, but she hoped profoundly that it was the former.

Now she had learned all that she was likely to, she did not want to remain longer and risk saying something that would give away the lie to Livia's explanation for her presence. The only charity with which she was connected was the house in Coldbath Square, and she did not think that Mr. Dalgarno would find it easy to believe that Livia was interested in that.

She rose to her feet. "Thank you, Miss Baltimore," she said with a smile. "You have been most gracious, and I shall call upon you again if you wish, or not trouble you further if you feel we have—"

"Oh, no!" Livia interrupted hastily, rising as well, her black skirts rustling stiffly. "I should very much like us to speak again, if . . . if you would be so kind?"

"Of course," Hester agreed. "Thank you again for your graciousness." She turned to him. "I am delighted to have made your acquaintance, Mr. Dalgarno." He moved to open the door for her. She went out and was conducted to the entrance by a footman. She passed a tall, fair-haired young man coming in. He was remarkable for his vigor and his large ears. He took no notice of her, but strode toward Dalgarno and started to speak before he reached him. Unfortunately, Hester was obliged to go out into the street before she could overhear anything.

*   *   *

The following evening Hester and Margaret kept their appointment to meet in Margaret's sister's home and learn what more they could about Nolan Baltimore.

Accordingly, Hester dressed carefully in her most sober jacket and skirt, the one which she would have worn were she seeking a position of nursing in a private house. Margaret wore a becoming gown of a dark wine shade and a highly fashionable cut. They took a hansom together and arrived in Weymouth Street, south of Regent's Park, just after six. It was a very imposing house, and even as they crossed the footpath and mounted the steps up to the front door, Hester felt a subtle change come over Margaret. She moved less briskly, her shoulders were not quite so square, and she pulled the brass knob of the bell almost tentatively.

The door was answered straightaway by a footman of towering height and excellent legs, the qualities most admired in his calling.

"Good evening, Miss Ballinger," he said stiffly. "Mrs. Courtney is expecting you and Mrs. Monk. If you would care to come this way." He ushered them in, and Hester could not help glancing around the perfectly proportioned hallway with its black-and-white flagged floor leading to a magnificent staircase, and the walls hung with ancient armor, decorated swords, and flintlocks, stocks inlaid with gold wire and mother-of-pearl.

The footman opened the withdrawing-room door, announced them, and then showed them in. Hester saw Margaret draw in a deep breath and go forward.

Inside the room, oak-floored with paneled walls, heavy plum-colored curtains framed high windows onto formal gardens beyond. Three people were awaiting them. The woman was obviously Margaret's sister. She was not quite as tall, and judging by her skin and slightly more ample figure, the elder by four or five years. She was handsome in a conventional way, and gave the air of being extremely satisfied with all about her. She was fashionably dressed, but discreetly so, as if she had no need to make herself ostentatious in order to be remarked.

She came forward as soon as she saw Margaret, her face beaming with welcome. Either she was genuinely pleased to see her sister or she was a most accomplished actress.

"My dear!" she said, giving Margaret a swift kiss on the cheek, then stepping back to regard her with great interest. "How delightful of you to have come. It has been far too long. I swear I was quite giving up hope!" She turned to Hester. "You must be Mrs. Monk, Margaret's new friend." This welcome was not nearly so warm—in fact, it was merely courteous. There was something guarded in her eyes. Hester realized immediately that Marielle Courtney was not at all sure that Hester's influence upon her sister was a good one. It might have replaced some of her own, and with less desirable effects. And of course she could not place Hester socially, which set her at a disadvantage in estimating her desirability.

"How do you do, Mrs. Courtney," Hester replied with a polite smile. "I think so highly of Margaret that to meet any member of her family is a great pleasure to me."

"How kind of you," Marielle murmured, turning to the man to her right and just behind her. "May I introduce you to my husband, Mr. Courtney?"

"How do you do, Mrs. Monk," he responded dutifully. He was a bland-faced man of approximately forty, already a little corpulent, but full of assurance and general willingness to receive his wife's family, and whoever they might bring with them, civilly enough.

The third person in the room was the one they had come to see, the man who might be able to tell them more about Nolan Baltimore. He was slender and unusual in appearance. His thick hair waved back off a high brow and was touched with gray at the temples, suggesting his age was more than his ease of carriage and elegance of dress portrayed. His features were very aquiline, his mouth full of humor. Marielle introduced him as Mr. Boyd, and laid rather more emphasis on Margaret than Hester was prepared for.

She saw Margaret stiffen and the color rise to her cheeks, although she masked her discomfort as well as possible.

The usual formalities of refreshment were offered and accepted. Marielle invited them to remain for dinner also, and Margaret declined without even referring to Hester, stating a previous engagement which did not exist.

"It is very good of you to come in order to furnish us with assistance and information, Mr. Boyd," she said a little stiffly. "I hope it has not spoiled your evening."

"Not at all, Miss Ballinger," he replied, smiling very slightly, the humor going all the way to his eyes, as if he saw some joke that might be shared, but not spoken of. "Please tell me what it is you wish to know, and if I can answer you, then I will do so."

"I understand the restrictions," she said hastily. "I am sure you are aware that Mr. Baltimore died tragically just over two weeks ago . . . in Leather Lane?"

"I am." If he felt any distaste he was too well schooled to show it.

Hester's regard for him increased. She glanced at Marielle and saw her intense interest. She was watching Boyd, and then Margaret, and then Boyd again, as if the outcome was of the greatest importance to her. Hester was filled with a fierce understanding of why Margaret longed to escape from her home and the pressure to marry suitably . . . as Marielle had done, and possibly whatever other sisters she had. She recalled some mention of a younger one, who was no doubt impatient for her turn.

Was Boyd aware of this also? Did he know he was being gently but very firmly engineered into the desired place? He looked like a man supremely able to make his own decisions. No ambitious mother, or sister, would maneuver him, of that Hester was certain. But it was Margaret's feelings that concerned her.

"I work in a charity in that area," Margaret went on with a candor that made Marielle wince and her husband look startled, and then unhappy.

"Really, Margaret . . ." he said with disapproval. "Gaining a little money for those who are unfortunate is one thing, but you should not become involved in any personal way, my dear . . ."

Margaret ignored him, keeping her attention on Boyd. "Mrs. Monk was a nurse in the Crimea," she went on relentlessly. "She offers medical assistance to women who cannot afford to pay a doctor. I am privileged to give what additional help I can, as well as to raise money for the rent of the rooms and for medicines."

"Admirable," Boyd said, seemingly with sincerity. "I don't see what I can contribute, beyond an offering of money, which I am happy to do. What has Nolan Baltimore's business to do with this? He did well, but not extraordinarily so. And anyway, as you observed, he is dead now."

Hester searched his face but saw no personal grief in it, and no trace of surprise or alarm. Neither did she see the outrage she had at least half expected.

"He was murdered," Margaret added. "As you may imagine, it has caused some upheaval in the area, an intense police presence—"

"Of course it has!" Marielle said sharply, moving forward a step as if to come between Margaret and Hester, who represented this regrettable involvement of her sister's. "It is completely shocking that a respectable man should be attacked in the street and done to death by the immoral and predatory creatures who inhabit such places." She turned her shoulder toward Hester. "I don't know why you wish even to discuss such subjects, Margaret. You never used to be so bold in your conversation." She looked at Boyd. "I am afraid Margaret's soft heart at times leads her into some strange, not to say misguided, avenues. . . ."

"Marielle . . ." Courtney began.

"I do not need you to apologize for me!" Margaret snapped. Then she looked candidly at Boyd before her sister could respond. "Mr. Boyd, Mrs. Monk and I have reason to believe that Mr. Baltimore may have been murdered by a business rival rather than a prostitute." She ignored Marielle's sharp intake of breath at the word. "And we would both be most obliged if you could tell us more of his business interests and his character as you may have heard it. Is it possible he went to meet someone he was dealing with in such a place as Leather Lane, or its environs, rather than in his customary offices?"

Hester felt obliged to interject. "We know what his family says of his business interests and conduct. I am acquainted with his daughter. But their view cannot help but be biased. What was his reputation in the City?"

"You speak very plainly, Mrs. Monk." Boyd turned his gaze to her, and she knew instantly that he remarked it in respect, not disapproval, although the faint ghost of humor was still there in his eyes. She found herself liking him. Had she been in Margaret's place, and had she not already met Oliver Rathbone, she might have been acutely uncomfortable at being so foisted upon this man, rather than having him choose her for himself. She believed closer acquaintance with him might prove a great pleasure.

"I do," she agreed. "The matter does not allow for misunderstandings. I apologize if it offends you." She knew it did not. "I am afraid nursing has blunted the edges of my good manners." Suddenly she smiled at him fully. "That is a euphemism. I never had any."

"Then I shall follow your example, Mrs. Monk," he replied with a very slight bending of his head, almost like a bow, his eyes dancing. "Nolan Baltimore was a man with great ambitions who took extraordinary chances in order to achieve them. He had courage and imagination, both of which were admired." He was watching her as he spoke, weighing what she made of his remarks.

"And . . ." she prompted him.

He acknowledged her understanding. "And some of his risks paid fairly well; others did not. He managed to survive rather better than some of his friends. He was not noted for his loyalty."

"In general?" Hester asked. "Or in particular?"

"I had no dealings with him myself."

She knew his tact was for Courtney, not for her. He expected her to understand his omissions as much as his words.

"From choice?" she said quickly.

"Yes." He smiled at her.

"Could any of his ... chances ... have taken him to Leather Lane?" she asked.

"Dubious finance?" His eyes widened. "It is not impossible. If one needs money and the usual services are not available, one goes elsewhere. A short-term loan that was to be paid off when an investment produced a high profit could be found in such a place. There is plenty of money in vice of one sort or another. People who come by it that way are often keen to invest it in a legitimate business."

"Really ... Boyd!" Courtney growled. "I don't think this is the sort of thing to discuss in front of ladies!"

"If Mrs. Monk has been an army nurse, and now works in the Coldbath area, James, I doubt I can tell her anything that she does not already know better than I," Boyd pointed out with more humor than annoyance.

"I was thinking of my sister-in-law!" Courtney said a trifle waspishly, his eye flickering to Marielle and back again, as if in actuality responding to her rather than his own thoughts. "And my wife," he added, perhaps unaware of the implied insult to Hester.

Boyd looked at him coldly for a moment, and noticed him color, then he turned to Margaret. "I apologize if I have distressed you, Miss Ballinger," he said with a slight smile, but a question in his eye.

"I shall require an apology, Mr. Boyd, if you think me less able to face the truth than Mrs. Monk!" Margaret replied with heat. "You have answered us very frankly, and for that I am grateful. Please do not spoil your respect for our sincerity by equivocating now."

Boyd ignored both Courtney and Marielle as if they had not been present.

"Then I must tell you, Miss Ballinger," he replied, "that I think Nolan Baltimore was as likely to have gone to Leather Lane for the reasons generally supposed as for any business purpose, honorable or otherwise. The quality of his living, the cost of his clothes, his carriages, his food and wine, did not suggest a company with any need to seek finance." He waved Courtney's proposed interruption away impatiently, and without taking his eyes from Margaret's, he continued. "Since I have seen him in the City he has never restricted himself. Rumor has it that his company is on the verge of a great achievement. Perhaps he has borrowed against his expectations, or else he had a backer with very deep pockets. But before you ask me who it might be, I have no idea whatever. Not even an educated guess. I am sorry."

An extraordinary thought occurred to Hester, only a flutter of darkness to begin with, but less and less absurd as the seconds ticked by. "Please don't apologize, Mr. Boyd," she said with sincerity. "You have been most helpful." She ignored Margaret's look of surprise, and Marielle's clear disapproval.

Boyd smiled at her, curiosity and satisfaction in his face.

"How fortunate," Marielle said coolly, indicating that the subject was closed. "Have you seen the new exhibition at the British Museum yet, Margaret? Mr. Boyd was just telling us how fascinating it is. Egypt is a country I have always wished to visit. The past must seem so immediate there. It would give one quite a different perspective upon time, don't you think?"

"Unfortunately, it would not give me any more of it," Margaret said, trying to sound casual and less embarrassed than she was at such an obvious ploy. She looked at Boyd. "Thank you for your candor, Mr. Boyd. I hope you will excuse us leaving so abruptly, but there is no one to take our places should any injured be brought into the house in Coldbath Square." She looked at her sister. "Thank you for being so generous, Marielle. I am extremely grateful to you."

"You really must stay longer next time," Marielle said resentfully. "You must come to dinner, or to the theater. There are many excellent plays on at the moment. You are allowing your interests to become too narrow, Margaret. It cannot be good for you!"

Margaret ignored her, bade everyone good-bye, and a few moments later she and Hester were outside in the cool air of the street, walking toward the corner where they might find a hansom easily.

"What did he say that was helpful?" Margaret demanded. "I don't see what any of it means that is really any use."

"Mr. Boyd hinted that Baltimore had other income, apart from the railway company," Hester said a little tentatively.

"He went to Leather Lane on business?" Margaret was uncertain. "Does that help? We have no idea what business, or with whom. And actually didn't you say his death wasn't in Leather Lane anyway?"

"Yes, I did. I said it might very well have been in Portpool Lane."

Margaret stopped walking abruptly and swung around to face Hester. "You mean . . . in the brothel that is run by the usurer?"

"Yes—I do mean that."

"His tastes were . . . to humiliate young women who used to be respectable?" Disgust and anger were very clear in Margaret's face.

"Possibly," Hester agreed. "But what if that was his other source of income? His family would not know of it, nor would any gatherer of taxes or anything else. It would explain very nicely why he had more funds to spend on his pleasures than Baltimore and Sons could supply. And his death coincides just about exactly with Squeaky Robinson's panic. Maybe the question has nothing to do with railways. Maybe the question is—was he killed as a client who went too far, or as a usurer who got too greedy?"

Margaret was tense, but her eyes did not waver even though her voice did. "So what must we do? How can we find out?"

"I don't have any plan yet," Hester replied. "But I will certainly make one."

She saw a hansom and stepped off the curb, raising her hand in the air.

Margaret followed after her with equal determination.

8

MONK ARRIVED at the station in London exhausted. His head ached so fiercely all he wanted to do was go home, take as hot a bath as he was able to, then have several cups of tea and go to bed to sleep properly, lying flat and between clean sheets. It would be best of all if Hester were beside him, understanding everything and holding no criticism or blame, and that would be impossible. To do that she would have to be without moral judgment. And what use would she be then, what real person at all? Or that she would be unaware of any of the fears that tangled in his mind, simply there, a gentle presence in the darkness.

Except that, of course, she would know what he was feeling: the fear of truth, of finding in himself a greed and a cowardice he would despise, a betrayal for which there was no excuse. Greater than his wrong to Dundas was his wrong to himself, to all that he had made and built out of his life since the accident. If she did not know that, then in what sense was she actually there at all? None that mattered. She might as well be in another place. They would speak, touch, even make love with each other, and the heart would remain utterly alone. It would be a worse loneliness than to have stayed apart, because it was a negation of what had been real, and mattered infinitely.

So he would go to a public bath, and simply buy a new shirt. He would visit a barber to make himself look fit to go this afternoon and meet Katrina Harcus, and tell her that there was no reason whatever to suspect Michael Dalgarno of anything that was not usual practice among businessmen. There was no record of his having bought or sold any land in his own name, or of having made any profit other than for the company for which he acted.

Monk would also report that he had investigated the crash in which Baltimore and Sons had been peripherally involved sixteen years ago, and the land fraud proved against one of its bankers had no connection whatever with it. The cause of that tragedy was not known, but the track had been repaired and was still in use. It had been examined minutely, and no flaws or inadequacies had been found in it.

He was so tired he longed for sleep, even on a park bench in the bright April sun, but he was afraid of what horror might return to him the moment he lost control of his thoughts. He did not know how he could be guilty of anything, but the guilt remained, the helplessness, the blood, the screams, the awful squeal of metal on metal, and the glare and smell of fire, and always the certain knowledge that he could have prevented it.

He drank coffee bought from a corner peddler, then made his way back to the gingerbread seller to see what he had learned from his notorious acquaintances. He found him dispersing slices of hot, spiced loaf to a group of children, and waited a few yards off until he had finished.

"Well?" he asked. There was no need to question if the man remembered him; his crooked face was alive with anticipation.

" 'E went out, all right," he said triumphantly. " 'Bout midnight. Face like thunder. Come back 'alf an hour later, no more."

Half an hour. Not time enough to get to Leather Lane, find Nolan Baltimore, kill him, and return. Monk was overswept with relief, so sharp it was physical. He could tell Katrina that Dalgarno was innocent.

"And he didn't go out again?"

"Not 'less it were close on daylight," the gingerbread seller said firmly. "Crows 'as got eyes like 'awks. Don't miss nothin'. Can't afford to!"

He was right. The lookout men for burglars survived on their ability to see, remember and report.

"Thank you," Monk said sincerely. He was so relieved he gave the man a sovereign, and added another half crown on top, then bought a piece of gingerbread.

At two o'clock he was tired and his feet were sore, but his step was light as he went in through the gate of the Royal Botanic Gardens, noticing briefly the blaze of color of the spring flowers. He had only five minutes to wait. She came to the entrance and stopped still, searching for him. Several other people turned to look at her. He was not surprised; she was most striking with her dramatic face and proud bearing, head high. She wore white muslin sprigged with dark blue, and the lines of the bodice echoed the same vivid color, accentuating the femininity of it. Her hat had roses on the brim, and her parasol was trimmed with blue ribbons. Several gentlemen stared at her, smiling for longer than was really polite, but their admiration robbed it of offense.

She saw Monk, and her face lit with pleasure, almost relief. He knew she must have been here many days, each time hoping to see him. He felt a welling up of satisfaction because at last he could tell her that as far as any investigation could show, Dalgarno was innocent of fraud, and even if there was land fraud by anyone else, it could have no connection with any crash. Her fears were honorable but needless.

She came toward him swiftly, stopping so close to him he could smell the perfume she wore, warm and musky, quite different from the sweet, fresh smell of the flowers around them.

"You have news?" she said with a gasp. "I can see it in your face."

"Yes." He smiled back at her.

There was a wildness in her eyes, and he saw her bosom rise and fall in the effort to control her breathing. He put his hand up as if to touch her arm, to reassure her, then realized how little he really knew her. The understanding of her fears, the feeling of identity with her, was on his side only. She would regard his touch as intrusive, which it would be. He let his hand fall again.

"Most importantly, I have been able to ascertain that Mr. Dalgarno did not leave his house at a time or for a duration where he could possibly be involved in Nolan Baltimore's death."

She was startled. "How?" she said incredulously. "How could anyone know that?"

"Burglars leave men on watch," he explained dryly. "They call them crows. There was at least one on that street between midnight and dawn."

She breathed out very slowly, her face very pale. "Thank you. Thank you very much. But . . . but what about . . ."

"I have searched exhaustively in London and in Liverpool, where the company was based earlier, Miss Harcus," he said. "And I can find no evidence of fraud at all."

"None . . ." She started, her voice high, her head moving very slowly in a gesture of denial, disbelief.

"A little oversharp profit on certain deals," he conceded. "But that is common." He stated it with authority, realizing only afterwards that he was speaking from memory. He was not guessing, he knew. "And everything was in the company name, not that of Mr. Dalgarno. He is a successful business-man, and as honest as most."

"Are you certain?" she pleaded, her face flooded with amazement and dawning joy. "Absolutely certain, Mr. Monk?"

"I am sure there is nothing whatever to raise doubt as to his honor," he repeated. "You may rest in confidence that his reputation is in no peril."

She jerked back, her eyes wide. An onlooker might have thought he had insulted her from the disbelief in her face, which seemed almost like anger. "Rest?" she said fiercely. "But the crash! What about the danger of another?"

"The Liverpool crash had nothing to do with the track," he said patiently. "It was driver error, with a possibility that the brakemen also were—"

Now she was angry, flinging her hand back, almost as if to strike the person behind her. "What—all of them?" she challenged. "They all chose the same moment to make a mistake?"

He caught her wrist. "No, they don't mean that. They mean

it was one of them, and possibly the others panicked and didn't know how to right it."

"Are you saying that Baltimore and Sons was innocent?" she demanded. "Always? Then and now?"

"Innocent of the crash, yes." He heard his own voice, and he sounded uncertain. Why? There was nothing to implicate Nolan Baltimore in the Liverpool crash or in the fraud that had ruined Arrol Dundas. It was his own emotions, his own shadow of guilt, trying to place the blame on someone he did not care about.

She took a step towards him. Now she seemed almost excited. Her eyes were bright, her body tense, her cheeks flushed with pink. She put her hands on the front of his chest, closing her fingers tightly over the edges of his jacket. "Is there proof of their innocence?" she said hoarsely. "Real proof? Something that would stand in a court? I have to be sure. An innocent man was convicted once before."

He felt his own body tighten and the blood pound in his veins. He clasped her wrists. "How do you know that?" he said between his teeth. He was startled to find that he was shaking.

She pulled away from him violently. He felt the button in her hand rip off his coat, but it hardly mattered. Her face was filled with emotion so intense her eyes blazed and her color was hectic. She stared at him for a long, desperate moment, then spun on her heel and all but ran back toward the gate.

Monk was aware that several people were staring at them, but he did not care. What did she know about Arrol Dundas? That question filled his mind to the exclusion of everything else. He strode after her, almost catching up with her at the gate out onto Inner Circle pathway, but she was moving rapidly. She crossed the path and followed it through the grass and trees past the Toxophilite Society grounds on the left, toward the bridge over an arm of the lake. He managed to stop her on the far side, again to the alarm and curiosity of passersby.

"How do you know that?" he repeated the demand. "What have you heard? From whom—Dalgarno?"

"Dalgarno?" she said incredulously, then she started to

laugh, a wild sound, close to hysteria. But she did not answer. Instead, she turned away from him again and half ran along York Gate towards the Marylebone Road and the general traffic with carriages and hansoms going in both directions. "I'm going home!" she called at him over her shoulder.

He ran after her, catching up again and walking beside her as she reached the road and raised her parasol to hail a cab. One pulled up almost immediately and Monk helped her in, climbing in after her.

She made no protest, almost as if she had expected him to.

"If it was not Dalgarno, then from whom?" he insisted after she had given the driver instructions to take her to Cuthbert Street in Paddington.

She turned to face him. "You mean the fraud case, all those years ago?"

"Yes, of course I do!" He kept his temper only with the greatest difficulty. It mattered intensely. What did she know? How could she know anything, except from Baltimore's records or something she had overheard him say?

She stared straight ahead, smiling, but there was a hollowness in her eyes. "Did you imagine I made no enquiries myself, Mr. Monk?" Her voice was hard-edged, grating. "Did you think I learned nothing about the past history of Baltimore and Sons when I knew how deeply Michael was involved in it, and expected to make his fortune through it?"

"You said that you knew an innocent man was convicted of fraud in that case," he said grimly, horrified at how his own voice betrayed the emotion choking him. "How do you know that? No one knew it then."

"Didn't they?" she asked, staring ahead of her.

"Of course they didn't, or he wouldn't have died in jail!" He grasped her arm. "How do you know? What happened?"

She turned in the seat to stare at him, her face twisted with a fury so intense he drew back from it, loosening his hold on her.

"A great wrong, Mr. Monk," she said softly, her voice trembling, her words almost a hiss. "People were wronged then, and are wronged now. But revenge will come—that I promise you. It will come . . . on my mother's grave . . . on mine if need be."

"Miss Harcus . . ."

"Please get out!" Her face was ashen now. "I need to think, and I must do it alone." She snatched her hand from him and, picking up the parasol, banged on the front of the hansom to draw the driver's attention. "I will tell you . . . this evening."

She banged on the front again, more fiercely.

"Yes, miss?" the driver answered.

"Mr. Monk is alighting. Would you be so good as to stop," she ordered.

"Yes, miss," he said obediently, and pulled in to the curb. They were at the corner of Marylebone Street and the Edgware Road, traffic streaming around them in both directions.

Monk was touched by a deep concern for her. She looked so torn by conflicting passions it was almost as if she had a fever. He wanted desperately to know what she meant by stating so vehemently that Dundas was innocent and that revenge would come, or what the present wrong was that he could not see. But now that he knew where she lived at least he could find her again when she was calmer. Perhaps he could even be of some help to her. Now she needed to rest and compose herself.

"I'll call upon you, Miss Harcus," he said far more gently. "Of course, you need time to consider."

She made an intense effort at self-control, breathing in very deeply and letting it out in a sigh. "Thank you, Mr. Monk. That would be very good of you. You are most patient. If you would call upon me this evening—after eight, if you would be so good—then I shall tell you what you wish. I shall speak to Michael Dalgarno again, and that will be the end of it, I promise. You have played your part perfectly, Mr. Monk. I could not have wished better. You will see me after eight? Do you give me your word—absolutely?"

"I do," he swore.

"Good." The faintest ghost of a smile touched her face. "At twenty-three Cuthbert Street. You have given me your word!"

"Yes. I will be there."

He alighted and stood on the pavement as the hansom pulled away from the curb immediately and was lost in the traffic.

Monk went home to Fitzroy Street and an empty house. He washed and slept at last. At ten past eight, as the light was fading, he took a hansom to twenty-three Cuthbert Street. He was startled back to attention from his thoughts when they stopped abruptly and the cabbie looked in and told him that he could not go any further.

"Sorry, sir," he said apologetically. "P'lice blockin' the road. Dunno wot's 'appened, but there's a big ruckus up front. Can't go no further. Yer'll 'ave ter walk, if they'll let yer."

"Thank you." Monk scrambled out, paid him, leaving the change of eight pence, and started to walk toward figures he could see standing under the street lamps. There were three men, two arguing with each other, the third, familiar in its tall, stiff outline, looking down at something like a bundle of clothes that lay at his feet. It was Runcorn, who had been Monk's rival in the old days, then his superior; who had always hated and feared him until the quarrel when he had dismissed Monk at the same moment Monk had resigned in fury. Then the case of the artist's model just months before had drawn them together again, and in shared emotions, painful and unexpected pity, they had formed an uneasy alliance.

But what was Runcorn doing here?

Monk lengthened his stride, only just restraining himself from running the last few yards.

"What is it?" he demanded, although as Runcorn swung around to face him, he could already see. The figure of a woman was sprawled on the ground. Her white muslin dress trimmed in blue was crumpled, and dirty, and deeply stained with blood. She lay half on her front, half sideways, as if she were broken. Her neck was at an awkward angle, one arm doubled under her, her legs crooked.

Instinctively, he looked upward and saw the flat roof of the building's third floor, and then the rest of it going up another

story beyond that. There was a railing as if it were an extended balcony from the upstairs room. He could not see the
door; it was hidden by the wall above them.

A wave of nausea overtook him, and then overwhelming,
consuming pity. He stared at Runcorn, his mouth too dry to
speak.

"Looks like she fell off," Runcorn replied to Monk's original question. "Except she's a bit far out, as the eye sees it. And
people usually fall backward. Might have twisted in the air."
He squinted upward. "It's a fair distance. Get a better idea
from up there. Could've jumped, I suppose."

Monk started to speak, then stopped.

"What is it?" Runcorn asked sharply.

"Nothing," Monk said hastily. He should say nothing . . .
not yet. His mind raced. What on earth could have happened?
She would never, ever have jumped! Not Katrina Harcus. She
was on the edge of exposing an ancient wrong. She wanted
revenge, and she had had it almost within her grasp. And Dalgarno was innocent, which was what she had wanted above
all from the beginning.

A uniformed constable came across the pavement, pushing
his way past the bystanders who had begun to gather. "Got a
witness, sir," he said to Runcorn. His face was pinched and
unhappy, expression exaggerated in the shadows cast by the
street lamp. "Says there were two people up there, quite defi-
nite. 'E saw them strugglin' back and forward. 'Eard 'er scream
out summink, and then she staggers back an' 'e comes after 'er,
an' next thin' 'e turns, an' she's gorn over the edge." He looked
down at the figure on the ground. "Poor creature. Looks like
she were youn' . . . an' right 'andsome too. It's a cryin' shame."

"What happened to the man?" Runcorn asked, glancing at
Monk, then back to the constable.

The constable straightened up. "Dunno, sir. I asked the
witness but 'e didn't see. Light was very fitful, like. 'E saw
'er partic'lar because of 'er wearin' white an' all. Man were in
summink very dark, an' 'e 'ad a cloak on, sort o' . . ." He
shrugged. "Well, a cloak. Witness says 'e saw it billowin' out
when they was fightin' just before she went over."

Monk felt sick imagining it, Katrina struggling with someone, crying out for help, and no one did more than watch! They did not even know who had been there on the roof fighting with her . . . killing her! Dalgarno? It must have been. He was the only person involved. He must have come here when she had contacted him, as she had told Monk she would. Something she had said, some evidence she had found and he had missed, for all his meticulous searching, had driven Dalgarno to defend himself this murderous way.

But what? How had he committed the fraud? Why had Monk not been able to find it? Why was he so stupid, so blind all over again? And now someone else was dead, another he had been doing everything he could to help. He had promised her . . . and failed.

Runcorn was still talking to the constable. Monk bent onto his knees beside the body. Her eyes were wide open. This side of her face was barely damaged at all; there was just a trickle of blood. He knew better than to touch her, but he wanted to brush back the hair from her cheek, as if she could feel it across her skin. One hand was under her, the other outstretched, and as he looked more closely he could see there was something held inside it, something very small. Had she clutched at her murderer the last moment before he pushed her over, and torn something from him?

Runcorn and the constable were still absorbed in conversation, facing each other. Monk put out one finger and moved Katrina's hand very slightly, just enough for the object to slip out of the slack grasp and fall onto the stones. It was a button, a man's coat button. He drew in his breath to tell Runcorn, then a wave of heat engulfed him, bringing the sweat out on his skin, and the instant after he was cold. It was his own button, the one she had torn off in a heated moment in the Botanic Gardens! But that had been hours ago!

"What have you got?" Runcorn's voice broke into his daze of horror, shattering his indecision. He could do nothing now, certainly not hide it. With clumsy fingers he fastened the lower buttons on his jacket so the top would be closed as well, hiding the fact that a button was gone, seeming as if it were simply not done up. He rose to his feet, his legs trembling. "A button," he said huskily. He cleared his throat. "There was a button in her hand."

Runcorn bent down and lifted it from the pavement, turning it over and over curiously.

Monk held his breath. Please God, Runcorn would not notice that it was exactly like the ones on Monk's coat! It was dark; he was half turned from the street lamp. He would leave as soon as he could.

"Man's coat button, by the look of it," Runcorn observed. "Must have pulled it off as she struggled with him." He put it in his own breast pocket. "Good piece of evidence." He gave his attention to the constable again. "You talk to the people around here. See what you can find. Do we know who she was yet?"

"No, sir," the constable answered. "They seen 'er comin' an' goin', but not to speak to, like. Seemed very respectable. A Miss Barker, or Marcus, or summink like that, but not sure."

To evade it was a pointless lie, and he would be caught in it sooner or later. "Harcus," Monk said quietly. "Katrina Harcus."

Runcorn stared at him. "You know her?"

"Yes. I was working on an investigation for her." Now the die was cast, but he could not have hidden it, and neither should he want to. It was one coat button, easily enough explained. There might even be people in the gardens who had seen them and would recall the gesture in which she had accidentally ripped it off. "I can help," he went on. Now that fierce anger overtook the initial shock, he wanted to. He wanted to be revenged for her, to find who had done this and see him punished. It was all he could do for her now. He had failed in everything else, but she had wanted revenge; he remembered very clearly the fury in her face. He could get at least that for her.

Runcorn's eyes were wide. He let out his breath slowly. "So you weren't here by accident. I should have known. What would you be doing in Cuthbert Street at this hour of the evening?" It was a rhetorical question to which he expected no answer. "What was it, this case you were working on?" he asked. "Do you know who did this to her?"

"No, I don't know," Monk replied. "But I've an idea, and I'll damn well find out . . . and prove it! She was betrothed to a Michael Dalgarno, a senior employee of Baltimore and Sons, a railway company—"

"Just a minute!" Runcorn interrupted him. "Wasn't there a Nolan Baltimore murdered in Leather Lane just a few weeks ago? Is that some connection with this?"

"None that I've been able to find," Monk admitted. "Looks like Baltimore simply went to enjoy his pleasures and got involved in a fight that ended badly. Perhaps he didn't pay enough, or more likely he was drunk and picked a quarrel."

"So what were you doing here?" Runcorn pressed.

"Nothing to do with that," Monk replied.

"There's no need to be secretive now, Monk. She's dead, poor creature." He glanced down at her. "The only help you can give her is to find out who killed her."

"I know that!" Monk retorted sharply. He steadied himself with an effort. "As I said, she was betrothed to Michael Dalgarno. She was concerned that there might be some fraud to do with the new line they are building between London and Derby." He saw Runcorn's start of interest. "Specifically to do with the purchase of land—"

"And was there?" Runcorn cut across him eagerly.

"None that I could find, and I looked very carefully." Monk knew he sounded defensive. He felt it. If he had found the proof, Katrina might still be alive.

Runcorn looked dubious. "If it were plain to see, others would have found it too."

"I know more about railways than most people," Monk responded, then instantly felt vulnerable. He had told too much about himself, opened up areas where he was guessing, piecing bits together one at a time—and to Runcorn, of all people!

Theirs was an uneasy truce; the old resentments were covered over, not gone.

"Do you?" Runcorn said with surprise. "How's that, then?

Thought you were in finance before you joined up with us ordinary police." His words were civil enough, even his tone, but Monk knew the envy of money, of self-assurance, of a life Runcorn had never had, with its social ease and elegance.

"Because railways have to be financed," he replied. "The last thing I did before leaving banking was a new railway line near Liverpool."

Runcorn was silent for a moment. Perhaps he heard the strain in Monk's voice or caught something of his grief and his anger.

"So you found no fraud," he said at last. "Does that mean for sure that there wasn't any?"

"No," Monk admitted. "It means that if it was there, then it was very well hidden indeed. But she was convinced it was . . . even more so the last time I met her than in the beginning."

"So she'd found something, even if you hadn't!" Runcorn eyed him sideways. "Did she give you any idea what it was?"

"No. But her whole conviction that there was something wrong arose from things she overheard in the Baltimore offices, or house. Being betrothed to Dalgarno gave her access to conversations I had not."

Runcorn grunted. "Then we'd better go in and find out what there is—except I daresay he took it with him! Probably why he killed her." He started forward toward the house.

Monk changed his mind about leaving and decided to accept it as an invitation to accompany Runcorn. He could not afford to refuse. He moved with alacrity to follow, catching up with him at the entrance and going in a step behind him.

It was still early in the evening, but by now word had spread that a woman had fallen or been thrown off the roof and was lying dead in the street. Neighbors waited in shocked silence or hasty, whispered conversations with each other. The uniformed constables were questioning them all, one by one, for anything they might have noticed either tonight or earlier.

Runcorn was shown up the stairs to Katrina's apartments.

Monk was close on his heels, as if he belonged, and no one challenged him.

"Right!" Runcorn said as soon as they were inside and the door closed. The gas was burning as she must have left it, but the corners were still full of shadows. Monk was grateful for it, conscious of the missing button as if it had been a bloodstain.

"Where'd she keep her papers, anything that would be likely to tell us about this railway?" Runcorn asked, looking about him.

"I don't know. I've never been here before," Monk replied, turning away from the light.

"I thought you said she employed you? And you were on your way here tonight. You told me." There was challenge in Runcorn's voice.

"It was the first time I'd come here," Monk explained. "She came to my office, or we met in the Royal Botanic Gardens." It sounded odd even as he said it.

"Why's that?" Runcorn said curiously, skepticism in his eyes.

"She was very careful of her reputation," Monk answered. "She was betrothed to an ambitious man. She wanted to be entirely discreet about having hired me. I imagine she intended it to appear that we were social acquaintances." He went to put his hands in his pockets, then realized it would alter the sit of his coat, perhaps showing the missing button, and changed his mind. "After the first time, we always met in public, and by chance. She walked in the gardens every day at the same time, and if I had anything to report I knew where to find her."

"Extremely careful," Runcorn agreed. "Poor creature," he added softly. "Maybe she knew then that this Dalgarno was dangerous." He shook his head. "Funny what attracts some women to a man. I'll never understand that. Well, we'd better get on with it. We'll just have to search."

Monk stared around at the room. It was simply furnished, but the taste was excellent and the few pieces were of good quality, giving it an air of spaciousness that was unusual. He was not surprised. Katrina herself had been a woman of character and strength, highly individual. Again his anger against

Dalgarno boiled over, and he went across to the desk and opened it. He kept his back to Runcorn, who was still staring around, gaining an impression of the style of the room, and going instinctively to the glass doors which opened onto the balcony from which she must have fallen.

The desk contained quite a few business papers, and Monk began leafing through them, only glancing at the subject. He did not know what he was looking for, and if Dalgarno had killed her because she had found proof of his fraud, then most certainly she would have shown it to him and he would have taken it to destroy. Nevertheless there might be more than one paper of interest, and he had to look.

He found something surprisingly quickly, but it was not what he expected. It was a letter written but obviously never sent, addressed to someone named Emma.

Dear Emma,

I promised to tell you all I learned, so I must keep my word, even though it is extremely painful for me to acknowledge such a mistake. I have discovered papers to do with the original fraud in Liverpool, and it now seems incontrovertible that Mr. Monk, whom I had trusted profoundly, was actually involved in that terrible affair himself. I found an old receipt among the Baltimore papers, and it was signed by him!

Upon further investigation, I learned that he once worked in merchant banking, and was connected with the loan for the railway Baltimore and Sons were building. He had kept it concealed from me, and no wonder—the fraud was profound and far-reaching. One man died for it, and a great deal of money is still unaccounted for, even to this day. And of course there was the crash! Mr. Monk is deeply implicated. You can only imagine how it grieves me.

I have not confronted him yet, but I believe I must. How else can I behave honorably?

Dear Emma, I wish you were here, so I could counsel with you what to do. I am suddenly deeply afraid.

There was no more written.

Monk stared at it. Who was Emma? Where did she live? There was no address. What else might Katrina have written to her?

He flicked very carefully through the other papers in the first drawer and found bills, an old invitation, and another letter, written in a cramped, sloping backhand:

My dearest Katrina,

It is so good to hear from you, as always, but I confess I do not care for the sound of this man, Monk, whom you have employed, and all you have told me only adds to my foreboding. Please, my dear, be very careful. Do not trust him.

He scanned the rest, but it was merely pleasant gossip about mutual acquaintances, mentioned only by Christian name. If Runcorn found these he would think Monk himself could have killed her. Fingers fumbling, moving slowly so as to not rattle the paper, he slid both of them off the pile and heard them rustle.

Runcorn had come in from the balcony. He was holding up a large, slightly crumpled man's cloak. In the gaslight it appeared to be black.

"What's that?" Monk asked, moving to shield the papers from Runcorn's view, and put out his other hand to leaf the pages and mask the sound of the two he was taking out. He folded them quickly and slid them inside his shirt, around the side of his body where movement would not make them crackle.

"It was out there," Runcorn said with a frown. "Lying on the ground near the edge where she must have gone over." He looked at it. "It's too long for her, and anyway it's not a woman's."

Monk was surprised. "That's a careless thing to do—leave it behind."

"Must have come off when he struggled with her." Runcorn wrapped it over, lining to the outside. "Doesn't have a tailor's name, but we'll find out where it comes from and whose it is. Did you find anything?"

"Nothing significant yet," Monk replied, keeping his voice perfectly level, unnaturally so. He leafed through another few sheets and saw a scribbled note. The sweat stood out on his skin as he read it.

Tell Monk of conversation I overheard which makes me certain that there is a fraud currently at Baltimore and Sons and that I am deeply afraid that Michael Dalgarno is involved. A very great deal of money is to be made shortly, but the matter must be kept completely secret.

The land fraud is basically the same as before—he will see that when he looks carefully enough. Questions to raise—is it cheaper, and therefore illegal profit to be made by diverting the line and somehow stealing the difference from investors? Or is there bribery, either by someone to use their land—or not to use it? There are several possibilities.

Again, Michael has to know of it! His signature is on the wages receipts and on the land purchase orders.

There was nothing more, as if it were written as an aid to her own memory.

Runcorn looked at Monk. "Well?" he demanded. "Are those the papers you looked into?"

"Yes."

"And yet you found nothing to incriminate this Dalgarno?" Runcorn was skeptical. "Not like you to miss something— 'specially if you know all about railways! You're slipping, aren't you?" There was only the very faintest trace of the old animosity in his voice, but Monk heard it. He was too sensitive to years of enmity not to know every shade and nuance of a jibe when it was there. He had made enough of his own; more often than not, Runcorn had been the victim.

"There wasn't any land fraud like the first," he said defensively.

Runcorn's eyes widened. "Oh—you found the first, then?"

"Yes, of course I did!" Monk desperately did not want to

tell Runcorn about Arrol Dundas or anything to do with his own past with all its secrets and its wounds. "That was land fraud, and this time it looked to be the same, but Dalgarno didn't buy the land himself, so there was no profit for him when it was sold."

Runcorn looked at him pensively. "And what was the fraud the first time, exactly?"

"A man bought poor land at a cheap price, then had the railway line diverted to it when it didn't have to be, and sold the land to the railway company at a much higher price," Monk replied, hating putting it into words.

"And she thought this was the same, but it wasn't?" Runcorn concluded.

"That seems so."

"Then why did this Dalgarno kill her?"

"I don't know." It did not occur to Monk that it might not be Dalgarno. She had spoken of him with such a consuming hunger for revenge; only someone she had once loved could have aroused such a fury in her. Strangers could never waken passion so deep.

"Well, I intend to find out," Runcorn said with scalding heat. "I'll hunt him down and I'll drag him all the way to the gallows. I promise you that, Monk!"

"Good. I'll help you—if I can."

"Help me look at the rest of this, in case you can explain any of it—to do with railways and so on," Runcorn said. "Then you can go home, and I'll go and find Mr. Dalgarno and see what he has to say for himself!"

By quarter past ten Monk was at home in Fitzroy Street again. Hester was sitting by a low fire, but she started up as soon as she heard him at the door. She looked tired and a little pale; her hair was pinned rather lopsidedly, as if she had done it without a looking glass. She stared at him, the question in her eyes. If she had intended to speak, the look in his face must have been sufficient to silence her.

The misery of his own failure was like a gray fog around him. He longed to be able to tell her all of it and allow her to comfort him, to say over and over that it did not matter, that it was not true of him, but only a collision of circumstances.

But even if she said all that, he would not believe her. He was afraid that it was true, and he was even more afraid that she would be denying it out of pity, and loyalty, not because in her heart she could believe it. She would be disappointed, let down. It was not her standard of integrity ever to have done such a thing, or been so dishonest at the core.

It was the past reaching out like a dark hand to pull him back from all he had built, staining the present, stopping him from being the man he tried to be.

But he had to tell her something, and it must be true, if not all the truth.

"I went to see Miss Harcus," he said, taking off his coat with its torn button. He would have to replace it if he could, or get rid of the coat. "To tell her that I can find no proof that Dalgarno is guilty of anything . . . in fact, there doesn't seem to be anything to be guilty of."

She waited, her face pale, eyes wide.

"She was dead," he told her. "Someone threw her off the balcony of her apartment. Runcorn was there."

"William . . . I'm so sorry . . ." She meant it; the pity was there in her face—for him, but far more for the woman she had never met. "Do you have any idea who—"

"Dalgarno," he said before she had finished. He suddenly realized how cold he was, and walked over to the fire.

"Michael Dalgarno?" she said slowly, turning so she was still facing him.

"Yes. Why?" He studied her face, the profound unhappiness in it more intense than even a moment before. "Hester?"

"What relationship does she have to Dalgarno?" she asked, her eyes not leaving his. "Why did she think he was guilty of something, and why do you think he killed her, William?"

"She was betrothed to him. Did I not tell you that?"

"No, not by name."

"Why do you ask? Tell me!"

She looked down, then up at him quickly, her face full of pain. "I went to see Livia Baltimore to tell her a little about what I have discovered regarding her father's death. It isn't much . . ." She must have seen his impatience. "I met Michael Dalgarno. He was there."

"He works for Baltimore and Sons. It's not surprising." He knew as he said it that she had not told him all that mattered.

"He was paying court to Livia," she answered. "And from the way she received him, she was expecting it, so he has been doing so for some time. If he was betrothed to Miss Harcus, then he was behaving disgracefully."

He knew she would not be mistaken in such a thing. She understood the nuances of courtship, even if she had never flirted in her life. She also knew the correct way for a young woman to behave, and what was acceptable for a man to do, and what was not.

So Dalgarno had betrayed Katrina in love as well as in financial honesty. Had she known that? Had she found out that very night when she had challenged him over the land fraud? Had he shown himself the ultimate opportunist, and knowing that he had no intention of marrying her now that Baltimore's daughter would accept him, had she threatened to expose the fraud? And so had he killed her?

Monk bent to poke the fire, glad of the flames as it burned up, and of the excuse to look away from Hester.

"Poor Katrina," he said aloud. "He betrayed her in every way. First he was a thief, then he jilted her for another woman, and when she faced him with it—he murdered her." He found it difficult even to say the words.

"But you'll prove it . . . won't you," Hester said quietly. "You won't let it go . . ."

"No, I won't," he promised, standing up again. "I couldn't save her, but by God I'll have justice for her!"

"I wish that were more comfort," Hester replied. She stepped toward him almost tentatively, then very gently put her head on his shoulder and slid her arms around him, holding him softly, as if he were so physically hurt that she might cause him pain.

It did comfort him, but the pain was too deep inside to be touched. That she should love him was so infinitely precious that he would give anything he owned not to lose it, but there was nothing to give it to, no bargain to make. He lifted his hands and stroked her hair, her neck, and held her.

Monk slept late. It was a long time since he had lain in his own bed with Hester beside him and any kind of peace in his mind, even if it were only the peace of exhaustion, and the knowledge that he could do nothing more to help Katrina Harcus. Avenging her was a different matter. It was important, but he was not alone in it. Runcorn would not let go. Monk could and would help him as the occasion arose.

When he got up in the morning he offered to riddle the kitchen stove and get it going well enough for breakfast. Hester accepted with slight surprise. Monk carried heavy things willingly enough for her, but he was not naturally domestic. He was used to being cared for and accepted it without question, barely noticing the detail.

When he was alone in the kitchen he worked hard at shaking loose the old ash, then took it out on the shovel and put it in the ash can. He brought in a little kindling to get the flames going quickly, then light coal, and as soon as he had the fire burning well enough, he pulled the papers out of his shirtfront, where he had concealed them when dressing, and poked them into the fire. Within moments they were consumed, but they were only two letters, and obviously there had been others. Who was Emma? How could he find her? Where could he even begin to look? He closed the stove door and stood up just as Hester came back from the dining room.

"It's going well," he said with a smile.

"That was quick!" She regarded him with surprise. "If you are so good at it, perhaps I should have you do it every day."

It was meant as teasing, and he relaxed at the ease of it, the old banter returned. "Chance," he said airily. "Just good luck. Might never happen again."

"Don't be so modest!" she retorted with a sideways look at him.

The papers were burnt. He felt guilty about it, they were

evidence, but he also felt a wave of relief, at least for the moment. It gave him time. He did not yet know what he would do about the jacket and its missing button. "I thought you admired modesty," he said, raising his eyebrows.

She rolled her eyes, but she was smiling.

They had only just finished breakfast when Runcorn arrived. He looked tense and angry. At first he refused Hester's offer of tea, then almost straightaway changed his mind and sat down heavily at the table while she went to brew a fresh pot.

"The man's a swine!" he said savagely. He had not even removed his coat, as if he were too knotted up to relax sufficiently. "I'll see him hang for this if it's the last thing I do!" He glared at Monk. "He's a liar of the worst sort. He says he never had any intention of marrying Katrina Harcus. Can you believe that?"

"No," Monk said coldly. "But I can believe that when he found he had a chance to marry Baltimore's only daughter he seized it with both hands, and suddenly found Katrina something of an embarrassment."

Runcorn stiffened. "You knew!" he accused him. "You lied. For God's sake, Monk, what were you thinking of? Trying to protect her feelings or her dignity? She's dead! And a pound to a penny Dalgarno killed her! It—"

"I only found out last night after I got home!" Monk cut across him, his voice sharp with anger at Runcorn for prejudging him, at Dalgarno for being greedy, dishonest and cruel, and at Katrina for loving so passionately a man unworthy of her, or of anyone.

Runcorn was regarding him with disbelief.

"Hester told me," Monk snapped at him. Then, seeing Runcorn's continued doubt, he went on. "She knew something was wrong. I told her Katrina Harcus was dead and that it looked as if Dalgarno had killed her. When she heard his name she said that she had been to see Livia Baltimore—"

"Why?" Runcorn interrupted.

"Because Livia Baltimore's father was murdered in Leather Lane, everyone assumes by a prostitute," Monk replied curtly. "You knew that. Hester has set up a house in Coldbath Square

where injured women can get some medical help." He felt a
certain satisfaction at seeing the amazement, and then the admiration, in Runcorn's face. He remembered the deep and
powerful change of heart he had seen in him over the women
driven to prostitution when they had investigated the death of
the artist's model together. It was the moment when Monk
had been obliged, intensely against his will, to see a goodness
in Runcorn that he could not ignore, or disdain. He had liked
him for it, genuinely.

"So she went to see Miss Baltimore . . ." Runcorn
prompted.

Hester came back with a fresh pot of tea and without
speaking poured for Runcorn and passed the cup to him. He
nodded his appreciation, but his eyes were on Monk.

"Yes," Monk answered the question. "Dalgarno was there,
and their feelings for each other were quite open."

They both glanced at Hester and she nodded.

Runcorn made a noise of disgust in the back of his throat,
wordless and eloquent of his fury and contempt.

"Where was he last night?" Monk asked, knowing Runcorn would have found out.

Runcorn's face split into a sudden smile. "Alone in his
rooms," he said with profound satisfaction. "Or so he claims.
But he can't prove it. Manservant out, no porter, no callers."

"So he could have been in Cuthbert Street?" Monk was
surprised at the mixture of emotions that awoke in him. Had
Dalgarno been able to account for his time it would mean he
could not be guilty, at least not in person, and that would have
thrown the whole question wide open. Monk knew of no one
else with any reason to harm Katrina. But it also caused him
more distress than he would have imagined, because he
thought of her facing the man she had loved so deeply, and
seeing in his eyes that he meant to kill her. Had she known it
immediately? Or had she waited, standing in the room, or out
on the balcony, even until the last moment unable to believe
he would, and then she had felt his hands on her and his
strength, and knew she was pitching backward, falling?

"Monk!" Runcorn's voice broke into his thoughts.

"Yes . . ." he said sharply. "What else did he say? How did he react?"

"To her death?" Runcorn's loathing was quite open. "With affected surprise—and indifference. He's the coldest swine I've ever dealt with. One would have judged from his manner that the whole thing was a tragedy that barely touched on his life, a matter of regret for decency's sake, but in reality of complete indifference. He's got his eye on being part of the Baltimore company, and that's all he cares about. I'll get him, Monk, I swear it!"

"We've got to prove his motive," Monk said, concentrating his mind on the issue. Fury, outrage, and pity were all understandable emotions, but they accomplished nothing now.

"Greed," Runcorn said simply, as if the one word were damnation in itself. He picked up his tea and sipped it gingerly, afraid of burning himself.

"That doesn't prove he killed her," Monk pointed out with controlled patience. "Lots of people are greedy. He wouldn't be the first man to have broken his promise to a woman of little means in favor of an heiress, once he realized he had the chance. It's despicable, but it's not a crime."

"He has no proof where he was." Runcorn put down his cup and touched the points off on his fingers. "He had the opportunity to have been in Cuthbert Street. He resembles the figure seen on the roof by the witnesses. Only an impression, but elegant, dark, taller than she was, but not by a great deal. But she was quite a tall woman." Runcorn held up his second finger. "He needed nothing to kill her with except his own weight and strength. And of course there was the man's coat button we found in her hand. We'll look at all his clothes."

Monk felt the chill run through him and then the sweat break out on his body. He prayed Runcorn did not notice it. The jacket with the missing button was in his wardrobe in the bedroom. Thank God he had not stuffed it into the stove with the paper. He had thought about it!

"Hope he hasn't destroyed it," Runcorn went on. "But even if he has, people will know he had another coat, and how will he explain its disappearance?"

Monk said nothing. His mouth was dry. Where could he find another button and replace it? If he went to a tailor Runcorn might find out.

Runcorn held up a third finger. "And she had accused him of being involved in fraud; we know that she hired you to prove it!"

Monk licked his lips.

"Disprove it, actually," he countered.

"And he wanted to cast her aside and marry the Baltimore heiress," Runcorn went on relentlessly. "That's more than motive enough."

Hester was looking silently from one to the other of them.

"Only if we prove the land fraud," Monk argued. "And Livia Baltimore is probably quite comfortably off, but she's not an heiress."

"She will be when Baltimore and Sons sells its railway components to India," Runcorn answered vehemently. "It will make them all rich, and it will only be the beginning. The money will go on and on."

Something flickered in Monk's brain, then vanished.

"What is it?" Runcorn demanded, looking at him more closely.

Monk sat motionless, trying to bring it back, to catch something of it from the edge of his mind, but it was gone. "I don't know," he admitted.

Anger flared for an instant in Runcorn's eyes, then was replaced by understanding. "Well, if you remember, tell me. In the meantime, I've got to tie Dalgarno into the fraud better." His tone of voice had a lift at the end, as if waiting for Monk to complete the thought for him.

"I'll help," Monk said immediately. It was a statement. He intended to whether Runcorn agreed or not; it would simply be easier if he did.

Runcorn must have searched the rest of Katrina's house. Had he found any letters from Emma? There would be a return address on them. Dare he ask? What excuse could he give?

The moment slipped away.

Runcorn gave a wry smile. "Thought you would." He pulled a sheaf of papers out of his pocket, maybe half a dozen or so, and for an instant Monk felt as if he must have spoken aloud. "Got these from Miss Harcus's rooms." Runcorn looked at him, all shadow of even the most bitter humor gone from his eyes. "They're order forms and receipts from Baltimore and Sons. She really suspected him. She must have gone to a lot of trouble, and risk, to take these. She was a brave woman with a passionate love of honesty." He held the papers high in his hand. "No matter how much she loved him, she wasn't going to protect him from fraud. Even though when she started out suspecting, she was still betrothed to him, so in time she would have shared with him whatever he got out of it." He shook his head very slowly. "Why are people such fools, Monk? Why did he want dishonest money more than a really fine woman? Not as if she wasn't handsome as well, and young."

"Precisely because she was honest, I expect," Hester replied for him. "She loved him in spite of what he was, not because of it. Maybe his pride couldn't live with that. He wants admiration."

"Then he'd have to have been a saint," Runcorn said in disgust. "As it is, he'll swing for her. Sorry, Mrs. Monk, but he will." He held the papers out to Monk. "Here, take these and see if you can find anything. I'm going to follow the Baltimore money and see just how much of it ends up with Dalgarno, either now or if he marries Miss Baltimore." He turned to Hester. "Thank you for the tea. I apologize for disturbing you."

She smiled and rose to see him to the door.

Monk stood in the center of the room with his hands clenched and shaking, the papers crumpled by the power of his grip.

Monk read very carefully through everything Runcorn had left with him. There were no letters to implicate Dalgarno in anything but the desire to make as large a profit as possible, and that was common to all businessmen. There was nothing

illegal, nothing even underhanded. All they showed was that
Dalgarno was involved in every aspect of the survey, bargain-
ing for and purchasing the land. But that was part of his duty.
Jarvis Baltimore had apparently dealt with the purchase of
timber, steel and other necessary materials for the track itself,
and Nolan Baltimore had overseen the whole enterprise and
concerned himself with the government and the competition.
The fiercest rivalry between railway companies lay in the great
days of expansion, a generation or so before, but it still required knowledge now, ability and the right connections, to
achieve any success.

The one thing that impressed itself upon Monk as he
looked over the papers a third time, reading the principal
pieces aloud to Hester, was that the amounts of profit were
not undue.

"The Baltimores must be comfortably off," she observed.
"But it is not really a fortune."

"No," he agreed wryly. "Not by railway standards, I
suppose."

Memory teased him that Dundas had been accused of defrauding for much larger profits than anything written here. It
was only glimpses so brief they were gone again before he
could understand them. They might have no connection with
the present issue, but something in them could be the key, the
one element still missing. And there was something that would
tie them all together and make sense of them, but it floated always just beyond his reach, melting into shapelessness one
moment, on the verge of identity the next. He grasped for it,
and it melted into fear without meaning.

But there was another fear with very precise shape—
Emma, to whom Katrina had written so frankly and in whom
she had confided that she did not trust Monk. Who was she,
and why had she not come forward? Someone would tell her
Katrina had been murdered, friends, gossips, even possibly
some lawyer with whom Katrina had entrusted her affairs.
From his brief sight of her rooms, and the clothes she had
worn to meet him, she was not without means.

If they corresponded with such candor then they were close,

wrote frequently. There would surely be some note among Katrina's papers—of her address, or at least something from which he could deduce where she lived.

She might even know more about Dalgarno than Katrina had told him, something to help Runcorn.

He must go back to her rooms. The question was: would it be wiser to go brazenly in daylight, lie that he had authority, or break in at night and trust to his skill not to be caught? Either way he had no honest explanation. Worst of all could be if he were caught having found Emma's address, or some further damning letter from her.

But the risk of leaving it was too great, not only if Runcorn found it, but for the first time in his life that he could remember, his nerves were raw enough to betray him, to Hester at least, and it was she who mattered, even above the law.

He did not know if it was the braver of the two ways or not, but he chose to go by daylight. He would have a better chance of bluffing his way if he was questioned, and it was quicker. He wanted it over with. The waiting was almost as hard as the preparation and the doing.

He found no one on duty at the door of Katrina's building, but there was a beat constable twenty yards away. He hesitated. Should he wait until the man moved on, then try to sneak in, and if he was caught think of some excuse for not being honest? Or would it be better to go up to him boldly, lie about having thought of something useful and having Runcorn's permission to search? Implicitly he did have. Runcorn wanted him to prove Dalgarno's guilt.

There were only two choices; the latter had dangers, but it was the better of the two. He forced the consequences out of his mind. Fear would show in his face, and if the constable was very good he would see it. He walked firmly up to the constable and stopped in front of him.

"Good morning, Constable," he said with a very faint smile, no more than a gesture of civility. "My name is Monk. You may remember me from the night Miss Harcus was killed." He saw recognition in the man's face with a wave of relief. "Mr. Runcorn has asked for my assistance, since I knew Miss Harcus and was working on a case for her. I need to go into the house again and make a further search. I do not require your assistance. I am simply informing you so that you are not concerned if you see me there."

"Right, sir. Thank you," the constable said with a nod. "If you need me, sir, I'll be 'ere."

"Good. I'll send for you if there's anything. Good day." And before the man could sense his tension, he turned and left, going as rapidly as he dared toward the house. He had no keys. He was going to have to fiddle with the lock and pick his way in, but that was an art he had learned from a master in the days before the accident, and the skill had not left him.

He was inside the house within seconds, and retraced his steps up to Katrina's rooms. It took him even less time to pick the lock on her door, and then he was in the room. The sense of tragedy closed around him, the silence, the very faint film of dust showing on the wooden surfaces in the sunlight through the bay windows. Perhaps to someone else it would simply have looked like the room of someone on holiday; to him the presence of death was as tangible as another person watching him, waiting.

He jerked his attention back to the moment. There was no time to think about what had happened here, to try to picture Dalgarno, if it had been him, standing probably where Monk was now, charming her, quarreling, whatever it had been, then going out onto the balcony with her, the last furious words, the struggle, and her falling . . .

He was looking for papers, letters, address books. Where would they be? In the desk where Runcorn had already looked, or in some other similar kind of place. He moved quickly to the desk, opened it and started with the pigeon-holes, then the drawers. There was surprisingly little for a woman who conducted her own affairs, and nothing dating farther back than a few months. Presumably that was when she had come to London.

There was nothing else to Emma, which was not surprising. They would naturally all have been posted. He was chilled inside at the thought of what Emma might have. And it seemed Katrina had not kept Emma's other letters, at least not in the desk. Nor was there any note of her address. Was it one that she knew so well there was no need to note it down?

He stood in the middle of the floor, staring around him. Where else might she keep anything on paper? Where did she cook? Did she have recipe books, kitchen accounts that were separate? A diary? Where did women keep diaries? Bedside table or cabinet? Under the mattress, if it were private enough.

He searched more and more frantically, trying to steady his hands and be methodical, miss nothing, replace everything as he had found it. There were no other letters, no address book, only the cooking notes any woman might have, a book of recipes handed on from Eveline Mary M. Austin, and brief memos on how to launder certain difficult fabrics.

He found the diary just as he was about to give up. He had actually sat down on the bed, sweat on his face, frustration making his hands stiff and clumsy, when he felt a hardness in the lace-covered decorative pillow at the head, over the coverlet. He fished inside the fold at the back and drew out the hardcovered little book. He knew instantly what it was, and opened it, gulping his breath at fear of what he would find. It could be anything, more doubts of himself, words that would prove Dalgarno's guilt, or even someone else's, or nothing of use at all. And he hated the intrusion. Diaries were often intimate and shatteringly private. He did not want to read it, and he had to.

Inside the flyleaf was an inscription: "To my dearest Katrina, from your Aunt Eveline." He only glanced at the pages. The first date was over ten years ago, and the entries were sporadic, sometimes merely the notation of a date, at others a page or more, even two for events of great importance to her. He had not time to read them all, and he concentrated on the more recent ones, particularly since meeting Dalgarno.

He felt guilty reading what were in some cases the inner thoughts of a young woman on the people in her life and the emotions they caused in her, but often her words were so cryptic he could only guess, and he preferred not to. He imagined what he would have felt, had he ever committed his own thoughts to paper like this, and some mere stranger had read them.

He found the letter from Emma almost at the end. It was in the same cramped backhand as the one he had destroyed. It was far less specific, only words of any general sympathy, as if in answer to a letter from Katrina which did not need repeating for her responding emotions to be understood.

He read it twice, then folded it up again, put it in the diary and then put the diary carefully in his pocket. Apparently, Runcorn had not found it so he would not now miss it. He could read it later, and see if anything in it would lead to Emma.

Within half an hour of going in, he was out in the street again, telling the constable that unfortunately he had found nothing, and then wishing him good day and walking rapidly back towards the main thoroughfare.

The news broke in the late edition that evening: MICHAEL DALGARNO ARRESTED FOR BRUTAL MURDER OF KATRINA HARCUS IN SECOND TRAGEDY FOR BALTIMORE AND SONS.

Runcorn must think he had enough to go to trial. Please heaven he was right!

But Runcorn was not certain. Monk knew that the moment he spoke to him the next morning, even though he denied it. They were in Runcorn's office, papers scattered on the desk and the sunlight coming through the window making bright patterns on the rest of the floor.

"Of course it's enough!" Runcorn repeated. "He was pulling a land fraud against the investors in Baltimore and Sons, and Katrina Harcus knew it. She told him so, begged him to stop. He had two reasons for wanting her dead." He held up his fingers. "To keep her quiet about the fraud, for which she may well have had proof—and he destroyed it, she as good as told you that. And because he now had a chance of marrying Livia Baltimore, who was shortly going to be a rich woman." He looked across at Monk challengingly. "And whether he had anything to do with Nolan Baltimore's death or not, we'll probably never know, but it's possible." He drew in his breath. He held up a third finger. "Added to that, he can't prove where he was at the time of her death. He says he was at home, but there's no one who can swear to it."

"What about the cloak?" Monk asked, then instantly wished he had not. It had to remind Runcorn of the button as well, and he had not yet destroyed the jacket, or had a chance to find a replacement button, if he dared do that.

Runcorn sighed irritably. "No trace of it," he said. "Can't find anyone who saw him with a cloak anything like that. He had a cape for the opera." His tone of voice suggested what he thought of that. "But he's still got it."

Monk was disappointed.

"Nothing with the button either," Runcorn went on. "All his coats and jackets are complete, and his manservant says there's nothing missing."

"Then it all hangs on there being a fraud," Monk pointed out. He hated having to say it, but it was the truth. "And we can't prove that."

"The land!" Runcorn said truculently, his chin forward. "You said there are rabbits in it. You told me you saw them yourself. Is there some kind of a rabbit that can build tunnels through a hillside that a team of navvies couldn't blast through with dynamite, for God's sake?"

"Of course there isn't. At least I hope not," Monk said wryly. "But even if there was a bit of sharp profit made on that, it wasn't because Dalgarno owned the land they had to divert to."

"If there was no profit, why do it?" Runcorn demanded.

Monk was patient. "I didn't say there was no profit, only that it wasn't because Dalgarno owned the land. He didn't; neither did either of the Baltimores. It may have been a matter of bribery. Someone paid very nicely to have the line diverted from his land, but we haven't any proof of it, and I don't think Katrina did either. At least she didn't tell me about it—" He stopped.

"What?" Runcorn said quickly. "What is it, Monk? You've remembered something!"

"I think she knew something more that she had not yet told me," he admitted.

"Then that was it!" Runcorn's face was alight. "That was the proof she was going to give you, but Dalgarno killed her before she could! She wanted to try one more time to persuade him to give it up—"

"We have no evidence of that!" Monk cut across him.

"Look!" Runcorn clenched his fist and stopped just short of banging it on the table. "This fraud is a copy of the first one, for which Arrol Dundas was jailed sixteen years ago—yes?"

Monk felt his body tense. "Yes," he said very quietly.

"Which Nolan Baltimore had to have known about, either at the time or when it all came out in court?" Runcorn pressed.

"Yes . . ."

"All right. Now, this Dundas wasn't a fool. He got away with it for quite a long time—in fact, he nearly got away with it altogether. Nolan Baltimore knew all about it, presumably so did Jarvis Baltimore—and so very possibly did Michael Dalgarno. It's all part of the company's history, after all. Find out how Dundas got tripped up, Monk. Find the details of it, piece by piece."

"It was his land," Monk said wearily. "He bought it before the railway was diverted, and then sold it to them expensively after falsifying the survey report as to the height and composition of the hill."

"And Baltimore and Sons is doing exactly the same thing this time, and diverting the track again?" Runcorn's eyes were wide with disbelief. "And I'm supposed to believe that's just a coincidence? Balderdash! Dalgarno knew all about the first time, and he pulled exactly the same trick . . . for a very good reason. There's profit in it for him somewhere. And Katrina found proof of it. You know railways, you know banking—find it, and before we go to trial! I'll see you get the money for going to Liverpool, or wherever it takes you. Just come back with proof."

Monk could not refuse, for his own sake as much as Runcorn's, or Katrina's. He held out his hand and after a moment's blank stare, Runcorn pulled open his desk and came out with six guineas which he put into Monk's palm. "I'll send you more if you need it," he promised. "But don't take any longer than you have to. They'll put him up pretty soon."

"Yes," Monk agreed. "Yes, I imagine they will." He put the money in his pocket and went out of the door.

9

Wʜᴇɴ Hᴇsᴛᴇʀ ʀᴇᴛᴜʀɴᴇᴅ home and found a message from Monk that he had gone to Liverpool hoping to find proof of Dalgarno's guilt in the fraud, she understood exactly why he had done so. In his place she would have done the same. Still, she felt a great emptiness in the house, and within herself also. She had not been able to help him in this case, and for all the superficial explanation and understanding, she knew there were deep and intense feelings he had not shared with her, and most of them were painful.

Perhaps she had been so absorbed in the problems facing Coldbath Square that she had not insisted he tell her in the way that he had needed her to. He could not speak easily of the truth because it trespassed on that part of his life that hurt him, and in which he was afraid he had been so much less than the man he was now.

Why did he still not trust her to be generous of spirit, to hold back willingly and genuinely from needing to know that which was better buried? Did part of him still think she was critical, self-righteous, all the cold and pinched things of which he used to accuse her, before either of them would acknowledge that they were in love?

Or had she somehow failed to let him know that she had accused him of arrogance, cynicism, and opportunism only because she was afraid of her own vulnerability? She had been looking for something comfortable, a man she could love while retaining her inner independence. A love which would be agreeable, safe, never take from her more than she wished to give, never cause her pain that was as great as the laughter and the joy.

He had pulled back for the same reasons!

He had pursued women who were soft and compliant, pretty, who did not challenge him or hurt him or demand of him all he had to give, and more, who did not strip away the pretenses and the shields to reach his heart.

When he was back she would do better—stop playing games of accommodation, politeness, skirting around the truth. She would get back to the passion of honesty they had had in the beginning, things shared with such intensity that touch, words, even silence, was like an act of love.

But for now she must occupy herself, and do something about the women who owed money to the usurer and were being beaten because they could not pay. She was almost certain that Squeaky Robinson was the culprit. But until she had spoken to him again and probed a good deal deeper, her suspicions were not enough. He was afraid of something. It would be very helpful to know what it was.

It was a warm day outside. She barely needed a shawl, let alone a coat, and the streets were crowded as far as the Tottenham Court Road, where she looked for a hansom.

She thought of buying a peppermint water from a peddler—it looked inviting—but then she thought better of spending the money. She passed a newsboy and her eye caught an article on the war in America. Guiltily she hesitated in her step long enough to read at least the beginning, remembering with vivid horror being caught up in that war's first fearful battle. It seemed that the Union forces had been profoundly embarrassed that many of the guns bristling out of miles of Confederate fortifications were actually only painted logs of wood. The cannoneers had retired south some considerable time before.

She smiled at the irony of it and hurried on, finding a hansom at the next corner.

She went into the house in Coldbath Square, really only to tell Bessie where she intended to be, so that if she was needed she could be sent for, and also so that someone would know where she had gone. It was the nearest she could come to any kind of security. Not that she thought Squeaky Robinson was any threat to her. He had no reason to wish her harm—they were ostensibly on the same side, at least he thought they were. Still, it was a kind of precaution.

Bessie was highly dubious about it. She stood with her arms folded, her lips pursed. "Well, all I can say is if yer in't back 'ere safe an' sound in two hours—an' I can tell the time—then I'm goin' fer Constable 'Art! An' I'll not mince me words! I'll let 'im know w'ere yer are an' wot's goin' on. I swear! An' 'e'll come right arter yer! Likes yer, 'e does!" She said that fiercely, as if it were a threat in itself. But that Bessie would speak willingly to a policeman at all, let alone confide in him and ask his help, was eloquent witness to the gravity with which she viewed Hester's undertaking.

Satisfied that she had made her point, Hester thanked her, and wrapped her shawl over her head in spite of the sun, and set out for Portpool Lane.

Squeaky received her stiffly, sitting upright in his chair behind the desk. A tray of tea sat in the only space clear of papers. He had spectacles perched on the end of his long nose, and there were ink stains on his fingers. He seemed profoundly unhappy. His hair stood on end as if he had been continually running his fingers through it.

"What do you want?" he said abruptly. "I haven't got anything to tell you. I haven't seen Jessop."

"I have," Hester said quickly, sitting down on the chair opposite him and arranging her skirts more elegantly, as if she meant to stay for some time. "He is still greedy for more money . . . which we don't have."

"Nobody has money!" Squeaky said resentfully. "I certainly don't, so there's no use looking to me. Times are hard. You of all people ought to know that."

"Why me?" Hester asked innocently.

" 'Cos you know there's hardly a soul on the streets!" he said savagely. "Toffs are starting to go other places for their pleasure. We're all going to end up in the workhouse, an' that's a fact!" It was an exaggeration. He would steal long before he allowed such a disaster to happen, but there was an underlying note of panic in his voice which was real.

"I know it's serious," she said gravely. "Political pressure is still keeping the police all over the place, although no one expects them to find out now who killed Baltimore."

A curious expression flickered over his face, a kind of suppressed fury. Why? If he knew who it was, why did he not inform, secretly of course, and get the whole thing over with? Then he and everyone else could get back to normality.

There was only one possible answer to that—because it implicated him in some way, or at least his house. Did he protect his women, even at the cost of business? She found that very hard to believe. He used women until they were of no value anymore, then discarded them, as all pimps did. They were property.

But his were particularly valuable property, not easily replaced. He could not go out and get them; they had to walk into this trap.

"They won't find out," he sneered, but there was rising tension underneath it, and he watched her every bit as closely as she did him. "If they'd had any idea at all they'd have sewn it up by now," he went on. "They're here to please some bleedin' toff's feelings of outrage 'cos a tart dared to hit back." There was hatred in his eyes, but for whom she could not tell.

What had happened to the woman who had killed Baltimore, if it was a woman? Or had she simply struck him, and perhaps screamed, and someone like the would-be butler at the door had actually killed him? Perhaps even unintentionally, in a fight at the top of the stairs, Baltimore had lost his balance and fallen.

"Somebody must be sheltering her," she said aloud, then stopped, seeing the instant denial in his face. "You think not?"

He wiped his expression blank. "How'd I know? Mebbe."

"You'd make it your business to know," she replied, her eyes never leaving his. "Do you wish to be thought incompetent—stupid?" she added for clarity in case he misunderstood.

He flushed with anger—or possibly a kind of embarrassment?

"You've a reputation to keep up," she continued.

"What do you want?" he snapped, his voice high with barely controlled tension. "I can't stop Jessop, I told you that. If you want someone to go an' beat a little consideration into 'im, it'll cost you. I don't care whether you've got money or not, you'll get nothin' for nothin'."

It was not just greed driving him, it was fear as well; she could see it and hear it, almost feel it in the room. Fear of what? Not the police; they were nowhere near any kind of solution. She knew that from Constable Hart. Fear of the silent man who loaned money to young women and then blackmailed them into prostitution? A man who would do that must be a cruel and possibly dangerous partner. Was he threatening Squeaky if he did not produce the usual income in spite of the circumstances?

She smiled slowly. The idea of the would-be butler's giving Jessop a couple of black eyes and a thoroughly good fright was very appealing. She could be tempted.

Squeaky was watching her as a cat does a mouse.

"Five pounds," he said.

It was, relatively speaking, a modest enough sum. Margaret would be able to come by it. Why was Squeaky offering to do such a thing for only five pounds? Was the partner really so demanding? He was a usurer. Money was his stock-in-trade. Was Squeaky down to so little that five pounds made a difference?

"For you, in your position?" she asked.

"Me!" he snapped. "He's . . ." Then the derision vanished from his face and he conceded everything. "Me," he repeated.

It was a second or two before she realized what he was saying, then it came in a flood of understanding—he was alone. For some reason the partner was no longer there. That was his panic—the fact that he did not know how to run the business by himself.

The wild idea gained at Marielle Courtney's house hardened into close to a certainty. Nolan Baltimore had been Squeaky's partner, and his death, murder or accident, had left Squeaky without anyone to run the usury side of the business.

He needed a new partner, someone with access to the sort of young women who might get into debt, the polished manner to earn their confidence, and the business acumen to loan them money and insist on its repayment in this way.

An even wilder idea came almost unbidden into her mind. It was outrageous, but it just might work. If it did, if she could persuade him, it could solve their own problem. It would not reveal who killed Baltimore, or get the police out of the area, but she found to her surprise that she did not care greatly. If Baltimore had been the usurer, and also a client of his own appalling trade, then she could not mourn his death.

"I will consider your offer, Mr. Robinson," she said with aplomb. She rose to her feet. Now that she had thought of a plan, she was in a fever to put it to the test.

He looked vaguely hopeful. Was that for the money or the prospect of seeing Jessop severely frightened? Either would do. "Let me know," he said with a very faint smile.

"I will," she promised. "Good day, Mr. Robinson."

Hester had to wait until the evening before she could put her idea to Margaret. After the initial business of the house was over, Alice and Fanny were resting fairly easily. The two were actually talking to one another; Hester heard the occasional soft giggle. Hester sat down with Margaret to a cup of tea, and she could contain herself no longer.

Margaret stared at her wide-eyed with disbelief. "He'll never do it! Never!"

"Well, he might not," Hester admitted, reaching for the butter and jam for her toast. "But it could work, don't you think—if he would?"

"If . . . do you think . . ." Margaret could scarcely admit the possibility, but she was glowing with excitement, her cheeks pink.

"Will you come with me to try?" Hester asked.

Margaret hesitated. Her eagerness was plain in her face, also her fear of embarrassment, and of failure. She might be thought too forward, and invite a rebuff which would hurt more than she would find easy to accept.

Hester waited.

"Yes," Margaret agreed, then took a deep breath as if to retract it, and let it out in a sigh and picked up her tea.

"Good." Hester smiled at her. "We'll go tomorrow morning. I shall meet you at Vere Street at nine o'clock." She gave Margaret no chance to change her mind. She stood up and, carrying her toast with her, went to speak to Fanny as if the whole matter were settled and there could be nothing more to discuss.

The morning was bright and chilly again, and Hester dressed smartly in a plain dark blue dress and coat. She took a hansom to Vere Street to be there just before nine. She knew Margaret would be on time, and trembling with tension. She cared for her feelings, but apart from that, she did not wish to give her any opportunity to retreat.

Actually, Margaret was late, and Hester had begun to pace up and down the pavement anxiously. At last the hansom drew up and Margaret, beautifully dressed, scrambled out with less grace than usual.

"I'm sorry!" she said hastily after paying the driver. "The traffic was terrible. Somebody clashed wheels and broke an axle in Trafalgar Square, and they started shouting at each other. What a mess. Are we . . ."

"Yes," Hester replied, too relieved to be angry. "We are! Come on!" And she took Margaret by the arm and entered Rathbone's chambers.

They were too early, as Hester expected they would be. She was immensely relieved simply to find that Rathbone was not due in court that morning, and if they waited, there was an excellent chance he would be able to see them after his first client, who was due at half past nine, exactly the time the clerk expected Rathbone himself.

As it transpired, they were invited to go into his office

shortly after ten o'clock, but Hester had the feeling that had Margaret not been with her he might have kept her waiting longer.

Rathbone came forward to greet them, hesitating an instant as to which of them he should speak to first. It was so slight Hester barely saw it, but she knew him far better than Margaret did, and she had not mistaken it. He addressed Hester, because of their long friendship, but he had wanted to go to Margaret.

"Hester, how pleasant to see you," he said with a smile. "Even if I am perfectly sure that at this time in the morning you must have come on business, no doubt to do with your house in Coldbath Square." He turned to Margaret. "Good morning, Miss Ballinger." There was the very faintest flush on his cheeks. "I am glad you were able to come also, although I am afraid I have not yet thought of any way in which your usurer can be stopped by the law. And believe me, I have tried."

Margaret smiled back at him, meeting his eyes with candor, and then suddenly realizing how bold she was and moderating her gaze. "I am sure you have done all that could be . . ." she started, then stopped. "We have thought about it a great deal also, and certain events have changed matters considerably. Hester will tell you; it is her idea . . . although I do heartily agree."

Rathbone turned to Hester with his eyebrows raised and a distinct look of apprehension in his face as he invited them to be seated. He turned to Hester. "Well?"

She knew time was limited and she must not waste words or choose the wrong ones. There would be little opportunity to retrieve a mistake. She was prepared to risk a touch of overstatement. If she was wrong she could apologize later. She plunged in.

"I know who the usurer is . . . was," she stated with assurance. "It was a partnership, one man who found the young women and lent them the money, the other who actually ran the brothel and did the day-to-day management of affairs. He collected the repayments and exacted the punishment if they were late. It is the one who did the lending who is dead," she added.

"Then is the business ended?" he asked, doubt in his face. "Will he not find another usurer, or plan that part of it himself?"

"He can't take it over himself," she answered. "He has not the skills, nor has he the opportunity to meet the sort of young women most vulnerable. He is a brothel-keeper, and he looks and sounds like one." She leaned forward a little. "What he needs, desperately at the moment, is someone who appears to be a gentleman but who has business ability and a degree of charm to deceive young women in debt into borrowing from him in the belief that they can repay with money honestly earned." She watched him carefully to make sure she was putting the case clearly and yet not so obviously that he was ahead of her, and would refuse before she had had the opportunity to explain the whole plan.

"I expect he will find one," he said, his face filled with the rueful humor she knew so well. "It would be very pleasant to think that he will not, but not realistic. I'm sorry."

"I agree." She nodded. "If he could not, then we would have no concern."

"I cannot prevent it, Hester," he said gravely. "Nor can I reasonably find out who it will be. I wish I could. Or are you saying that if we are to stop this business we have only a small amount of time in which to act?" He looked genuinely grieved. "I would, if I knew of anything that would help. It is not practical to try closing him down. London is full of prostitution, and probably always will be, like all large cities." There was apology in his eyes, in the line of his mouth. He did not look at Margaret.

"I know that," Hester answered softly. "I am not so idealistic as to aim at changing human nature, Oliver, only at putting Squeaky Robinson out of this particular business."

"Miss Ballinger suggested that you had an idea," he said with care, the slight frown back between his brows.

She could not help a flash of humor. He had been involved in one or two of her plans before and was wise to be wary.

She plunged in. "We must strike before he finds a partner,"

she said firmly, praying she would phrase her plan in such a way as to make him believe it was not only possible but perfectly moral and reasonable, which would not be easy!

"Strike?" he said warily. He glanced at Margaret.

She smiled with magnificent innocence.

He looked uncomfortable and turned back to Hester.

She took a deep breath. This was the moment. "Before he finds a partner himself," she said, "we must provide one . . . who will need to examine the books, of course, before he commits himself. . . ."

Rathbone said nothing.

"And will thus have the opportunity to destroy them," she finished.

He looked puzzled. "He won't believe you," he said with grave regret. "Your reputation is too well known, Hester. And unless he is a complete fool, he wouldn't believe Monk either."

"Oh, I know that," she agreed. "But he would believe you, if you did it well enough."

He froze, eyes wide.

There was nothing to do but continue. "If you were to go to him with us, of course, and say you would be interested in investing a little money in such a profitable sideline." She knew she was speaking too quickly. "Providing an examination of the books, the debts still to be collected, and so on, were satisfactory, then you would also be able to provide suitable young women in the future. You come across them often enough in your practice—"

"Hester!" he protested, aghast. "For God's sake . . ." He swiveled to Margaret. "I apologize, Miss Ballinger, but I couldn't possibly involve myself in usury and prostitution! Not to mention sanctioning the brutal punishment of people unable to pay their debts . . ."

"Oh, but you wouldn't be!" Margaret said sincerely. "You would only have to go there once." Her eyes did not leave his. "And surely lawyers deal with some very questionable people a lot of the time? You can hardly defend people who haven't at least been charged with a crime, whether they are guilty or not?"

"Yes, but that's . . ." he protested.

Her smile lit her face with a softness and a warmth which were unmistakable. She could not have hidden her admiration for him then even had she tried, and at the moment she was oblivious of it. "If anyone were to mention it, should they know, you could be perfectly candid afterwards as to why you were there," she said reasonably. "Could anything be more justified than rescuing perfectly honest young women from a life on the streets?"

His face was filled with confusion both intellectual and emotional. Hester, who knew him so well, could see it clearly.

"That's not exactly what you're suggesting," he pointed out reluctantly, looking from one to the other of them. "I need to go to this . . . Squeaky?"

"Yes . . . Squeaky Robinson." Hester nodded.

"And offer to be his partner in usury and pimping?" he finished.

"Only offer," Hester said, as if it were the most reasonable thing in the world. "Not actually do it."

"The difference between intent and execution would be difficult to prove," he said with a touch of sarcasm.

"To whom?" Hester argued. "Who is going to know, except Squeaky Robinson, who will be in no position to retaliate, and Margaret and I, who will be undyingly grateful. And of course we know exactly where your real morality lies."

"Hester, it is . . ." he tried again.

"Ingenious and unpleasant," Margaret answered for him. "Of course it is." Her voice conveyed understanding and disappointment. Her eyes were wide, full of gentleness, as if she knew she had expected too much.

Rathbone flushed. He was perfectly well aware that she and Hester worked in Coldbath Square almost every day, regardless of dirt, danger, or risk to their reputations.

"When were you planning on doing this?" he asked tentatively.

"Tonight," Hester replied without hesitation.

Margaret smiled hopefully and said nothing.

"Tonight! I . . ." Rathbone was momentarily nonplussed. "I . . ."

"Thank you," Hester murmured.

"Hester!" he protested, but he had already surrendered and all three of them knew it.

Margaret's eyes were gleaming, her cheeks faintly flushed, although no one could have told whether the cause was anticipation of the possible victory tonight or her knowledge that Rathbone had succumbed largely because of her.

Hester stood up, and Rathbone and Margaret did likewise. Time was short, but quite apart from that, it was wise to withdraw before triumph could be turned into defeat by a thoughtless additional remark.

"Thank you very much," Hester said sincerely. "Where would you like to meet us? Coldbath Square might not be the most advisable."

"What about Fitzroy Street?" Margaret suggested. "I can be there at whatever time you wish."

"Then I shall join you at nine o'clock," Rathbone replied. He looked at Hester with a twisted smile. "What does one wear to buy into a brothel?"

She regarded his extremely elegant gray suit and white shirt with its perfectly tied cravat. "I would not change, if I were you. Dressed like that, he will believe you have money and influence."

"How about greed, immorality and perverted tastes?" he asked with a slight curl of his lip.

"You cannot dress for that," she replied with perfect seriousness. "Regrettably."

"Touché," he murmured. "Until nine o'clock. I presume you will tell me then whatever else I am required to know?"

"Yes, of course. Thank you, Oliver. Good-bye."

He bowed very slightly. "Good-bye."

Hester and Margaret walked away side by side, heads high, without speaking, each lost in her own thoughts. Hester assumed Margaret's were of Rathbone, perhaps driven by emotions rather than reason. Her own were also emotional, the full realization that whether Rathbone knew it or not, he was falling in love with Margaret Ballinger quite as much as he had ever been with Hester herself. She felt a powerful mixture of regret and pleasure, but she knew in a while the pleasure would win.

By the time the hansom stopped in the Farringdon Road at just after half past nine, Hester, Margaret and Rathbone knew exactly what part each was going to play in what they hoped was going to be the downfall of Squeaky Robinson's business. They alighted and walked the short distance in the fitful lamplight along Hatton Wall and across Leather Lane to the darkness of Portpool Lane, under the shadow of the brewery. None of them spoke, each concentrating on what he or she was going to say and how to assume their various roles.

Hester was nervous. It had seemed a brilliant idea when she first thought of it. Now that it was about to become a reality, she could see all the difficulties that she had so eagerly persuaded Margaret, and then Rathbone, did not matter.

She led them through the alley entrance, which was still remarkably clear of rubbish, and up the steps to the door. As usual it was opened by the man in the cast-off butler's suit.

"You again," he said somewhat ungraciously to Hester, then looked beyond her to the other two. His face clouded. " 'Oo are they?" he demanded.

"Friends of mine," she replied confidently. "The gentleman is in a way of business which might interest Mr. Robinson. I am aware of certain"—she hesitated delicately—"requirements, at the moment. You had better tell him I am here."

He was empowered to make decisions; it showed in his face. It was also more than likely that he was fully aware of the problems occasioned by Baltimore's death. It was probably he who had moved the body and left it in Abel Smith's house. He swung the door wide, slight surprise registering in his face. "Then yer'd better come in," he suggested. "But don't take no liberties. I'll find if Mr. Robinson'll see yer."

He left them in the small side room in which Hester had waited before. There was not even space or chairs for all three of them to be seated.

Rathbone looked around him with curiosity and a slight puckering of his nose with distaste.

"Did you come here by yourself, Hester?" he said anxiously.

"Yes, of course I did," she replied. "There's no one to come with me. Don't look like that. I didn't meet with any harm."

"Did Monk know?" he asked.

"No. And you are not going to tell him!" she said hotly. "I will do so myself, when the time is right."

He smiled very slightly. "And when will that be?"

"When the matter is closed," she said. "It is not always a good idea to tell everybody everything, you know. One should keep one's own counsel at times."

He gave her a pointed look.

"Hester is very brave," Margaret said loyally. "Far braver than I am . . . in some things."

"I hope you have more sense!" he said sharply.

Margaret blushed and looked down, then up again at him quickly. "I do not think you should criticize Hester, Sir Oliver. She does what she has to in order to protect people who have no one else to care for their interests. The fact that in some cases they may have made errors of judgment does not set them apart from the rest of us."

Suddenly he smiled. It was a warm and charming gesture. "You are quite right. I'm not used to women who take such risks. It is my fear for her which speaks. I am very slow to learn that my discomfort may concern her, but it certainly will not stop her."

"Would you wish it to?" Margaret challenged.

He thought for several seconds.

Hester waited, surprisingly interested in what he should reply.

"No," he said at last. "I used to wish it would, but I have learned at least that much."

Margaret smiled back at him, then looked away, conscious of his eyes upon her.

The butler returned. "Yer'd better come," he said, jerking his head toward the corridor and leading them deeper into the warren of passages and stairways.

Squeaky Robinson was sitting in the same room as when Hester had seen him before. Piles of papers were strewn around him, and one gas lamp was lit, throwing a pool of yellow onto the desk. And again there was the tray with tea. He looked tired to the point of exhaustion; his skin was papery with dark smudges under his eyes. Had he been in ordinary trade Hester would have been sorry for him, but she was too aware of Fanny and Alice, and others like them, to allow herself such a feeling.

Squeaky stood up slowly, only glancing at Hester, then his eyes went straight to Rathbone. He barely noticed Margaret at all. Perhaps women were largely invisible to him if he was not inspecting them as goods.

"Good evening, Mr. Robinson," Hester said as calmly as she could. "I have brought this gentleman, whose name you do not need to know as yet, because he is interested in investing money in a business a little out of the ordinary, where he can have a fast and safe return. It will also be desirable if it can escape the attention of the tax inspectors and not have to be explained to certain members of his family with whom he might otherwise have to share it." She indicated Margaret. "And this lady is good with books and figures, always an advisable attribute to have when considering an investment."

Squeaky stood up slowly, his face like that of a man who has walked long across an arid plain and at last thinks he sees water. He stared at Rathbone, taking in his immaculate boots, his perfectly cut suit with its excellent cloth, his cravat as clean as snow, the humor and intelligence in his face.

"How do you do, Mr. Robinson." Rathbone did not offer his hand. "Mrs. Monk tells me that your previous partner in business met with an unfortunate accident, and therefore the position is now vacant. Is she correct?"

Squeaky licked his lips. His indecision was palpable. Whatever answer he made, there was risk attached. On one hand he might give away too much about himself, on the other he might lose Rathbone's interest, and thus the new partner necessary for his survival.

The silence was heavy in the room. The building seemed to

sag and creak as if settling itself deeper into unseen mire beneath it.

Rathbone glanced at Hester impatiently and frowned.

Squeaky saw it. "Yes!" he said abruptly. "He died. Suddenly."

"A euphemism, surely?" Rathbone raised his eyebrows. "Was he not murdered?"

"Ah!" Squeaky gulped, his throat jerking. "Yes. Nothing to do with his investment here! A purely private matter. A quarrel . . . his own . . . appetites. Most unfortunate."

"I see." Rathbone looked as if he did, although Hester knew he had not the slightest idea. "Well, that will not affect me. I have no desire to avail myself of your services. I mean simply to invest money and reap the reward. But I would prefer to think that you did not have many clients who meet with accidents. It attracts the wrong kind of attention. I am in a position to ride out one term of police presence due to murder, but not two."

"Oh, it won't happen again!" Squeaky assured him. "It's never happened before, and I'll take care of it. The woman's gone, I assure you."

"Good!" Rathbone almost smiled. "Satisfactory so far. But naturally I require to know rather more about your business—for instance, the financial side of it, the incomings and outgoings, the general history—before I commit myself."

"Of course . . . of course!" Squeaky nodded vigorously. "Anyone would. It needs a careful man."

"I am a careful man," Rathbone said with the barest smile.

Hester had a sudden suspicion that part of him was enjoying playacting the role. There was a casual elegance in the way he stood, and his hands by his sides were relaxed, his fingers loose. She might tease him about this afterwards, when it was all over. He would probably never admit to it.

"It's a good business," Squeaky assured him. "Very profitable, and strictly legal, mind. Just a matter of lending a little money to people who need it. Could almost be viewed as a charity." He saw the look on Rathbone's face and amended his expression. "Well . . . there's no matter what anyone thinks, is there, 'cos nobody's going to know."

"Not from me," Rathbone replied dryly. "And if you are wise, not from you either."

"Oh, rest easy, sir!" Squeaky nodded vehemently, his eyes wide. "Rest easy!"

"You won't get any money until I do," Rathbone promised him. "How did your deceased partner become involved?"

Hester shot a quick look at him. It did not matter how Baltimore had started in this. In fact, she really no longer cared who had killed him, if it was one of his own victims, and not only for the money but for his appetites as well. A certain kind of justice had already been served.

"Some gentlemen have different tastes," Squeaky said with a wry leer. "He was one of them."

"And you take all such men into your confidence?" Rathbone said with disgust. Hester saw his hand clench by his side. She was afraid now that the answer Squeaky would give would make it far harder for him to remain as an investor. He had pushed too far. Should she say something to help? But what?

"You set up the business with him?" she interrupted. "I daresay it was his idea?"

"No, it was not!" Squeaky said angrily, his voice rising alarmingly in pitch. "It was already a very good concern when he came in." He resented her intrusion.

"That's hard to believe," she said scathingly.

Squeaky pointed his finger at her. "Look, miss, you just keep to your good works in Coldbath and leave the business to them as know about it. I had a very good thing going here before Mr. Baltimore ever came along. I was just unlucky. My partner then, Preece, his name was, was a greedy man. He tried to blackmail one or two of the better-off customers. That's a fool thing to do. Kill the goose that way. Enough's enough." He sliced the air with his stringy hand and its ink-stained fingers. "Anyway, Baltimore got very angry and they set at each other like prizefighters." His lips pursed in a gesture of disgust, but he looked a little pale at the memory. "Preece was a big fat bastard, and he took an attack. Went all colors and fell down on the floor, clutching his chest. Died right there." He looked past Hester, directly at Rathbone. "Heart!" he said savagely. "Too much belly and no brain. His own fault."

Rathbone nodded. "Apparently," he agreed.

Hester saw him relax so very slightly it was barely perceptible. She shot a glance at Margaret in the shadows behind him, and read the relief in her face also.

"Anyway," Squeaky resumed, "I needed someone to take his place, and Baltimore needed the business to continue—in his own interest, like. We were the only ones offering exactly the service he wanted, otherwise he'd have to start all over again, looking from scratch, as it were. Worked out very well all 'round."

"Until he died as well. . . ." Rathbone observed.

"That was his own fault too!" Squeaky said immediately. "He got stupid, and thought just because he had a share in the place that he could go as far as he liked with the girls."

"One of them killed him?" Rathbone said very softly.

"Yeh. But she's gone. Too wild, that one. Pushed him out o' the window. Top story, an' all." He winced. "What a mess! It's all right, though, the police don't even know it happened here." He grinned. "We put the body in old Abel Smith's place, like he fell down the stairs."

"Very tidy," Rathbone observed. "You have a gift for making the best of bad luck."

"Thank you." Squeaky bowed.

Margaret drew in her breath sharply.

"Now all I require is to look at your accounts, if you please," Rathbone asked.

Squeaky hesitated, staring at Rathbone as if to hold his attention while he deliberated. He glanced at Hester, then Margaret in the background, barely moving, then at Rathbone again.

Rathbone understood his meaning instantly. "Miss . . ." Then he changed his mind. "I cannot enter a business unless I have a financial opinion upon the books, Mr. Robinson—one that I trust." He smiled very slightly, hardly more than an easing of his features. "I do not care to consult my usual bankers in this particular matter."

Squeaky grinned, then nodded slowly, satisfied. He turned and went to a cupboard on the far side of the overcrowded room. Taking a key out of his pocket—although it remained attached to him by a chain—he opened one of the doors. He lifted up a large ledger, relocked the door, and carried the ledger over to the table.

Margaret stepped forward. "I shall require a quiet place to study the figures." She said it coolly, but Hester knew from the tension in her shoulders and the slightly higher pitch of her voice that she was desperately aware that everything hung on this moment. "Alone, and no interruptions, if you please," Margaret added. "Then, if it is satisfactory, you can make the arrangements."

Squeaky regarded her with curiosity. It was perfectly plain that she was nothing he had expected, and he was confused. She did not belong in any preconceived part of his world.

She waited. No one interrupted the silence.

Rathbone moved from one foot to the other. Hester all but held her breath.

"Right," Squeaky said at last. He offered the ledger to Margaret, who took it with very slightly trembling hands and clasped it to her.

"Through there," Squeaky said, pointing to a corner of the room where another doorway was partially concealed by a curtain.

"Thank you," Hester accepted immediately, and to Squeaky's fairly obvious relief, she and Margaret left him alone with Rathbone.

The next room was small and enclosed. The turning up of the gaslight revealed one square, uncurtained window overlooking rooftops almost indistinguishable against the night sky.

There was one chair and a table on rickety legs. Margaret sat down and opened the ledger, and Hester leaned over her shoulder and read with her. It was written in a very neat crabbed hand, all the figures sloping backward a little.

Even at a glance the profits were plain to see, if the entries were honest. But it was the IOUs they needed. Whatever this proved was immaterial. It was not illegal.

Margaret started to turn the pages more hurriedly, then picked up the whole ledger and held it upside down. Nothing fell out.

"They're not here!" she said with a note of desperation.

"Give it a few moments more, as if we had read it all," Hester replied. "Then I'll go and ask for them. I'll say you need to get an idea of the future, as well as the past."

Obediently, Margaret returned her attention to the columns and perfunctorily added them up.

"Baltimore was turning a very nice profit on this," she said bitterly after another few moments. "This looks like Alice's repayments here." She pointed. "Stopping about the time of Baltimore's murder. Actually, there are hardly any repayments after that, only this one."

"Right," Hester said firmly. "That's all I need. I'll go to see Mr. Robinson." She went straight to the door and, without knocking, back into the room where Rathbone and Squeaky were sitting facing each other in what seemed to be earnest conversation. Squeaky looked excited and anxious, leaning forward so the gaslight threw his seamed face into heavy relief, and Rathbone relaxed back in his chair, half smiling.

They both turned as Hester came in.

"What is it?" Squeaky demanded.

Rathbone frowned, his eyes searching hers.

"It all looks very profitable, Mr. Robinson," Hester said smoothly. "There is just one matter to sort out."

"Oh?" Squeaky asked abruptly. "And what's that, then?"

"There has been almost a complete stop in repayments lately—over the last three weeks, to be exact," she answered.

"Of course there has!" Squeaky exploded. "Gawd sakes, woman, there's rozzers on every bleeding footpath! How d'yer think anyone's going to earn anything? Where are your wits at?"

Rathbone stiffened.

"At wanting to see your paper proof that there are still debts owed," Hester answered perfectly levelly, avoiding Rathbone's eyes. "No one wants to buy a business that has nothing coming in on a permanent basis."

Squeaky shot to his feet. "I have!" he said furiously, jabbing his finger in the air. "I've got lots o' money coming still, but nothing's forever! What do you think I need a partner for? When these run out, we gotter get more!" He went back to the cupboard where he had found the ledger and pulled the key from his pocket and opened the door. He poked his hand inside and fished around for a few moments, then withdrew it holding a sheaf of papers. He ignored the wide-open door and came back to Hester, holding them out. "There! All debts!" he said, waving them at her.

"So you say," she agreed, resisting the impulse to snatch at them. "We will add them up, deduct a little for . . . accidents, and come to a figure to present." She inclined her head at Rathbone, but carefully avoided using his name.

Squeaky still held tight onto the papers.

Hester looked at Rathbone again.

Rathbone pursed his lips and started to stand up.

"All right!" Squeaky thrust the papers at Hester. "But only in that room, mind. They're worth a lot of money."

"Of course," Rathbone agreed. "Or I would not be willing to put my own money into the venture."

Hester took the papers from Squeaky's reluctant fingers and walked straight over to the doorway, expecting any moment to hear Squeaky's footsteps behind her. She reached the door with relief and opened it, then closed it again behind her. Margaret looked up at her, her face pale and tight with tension. She gulped when she saw the papers in Hester's hand, and relaxed a fraction.

Hester looked at them just long enough to be certain that they were the original signed IOUs, not copies of anything in Squeaky's own hand. When she was satisfied that they were, she looked up and nodded to Margaret.

Margaret took them and went to the fireplace. She put a ta-per to the gas flame in the light, caught fire to it, then, sheltering it with her hand, bent down and set it to the papers, all in absolute silence.

Hester stood with her back against the door, her heart pounding.

The flames caught and flared up. Margaret watched until there was nothing left, then took the tongs and crushed the blackened pieces. She turned around to Hester, a smile of triumph on her face.

Hester picked up the ledger. "Do you want to?" she invited her.

Margaret shook her head. "It's yours," she replied. "But I want to watch."

Hester made a little beckoning gesture, then opened the door with her free hand and went back into the room with Squeaky and Rathbone.

Squeaky looked up. "Well?" he demanded. "Didn't I tell you?"

"You did," Hester agreed, putting the ledger down on the desk in front of him. "There was a lot of money owed. But since I have just burned the IOUs, you will not be able to collect it."

Squeaky stared at her in incomprehension. It was too terrible for him to grasp.

Even Rathbone seemed startled. He had expected her to leave Squeaky to find that out for himself when they were well outside the place. He looked a trifle taken aback.

"You . . . you fool!" Squeaky screeched as the truth of it dawned on him. "You . . . you . . ."

"Not a fool, Mr. Robinson," Hester said calmly, although her hands were sweating and she knew she was trembling. "It was precisely what I intended to do."

"I'm ruined!" Squeaky's face was red, his eyes bulging. He held out his hands as if he were thinking of actually grasping hold of her and strangling her.

She took a step backward just as Rathbone stood up. "No you won't," she said chokingly. "I have an idea how you could use this place . . . really quite well."

"You what?" Squeaky said with total disbelief. She was monstrous! Beyond credibility.

"I . . . I have an idea," Hester repeated. "We need new premises, better than we have now, and cheaper . . ."

"Cheaper?" Squeaky yelled. "You should pay me compensation! That's what you should do . . . you . . . you lunatic!"

"Nonsense!" she said briskly. "At least you will stay out of jail. You can run this place as a hospital for the sick and injured. There's plenty of room."

He gulped and choked.

"The money can be raised by charity," she went on in the deafening silence. "You've got lots of young women here who could learn to be nurses. It would—"

"Gawd Almighty!" Squeaky burst out in anguish.

"Hester!" Rathbone protested.

"It seems like quite a good bargain to me." Hester adopted an air of utmost reason.

Squeaky turned to Rathbone to appeal to him.

"I'm sorry," Rathbone said, a strange lift in his voice, as if he were teetering on the edge between horror and laughter. "I have no intention of investing in your business, Mr. Robinson. Unless, of course, you adopt Mrs. Monk's suggestion? I had no idea that she had such a thing in mind, but it seems to me something to which I could donate a certain amount, and possibly find others who would do the same." He took a deep breath. "I appreciate that it would ruin your reputation among your colleagues, but it might earn you a certain leniency in other directions."

"What other directions?" Squeaky wailed. "You're asking me to be worse than legitimate! It'd be downright . . . good!" He said the word as if it were damnation.

"The law," Rathbone said reasonably. "I am a barrister." He bowed very slightly. "Sir Oliver Rathbone, Q.C."

Squeaky Robinson let out a long, wordless groan.

"Then we will all be well suited," Hester said with satisfaction.

"We shall even be able to tell Mr. Jessop that his premises are no longer required," Margaret added. "I personally will enjoy that very much. We shall, of course, not pay you well, Mr. Robinson, but the donations will be sufficient, without that expense, to see that you are comfortable and properly fed and clothed. If you manage the place, it will give you something to occupy your time, and the other work will need to be overseen. The present young ladies can earn a modest living, quite honorably . . ."

Squeaky howled.

"Good," Margaret said with deep satisfaction. She glanced at last at Rathbone, and blushed at the admiration in his eyes. She looked at Hester.

Hester smiled back at her.

"You're all in it together!" Squeaky accused, his voice hitting falsetto in outrage.

"You are exactly right," Rathbone agreed gently, smiling as if extraordinarily pleased with himself. "And now you are fortunate to be in it with us also, Mr. Robinson. My sincere advice, for which I will not charge you, is to make the best of it."

Squeaky let out a last, despairing groan, and was utterly ignored.

10

THE JOURNEY TO LIVERPOOL was just like the others. He could hear the rattle of iron wheels over the joints in the rails even when he drifted into sleep, although he fought against it. He was afraid of what the dreams would bring back, the sense of horror and grief, the piercing, sick knowledge of guilt, although he still did not know for what.

He stared out of the window. The rolling countryside with its plowed fields was dark where the grain was sown but not yet through the ground, green like thrown gauze over the earth where the earlier crop had sprung. The cherry and wild plum and pear trees were mounded white with blossom, but all of them made no mark on his senses. He got out and back in again at every stop, eager to be there.

He reached Liverpool Lime Street just before dark, stiff and tired, and found himself lodgings for the night.

In the sharp chill of morning his mind was made up where to begin. Whatever pain it might bring, whatever revelations not only as to his life, but to Monk's also, he must start with Arrol Dundas. Where had he lived? Who had been his friends, or his associates? What had been the style and the substance of his life? Monk had wanted to know these things, and at the same time dreaded it, ever since the first splinters of memory had begun to return. It was time to realize both the hopes and the fears.

The newspaper accounts had stated where Dundas had

lived at the time of his arrest. It was a simple enough matter to check, and take a cab out to the elegant, tree-lined street. He sat in the hansom outside number fourteen, staring up and down at the beautiful houses, which were spacious and meticulously cared for. Maids beat carpets in the back alleyways, laughing and flirting with delivery boys, or arguing over the price of fish or fresh vegetables. Here and there a bootboy idled a few minutes, or a footman stood looking important. Monk needed no one to tell him this was an expensive neighborhood.

"This right, sir?" the cabbie asked.

"Yes. I don't wish to go in. Just wait here," Monk answered. He wanted to think, to let the air of the place, the sights and sounds, swirl around him and settle in his mind. Perhaps something here would rip away the veils in his mind and show him what he hoped and dreaded to see—himself as he had been, generous or greedy, blindly loyal or a betrayer. The past was closing in. Only another fact, a smell, a sound, and he would be face-to-face with it at last.

Who lived in this house now? Was there still a stained-glass window at the top of the stairs, before the flight turned up another story? Was there still a pear tree in the garden, white with spring blossom? There would be a different carpet in the withdrawing room, not red and blue anymore, probably not red curtains either.

Suddenly, with a jolt of clarity, he remembered perfectly sitting at the dining room table. The curtains were blue all along the row of windows opposite him. The chandeliers were blazing with candles, reflecting on the silver cutlery and the white linen below. He could see the patterns on the handles as if he held one right now, ornate, with a *D* engraved in the center. There were fish knives as well, a new invention. Before that people had eaten fish with two forks. Mrs. Dundas was extraordinarily pleased with them. He could see her face, calm and happy. She had been wearing a sort of plum color; it complimented her rather sallow skin. She was not beautiful, but there was a dignity and an individuality about her he had always liked. But it was her voice that pleased most, low and a little husky, especially when she laughed. There was pure joy in it.

There had been a dozen people around the table, all perfectly dressed, jewels glittering, faces smooth and happy, Arrol Dundas at the head, presiding over the good fellowship.

There had been money, plenty of it.

Had it been the product of fraud? Had all that elegance and charm been bought at the expense of other people's loss? It was a thought so ugly he was surprised he could entertain it without it leaving him with a raw wound. And yet it did not. Perhaps he was too anesthetized by Katrina's death and the snatched memories and imagination of the crash to be capable of still more hurt.

He leaned and tapped hard to get the cabbie's attention.

"Thank you. Take me back to the records office, please," he instructed him.

"Yes, sir. Right." The cabbie had had his fair share of eccentrics, and it made no difference to him, as long as they paid. He flicked the whip lightly and the horse moved forward, glad to stand no longer in the sharp sunlight. The overnight frost had not yet melted on the cobbles in the shade.

Had the house been Dundas's, or merely rented? Monk had followed enough other people's affairs to know that all kinds of men lived on credit, sometimes the last ones you would expect. He remembered Mrs. Dundas somewhere quite different when she had told him of her husband's death. Had she left this beautiful place for financial reasons, or because she could no longer bear to live so close to her old friends after her husband was disgraced? There would be no invitations anymore, no calls, no conversations in the street. Anyone might choose to move—he would have!

Dundas must have left a will. And there would be records somewhere of the house's being sold, with the date.

It took him till the middle of the afternoon to trace what he was looking for. It left him puzzled and acutely aware of a mystery he should already have solved, but if he had there was nothing of it left in his memory. The house had been sold before Dundas's death. In fact, by then his estate had been worth no more than the new, very modest house in which his widow had lived, and a very small annuity, sufficient only to keep her in the necessities, and even to do that she would have had to spend with care.

What startled him, and left him with shaking hands and a tightness in his chest, was that the name of the executor of the will was William Monk.

He stood in front of the shelf with the book open in front of him, and leaned over it, his legs weak.

What had happened to the money from the sale of the house? The court had not taken it. The profit from the sale of land which had been charged as fraud was still to be realized. Dundas had owned the house for twelve years. There was no shadow or taint upon his purchase of that.

So where had it gone? He looked again, and again, but search as he might, he could find no record of it. If he had handled it himself, and it seemed that Dundas had trusted him to do just that, then he had concealed all trace of it. Why? Surely the only reason a man hid his dealings with money was because they were dishonest?

It had been a fortune! If he had taken it himself, then he would have been an extremely rich man. Surely that was not something he could have forgotten? When he joined the police he had owned nothing but the clothes he stood up in— and a few others besides. Clothes—Dundas had taught him to dress well, very well, and he had never lost the taste for it.

Glimpses of memory returned of fittings at tailors, Dundas leaning back elegantly and giving instructions, a lift here, an inch in or out there, a little longer in the legs. *Yes—that's right! This cut of shirt is best, Egyptian cotton, that is how to tie a cravat. Smart but vulgar—don't ever wear one like that! Understated, always understated. A gentleman does not need to draw attention to himself. Discreet but expensive. Quality tells in the long run.*

Monk found himself smiling, against his will, a lump in his throat so high and hard it stopped him from swallowing.

The legacy was still with him; he spent too much on clothes even now.

What had happened to the money?

What had Mrs. Dundas bequeathed at the time of her death?

That too was easily discovered when he found her will: very little indeed. The annuity died with her. The house was worth a small amount, but some of that went to settle outstanding debts. She had lived to the meager limits of her income.

If he had been Dundas's executor, had he disposed of the money somehow? Where? To whom? Above all, why? That question beat in his mind at every turn like the scrape of leather on a bleeding blister.

He drank hot coffee and was too tense to eat.

What did it have to do with Baltimore? Perhaps the affairs of Baltimore and Sons would give him some of the answers or lead him to another avenue to follow in his search.

It took him until the next day to find someone both willing and able to discuss the subject with him: Mr. Carborough, who made a study of the finances of such businesses with a view to investment in them for himself.

"Good company," he said enthusiastically, waving a pencil in the air. "Small, but good. Made a nice profit from the land deals, not excessive, and better, of course, from the railways themselves. Headquarters in London now, I believe. Building another nice line to Derby."

They were sitting in Carborough's office overlooking a narrow, busy street down near the docks. The smell of salt drifted up to the half-open window, and the shouts and clangs of traffic, winches and bales being loaded and unloaded.

"What about Dundas and the land fraud?" Monk asked, keeping his voice casual, as if it were of no personal interest to him.

Carborough curled his lip. "Stupid to get caught in something as trivial as that," he said, shaking his head. "Never understood it myself. He was brilliant. One of the best merchant bankers in the city, if not the best. Then he goes and does a foolish thing like changing the grid reference on a survey so they move the course of the track onto his own land,

and he makes . . . what?" He shrugged. "A thousand pounds at most. Hardly as if he needed it. And at the time he did it, he'd have expected to get an interest in whatever the company made on the new brakes. He found the money to develop them."

"What new brakes?" Monk said quickly.

Carborough opened his eyes wide.

"Oh . . . they invented their own system of braking for carriages and goods wagons. Quite a bit cheaper than the standard ones used now. Would have cleaned up a fortune. Don't know what happened there. They never followed through with it."

"Why not?" he asked. The same flicker of memory woke in Monk and died in the same instant.

"Don't know that, Mr. Monk," Carborough replied. "After Dundas's trial everything seemed to stop for a while. Then he died, you know?" He put the pencil down next to his pad, making it perfectly level. "In prison, poor devil. Maybe the shock of it all was too much. Anyway, after that they concentrated on new lines. Seemed to forget all about brakes. Built their own wagons and so on. Did pretty well out of it. As I said, moved down to London."

Monk asked him more questions, but Carborough knew nothing about Dundas personally and had not heard Monk's name before that he recalled.

Neither was there any sign of the money that Dundas must have received for his house. It had vanished as completely as if the treasury notes it was paid in had been burned.

The next step was to pursue the Reverend William Colman, who had given such telling evidence against Dundas. It might be an unpleasant encounter, since Colman would certainly remember Monk from the trial. He would be the first person Monk had spoken to who had known him from that time. Dundas and his wife were both dead, and so was Nolan Baltimore. Monk would be coming face-to-face with the reality of who he had been, and finally there would be no escape from whatever Colman remembered of him.

Had he hated the man then, for his evidence? Had he been offensive to him, tried to discredit him? Had Colman even believed him equally guilty with Dundas, but simply been unable to prove it?

Colman was still in the ministry, and it was not a difficult matter to find him in Crockford's, the registry of Anglican priests. By late afternoon Monk was walking up the short path to the vicarage door in a village on the outskirts of Liverpool. He was aware of a fluttering in his stomach and that his hands were clammy and aching from the frequency with which he was clenching them. Deliberately, he forced himself to relax, and pulled the bell knob.

The door opened surprisingly quickly and a tall man in slightly crumpled clothes and a clerical collar stood staring at him expectantly. He was lean with gray hair and a vigorous, intelligent face. Monk knew with a thrill of memory so sharp it caught his breath that this was Colman—the face he had seen sketched with the protesters against the railway. Immeasurably more vivid than that, it was the face he had seen in his dreams, and desperate, fighting through the wreckage of the burning train.

In that same instant Colman recognized him, his jaw momentarily slack with amazement.

"Monk?" He stared more closely. "It is Monk, isn't it?"

Monk kept his voice steady with difficulty. "Yes, Mr. Colman. I would appreciate it if you could spare me a little of your time."

Colman hesitated only a moment, then he swung the door wide. "Come in. What can I do for you?"

Monk had already decided that the only way to achieve what he needed was for the complete truth to come out, if indeed it was possible at all. The truth necessarily involved being honest about his loss of memory, and that bits and pieces were now coming back.

Colman led the way to the room in which he received parishioners and invited him to be seated. He regarded Monk with curiosity, which was most natural. He had not seen him in sixteen years. He must be looking at the changes in him, the character more deeply etched in his face, the tiny differences in texture of skin, the way the lean flesh clothed the bones.

Monk was acutely aware of Colman's personality and the force of emotion he had felt in him before—nothing had diminished it. The grief was all still there, the memory of burying the dead, of trying to scrape together some kind of comfort for stricken families.

Colman was waiting.

Monk began. It was difficult, and his voice stumbled as he summarized the years between then and now, ending with the story of Baltimore and Sons and the new railway.

As Colman listened the guardedness was there in his face, the echoes of old anger and shattering grief. They had been on opposite sides of the issue then, and it was clear in his expression, in his careful eyes and slightly pinched lips, and above all in the tightness in his body as he sat, one leg still crossed over the other. His fists were closed, his muscles rigid. They were opponents still. That would never be forgotten.

"Nolan Baltimore has been murdered," Monk stated. He saw Colman's start of surprise, then a gleam of satisfaction, and immediately afterwards guilt for it, even a flush in his cheeks. But he was in no haste to express the usual regrets. There was an honesty in him which prevented it.

"By a prostitute," Monk added. "While in the pursuit of somewhat irregular pleasures."

Disgust was plain in Colman's eyes.

"And that brings you here?" he said in disbelief.

"Not directly," Monk replied. "But it does mean we cannot question him about anything to do with what very much appears to be another fraud in Baltimore and Sons, almost exactly like the first."

Colman sat upright with a jolt. "Another? But Dundas is dead, poor soul. You, of all people, must know that. Surely your memory cannot be so affected ... I mean ..." He stopped.

Monk rescued him in his embarrassment. "I remember that. But what I don't recall is how the fraud was discovered ...

not in detail. You see, it seems this time as if a man named Dalgarno is responsible, only the person who was his main accuser is also dead . . . murdered." He saw the pity in Colman's face, this time unmixed with anything else. "A woman," Monk continued. "She was betrothed to him, and because of her privileged position as his fiancée, discovered certain things about the business, overheard conversations, saw papers, which made her realize there was something seriously wrong. She brought it to me. I investigated it as far as I was able, but I could find no fraud. A little questionable profiteering, but that's all."

"But she was murdered?" Colman interrupted, leaning forward with urgency.

"Yes. And Dalgarno is charged with it. But in order to prove his guilt we need to show the fraud beyond question."

"I see." It was clear from his expression that he understood perfectly. "What is it that you want of me?"

"You were the one who first suspected fraud. Why?"

Colman frowned. He was clearly fascinated by the concept of such total loss from the mind of something in which Monk had been passionately involved. "You really remember nothing of it?" His voice thickened with emotion; his body became rigid. "You don't remember my church? In the valley, with the old trees around it? The graveyard?"

Monk struggled, but nothing came. He was picturing it in his mind, but it was imagination, not memory. He shook his head.

"It was beautiful," Colman said, his face tender with sorrow. "An old church. The original was Norman, with a crypt underneath where men were buried nearly a thousand years ago. The graveyard was full of old families, over fifteen or twenty generations. It was the history of the land. History is only people, you know." He stared at Monk intensely, reaching for the man behind the facade, the passions which could be stirred—and wounded—deeper than the analytical brain. "They sent the railway right through the middle of it."

Now something clicked in Monk's mind, a bishop mild and reasonable, full of regret, but acknowledging progress and the need for work for men, transport, the moving forward of society. There had been a curate, shy and enthusiastic, wanting to keep the old and bring in the new as well, and refusing to see that to have both was impossible.

And caught between the two of them the Reverend Colman, an enthusiast, a lover of the unbroken chain of history who saw the railways as forces of destruction, shattering the cement of family bonds with the dead, vandalizing the physical monuments that kept the spiritual ties whole. Monk could hear voices raised—shouting, angry and afraid, faces twisted with rage.

But Colman had done more than protest, he had proved crime. Was this it, the elusive memory at last—the proof? Who would it blame—Baltimore, or Monk himself? He cleared his throat. It felt tight, as if he could not breathe.

"They destroyed the church?" he asked aloud.

"Yes. The new line goes right over where it used to be." Colman did not add anything; the emotion in his voice was sufficient.

"How did you discover the fraud?" Monk forced himself to sound almost normal. He almost had the truth.

"Simple," Colman replied. "Someone told me he watched rabbits on the hill they said they had to go around because it would be too expensive to tunnel through. He was a parishioner of mine, in trouble for poaching. When I asked where he'd been caught, he told me. Rabbits don't tunnel in granite, Mr. Monk. Navvies can blast through pretty well anything; solid mountains just take longer, and therefore cost more.

"I found the original survey. When one looked more carefully at the one Baltimore was using, it was falsified. Whoever did it had been too clever to alter the heights or composition— he found a hill that was exactly right somewhere else and altered the grid reference. It was an extremely skilled job."

Monk asked the question he had to, but he had to clear his throat again to make his voice come. "Arrol Dundas?"

"It looked like it," Colman said with regret, as if he would rather it had been someone else.

"Did he ever admit to it?"

"No. Nor did he blame anyone else, but I think that was more a matter of dignity, even morality, than because he had no idea who it might have been."

It was a moment before Monk realized the full meaning of what Colman had said. He had begun his own next question, and stopped in the middle of the sentence.

"You mean you doubted Dundas was guilty?" he said incredulously.

Colman blinked. "You always maintained he wasn't. Even after the verdict, you swore he was not the one who had changed the survey, and that his profit was through good speculation but not dishonesty. He simply bought low and sold high."

Monk was confused. "Then who forged the survey references? Baltimore? Why would he? He didn't have any land!"

"Nor money in the bank from it afterwards," Colman agreed. "I don't know the answer. If it wasn't Dundas, then the real money probably came in bribery somewhere, but no one will ever prove it."

"Why would anyone else falsify the surveys?" Monk pressed.

Colman frowned, weighing his answer before he gave it, and then his words were picked with great care. "The railway cut through the middle of my church, and that was all I could think of at the time." His eyes filled with sudden tears. "And then the crash . . . the children . . ." He stopped. There was no way to express it, and perhaps he saw some recognition of horror in Monk, and words became unnecessary.

Monk's recollection of him was growing sharper. He had wanted to like him before; it was his testimony against Dundas that had made it impossible. Now all that had receded into history for both of them and there was no issue to be fought anymore.

Colman blinked and smiled in apology. "I am afraid I am not much help in gaining the evidence you need to prove Dalgarno's guilt for murdering the young woman, or whether Baltimore was the one practicing the fraud. But if I understood you correctly, he was already dead himself by the time she was killed."

"Yes, by two or three weeks," Monk agreed.

"Then possibly Dalgarno was in the fraud with Baltimore, and once Baltimore was dead he would take all the profits to himself?" Colman suggested.

"Or share them with the son, Jarvis Baltimore," Monk amended. "It seems likely, especially since Dalgarno is now courting the daughter, Livia, according to my wife's observation."

Colman's eyes widened. "Your wife is acquainted with the Baltimores?"

Monk did not bother to hide his smile, or the bubble of pride springing up inside him, high and bright, and with a pain like a dagger for what he could lose. "No. She is running a house of refuge and medical treatment for prostitutes in Coldbath Square, and Livia Baltimore went to her for help, and in considerable anger and distress, after her father's murder. Hester learned some information and went to call on her. She nursed in the Crimea. There is not much that deters her once she is convinced she is right."

Colman shook his head, but his eyes were shining. "I hope she does not have to enlighten Miss Baltimore as to the true nature of her father," he said. "I think he may well have tried the same fraud a second time. But I don't know how you will prove it to a jury without evidence of profit. He escaped the first time because it was plain he had no financial gain from it, and Dundas did."

"Dundas died with very little," Monk pointed out, old sadness and anger washing over him in a tidal wave.

Colman became suddenly very solemn also. "I heard that, although it was extraordinary. He was an excellent banker, quite brilliant. But you can't have forgotten that, surely?"

"I had. But not now. Where did the money go?"

Colman stared at Monk somberly.

"I have no idea. No one had. And shortly after that the crash put all such things out of everyone's thoughts." Suddenly his face was pinched and the color went from his cheeks again. "It was the closest thing to hell I think this life could offer. I shall remember the screams as long as I live.

The smell of burnt hair still brings me out in a sweat and I feel sick. But you know that. You were there."

He looked ill. Monk lowered his eyes. He knew what Colman meant. He had tasted something of it in his own nightmare. It was strange, an almost irrelevant reality, to hear Colman say that Monk had been there; he knew it far more urgently and terribly from the nightmare of his hidden mind.

"What caused it?" he said aloud.

Colman looked up slowly. "They never found out. But it wasn't the new track. That was perfectly good. At least . . . as far as anyone could tell." The last vestige of blood drained out of his face and his body stiffened. "Oh, no! You don't think it's going to happen again? Please God—no! Is that what you're afraid of?"

"It is what Katrina Harcus was afraid of," Monk replied. "But I've searched everything I can; I've walked the track myself and I can't see anything wrong with it at all. Tell me, Mr. Colman—how can I prove this fraud? It's happened again—and I still can't see it!"

Colman looked at him with intense pity. "I don't know. Do you think if I did I would have stayed silent all these years? Whoever it hurt, I would have spoken. I simply don't know!"

Monk stared at him helplessly, his mind caught like a runner through the breaking surf, feeling the tide drag at his feet, taking away his balance, and still no sense came out of it.

"Look for the bribe," Colman urged. "That's all it can be."

Monk did not argue as to whether there had been a bribe or not. Colman had long ago made up his mind. He stayed a little longer, then thanked Colman and left, walking more easily, with lighter feet. One old enmity had been exorcised. Now he would not dread seeing Colman's face in his dreams.

But he had not found that one fact which he was convinced would let him unravel all the others from the fast-tied knot of his memory. There was something which he dared not bring back because of the pain, and yet until he knew what it was, and faced it, all the rest was just beyond his reach.

He had the courage to look at it, and the will in his conscious mind, but that tiny part of him which looked too deep to touch, which knew what it was, still held it just beyond his reach.

Was it defying him . . . or protecting him?

He went back to London through Derby, checking once more on the original route, before the alteration, and seeing exactly whose land it had crossed. There was a large and wealthy farm it would have cut in half, making it impossible to have taken cattle from one side to the other, effectively ruining the unity of it.

It would also have sliced through a spinney of trees, one of the best in the area for drawing a fox, a favorite place of the local hunt. Would it have needed bribery to divert the track a mile or two through unused land? On the whole, he thought not. It seemed the obvious thing to do. Not to would have been an act of vandalism, and earned a dangerous enmity among the people of the nearest town.

Was any of this really a crime? Was it even a sin worth caring about more than with a passing regret?

Michael Dalgarno was a worthless man in his relationship with Katrina. He had taken her love while it suited him, and then cast her aside when a financially better prospect had presented itself in Livia Baltimore. But that was not a crime either . . . a sin certainly, but one many men were guilty of. As men had married for beauty, so many an empty woman had married for wealth.

None of that was motive for Dalgarno to have murdered Katrina.

To conceal fraud was, certainly, but where was the fraud? None that Monk could prove. It was all only suggestion and suspicion. Monk remembered the letter with his own name in it that he had removed from Katrina's. His hand stung as if it had burnt him. Had he left it there, it would be he that Runcorn was after now, and were it anyone other than Runcorn, with as much certainty of his guilt!

"Of course he's guilty!" Runcorn said indignantly when Monk went straight from the station to see him and report his failure. As always, his office was crowded with papers, but they were all neatly stacked, as though studied and dealt with. He was too busy to offer Monk tea. Anyway, he seemed to regard him now as a colleague rather than a guest. He looked at him skeptically and with some disappointment. "The fact that you still didn't bring back any proof of the fraud doesn't mean he's innocent," he said grimly. "It just means he hid it too well for you to uncover. Presumably he learned from Dundas's mistakes. Two farms, or estates or whatever, you said?"

"Yes," Monk replied stiffly. "And if I'd been planning that line you wouldn't have had to bribe me to divert around a hill rather than go through it, if it meant not vandalizing a stretch of land like that."

"And you think Dalgarno is the same as you, do you?" Runcorn lifted his eyebrows in a mixture of surprise and disbelief.

Monk hesitated. The question had been meant sarcastically, but he realized how much truth there could be in it. There was a physical resemblance, increased by their similar self-assurance—one might say arrogance, the love of good clothes, a certain grace of movement. If the witnesses to Katrina's death had really seen someone on the roof, if their descriptions fitted Dalgarno, they would just as easily fit Monk. Plenty of people had seen him with Katrina—ask anyone in the Botanic Gardens. And to an onlooker they could have appeared to be quarreling. With a chill in the pit of his stomach, Monk remembered how she had put her hands up and grasped his coat, pulling off the button. He knew when it had been torn—but she had died with it in her hand. Why? What was she doing still holding it so long after?

Without the motive, Dalgarno was no more proved guilty than was Monk himself. Perhaps the evidence against Dalgarno was just as rooted in chance—or mischance?

"Monk!" Runcorn said loudly. "Are you saying Dalgarno was like you?"

Monk returned to the moment with a jolt. "Somewhat," he answered.

"Somewhat like you?" Runcorn said, amazement showing in his face that Monk was considering it seriously.

Monk felt himself on the brink of a precipice and pulled back. "Superficially," he answered. Already his mind was enmeshed in other thoughts, farther into his own doubts and necessities. "Only superficially." He wanted to excuse himself as soon as he could. He was feeling more and more impelled to see Rathbone. It was imperative. Perhaps it was almost too late now.

"There isn't anything more," he said aloud. "You'll have to trust your prosecution. Sorry."

Runcorn grunted. "I suppose I should be grateful that you tried."

He had to wait an hour and a half before Rathbone was free to see him. It was a wretched time, far too long to sit and consider the difficulty and the embarrassment of what he must do.

When eventually Rathbone came and he was conducted into his familiar, elegant office, he began without preamble.

"Michael Dalgarno has been charged with murdering Katrina Harcus, but the proof depends on his having a motive," he said bluntly.

"Of course." Rathbone nodded, looking at Monk with sharpening interest. They knew each other well enough for him to be aware that Monk would not be there to say something so obvious, nor would he be so tense, his body tight, his voice on edge, were it not of acute personal importance, even pain, to him. The relationship between them was deep, at times troubled by rivalry between the smooth, socially and intellectually confident Rathbone, who nevertheless lacked emotional courage, and the arrogant, uncertain Monk, who looked and behaved almost like a gentleman, yet had the inner passion to commit his heart, win or lose, and was now so desperately afraid that after all the effort, the change, the hope, it would be lose.

Rathbone was regarding him gravely, waiting for him to explain.

"Runcorn assumes it was because Katrina had proof of his

being involved in fraudulent purchase and sale of land for Baltimore's railway line to Derby," he began. "I thought so too, but I've searched as thoroughly as I can, even comparing all the dealings with the fraud in Baltimore and Sons in Liverpool sixteen years ago, when I worked for the banks concerned myself." He saw Rathbone's slight start of surprise, concealed almost instantly. "But I can find no proof," he went on. "Certainly not sufficient to hang a man for murder."

Rathbone looked at his hands, then up at Monk. "Exactly what was your involvement in the first fraud, as much as you know?" he asked.

Now was the time when only the naked truth would do. Any evasion might come back as guilt, like a knife to destroy whatever good was left.

"Arrol Dundas, the man who taught me everything I knew and was almost a father to me, was accused of buying land cheaply and then selling it at huge profit after falsifying the surveys so the railway would divert its course," he replied. "He was found guilty, and died in prison." It was odd, put so baldly, devoid of the reality of passion that had made it acutely and irrevocably painful. It sounded like a legal issue, not people's lives torn apart. Best to add the ugliest part of that now, get it over. "And while he was in prison, there was one of the most terrible rail crashes in history. A coal train collided with an excursion train full of children."

Rathbone was so moved by his own imagination of the horror of it that for a moment or two he did not speak. "I see," he said at last, his voice low enough to be almost inaudible. "And did it have anything to do with the fraud?"

"Not that I could tell. It was attributed to human error—possibly both driver and brakeman."

"Proof?" Rathbone raised his eyebrows very slightly.

"None. No one ever knew for certain. But navvies have never been known to build a faulty track. There are too many checks, too many skilled people involved."

"I see. And was Dundas guilty of the fraud, or was it someone still alive now? Dalgarno?"

"Not Dalgarno, he would have been a schoolboy sixteen

years ago. I don't know whether Dundas was guilty. I was certain he was innocent at the time . . . at least I think I was." His eyes did not leave Rathbone's. "I fought to get him acquitted . . . and I can remember the grief and the sense of helplessness when he wasn't."

"But . . ." Rathbone probed gently, like a surgeon with a knife, and like a knife, it hurt.

"But I can't remember. I feel guilty about something. I don't know whether it was because I couldn't help. In Liverpool just now I looked into his financial affairs as far as I could with no authority. He was very wealthy while I knew him, and up until the time of the trial. He was supposed to have made a profit out of the land deal. . . ."

Rathbone nodded. "Naturally. One presumes that was part of the evidence of fraud. What about it?"

"He died with very little." This time Monk did not look at Rathbone as he said it. "He sold his large house and his widow lived extremely modestly in a far less salubrious area. When she died she left nothing. She had lived on an annuity which ended with her death."

"And you don't know where the money went?"

Monk looked up. "No, I don't. I've done everything I can to remember, been to the places again, read the newspapers, and it still won't come."

"What are you afraid of?" Rathbone spared him nothing. Perhaps that was as necessary as a doctor pushing to see where it hurt most.

Could he lie? At least about this? What was the point? He had to tell Rathbone that he had burnt the letters which implicated him—falsely. And there could be others saying that.

"That I did know at the time," he replied. "I was executor of his will. He must have trusted me."

Rathbone did not stay his hand at all, although the reluctance, the hurt at having to do it was in his voice. "Could you have taken this money yourself?"

"I don't know! I suppose so. I can't remember." Monk sat forward, staring at the floor. "All I can see clearly in my mind is her face, his widow, telling me he was dead. We were in a very ordinary house, small and neat. I didn't have the money, but I don't know if I did something with it. I've racked my mind, but I just don't remember!"

"I see," Rathbone said gently. "And if Dundas were innocent, as you thought at the time, then was the truth that there was no fraud or that someone else was guilty?"

"I think that's the difference," Monk said, straightening up slowly and meeting Rathbone's eyes. "Sixteen years ago there was definitely fraud. The grid references on the survey map were altered. If it wasn't Dundas, then it was someone else, possibly Nolan Baltimore—"

"Why?" Rathbone interrupted. "If Dundas profited personally, why would Baltimore have forged a survey report?"

"I don't know. It makes no sense that I can see," Monk admitted, defeated again. It closed in on him on every side. "But I don't believe there was fraud this time. The track was rerouted, but Dalgarno didn't own the land. If there was illegal profit, then it was bribery in order to change the route and not divide farms or estates. And placed as they are, anyone could have done that out of a sense of preservation of the land, without being bribed to."

Rathbone stared at him, his face very grave. "Monk—what you are saying is that Dalgarno had no reason that you know of to kill this woman. If he had no motive, and no one saw him do it, then there is no evidence to tie him into the crime at all."

"There is a little," Monk said slowly, very distinctly, hearing the words drop like stones, irretrievable. He must tell Rathbone all of it. "There is the paper Katrina Harcus left accusing him. But she also left one which, on the face of it, accuses me. And the button." Now it would be impossible to retract. Rathbone would force him to tell the whole truth.

"Button?" Rathbone frowned.

"She died with a man's coat button in her hand."

"Torn off in the struggle? Why the devil didn't you say so?" Now Rathbone's face was keen, his eyes alight. "That ties him in completely—motive or not!"

"No, it doesn't," Monk said flatly, even at this awful moment aware of the bitter humor of it.

Rathbone opened his mouth to speak, then sensed something deeper and beyond words, and said nothing.

"I met her in the Botanic Gardens earlier in the day," Monk went on. "She was very distressed, and still passionately convinced that Dalgarno was guilty. We more or less quarreled about it, at least that is what it would appear to be to any onlookers, and there were many."

Rathbone leaned forward a little across the desk, concentrating intensely.

Monk felt hot, and then cold. He was shivering. "She grasped at me, as if to demand my attention. Then, in pulling away she tore the button off my coat. It was my button in her hand."

"Several hours later? When fighting with her murderer?" Rathbone said softly. "Monk, are you telling me the whole truth? If I am to defend you, I need it."

Monk looked up at him slowly, dreading what he would see. "I came to ask you to defend Dalgarno," he said, ignoring Rathbone's surprise. "I think he may be innocent. Either way, I need him to be defended to the best of anyone's ability. If he hangs, I have to be certain, beyond any doubt at all—reasonable or otherwise, that he killed her."

"I am more concerned about keeping your neck out of the noose," Rathbone said earnestly. "You knew this woman, you were seen to quarrel with her the day of her death, and your coat button was in her hand. And you didn't tell me what happened to the letters which incriminated you."

"I took them," Monk told him. "Runcorn asked me to show him the rooms where she lived. I saw them before he did. I took them, and burnt them when I got home."

Rathbone let out a long sigh. "I see. And to whom were these letters written?"

"Someone called Emma, but I don't know anything else, except that she did not live in London. I went back"—he saw Rathbone wince, and ignored it—"and looked for more, an address book, but I didn't find one."

"Were they regular correspondents?"

Monk's voice was hoarse. "I don't know!" He did not mention the diary. No one had heard about it, and he clung to the tiny thread of hope that somehow it would still tell him something about Katrina which could provide a link, however fragile. And there was something of her dreams in it he wanted to protect. Perhaps if he were honest, that was it.

"I see," Rathbone repeated softly. "And you are afraid your actions will hang a man who may be innocent." That was not a question. He knew Monk well enough for it not to need to be.

Monk looked at him steadily. "Yes. Please?"

"He may have his own barrister already," Rathbone warned. "But I will do everything I can, I promise you."

Monk started to say "You've got to," and realized how foolish that was. He was asking a favor for which he could not pay, perhaps an impossible one. "Thank you," he said instead.

Rathbone smiled slightly, like a moment's sun on a winter landscape. "Then let us begin. If Dalgarno did not kill her, and you did not, then who did? Do you have any idea at all?"

"No," Monk said simply. It was the bare truth. He realized how very little he knew about Katrina Harcus. He could have described her to the minutest detail—her hair, her face, her remarkable eyes, the way she moved, the inflections of her voice. He could have told Rathbone what she had worn almost every time he had seen her. But until the day of her death he had not even known where she lived, let alone where she came from or anything of her daily life, her family or her past.

Rathbone tightened his lips for a second, then with an effort forbore from making any comment on Monk's gullibility. Perhaps if he considered it, he knew as little about some of his own clients. "Well then, the first thing you can do is find out everything else you can about her, and as rapidly as possible," he said bleakly. "Go wherever it takes you, but report to me every day." He knew he did not need to emphasize that.

Monk stood up. Rathbone had been light in his condemnation, saying nothing of criticism or blame, but Monk knew him well enough to be aware of his thoughts. He felt as crushed by the mere fact of them as if they all had been put into speech.

Rathbone handed him the funds he would need.

"Thank you," Monk accepted, hating it. Whether Rathbone would get any of it back from Dalgarno was still an open question, but Monk could not afford to refuse. He had no idea where his search would take him. Not only would Dalgarno's life depend on it, but his own conscience, his identity, and if things came to the worst, his life too. If it seemed Dalgarno would be convicted, then he would have to tell the court of the paper he had found at Katrina's rooms, and destroyed, and show them that the coat button was his. Then how could even Rathbone save him from the rope?

And yet he was innocent. Perhaps Dalgarno was also.

"I need to start with Dalgarno himself," he said aloud. "Get me an interview with him."

The clock had struck nine by the time Monk stood in the Newgate cell, Rathbone sitting to the side in the only chair. Dalgarno, pale and unshaven, paced back and forth restlessly, his face already haggard from the shock of realization that ahead of him lay the possibility of the gallows.

"I didn't kill her!" he said desperately, his voice rising, close to breaking.

Monk kept his own emotions icily under control. It was the only way to approach thinking with any clarity.

"Then someone else did, Mr. Dalgarno," he replied. "No jury will acquit you unless you provide them with an alternative."

"I don't know who did, for God's sake!" Dalgarno cried out wildly. "Do you think I'd be standing here in prison if I did?" He stared at Monk as if he were a complete fool.

Monk felt a pity for him, and a guilt for his own part in it, but he also could not like the man. He had treated Katrina Harcus badly, whether he had killed her or not.

"Hysteria won't help," he said with chill. "Logic is the only thing that may. What do you know about her? And please tell me everything, and the truth, whether it is flattering to you or not. Your life may depend upon it. It is no time for protecting your reputation or your vanity."

Dalgarno glared at him, then at Rathbone.

Rathbone nodded almost imperceptibly.

"I met her at a garden party," Dalgarno began, his tone now subdued. "She was charming, full of life. I thought she was the most interesting woman I had ever seen. But I knew nothing of her social background, except that she was obviously well-bred and had sufficient means to dress in the height of fashion."

"Who were her friends?" Monk asked.

Dalgarno rattled off half a dozen names. They meant nothing to Monk, but he saw Rathbone register recognition.

"Maybe one of them killed her," Dalgarno said desperately. "I can't think why, but God knows I didn't. Why would I? I didn't want to marry her, and she seems to think I did." He colored faintly. "But there was no fraud—I swear!" He waved his hands jerkily. "We may have shaved a little here and there, but everyone does."

Monk did not comment on that. It was irrelevant now. "That is precisely why I need to know more about her, Mr. Dalgarno. Someone killed her. Where did she come from? What about her family?"

"I don't know!" Dalgarno said impatiently. "We didn't discuss it."

"But you were intending to marry her," Monk pointed out. "As an ambitious young man, surely you enquired?"

Dalgarno blushed. "I . . . I believe she came originally from the Liverpool area. She said both her parents were dead."

It made excellent sense. The fraud she had accused Dalgarno of practicing was almost an exact copy of the one for which Dundas had been convicted. Had she grown up in the Liverpool area she could have heard of it, and of the crash she had told Monk about with such horror.

He asked other questions, but for a man who had claimed to be in love, Dalgarno knew surprisingly little about her. But then Monk recalled with brutal honesty how little he had known, or cared, about some of the young women with whom he had thought himself in love.

Perhaps it was because he had known Hester since the first months after the accident, and she had crowded all others out of anything but the surface of his mind. She was real; they were only idealizations he had thought he wanted.

Had Dalgarno been like that with Katrina Harcus? If he had, Monk could not blame him for it. There was little point in asking Dalgarno about their relationship; he would say what he wanted them to believe, and there was nothing against which to check it.

"What about your own family, Mr. Dalgarno?" he asked. "Did you introduce Miss Harcus to them? Surely your mother enquired? Perhaps she would know more about her?"

Dalgarno looked away. "My family are in Bristol. My father is in poor health, unable to travel, and my mother does not leave him."

"But you and Miss Harcus could travel," Monk argued.

Dalgarno swiveled around, his eyes angry. "I did not ask Miss Harcus to marry me!" he snapped. "She may have imagined I was going to, but women do that!"

"Especially if you give them cause to," Monk said equally sharply.

Dalgarno opened his mouth as if to deny it, then closed it again in a thin line.

Monk could learn nothing more of use. In the end he left the overpoweringly oppressive air of the prison and walked side by side with Rathbone along Newgate Street. Neither of them mentioned a like or dislike for Dalgarno, or the fact that he had shown no pity for Katrina Harcus, no remorse that he had used her badly.

"Liverpool," Rathbone said succinctly. "If it has anything to do with her past it will begin there. The police will be looking into everything in London, so don't waste your time with that. Honestly, Monk, I don't know what you are looking for."

Monk did not answer. He did not know either, but to admit it seemed like a surrender he could not afford.

* * *

When Monk reached Fitzroy Street, the house was empty, but he had been there not more than ten or fifteen minutes when Hester came in in a whirl of excitement. Her face lit when she saw him, and she dropped her parcel of shopping on the table and went straight to him as if she had no flicker of hesitation that he would take her in his arms.

He could not help himself from doing so, clinging onto her hard, feeling the strength of her answering embrace.

She pulled away and looked up at him. "William, I have solved the murder of Nolan Baltimore, at least in part. I don't know exactly who did it, but I know why."

He could not help smiling. "We all know that, my darling. We always knew. Ask any bootboy or peddler. He didn't pay his bills. Some pimp took exception and there was a fight."

"Not quite," she said like a displeased governess. "That is only an assumption. I told you there is a brothel where one partner hands money to respectable young women who have got into debt for one reason or another . . ."

"Yes, you did. What has that to do with it?"

"He was the partner!" she said. Then, seeing the disgust in his face, "I thought you'd think so. He lent the money, and Squeaky Robinson ran the brothel. But Baltimore was a client as well! That was why he was killed, for taking his tastes too far. One of the girls rebelled, and pushed him out of a top-floor window. Squeaky had the body moved to Abel Smith's place."

"Have you told the police?"

"No! I had a much better idea."

She was glowing with satisfaction. He had a sinking dread that he would have to destroy it. "Better?" he said guardedly.

"Yes. I have burnt the IOUs and put Squeaky Robinson out of business. We shall take over the premises, without rent, and the young women there can nurse the others who are sick or injured."

"You did that?" he said incredulously. "How?"

"Well, not by myself . . ."

"Indeed?" His voice rose in spite of himself. "And whose

help did you enlist? Or would I very much prefer not to know?"

"Oh, it is perfectly respectable!" she protested. "Margaret Ballinger and Oliver!"

"What?" He could not grasp it.

She smiled up at him and kissed him gently on the cheek. Then she told him precisely what they had done, ending with an apology. "I'm afraid it doesn't help with the railway fraud. It doesn't have anything to do with it."

"No," he agreed, but there was a tiny spark of pride warm inside him. "I have to go back to Liverpool for that."

"Oh . . ."

Then, in turn, he told her what Runcorn had said.

"It isn't proof, is it?" she agreed. "But they must have rerouted the track for some reason, and Miss Harcus said they were expecting an enormous profit which must be kept secret." She looked at him very steadily. "What are you going to do?"

It made it easier for him that without question she assumed he was going to do something.

"Go back to Liverpool," he replied. "Try to find out exactly what mistakes Arrol Dundas made that he was caught." He saw her eyes widen and heard her indrawn breath, let out again without speaking. "For this case," he replied. "Not the past."

She relaxed and smiled.

He went back to the same lodgings in Liverpool where he now felt familiar, even welcome. The first thing was to find if Katrina Harcus had been born here. It would be in the early 1830s, to judge from her age. That was just before the compulsory registration of births, so it would be a matter of finding a record of her baptism in a local church. There was nothing to do but go from one parish to another enquiring. He telegraphed Rathbone to that effect.

It took him four weary and tedious days to find the entry in the records of a small Gothic church on the outskirts of Liverpool. Katrina Mary Harcus. Her mother was Pamela Mary

Harcus. Her father was not listed. The inference was obvious. Illegitimacy was a stigma from which few recovered. He felt a stab of pity as he saw the solitary entry. He stood in the faintly dusty aisle where the sunlight fell in vivid jewel patches from the stained-glass windows, watching the parish priest walking towards him. Perhaps it was not so surprising that Katrina had left home and gone to London, where she was unknown, even friendless, to seek some future better than the taint of being a bastard which would follow her everywhere here.

"Did you find it?" the minister asked helpfully.

"Yes, thank you," Monk replied. "Does Mrs. Harcus still live in the parish?"

The Reverend Rider's bland, pleasant face filled with sadness. "No," he said quietly. "She died nearly three months ago, poor woman." He sighed. "She used to be such a charming creature, full of life, full of hope. Always saw the best in everything. Never the same after . . ." He checked himself just before speaking. "After her benefactor died," he finished.

Was that a euphemism for her lover, Katrina's father?

"Were things hard for her after that?" Monk asked solicitously. He was affecting pity for the vicar's sake; ordinarily he would have felt it, but at the moment he simply could not afford the emotional energy to let it fill him as it should.

"Yes . . . yes." Rider pursed his lips and nodded his head. "To be alone, in failing health and with little means is a hard thing for anyone. People can be very unkind, Mr. Monk. We tend to look at our own weaknesses with such charity and other people's with so little. I suppose it is because we know the fierceness of the temptation to our own, and all the reasons why that exception to the rule was understandable. With other people we know only what we see, and even that is not always the truth."

Monk knew more exactly what he meant than the vicar could have known. His loss of memory had forced him to see his own actions with that partial and outward eye, mostly through the lens of others, and understanding nothing. To be judged that way was acutely painful. He could feel closing on him the threat of answering for wrongs committed in a time he could not remember, and as if by another man. He had tried so hard to shed the old ruthlessness, the indifference. Was the past not now going to allow him that?

But he had no time for indulgence of his own feelings, however crowding and urgent.

"Yes," he agreed, to avoid the appearance of abruptness. "It is a narrowness common to most of us. Perhaps a little time being judged, instead of judging, would be a salutary thing."

Rider smiled. "Perceptive of you, Mr. Monk."

"Do you know who her benefactor was? Perhaps the father of her daughter, whom I knew, and attempted to help with a particular problem she was seeking to address."

"Knew?" Rider said quickly, catching the past tense.

"I am afraid she is dead." Monk did not have to pretend the grief. And it was more than guilt that he had not prevented it; it was a loss for someone who had been full of passion and urgency, much of which he had shared, even though she had not known it.

Rider looked crushed, a great weariness filled him. "Oh, dear . . . I am sorry," he said quietly. "She was always so very full of life. Was it an accident?"

"No." Monk risked the truth. "She was murdered . . ." He stopped as he saw the shock in Rider's eyes, almost as if he had walked into something unseen and without any warning found himself bruised and on the floor.

"I'm sorry," Monk apologized. "I should have told you less frankly. I am concerned because I fear they may have arrested the wrong man, and there is little time to learn the truth."

"How can I help?"

Monk was not sure, but he asked the obvious question. "Who was her father? And how long ago did she leave here?"

"About two years ago," Rider answered, frowning in concentration.

"And her father?" Monk pressed.

Rider looked at him ruefully. "I don't see how it can have anything to do with her death. It was many years ago. All those involved are dead now . . . even poor Katrina. Allow them to rest in peace, Mr. Monk."

"If they are dead," Monk argued, "then they cannot be hurt by it. I will tell no one, unless it is necessary in order to save the life of a man who will be hanged for killing her, and may be innocent."

Rider sighed, his face crumpled with regret. "I'm sorry, Mr. Monk, but I cannot break the confidences, even of the dead. You already know from the baptismal record more than I would have told you. Apart from my personal regard, these people were my parishioners, and their trust was my charge. If the young man is innocent, then the law will find him so, and for poor Katrina's sake, find the one who was guilty. Perhaps for his sake also, although it is not ours to judge." He took a long, deep breath. "I am deeply sorry to hear of her death, Mr. Monk, but I cannot help you."

Monk did not pursue it. He could see in Rider's gentle, sad face that his conviction would not waver.

"I am sorry to have brought you such news," he said quietly. "Thank you for your time."

Rider nodded. "Good day, Mr. Monk, and may God guide you in your quest."

Monk hesitated, steeling himself, and turned back.

"Mr. Rider, did Katrina have a friend named Emma?" His heart was beating so wildly he could feel it lurch inside him. He saw the answer in Rider's face before he spoke.

"Not that I am aware of. I am sorry. To my knowledge there was only herself and her mother—and her aunt, Eveline Austin. But she died some ten or twelve years ago. But of course I shall mention her death in church next Sunday, and no doubt word will pass." He smiled sadly. "Bad news so quickly does."

Monk swallowed, his mouth dry. He could feel everything precious, all the life he knew, infinitely precious, slipping away like water between his fingers, and there was nothing he could do to hold on to it.

"Are you all right, Mr. Monk?" Rider said anxiously.

"You look a little unwell. I am so sorry to be of . . . of so little assistance."

"No!" Monk steadied himself. This was an escape, but he was far from free yet. "Thank you. You have simply told me the truth. Thank you for your time. Good day."

"Good day, Mr. Monk."

11

T *HE ARRANGEMENT* with Squeaky Robinson, at least so far, was working very well. It had been a major undertaking to move all the beds, other furniture, and medicines and equipment from Coldbath Square to Portpool Lane, but the women who were now released from debt were mostly overjoyed to find a way of earning their living which was completely admirable and required of them no lies or evasions. Nor was there fear of being dismissed for not meeting with the moral standards of some mistress because of a past which must be hidden.

Squeaky complained bitterly, but Hester believed that at least part of it was because he thought it was expected of him. His most urgent concern was gone, and he was immensely relieved, even if he refused to admit it.

She had had great satisfaction in telling Jessop that he would no longer be troubled by the questionable tenants in his Coldbath house, since they had found alternative premises, which were larger, and at better rental—in fact, at no rental at all—and would be leaving as soon as was possible, a day or two at the most.

He had looked nonplussed. "It was an agreement, Mrs. Monk!" he protested. "You still owe a month's notice, you know."

"No, I don't," she had said flatly. "You threatened to evict us, and I believed you. I have found another place, as you said I should."

He had blustered, and refused to pay back the rent for the week paid for but apparently not to be used.

She had smiled at him, perhaps not as sweetly as she had meant to, and told him it did not matter in the slightest, which confused him. That in turn had made him angry. By the time the exchange was completed they had gathered quite an audience, all very plainly on Hester's side.

Jessop had left enraged, but knowing better than to make any threats. It was not a neighborhood in which to incur enemies who might have more power than you did yourself, and Jessop knew his limitations. Whoever had given Hester and Margaret premises, at no charge, must have a good deal of money to waste, and money was power.

They watched him go with immeasurable satisfaction, Bessie chortling with joy.

She also assured both Hester and Margaret that she could manage very well without them during the daytime once the trial of Michael Dalgarno began. Should there be an emergency she would send one of the local urchins for Mr. Lockhart, and then if that was still not enough, for one of them as well. However, since there was still little business going on, and the people of the streets were generally allied together against circumstances, at least as long as this crisis lasted, there was greater peace than usual among them.

Constable Hart also promised to give discreet assistance, if such were needed. Hester thanked him profusely, to his embarrassment, and gave him a jar of black currant jam, which he accepted, taking it with both hands. Even Bessie decided that perhaps he was an exception to the general rules about police.

So when the trial opened, Margaret, Hester and Monk were all sitting in the public gallery. Dalgarno was white-faced in the dock, Jarvis Baltimore fidgeting unhappily a few rows in front of them, Livia silent and wretched beside him, as Mr. Talbot Fowler began the case for the prosecution.

He was extremely efficient. He called witness after witness to show that Dalgarno was talented, ambitious, gifted with figures, and that he was undoubtedly the one who had accomplished most of the land negotiations for Baltimore and Sons with regard to the London-to-Derby railway.

On the second day he demonstrated that Dalgarno had paid court to Katrina Harcus, albeit not as openly as he might have done. They had been seen together quite often enough to substantiate her belief in his affection for her. Indeed, two of the witnesses had expected them to announce an engagement within the month.

Margaret sat beside Hester, leaning forward a little. Several times she seemed to be on the edge of speech, and Hester knew she was wondering why Rathbone did not cross-examine the witnesses, at least to appear to offer some kind of a defense. It was only her care for Rathbone which prevented her each time from putting her anxiety into whispered words. It would seem like a criticism.

On the other side of Hester, Monk was sitting equally tense, his shoulders high and stiff, his eyes strained forward. He must be thinking the same thing, but for entirely different reasons. If Rathbone failed, for him it was far more than disappointment in someone with whom he was falling in love; it would almost certainly mean changing places with the man in the dock.

And yet as Fowler paraded one witness after another, Rathbone said and did nothing.

"For God's sake!" Monk said desperately that evening as he paced his sitting room floor. "He can't be going to let it go by default. He's got to do more than just hope they can't prove it. Does he want to get accused of an incompetent defense?" He was ashen-faced, his eyes hollow. "He's not doing that to save me, is he?"

"No, of course not," Hester said instantly, standing in front of him.

"Not for me," Monk said with painful humor. "For you."

She caught his arm. "He's not still in love with me."

"The more fool he!" he retorted.

"He's in love with Margaret," she explained. "At least he soon will be."

He drew in his breath, staring at her. "I didn't know that!"

A flash of impatience crossed her face and disappeared.

"You wouldn't," she replied. "I don't know what he's going to do, William, but he'll do something—for honor, pride, all kinds of things. He won't let it go without a fight."

But Rathbone was unavailable all weekend. When Hester went to fetch fresh milk on Saturday morning, Monk snatched a few moments alone to look again at Katrina's diary. He hated doing it, but he was desperate enough to grasp after any clue at all.

But he still could understand only fragments of it. It was cryptic, scattered words as if simply to remind herself of emotions; the people who inspired them were so woven into her life she needed nothing more to bring them back to her. Nothing made a chain of sense.

He struggled with his own memory. There was something just beyond his grasp, something that defined it all, but the shadows blurred and the harder he looked the more rapidly it dissolved into chaos, leaving him dependent on the slow, minute process of the law.

On Monday morning, when the trial resumed for the third day, it looked as if letting go without a fight was exactly what Rathbone was going to do.

Monk, Hester and Margaret all sat in an agony of impatience as Fowler brought on the police witnesses, first the constable called to the scene who found the body, then Runcorn, who described his own part in the proceedings.

At last Rathbone accepted the invitation, now offered somewhat sarcastically, to cross-examine the witness.

"Good gracious!" Fowler said in amazement, playing to the jury, who until now had had nothing to consider but uncontested evidence.

"Superintendent Runcorn," Rathbone began courteously. "You described your conduct in excellent detail. You appear to have overlooked nothing."

Runcorn eyed him with suspicion. He was far too experienced at giving evidence to imagine a compliment was merely that. "Thank you, sir," he said flatly.

"And presumably you tried to find evidence proving that

this cloak found on the roof from which Miss Harcus fell belonged to Mr. Dalgarno?"

"Naturally," Runcorn conceded.

"And did you succeed?" Rathbone enquired.

"No, sir."

"Mr. Dalgarno doesn't have a cloak?"

"Yes, sir, but it's not that one."

"Has he two, then?"

"Not that we can trace, sir. But that doesn't mean it wasn't his," Runcorn said defensively.

"Of course not. He purchased this one secretly in order to leave it on the rooftop after he had thrown Miss Harcus off it to her death."

There was a nervous titter around the room. Several jurors looked confused. Jarvis Baltimore reached across and slid his hand over Livia's.

"If you say so, sir," Runcorn replied blandly.

"No, no, I do not say so!" Rathbone retorted. "You say so! I say it belonged to someone else . . . who was on the roof and was responsible for Miss Harcus's death . . . someone you never thought of trying to trace."

"No one else had reason," Runcorn said calmly.

"That you know of!" Rathbone challenged him. "I will presently show you a completely different interpretation of circumstances, Superintendent, one beyond your wildest ideas . . . which you would never seek to prove because it is extraordinary beyond anything else I have ever heard, and no man could be expected to think of it. Thank you. That is all."

Monk swiveled to look at Hester, his eyes wide.

"I don't know," she whispered back. "I've no idea."

The jurors were staring at each other. There was a buzz of speculation in the body of the court.

"Grandstanding!" Fowler said audibly, disgust heavy in his voice.

Rathbone smiled to himself, but Hester had a hideous fear that he was doing exactly that, and that Fowler was not blustering, but knew it.

Margaret sat with her knuckles white, leaning forward a little.

Fowler called his next witness—the police surgeon, of whom Rathbone asked nothing—and then began on the neighbors who had seen or heard something that evening.

Rathbone glanced at his watch now and then.

"What is he waiting for?" Monk hissed.

"I don't know!" Hester said more sharply than she had intended. What could Rathbone hope for? What other solution was there? He had not shaken any of the testimony at all, let alone suggested the alternative he had spoken of so dramatically.

They adjourned for the day and people trooped out into the halls and corridors. Hester overheard more than one say that they would not bother to return.

"I don't know why a man like Rathbone would take such a case," one man said disgustedly as he began down the broad steps into the street. "There's nothing in it for him but defeat, and he knows it."

"He can't be doing as well as we thought," his companion replied.

"He knows his client's guilty!" The first man pursed his lips. "Still, I'd have thought he'd try, for the look of it."

Hester was so angry she started forward, but stopped as she felt the pressure of Monk's hand on her arm. She swung around to face him.

"What were you going to say?" he asked.

She drew breath to reply, and realized she had nothing prepared that made sense. She saw Margaret's misery and growing confusion. "He'll fight!" she assured her, because she knew how badly Margaret wanted to believe it.

Margaret made an attempt at a smile, but excused herself to find a hansom home before facing the evening in Coldbath Square.

Hester began the fourth day of the trial with a sinking heart. She had lain awake in the night wondering whether to go to Rathbone's house and demand to see him, but realized there was nothing she could learn that would help, and certainly she had nothing to offer him. She had no idea who could have killed Katrina Harcus, or why. She knew it was not Monk, and was less and less certain that it was Dalgarno, although she could not like the man. Looking at him through the days so far she had seen fear in his face, in the hunched angle of his shoulders, the tight lips and pallor of his skin, but she had not seen pity for the dead woman. Nor had she seen any concern for Livia Baltimore, who was growing more miserable with each new piece of testimony that showed how callously he had treated a young woman who had believed he loved her, and whom, all evidence showed, deeply loved him.

In court in the morning she looked at Livia. Her skin was pale and puffy around the eyes, her body rigid, and Hester knew she was still clinging to hope. But even if Rathbone could somehow perform a miracle and gain an acquittal of murder for Dalgarno, was there anything on earth he could do to show him innocent of duplicity and opportunism?

Fowler concluded for the prosecution.

Hester slipped her hand over Monk's briefly. It was easier than trying to find words when she had no idea what to say.

Rathbone rose to begin the defense. The public gallery was almost half empty. He called the surveyor again.

Fowler complained that he was wasting the court's time. The surveyor had already testified in great detail. The subject had been more than exhausted.

"My lord," Rathbone said patiently, "my learned friend knows as well as the rest of us that I was able only to cross-examine him on the subjects already spoken of in direct examination."

"Can there possibly be any other subjects left?" Fowler asked to a ripple of laughter from the crowd. "We already know far more about the building of railways than we need to, or I imagine than we wish to."

"Possibly than we wish to, my lord." Rathbone smiled very slightly. "Not than we need to. We have still reached no unarguable conclusion."

"You are lawyers," the judge said dryly. "You can argue

any conclusion on earth! However, proceed, Sir Oliver, but do not waste our time. If you appear to be talking for the sake of it I shall sustain Mr. Fowler's objection—indeed, I shall object myself."

Rathbone bowed with a smile. "I shall endeavor not to be tedious or irrelevant, my lord," he promised.

The judge looked skeptical.

Rathbone faced the surveyor when he had been duly reminded of his previous oath and had restated his professional qualifications. "Mr. Whitney," he began, "you have already told us that you surveyed both the originally intended route for the railway of Baltimore and Sons from London to Derby and the route now taken. Is there a significant difference in cost between the two?"

"No, sir, not significant," Whitney replied.

"What do you consider significant?" Rathbone asked.

Whitney thought for a moment. "Above a few hundred pounds," he replied at length. "Hardly as much as a thousand."

"A lot of money," Rathbone observed. "Sufficient to buy several houses for an ordinary family."

Fowler rose to his feet.

The judge waved him down again and looked at Rathbone. "If you are intending to reach any conclusion, Sir Oliver, you have diverted further than the railway in question. You would be better occupied justifying your own circuitous journey."

There was a titter from the crowd. This, at least, was mildly entertaining. They were happy to see Rathbone baited; he was better game than the accused, who had long since lost any sympathy they might have felt for him.

Rathbone took a deep breath and steadied his temper. He acknowledged the judge's remark and turned again to the witness stand. "Mr. Whitney, would it be technically possible to commit a far greater fraud than the one suggested here, one worth several thousands of pounds, by this same means of diverting a proposed route?"

Whitney looked startled. "Yes, of course it would. This was only a slightly greater length, a few hundred yards. One could do far more to make money."

"For example?" Rathbone asked.

Whitney shrugged. "Buy land oneself, prior to the rerouting, and then sell it back at an inflated price," he answered. "Many things, with enough imagination and the right contacts. Choose a stretch where a lot of construction was necessary, bridges, viaducts, tunnels, even long cuttings, and take a percentage on materials—the possibilities are numerous."

"My lord!" Fowler said loudly. "My learned friend is simply showing that the accused is incompetent even at fraud. That is not an excuse."

There was open laughter in the room. No one pretended not to be amused.

When it had died down Rathbone turned to him. "I am attempting to prove that he is innocent of murder," he said politely, but with an underlying anger. "Why is it that you seem unwilling to allow me to do that?"

"It is circumstances that are preventing you, not I," Fowler returned to another rustle of laughter.

"Your circumstances!" Rathbone snapped. "Mine not only allow me to, they oblige me to."

"Mr. Fowler!" the judge said very clearly. "Sir Oliver has a point. Unless you have some objection of substance in law, will you cease from interrupting him, or we are likely to be here indefinitely!"

"Thank you, my lord," Rathbone said ironically. Hester believed that he was, in fact, spinning out time, but she had no idea what for. What, or whom, was he expecting? She felt the first sudden shiver of hope.

Rathbone looked up at Whitney. "You have given us examples of other ways in which a more efficient fraud could be perpetuated. Have you knowledge of any such fraud—I mean a specific circumstance?"

Whitney looked slightly puzzled.

"For example," Rathbone assisted him, "in Liverpool almost sixteen years ago? The company involved was Baltimore and Sons. There was a falsification of a survey, the grid references were changed . . ."

Fowler stood up again.

"Sit down, Mr. Fowler!" the judge commanded. He looked at Rathbone sternly. "I presume you have facts, Sir Oliver? Be careful you do not slander anyone."

"It is a matter of record, my lord," Rathbone assured him. "A man named Arrol Dundas was convicted of the crime, and unfortunately died in prison of jail fever. But the details of the crime were made public at the trial."

"I see. The relevance to this present case may easily be guessed, nevertheless we require you to prove it."

"Yes, my lord. I shall prove that records of it were kept by Baltimore and Sons, therefore it was known to senior members of the present company, even though they were not involved—in fact, not even out of school—at the time."

"Very interesting. Be sure that it is also relevant to Mr. Dalgarno's innocence."

"Yes, my lord." Rathbone drew out a few more details from Whitney, then excused him. Fowler looked as if he were considering asking him something, then declined, and Whitney left the stand.

Hester looked at Monk, but it was obvious from his tense, white face and the confusion in his eyes that he did not know what Rathbone was planning any more than she did. He was frowning, and staring at the court clerk, busily taking notes, his right hand bandaged. Fortunately, he wrote with his left.

Rathbone then called a junior clerk from Baltimore and Sons and drew from him the statement that the records of the earlier dealings were available—not easily, but a diligent search by a company member would elicit them all.

"And was the case public knowledge?" Rathbone said finally.

"Oh, yes, sir."

Fowler tried to show that it was an abstruse piece of information, never discussed and unlikely to come to the attention of Dalgarno.

"I couldn't say, sir," the clerk replied soberly. "I would think such things would be known, sir, even if only as an object lesson in what not to do."

Fowler retreated. "I still say, my lord, that incompetence

does not equal innocence!" he said tartly. "The Crown does not say that the accused committed fraud well, merely that he did it!"

Rathbone opened his eyes very wide. "If the Crown wishes, my lord, I can call a number of witnesses to demonstrate that Mr. Dalgarno was an ambitious and extremely able young man, that he rose from a relatively minor position to become one of the partners—"

The judge held up his hand. "You have already done so, Sir Oliver. We take the point that the nature of the fraud with which he is charged is far less efficient than the earlier example for which Mr. Dundas was found guilty. The only thing relevant to this case appears to be the fact that the earlier case may well have been known to Mr. Dalgarno, and one wonders why he did not emulate it, if fraud was his intention. So far you have not completed your task. Please be succinct!"

"Yes, my lord." Rathbone recalled the foreman of the team of navvies who had worked on the Derby line, and drew from him greater and more tedious detail of the cutting and blasting necessary to drive a track through a hillside, coupled with the labor and cost of building a viaduct. He could equally easily have asked Jarvis Baltimore, but the navvy was not only more skilled in detail, he was demonstrably impartial.

The court did not bother to hide its total lack of interest.

They adjourned for luncheon. Monk told Hester to go with Margaret and he would join them later. Unwillingly, she obeyed, and he strode forward, shouldering his way through the crowd moving in the opposite direction until he was standing in front of the court clerk.

"Excuse me," he said, trying not to be abrupt, and yet his voice was sharp.

The man made an effort to be civil. He was still trying to catch up with his notes. His writing was cramped, awkward, and with an odd, backward slope. Monk felt a strange dizziness in his mind as if there was something familiar about it. Could his idea be right?

"Yes, sir?" the clerk said patiently.

"What did you do to your hand?" Monk asked him.

"I burned it, sir." The clerk blushed very slightly. "On the cooking stove."

"You were writing with your other hand yesterday, weren't you?"

"Yes, sir. Fortunately, I can write with either hand. Not so neatly, but it'll do."

"Thank you," Monk said with a surge of understanding like a blaze of sunlight. He could picture exactly the odd characteristic capital *G*'s and *E*'s in Katrina's diary, and sloping back, but still the same, in Emma's. And suddenly the inscription in the recipe book—Eveline Mary M. Austin—EMMA! She had loved Katrina, and Katrina had kept her alive in her imagination by writing to her, and even from her, using her left hand.

It was a painful and eccentric thing to do, and even with the explanation, it troubled him.

At the beginning of the afternoon there were even fewer people in the public seats.

"I call Miss Livia Baltimore," Rathbone said to an immediate hiss of speculation and distaste. Livia herself looked startled, as if she were unprepared, but there was interest again from the crowd. Several jury members straightened in their seats as she made her way across the floor of the court and climbed the steps to the stand, pulling herself a little on the handrail as if she needed its support.

"I apologize for putting you through this ordeal, Miss Baltimore," Rathbone said gently. "Were it avoidable I would not do so, but a man's life hangs in the balance."

"I know," she said so quietly it was barely audible. The slight rustle of movement in the body of the court ceased, as if everyone were straining not to miss a word. "I will do anything I can to help you prove that Mr. Dalgarno did not do this terrible thing."

"And your testimony will assist me greatly," he assured her. "If you tell the exact truth as you know it, absolutely exact! Please trust me in this, Miss Baltimore."

"I do," she whispered.

The judge asked her to speak more loudly, and she repeated it: "I do!"

Rathbone smiled. "I imagine you have a natural sympathy for Miss Harcus. She was young, like yourself, not more than four or five years older, and very much in love with a charming and dynamic man. You must know how she felt, her whole future before her, full of promise."

She swallowed convulsively, and nodded.

"I am sorry, but we need you to speak," Rathbone said apologetically.

"Yes, I do," she said huskily. "I can imagine it very well."

"Have you ever been in love, Miss Baltimore, even if it had not yet reached more than a matter of understanding between you?"

Fowler was on his feet. "My lord, that is completely irrelevant to the issue of this court, and it is grossly intrusive! Miss Baltimore's personal feelings have no place here and should be respected by—"

The judge flapped his hand at him impatiently. "Yes, yes, Mr. Fowler. Sir Oliver, your point? Or you may continue no further on this rambling excursion of yours."

"My lord." Rathbone looked up at Livia. "Miss Baltimore, has Mr. Dalgarno paid court to you? Please do not be modest or discreet to the detriment of the truth. Trust me. And do not oblige me to ask other witnesses to refute any denial made in the effort to protect your reputation. There is nothing to be ashamed of in someone's paying court to you, even professing love and asking you for your hand in marriage."

Her face was scarlet, but she looked directly at Rathbone. "Yes. Mr. Dalgarno has done me the honor of asking me to marry him. We are simply not in a position to make the matter public so soon after my father's death. It would be insensitive . . . and . . . wrong."

There was a gasp of breath around the court. Now, at last, Rathbone had their attention. The judge's eyes opened very wide, and he shook his head slowly from side to side, not in denial but in surprise.

Fowler rose to his feet, and then before anyone directed him, sat down again.

"Just so," Rathbone said when the noise permitted him. "Not to mention the death of his previous fiancée, who heard of his change of heart only weeks earlier, but still kept her own passionate feelings toward him. I assume, Miss Baltimore, that although she must have been made aware of you, you were not aware of her?"

Hester looked across at Dalgarno and saw the tight, desperate look in his face. He had to see the jurors' increasing contempt for him. In law, to have deceived and discarded a woman, unless there were a promise, was not an offense. But he also knew that logic does not always override emotion. He shot a look of pure loathing at Rathbone, which had he seen it, should have scorched his tongue into silence.

Livia looked as if Rathbone had struck her. The blush faded from her face, leaving her ash pale, struggling to catch her breath. "Michael wouldn't kill her!" she gasped. "He wouldn't!" But it sounded more like a plea than an assurance.

"No, Miss Baltimore," Rathbone agreed loudly and very clearly. "Of course he wouldn't. He had no cause to wish her harm, merely to desire that she leave him alone to pursue a more fitting bride. Did you ever see her in your home after the time Mr. Dalgarno began to court you?"

She shook her head, her eyes brimming with tears.

"No," Rathbone repeated for her. "Or in any public place, seeking to embarrass or pursue Mr. Dalgarno?"

"No," she whispered.

"In fact, you were unaware of her interest in him at all?"

"Yes . . . I was."

"Thank you, Miss Baltimore. That is all I have to ask you."

Fowler shook his head. "This is irrelevant, my lord. We are chasing ghosts. All my learned friend has demonstrated is Dalgarno's abandonment of his commitment to a relatively poor woman when a richer one gave him hope that he might woo her successfully."

"No, my lord," Rathbone contradicted him. "I am showing the court that Miss Harcus had every reason to feel desperately betrayed by a man she loved, and whom she had sincerely believed loved her. That, with other facts I shall also bring witnesses and documents to prove, will explain what happened on the night of her death, and why. And it will show that Mr. Dalgarno had no intentional hand in it. He is guilty of no more than abusing a woman's love, which I regret to say is something many men have done and walked away from. It is regarded by most of us as contemptible, but not as criminal."

"Then do so, Sir Oliver," the judge instructed. "You have still some way to go."

"Yes, my lord," Rathbone said obediently.

He was bluffing, Hester knew it with certainty. A coldness gripped her.

"A witness, if you please, Sir Oliver," the judge said plaintively. "Let us proceed. We still have at least an hour before we may reasonably adjourn."

"Yes, my lord. I call Mr. Wilbur Garstang."

"We have already heard from Mr. Garstang . . . at some length!" Fowler protested.

"We have already heard from everybody at some length, yourself included," the judge retorted. "Please keep your interruptions to the minimum, Mr. Fowler. Sir Oliver, is there really anything Mr. Garstang can do beyond fill the time?"

"Yes, my lord, I believe so," Rathbone answered, although there was surely more truth in the judge's comment than he could afford to admit.

"Call Wilbur Garstang," the judge said wearily.

Mr. Garstang climbed the steps and was advised by the judge that he was still under oath. He was a precise little man with a carping attitude and an inclination to pick fault.

"I have already told you what I observed," he said to Rathbone, looking down at him over the top of his gold-rimmed eyeglasses.

"Indeed," Rathbone agreed. "But I wish to reestablish it in the minds of the jury, with rather a different emphasis. You are an exact and acute observer, Mr. Garstang, that is why I chose you to speak yet again. I apologize for the inconvenience no doubt it causes you."

Garstang grunted, but a look of satisfaction smoothed out his features a little. He did not consider himself susceptible to flattery, in which he was profoundly mistaken.

"I shall do my best," Garstang said, straightening his lapels a trifle and assuming an expression of readiness.

Rathbone hid a smile, but he was tense. Even his movements lacked their usual grace. "Thank you. Mr. Garstang, you were at your window on the night of Miss Harcus's death. Would you please remind us of the reason for this?"

"Certainly." Garstang nodded. "My sitting room is opposite her rooms, and very slightly below, the stories of the house in which my apartment is situated being a foot or two less in height. I heard a noise, as if someone were crying out. In case that were so, and they were in need of assistance, I went to the window and drew the curtains so that I might see."

"Just so," Rathbone cut across him. "Now, would you tell us exactly what you did see, as precisely as if you were painting a picture? Please do not tell us what you believed or have since heard that it was. I realize that this is difficult, and takes a very exact and literal mind."

"Oh . . . really . . ." Fowler groaned.

Garstang shot a look of acute dislike at him. He felt insulted, cut short and dismissed before he had even begun.

"Please, Mr. Garstang," Rathbone encouraged. "It is of the utmost importance. Indeed, someone's life is at stake."

Garstang assumed an attitude of intense concentration and held it until the court was silent, then he cleared his throat and began.

"I saw a dark shape on the balcony opposite. It seemed to heave and change outline violently, and to move from the open doorway across towards the edge. It surged back and forth for several moments, I cannot tell how long because I was horrified by the prospect of the tragedy about to happen."

"Why was that?" Rathbone said.

"You asked me to be literal," Garstang said crossly. "I described to you exactly what I saw, but it was perfectly obvious to me that it was two people struggling with each other, one intent upon hurling the other off the balcony onto the stones beneath."

"But you did not see two separate figures?" Rathbone asked.

"I did not. They were locked in mortal combat." Garstang's voice was schoolmasterly, as to a particularly stupid child. "If he had even once let go of her she might have escaped him, and we should not be here to see justice done after the event."

"Let us remember that we are here to see justice done," Rathbone reminded him. "Not to exercise our personal feelings. You have described what you saw very precisely so far, Mr. Garstang. Did you see a figure go off the balcony and actually fall?"

"Yes, of course I did. That is when I left the window and ran out of the room and down the steps to see if I could help the poor woman, or on the other hand apprehend her murderer," Garstang replied.

Rathbone held up his hand. "Just a moment, Mr. Garstang. I am afraid I need you to be more precise than that. I apologize for what must be distressing to any decent person. I assure you I would not do it were there any other way."

Fowler stood up. "My lord, this witness has already told us in overlong detail what he saw. My learned friend is flattering—"

"I am not flattering the witness at all, my lord!" Rathbone cut across. "Mr. Garstang may be the only man who observed exactly what happened and is capable of telling us not what he has since concluded but what actually was."

"If you do not have a point, Sir Oliver, I shall not indulge you again!" the judge warned. "Proceed, but be brief."

The relief in Rathbone was visible even from where Hester sat, but she had no idea why. She could see nothing whatever changed. She glanced at Monk, and saw equal confusion in his face.

Rathbone looked up at Garstang. "Mr. Garstang, you saw her go off the balcony. You are sure it was she who went off?"

There was a moment of silent incredulity, then a rush of sound, a babble, disgust, laughter, anger.

Garstang stared at him, disbelief giving way to a slow, terrible memory.

The noise in the room subsided. Even Fowler sank back into his seat.

Monk craned forward.

Hester sat with her hands clenched.

"I saw her face . . ." Garstang said hoarsely. "I saw her face as she fell . . . white . . . she was . . ." He shuddered violently. "She was between murder . . . and death." He put both hands up to his eyes.

"I apologize, Mr. Garstang," Rathbone said gently and with sudden sincerity that was like a warmth in the room. He was speaking for an instant only to Garstang, not the court. "But your evidence is the key to the whole, terrible, tragic truth, and we all thank you for your courage of the mind, sir. You have saved a man's life today."

Fowler stood up and swiveled around as if looking for something that was not there.

Rathbone turned to him and smiled. "Your witness, Mr. Fowler."

"For what?" Fowler demanded. "He has said nothing! What on earth does it matter that he saw her face? We all know it was she who fell!" He looked at the judge. "This is preposterous, my lord. Sir Oliver is making a farce out of a tragedy. Whether he is legally in contempt of court or not, morally he is."

"I am inclined to agree," the judge said with apparent reluctance. "Sir Oliver, you have certainly caught our attention, but you have proved nothing. I cannot allow you to continue in this manner. We have the public in our courts in order that they may see that justice is done, not as a form of entertainment. I shall not allow you to yield any further to the temptation to become a performer, in spite of your obvious talent in that direction."

There was a murmur of nervous laughter around the court.

Rathbone bowed as if contrite. "I assure you, my lord, I shall shortly show how the fact that Mr. Garstang saw her face is of the utmost importance."

"Are you questioning her identity?" the judge said with amazement.

"No, my lord. If I may call my next witness?"

"You may, but this testimony had better be relevant or I shall hold you in contempt, Sir Oliver."

"It will be, my lord, thank you. I call the Reverend David Rider."

Hester heard Monk's gasp of indrawn breath and saw him lurch forward in his seat.

Margaret turned to stare at Hester, and then at Monk, the question in her face. Hester looked at her helplessly.

The court watched in silence as the vicar climbed the steps up to the witness-box, his hands gripping the rail as if to steady his balance. He looked tired, but worn out by emotion rather than any physical effort. His skin was pale and puffy around the eyes, and he looked back at Rathbone as if there was some profound understanding between them of more than grief, some overwhelming burden of knowledge which they shared.

Rider swore to his name, his occupation and his residence on the outskirts of Liverpool.

"Why are you here, Mr. Rider?" Rathbone asked gravely.

Rider spoke very quietly. "I have been wrestling with my conscience ever since Mr. Monk came to see me over a week ago, and I have come to the conclusion that my greater obligation is to tell that part of the truth that I know regarding Katrina Harcus. My duty to the living is too great to deny in order to protect the dead."

There was a slight rustle of movement in the court, and then total silence.

Hester looked across at Dalgarno, as did several of the jurors, but they saw only complete confusion.

"You knew Katrina Harcus?" Rathbone asked.

"From her birth," Rider replied.

Fowler shifted in his seat in apparent discomfort, but he did not interrupt.

"Then I presume you also know her mother?" Rathbone said.

"Yes. Pamela Harcus was my parishioner."

"You say was," Rathbone observed. "Is she now dead?"

"Yes. She died some three months ago. I . . . I am glad she did not live to see this."

"Indeed, Mr. Rider." Rathbone bowed his head in acknowledgment of the tragedy of it. "Did you also know Katrina Harcus's father?"

"Not personally, but I knew of him." Then, without waiting for Rathbone to ask, he added, "His name was Arrol Dundas."

Monk let out an involuntary cry, and Hester reached out and put her hand on his arm, feeling the muscles hard underneath her touch.

The judge leaned forward. "Is this the same Arrol Dundas who was convicted of railway fraud sixteen years ago, Sir Oliver?"

"Yes, my lord."

"Let me understand you," the judge continued. "Was she his legitimate daughter or illegitimate?"

Rathbone looked at Rider in the witness-box.

"Illegitimate, my lord," Rider replied.

"What has that to do with her death?" Fowler demanded. "We all know that illegitimacy is a stigma that ruins lives. The sins of the fathers are visited upon the children whether we wish them to be or not, but it is irrelevant to her death, poor creature. It excuses nothing!"

"It is not offered as an excuse," Rathbone said tartly. He turned back to Rider. "To your knowledge, was Katrina aware of her father's identity?"

"Most certainly," Rider replied. "He provided handsomely for both Pamela Harcus and her daughter. He was a wealthy man and not ungenerous. She knew both him and his colleague, who apparently regarded her as if she were his niece."

"He was a man her father's age, I presume?" Rathbone said.

"As closely as I could judge," Rider agreed.

"But in spite of this her father could not legitimize her," Rathbone went on.

Rider looked even more unhappy. He moved his weight slightly, and his hands, swollen-jointed, gripped the railing of

the box. It was obvious that he still struggled with revealing
such information, which in his view was private and painful.

Hester looked at Monk, seeing in his face the crumbling of
disillusion, the fighting for memory, hunting for any bright
shards to redeem the darkness that was closing in. She ached
for something to help him, but there was no shelter or balm
for the truth.

"He could have," Rider said so quietly that the silence became even denser as everyone strained to catch his words. "It
was perhaps a dishonorable thing to do. His wife was in no
way at fault. To leave her in her middle years would be bar-
barous . . . a breaking of the covenant he had made in his marriage. But it would not have been impossible. Men do put
away their wives. With money, and lies, it can be achieved."

"But Arrol Dundas did not?"

Rider looked wretched. "He intended to. He was very torn.
His wife had no children. Pamela Harcus had given birth to
one, and might have had more. But he had a protégé, a young
man whom he regarded almost as a son, who in the end persuaded him not to. I daresay it was for Mrs. Dundas's sake."

Monk was so white Hester was afraid he was going to
faint. He seemed scarcely to be breathing and was oblivious
of her fingers gripping his arm. She did not even glance at
Margaret.

"Do you know his name?" Rathbone repeated.

"Yes . . . it was William Monk," Rider replied.

Monk very slowly put his hands up to his face, hiding it
even from Hester. Rathbone did not turn, but he could not
have been unaware of the effect the words would have.

"I see," he said. "And do you know if either Pamela Harcus
or Katrina was aware of who stopped their financial comfort,
and far more than that, their honor, their legitimacy, their social acceptance?"

"Katrina was only a child, perhaps seven or eight years
old," Rider answered. "But Pamela was aware, that I know for
certain. It was she who told me, but I did verify it for myself. I
spoke to Dundas."

"Did you try to change his mind?"

"Of course not. All I said was that he should be certain to make financial arrangement for them in the event of his death. He swore to me that he had already done so."

"So they were financially supported after he died?"

Rider's voice dropped until it was almost inaudible. "No sir, they were not."

"They were not?" Rathbone repeated.

Rider gripped the railings. "No. Arrol Dundas died in prison, for a fraud I personally do not believe he committed, but the proof at the time seemed unarguable."

"But his will?" Rathbone argued. "Surely that was executed according to his decisions?"

"I imagine so. The provision for Pamela and Katrina must have been a verbal one, perhaps to protect the feelings of his widow. She may have known of them, or she may not, but since a will is a public matter, it would be deeply hurtful for them to be mentioned," Rider replied. He looked down at his hands. "It was a written note, or so he told me. A personal instruction to his executor."

"Who was?" Rathbone stared at him, not for an instant turning towards the gallery where Monk sat white-faced and rigid.

"His protégé, William Monk," Rider said.

"Not the colleague to whom you referred earlier?" Rathbone asked.

"No. He trusted Mr. Monk uniquely."

"I see. So all the money went to Dundas's widow?"

"No. Not even she received more than a pittance," Rider answered him. "Dundas was a rich man at the time of his trial. When he died a few weeks later he had barely enough to provide a small house and an annuity for his widow, and that ceased upon her death."

There was a low rumble of anger in the room. Several people turned and glared at Monk. There were ugly words, catcalls.

"Silence!" the judge shouted, banging his gavel with a loud crack of wood on wood. "I will not have this unseemly noise in here. You are to listen, not to make judgments. Any more of this and I shall clear the court."

The sound subsided, but not the anger in the air.

Hester moved closer still to Monk, but she could think of nothing to say. She could feel the pain in him as if it were communicable, like heat.

On the other side of her, Margaret put her hand gently on Hester's. It was a generous moment of friendship.

"Then unless someone else assisted them, I assume that Pamela and Katrina Harcus lived in extremely straitened circumstances after Dundas's death?" Rathbone asked relentlessly.

"Extremely," Rider agreed. "I am afraid there was no one else to assist them. Her aunt, Eveline Austin, was also dead by this time."

"I see. Just one more thing, Mr. Rider. Would you be good enough to describe Katrina Harcus for us, if you please?"

"Describe her?" For the first time Rider looked puzzled. Until now he had understood everything with tragic intimacy, but this escaped him.

"If you please? What did she look like, as exactly as you can tell us?" Rathbone insisted.

Rider floundered a little. He was obviously uncomfortable with the personal details of such a thing.

"She . . . was . . . she was quite tall—for a woman, that is. She was handsome, very handsome, in an unconventional way . . ." He floundered to a stop.

"What color of hair had she?" Rathbone asked.

"Oh . . . dark, dark brown, with a sort of shine to it."

"Her eyes?"

"Ah . . . yes, her eyes were unusual, very fine indeed. Sort of golden brown, very fine."

"Thank you, Mr. Rider. I appreciate that this has been very difficult for you indeed, both because it concerns the tragic death of a woman you knew since her infancy, and because it required you to speak publicly of matters you would very much prefer to have kept in confidence." He turned to Fowler, still not looking up at Monk, or Hester beside him. "Your witness, sir."

Fowler regarded Rider, shaking his head slowly. "A sad but

not uncommon story. Has any of it got anything whatsoever to do with Michael Dalgarno having thrown her off the roof of her house?"

"I do not know, sir," Rider replied. "I had assumed that was what we were here to decide. From what I have heard from Sir Oliver, I believe it may."

"Well, from what we have heard from Sir Oliver, it is simply a piece of very moving but totally irrelevant tragic theater," Fowler said dryly. "The poor woman is dead . . . they both are! And Arrol Dundas and his wife also, and all except Katrina herself were gone before the crime which brings us here."

"Do I assume that means you have no questions to ask, Mr. Fowler?" the judge enquired.

"Oh, I certainly have a question, my lord, but I doubt Mr. Rider is in a position to answer it," Fowler said tartly. "It is— when is Sir Oliver going to address the defense of his client?"

"I am addressing something a little higher, but which will answer the same purpose, my lord," Rathbone said, and perhaps Hester was the only one in the room who could hear the edge of tension in his voice. Even through her own fear, and her agony for Monk, she knew that Rathbone was afraid also. He was gambling far more than he could afford to lose— Monk's life still lay in the balance. Rathbone was traveling, at least partially, blind.

She felt the heat rush through her, and then the chill.

"The truth," Rathbone finished. "I am trying to uncover the truth." And before Fowler could do more than sound a jeer, he went on. "I call William Monk, my lord."

12

I*T WAS A MOMENT* before Monk even registered what Rathbone had said.

"William!" Hester whispered anxiously.

Monk rose to his feet. He had to be aware of the enmity of the court. Hester could feel it in the air, see it in the eyes and the faces of those who turned to watch him make his slow, almost stumbling way forward across the open space of the court and up the steps of the witness stand.

Rathbone faced him without expression, as if he were controlling himself with such an intense effort not even ordinary contempt could escape it.

"I have little to ask you, Mr. Monk, simply for you to tell the court how Katrina Harcus was dressed when she met you on the several occasions you reported to her your progress regarding your search for evidence of fraud."

"My lord!" Fowler said in an outburst of exasperation. "This is preposterous!"

Monk looked equally baffled. His face was as white as Dalgarno's in the dock, and the jurors were staring at him as if they would as willingly have seen him there alongside the accused.

"If you please!" Rathbone said urgently, at last his own near-panic breaking through. "Were her clothes good or poor? Did she wear the same things each time?"

"No!" Monk said quickly, as if breaking out of his stupor at last. "She dressed very well indeed. I wish I could afford to dress my wife as well."

Hester closed her eyes, wrenched inside with anger, pity, helplessness, fury with him for caring about something so trivial, and saying so in public. It was no one else's business to know that.

"And she paid you appropriately for the work you did for her?" Rathbone went on.

Now Monk looked surprised. "Yes . . . she did."

"Have you any idea where the money for this came from?"

"No . . . no, I haven't."

"Thank you. That is all. Mr. Fowler?"

"I am as lost as everybody else," Fowler said with rising temper.

The judge regarded Rathbone grimly. "This raises several unanswered questions, Sir Oliver, but I do not see how they bear any relevance to the poor woman's death."

"It will become clear, my lord, with the evidence of my final witness. I call Hester Monk."

She did not believe it. It made no sense. What on earth was Rathbone thinking of? Monk was staring at her. On her other side, Margaret was pale with fear, her lips red where she had bitten them. Her loyalties were tearing apart in front of her and she was helpless to control any of it.

Hester rose to her feet, her legs trembling. She walked unsteadily forward between the rows of people, feeling their eyes upon her, their loathing because she was Monk's wife, and she was furious with them for their blind judgment. But she had no power to lash out, or to defend him.

She walked across the open space, telling herself over and over again to trust Rathbone. He would never betray friendship, not for Dalgarno, nor to win a case, nor for anything else.

But what if he truly believed Dalgarno was innocent and Monk was guilty? Honor came before any friendship. You do not let the innocent hang for anyone. Not anyone at all.

She climbed up the steps, holding the rail just as Rider had done. She reached the top gasping for breath, but it was not from the physical effort, which was nothing, it was from the tight suffocation in her lungs because her heart was beating too hard, too fast, and the room was swimming around her.

She heard Rathbone saying her name. She forced herself to concentrate and answer, to state who she was and where she lived, and to swear to tell the truth, all of it, and nothing else. She focused on Rathbone's face in front and a little below her. He looked exactly as he always had, long nose, steady dark eyes, sensitive mouth full of subtle humor, a clever face, but without cruelty. He had loved her deeply not so long ago. As a friend, surely he still did?

He was speaking. She must listen.

"Is it true, Mrs. Monk, that you run a charitable house for the medical treatment of prostitutes who are ill or injured in the general area of Coldbath Square?"

"Yes . . ." Why on earth had he asked that?

"You have recently moved premises, but on the night of the death of Mr. Nolan Baltimore, was that house actually in Coldbath Square?"

"Yes . . ."

"Were you and Miss Margaret Ballinger in attendance there that night?"

"Yes, we were."

Fowler was getting noticeably restless. Rathbone very deliberately ignored him—indeed, he kept his back towards him with some effort.

"Mrs. Monk," he continued, "were there any women who came to your house injured on that night?"

She had no idea why he asked. Was it because he thought, after all, that Nolan Baltimore's death had something to do with the railway fraud? Something Monk had missed?

Everyone was watching her, waiting.

"Yes," she answered. "Yes, there were three women who came in together, and another two alone, later on."

"Badly injured?" he asked.

"Not as badly as many. One had a broken wrist." She tried to remember clearly. "The others were bruised, cut."

"Do you know how they came by their injuries?"

"No. I never ask."

"Do you know their names?"

Fowler could contain his impatience no longer. "My lord, this is all very worthy, but it is a total waste of the court's time! I—"

"It is vital to the defense, my lord!" Rathbone cut across him. "I cannot move any faster and make sense of it."

"Sense!" Fowler exploded. "This is the worst nonsense I have ever heard in twenty years in courtrooms—" He stopped abruptly.

The judge's eyebrows rose. "You may care to rephrase that observation, Mr. Fowler. As it stands it is somewhat unfortunate. On the other hand, you may wish to allow Sir Oliver to continue, in the hope that before tonight he may reach some conclusion."

Fowler sat down.

"Do you know their names, Mrs. Monk?" Rathbone asked again.

"Nell, Lizzie, and Kitty," Hester replied. "I don't ask for more than some way to address them."

"And do you tell them more than that about yourself?" he asked.

The judge frowned.

"Do you?" Rathbone insisted. "Would those women have known who you were or where you lived, for example? Please be very exact in answering, Mrs. Monk!"

She tried to think back, remembering Nell's banter, her admiration for Monk. "Yes," she said clearly. "Nell knew. She said something about my husband, his appearance, his character, and she called me by name."

Relief flooded Rathbone's face like sunlight. "Thank you. Did they by any chance also know, at least roughly, the area in which you live?"

"Yes . . . roughly."

"Did anyone happen to mention Mr. Monk's occupation?"

"Yes . . . yes, Nell did. She . . . finds him interesting."

The judge looked at Rathbone. "Are you making any progress toward a point, Sir Oliver? I fail so far to see it. I shall not allow this indefinitely."

"I am, my lord. I apologize for the time it takes, but if the whole story is not shown, then it will not make sense."

The judge made a slight grimace and sat back.

Rathbone returned his attention to Hester. "Did you continue to receive injured women in your house in Coldbath Square, Mrs. Monk?"

"Yes." Was he seeking to expose the fact that Baltimore had been the usurer in partnership with Squeaky Robinson? But why? His death had nothing to do with Dalgarno. Or Katrina Harcus.

"Were any particularly severely injured?" Rathbone pressed.

It must be what he was looking for. "Yes," she answered. "There were two in particular, we were not certain if they would live. One was knifed in the stomach, the other was beaten so hard she had fourteen broken bones in her limbs and body. We thought she might die of internal bleeding." She heard the fury in her own voice, and the pity.

There was a murmur of protest in the court, people shifting uncomfortably in their seats, embarrassed for a way of life they preferred not to know so much about, and yet stirred to emotion in spite of themselves.

The judge frowned at Rathbone. "This is appalling, but this court is not the place for a moral crusade, Sir Oliver, justified as it might be at another time."

"It is not a moral crusade, my lord, it is part of the case of the death of Katrina Harcus, and how it came about," Rathbone replied. "I have not a great deal further to go." And without waiting he spoke to Hester again. "Mrs. Monk, did you learn how these women had been so badly injured?"

"Yes. They had been respectable women, one a governess who married a man who put her into debt and then abandoned her. They both borrowed money from a usurer in order to pay what they owed, and when the debt to him could not be settled by honest means of work, he forced them into the brothel in which he was a partner, where they catered to the more unusual tastes of certain men . . ." She could not continue for the increasing sound of outrage and disgust in the courtroom.

The judge banged his gavel, and then again. Slowly the sound subsided, but the fury was still prickling in the air.

"Respectable young women, with some education, some dignity and a desire to be honest?" Rathbone said, his own voice rough with emotion.

"Yes," Hester replied. "It happens to many if they have been abandoned, put out of a job and have no reference to character—"

"Yes," he cut her off. "Did this cause you to take any action, Mrs. Monk?"

"Yes." She knew the judge's tolerance would not last a great deal longer. "I was able to learn exactly where this brothel was, and by means of questioning, who the partner was who practiced the usury. I never learned exactly who carried out the beatings or the knifing." She did not know if he wanted this part or not, but she added. "It does not continue any longer. We were able to put the brothel out of business and turn the house into better premises for the Coldbath refuge."

He smiled very slightly. "Indeed. What happened to the usurer?"

"He was killed." Did he want to know it was Baltimore? She stared at him, and could not tell.

"But his record of the debts?" he asked.

"We destroyed it."

"Did you then know he was killed?"

"Yes . . . he was a client as well as the usurer. He took his own tastes too far, and one of the women, who was new to the trade, was so revolted by what he asked of her that she lashed out at him, and he fell backwards out of the window onto the pavement beneath, to his death."

There was a rumble of profound emotion from the courtroom. Someone even cheered.

"Order!" the judge said loudly. "I will have order! I understand your outrage—indeed, I share it—but I will have respect for the law! Sir Oliver, this story is fearful, but I still see no connection to the death of Katrina Harcus, and Mr. Dalgarno's guilt or innocence in the matter."

Rathbone swiveled to face Hester again. "Mrs. Monk, among those records did you find those of the young woman, Kitty, who came to you with cuts and bruises on the night Nolan Baltimore's body was discovered in Leather Lane, near Coldbath Square?"

"Yes."

"Was she among the once-respectable young women who had been reduced to selling her body for a particularly repulsive type of abuse in order to pay the ever-mounting debt of such high rates of usury that she could never be free of it?"

"Yes."

"Could you describe her for the court, Mrs. Monk? What did she look like?"

Now she understood. It was so terrible she felt sick. The room swam around her as if she were at sea, the silence was a roar like waves. She heard Rathbone's voice only distantly.

"Mrs. Monk? Are you all right?"

She clung onto the rails, gripping them hard so the physical pain would bring her back to the moment.

"Mrs. Monk!"

"She was . . ." She gulped and licked her dry lips. "She was fairly tall, very handsome. She had dark hair and golden brown eyes . . . very beautiful. She gave me the name of Kitty . . . and the records said Kitty Hillyer . . ."

Rathbone turned very slowly to face the judge. "My lord, I believe we now know where Katrina Harcus obtained the money to dress as well as was necessary for a handsome but penniless young woman, born illegitimate, left destitute when her father died and his promised legacy did not come. She traveled south to London to try and make a fortunate marriage. However, within the space of two months her mother died, her fiancé rejected her for a richer bride, and her debts became so urgent she was drawn into the most repellent form of prostitution to satisfy the usurer, her father's colleague, a man she had known as a child and to whom she had turned for help in a strange city, and who had so betrayed her. Perhaps because of who he was, his demands revolted her so intensely that she fought him off, to his death."

The judge commanded silence in the growing swell of fury within the room, but it was several long seconds before he received it, so intense was the wave of emotion in the room. He nodded to Rathbone to continue.

"And that very night when she was taken by two other prostitutes to Coldbath Square to have her own injuries treated," Rathbone resumed, facing the jury now, "who should be the nurse who helped her, but the wife of the man who was, in her mind, the author of her grief, all the injustices against her from childhood? She heard the name of Mrs. Monk, and the description both of Monk's appearance and his nature, and his new occupation. I believe from that moment on she began to plan a terrible revenge."

A hideous, unbelievable thought danced at the edge of Hester's mind.

Fowler stood up, but did not know what to say. No one was listening to him anyway.

Hester could think only of Monk. Dalgarno, the jury, even Rathbone, melted from her vision. Monk was sitting motionless, his eyes wide and hollow, his skin bleached of every vestige of color. Margaret had moved closer to him, but she had no idea what to do to offer any word or gesture.

"Katrina Harcus had nothing left," Rathbone said quietly, but in the now total silence every word was clear. "Her mother was dead, the man she loved had deserted her, and she had no hope of ever winning him back because there was, only too obviously, nothing to win. He was incapable of love or even of honor. She was in debt beyond her means ever to repay, and she had sold her body to a particularly degraded form of prostitution from which she may well have felt she would never again be clean. And now she was also guilty of a man's death. She was wise enough in the ways of the world to know that society would see it as murder, regardless of the provocation she endured, or that she may not have intended him to die. It would be only a matter of time before the police found her, and she would live in fear of it for the rest of her life."

He spread his hands. "The one thing left for her was revenge. And fate handed her the perfect opportunity for that when she found Mrs. Monk in Coldbath Square. She knew all about the original fraud in Liverpool for which her father, Arrol Dundas, was convicted. She created the impression of another fraud almost exactly like it, knowing that Monk would not be able to resist the temptation to investigate it. The likelihood of his recognizing her was remote. She had been a child of eight when he had last seen her, if indeed he saw her at all."

He looked from the judge to the jury. "She took good care that they met in public, where they would be observed by impartial witnesses. She may have made certain Monk would be there at her house in Cuthbert Street that night. We can call Mr. Monk to the stand to testify of that, if necessary." He drew in a deep breath and faced the judge again. "That, my lord, is the purpose of Mr. Garstang's so very exact testimony. He saw her face as she fell. Inspector Runcorn described her on the ground, on her side . . . not her back. No one saw two distinct figures, and the cloak was left on the roof, my lord, because she was not thrown or pushed off—she jumped!"

He was momentarily prevented from continuing by the uproar of amazement, disbelief and horror that engulfed the room. But it faded quickly as the terrible truth sank into understanding, and then belief.

When he resumed, his voice fell into utter silence.

"My lord, Michael Dalgarno is innocent of murder, because there was no murder . . . at least not of Katrina Harcus when she went off the roof of her house and plunged to her death. As for the night she killed Nolan Baltimore, we shall—"

He was prevented from saying whatever he had intended by Livia, now lurching to her feet, her face gray.

"That's not true!" she screamed. "That's a wicked thing to say! It's a lie!" Her voice choked in a sob. "An evil . . . terrible thing to say! My father . . ." She lashed her arms left and right as if fighting her way through some physical obstacle. "My father would never have done anything like that! It's . . . it's filthy! It's disgusting! I saw those women—they were . . ." The tears were streaming down her face. "They were broken, bleeding . . . whoever did that was monstrous!"

Rathbone looked wretched. He struggled for something, anything, to say to ease her grief, but there was nothing left.

"That can't be how he died!" Livia went on, turning from Rathbone to the judge. "He quarreled dreadfully with Michael and Jarvis that night!" she said desperately. "It was over the railway again, the huge order we have for the new brakes they've invented. Michael and Jarvis did it together, and Papa only found out that night, my lord! He flew into a terrible rage and said they'd ruin the company, because years ago Mr. Monk had forced him to sign a letter promising he would never manufacture the brakes again. He'd paid a fortune to silence somebody, but the price was that nobody would ever use them . . ."

Monk shot to his feet. "Where's Jarvis Baltimore?" he shouted at Livia. "Where is he?"

She stared at him. "The train," she said chokingly. "The inaugural run."

Monk said something to Margaret, then looked at Hester once where she still stood in the witness-box, then he scrambled past the people next to him and ran up the aisle and out of the door.

The judge looked at Rathbone. "Do you understand, Sir Oliver?"

"No, my lord." He turned to the witness-box. "Hester?"

"The rail crash sixteen years ago," she answered. "I think . . . I think he knows what caused it now." She looked at Livia. "I'm sorry . . . I wouldn't have told you. I wish you hadn't had to know. Most people get to keep their secrets."

Livia stood for a moment, the tears running down her cheeks, then slowly she sank to her seat and buried her face in her hands.

"I'm so sorry . . ." Hester said again. She hated Nolan Baltimore as much for what he had done to his own family as for the injury to Katrina and Alice and Fanny, and the other women like them. They might recover. She did not know if Livia would.

Rathbone looked at Dalgarno, white and bitter in the dock, then to the judge. "My lord, I move that the charges against the accused be dropped. Katrina Harcus was not murdered. She took her own life in a desperate attempt to achieve the only thing she believed was left to her—revenge."

The judge looked at Fowler.

Fowler swiveled around to stare at the jury, then back at the judge. "I concede," he said with a shrug. "God help her. . . ."

Outside the courtroom the street was almost empty, and it took Monk only five minutes to find a hansom and scramble in, shouting to the driver to take him to Euston Station as fast as the horse would go. An extra pound was in it for him if he made the inaugural train on the new line to Derby. Monk would willingly have given him more, but he had nothing else to spare. He must keep what he had in case he had to bribe his way onto the train.

The cabbie took him at his word, and with a yell of encouragement at the horse, and a long flick of the whip practically between its ears, set off as if on a racetrack.

It was a hair-raising journey with several close shaves where they missed other vehicles by inches, and more than once pedestrians leaped for their lives, some hurling abuse as they went. The cab pulled into the station and lurched to a stop. Monk thrust the money at the driver because he felt the man deserved it whether they had made the train or not, and sprinted to the platform.

Actually he was there with more than five minutes in hand. He straightened his jacket, ran his hand over his hair, and sauntered up to the door of the rearmost carriage as if he had every right to be there.

Without glancing around to see if he had been observed, which could have given away his lack of invitation, he pulled the handle, swung the door wide, and climbed in.

The inside of the carriage was beautifully furnished. It was a long train, but only first- and second-class. This was second, and still of a luxury to be admired. No doubt Jarvis Baltimore would be in the first-class. Since his father's death this was his train, his entire enterprise. He would be busy talking to all the various dignitaries making this journey, boasting to them of the new track, the new carriages, and perhaps of the new braking system with its fatal weakness. Although presumably he did not know the full truth of that.

There would be several stops along the route. Monk would make his way forward on each of them until he found Jarvis.

He nodded to the other people in his compartment, then sat down on one of the polished wooden seats.

There was a jolt. Somewhere ahead the whistle blew and the carriage jerked forward, and again, then settled into gathering momentum. Billows of steam drifted past the windows. There were shouts from outside and cries of excitement and triumph from the other compartments, and through the open windows of the carriages ahead someone called out a toast and yelled "Hooray!"

Monk settled in for the journey, expecting the best part of an hour to elapse before he had an opportunity to find Baltimore. But they were on double track all of that distance. He knew the route probably as well as Baltimore himself.

The train was gathering speed. The gray streets and roofs of the city were sliding away. There were more trees, open land.

There were foot warmers in the compartment, one close by him, but he was still cold; in fact, he started to shiver. There was nothing he could do about Baltimore until the first stop. His mind was filling at last with the knowledge he had forced from it since the moment he had realized about the brakes, and that it could happen again.

There had been no murder of Katrina Harcus, at least not from the roof in Cuthbert Street. He could see her face with its brilliant eyes as if she were in the seat opposite him. But nothing was the same as it had seemed. It was clear now: she had orchestrated the whole thing with passion and extraordinary skill, even to tearing the button off his coat and clasping it in her hand when she fell—jumped.

It made him cold to the pit of his stomach to know that she had hated him enough to leap deliberately into the darkness and crash, breaking her body on the stones beneath, into the abyss of death and whatever lay beyond it, simply to know that he would be destroyed with her.

And how close she had come to succeeding!

It was a dark and fearful thing to be hated so deeply by another human being. It could never be retrieved, because she was dead. He could not explain himself, tell her why, soften any of the tearing, wounding edges.

And she was Arrol Dundas's daughter! That was an indelible wound never to be eased away.

He sat huddled, avoiding the eyes of the other man in the compartment, until the first stop, then he got out, as did everyone else. When the whistle blew for the next leg of the journey he got into one of the first-class carriages and moved from compartment to compartment through the polished wood, the warmth, the soft seats, but Baltimore was not there.

He got out again at the next station and moved forward, and at the next. Time was getting short. He felt a flutter of panic. He found him at last in the front carriage. He must have gone forward also, to speak to every one of his guests. Indeed, he was talking to a portly gentleman with a glass of champagne in his hand.

Monk must attract his attention, if possible in a manner which would not cause embarrassment. He moved discreetly until he was close enough to grasp Baltimore's arm by the elbow, firmly, so he could not brush him off.

Baltimore turned to him, startled by the pain. He recognized Monk after a second's hesitation, and his face hardened.

"Mr. Baltimore," Monk said levelly, staring at him without blinking. "I have news for you from London which you need to hear as soon as possible. I think privately would be best."

Baltimore took his meaning and was eager not to mar his moment of triumph with an awkward interview. "Excuse me, gentlemen," he said with a smile that did not reach his eyes. "I will only be a moment. Please enjoy yourselves. Accept our hospitality." He turned to Monk, saying something under his breath as he half pushed him out of the door into an unoccupied compartment of the carriage they were in.

"What the devil are you doing here?" he demanded. "I thought by now they'd be questioning you on Dundas's money! Or is that what you're doing? Attempting to escape!"

His face hardened. "Well, I'm damned if I'll help you. My father told me on the night of his death how you tried to put him out of business. What was that for? Revenge because he exposed Dundas?"

"I tried to save hundreds of lives—without putting you out of business!" Monk said between his teeth. He kept his grasp on Baltimore's arm. "For God's sake, just hold your tongue and listen. We haven't much time. If—"

"Liar!" Baltimore snarled. "I know you made my father sign a letter that he would never manufacture the brakes again. What did you threaten him with? He's not an easy man to frighten . . . what did you do to him?" He snatched his arm away from Monk's grip. "Well, you won't frighten me. I'll see you in jail first."

"Why do you think your father agreed to it?" Monk demanded, containing his temper with intense difficulty as he stared at Baltimore's arrogant, angry face, and felt the train sway and jolt beneath them as it gathered speed, hurtling towards the long incline, and the viaduct beyond. "Just because I asked him?"

"I don't know," Baltimore replied. "But I won't give in to you!"

"Your father never did favors for anyone," Monk said between his teeth. "He stopped manufacturing the brakes after the Liverpool crash because I paid to have the enquiry return a verdict of human error, not to ruin the company . . . but on condition he signed that letter never to make them anymore." He startled himself with the clarity with which he remembered standing in Nolan Baltimore's magnificent office with its views of the Mersey River, and seeing Baltimore sit at his desk, his face red, his head shaking with shock and fury as he wrote the letter Monk dictated, and then signed it. The sunlight had been streaming across the floor, picking out the worn patches on the lush, green carpet. The books on the shelves were leather bound, the wood of the desk polished walnut. This was the piece at last! This was it! It made sense of it all.

Now Jarvis Baltimore stared at him, his eyes round and

wide, his chest heaving as he fought for breath. He gulped and tried to clear his throat. "What . . . what are you saying? That the Liverpool crash . . ." He stopped, unable to put it into words.

"Yes," Monk said harshly; there was no time to spare anyone's feelings. "The crash was due to your brakes failing. There were two hundred children on that excursion train!" He saw the blood drain from Baltimore's skin, leaving it pasty white. "And there must be a hundred people on this one. Order the driver to stop while you still can."

"What money?" Baltimore argued, struggling to deny it, shaking his head. "How would you get enough money to silence an enquiry? That's absurd. You're trying . . . I don't know why—to cover yourself! You stole Dundas's money. You had charge of it all! You didn't even leave anything for his widow—damn you!"

"Dundas's money!" Monk tried not to shout at him. They were both swaying back and forth now. The train was gathering speed fast. "He agreed to it. You don't think I would have touched it otherwise, do you? The man was in jail, not dead. I gave them all there was, apart from the little bit for her, but hell—it wasn't much! It took almost everything there was to make them keep silent on the truth."

Baltimore was still fighting it. "Dundas was a fraudster. He'd already cheated the company of—"

"No, he wasn't!" The truth was there at last, bright and sharp as daylight breaking. "He was innocent! He warned your father that they hadn't tested the brakes well enough, but nobody listened to him. He had no proof, but he would have got it, only they framed him for fraud, and after that nobody believed anything he said. He told me . . . but there was nothing I could do either. It was only his word, and by then he was branded."

Baltimore shook his head, but the denial died on his lips.

"It took all the money I could scrape together," Monk went on. "But it saved the company's reputation. And your father swore he'd tar Dundas with the same brush if I didn't succeed. We couldn't sue the driver. Better he be blamed than everyone put out of work. We took care of his family." He felt a stab of shame. "But that wasn't good enough. It wasn't his fault . . . it was your father's. And now you're going to do the same—unless you stop this train."

Baltimore shook his head more fiercely, his eyes wild, his voice high-pitched. "But we're supplying those brakes all over India! There's tens of thousands of pounds of orders!" he protested.

"Recall them!" Monk shouted at him. "But first tell the driver to stop this bloody train before the brakes fail and we come off the viaduct!"

"Will . . . will they?" Baltimore said hoarsely. "They worked perfectly well when we tested them. I'm not a fool."

"They only fail on an incline, with a certain load," Monk told him, shards of memory falling into place more vividly every moment. He could remember this same feeling of urgency before, the same rattle of wheels over the rail ties, the roar of movement, steel on steel, the knowledge of disaster ahead.

"Most of the time they're excellent," he went on. "But when the weight and the speed get above a certain level and with a curve in the track, then they don't hold. This is a far heavier train than usual, and there's exactly such a place just before the viaduct ahead. We can't be far from it now. Don't stand there, for God's sake! Go and tell the driver to slow up, then stop! Go on!"

"I don't believe it. . . ." It was a protest, and a lie. It was clear in Baltimore's frantic eyes and dry lips.

The train was already gathering speed. They were finding it harder to stand upright, even though Baltimore had his back against the carriage wall.

"Are you sure enough of that to risk your life?" Monk asked, his voice ruthless. "I'm not. I'm going, with or without you." And he backed away, almost losing his balance as he turned and started towards the other compartments and the front of the carriage next to the engine.

Baltimore jerked around and plunged after him.

Monk charged through the next compartment, scattering

the few company men along for the inaugural ride. They were too startled to block his way.

He felt a wild exhilaration unlike anything he had known in years. He could remember! Dreadful as some of the memory was, filled with pain and grief, with helplessness and the knowledge that Dundas was innocent and he had not saved him, it was no longer confusion. It was as clear as the reality of the moment. He had failed Dundas, but he had not betrayed him. He had been honest. He knew that, not from evidence or from other people's word, but from his own mind.

He was in the next compartment, pushing through the men, who were angry at his intrusion. The train, hurtling through the countryside toward the incline and the single track of the viaduct, brought back the time before when he had been on that other train, as if it had all been only weeks ago. He remembered Dundas telling him how he had tried to persuade Nolan Baltimore to wait, test the brakes more carefully, and Baltimore had refused. There was no proof, only Dundas's fear.

"Excuse me! Excuse me!" he cried more sharply. They parted for him.

One caught at his sleeve. "What's wrong?" he said anxiously, feeling the carriage pitching from side to side.

"Nothing!" Monk lied. "Excuse me!" He jerked free and went on forward, Baltimore on his heels now.

Then Dundas had been accused of the fraud, and Monk had forgotten about brakes in the fear and dismay of trying to prove his innocence. But there was too much evidence, carefully placed. Dundas was tried, convicted, sent to prison.

Less than a month later there had been the crash . . . a day exactly like this one, another train roaring through the peace of the countryside, belching steam and sparks, blindly careering toward a death of mangled steel and blood and flames.

Monk had realized it all, but it was too late to do anything but save what he could out of the pieces, and stop Baltimore from doing it again. Dundas had been more than willing to give everything he owned to stop it.

That was it! The last piece falling into place, sickeningly, making Monk halt where he stood at the end of the carriage behind the engine. Baltimore, a step behind, knocked against him and all but drove the air out of his lungs.

He had not known it at the time he had handed the money to Baltimore to bribe the enquiry, he had known it afterwards, when it could not be undone. It was not to protect Dundas's reputation, or the Baltimore company, although that mattered, a thousand men and their families. Nolan Baltimore had said he would implicate Monk in the faulty brakes. It had been his signature on the banking forms that had provided the money for their development. It had been to save Monk that Dundas had been prepared to sacrifice everything he had left.

As he lunged forward, forced open the carriage door against the onrushing air and stepped out onto the narrow ledge at the side, clinging to the door frame, it was more than the wind, the steam and the smuts that stung his skin and his eyes, it was an agony of memory, a sacrifice, a loss, the price of his own escape from ruin and prison as well.

He turned to see how far he had to inch along the carriage until he could scramble onto the plates that connected the carriage to the coal wagon and the engine.

Baltimore was screaming something behind him.

By then Dundas had understood what the price was. He might even have felt the jail fever in his bones and known he would die there. Certainly he knew the hatred of the injured and the bereaved after the crash. Blame for it would have destroyed any man, dogged him for the rest of his life. Poverty was a small price in comparison. Perhaps he trusted that his wife would have borne that lightly compared with Monk's ruin. He might even have discussed it with her.

Maybe that was why she had smiled even as she wept for him when she told Monk of his death.

He must move. The train was still increasing speed. If his hand slipped, if he lost his hold on the door frame, he would be dead in seconds. He must not look down. The countryside was a blur, like something seen through a rain-smeared window.

He started to inch along, moving his hands then his feet. It was not far to the front of the carriage, two yards maybe, but they were the longest two yards on earth.

There was no time to delay, no time to think. He put one hand along as far as he dared, and stretched his foot to grip. He let go with the other hand and jerked his body forward. The carriage swayed and he slipped, and grasped again. He almost fell onto the footplate behind the coal wagon, the sweat breaking out on his body until his clothes were cold and wet against his skin.

He turned to see Baltimore teetering on the edge, white with terror, and shot out his hand to haul him in. Baltimore's knees crumpled and he sank down onto the plate.

The noise was indescribable. Monk gestured toward the coal wagon.

Baltimore clambered to his feet, waving his hands.

"He'll never hear us!" he shouted desperately. His hair flying, whipped about his head, his face wild-eyed, wind stung, already splotched with smuts.

Monk waved at the coal wagon again and moved toward it.

"You can't!" Baltimore screamed at him, shrinking back against the carriage wall.

"I damn well can!" Monk yelled. "And so can you! Come on!"

Baltimore was plainly terrified of the thought of struggling to climb up the wagon into the loose coal and trying to crawl on hands and knees over it in the teeth of the choking steam as the train careered over the rails, growing faster and faster, lurching from one side to the other. The long slope was steepening ahead of them, and Monk could see the sweep beyond and down to the viaduct as if it were in his mind's eye.

He swiveled around to face Baltimore. "Is there anything else due on this line?" he shouted, driving his hand the other way to illustrate his meaning.

Baltimore put his hand up to his face, now ashen gray. He nodded very slightly. Like a man in a nightmare, he stepped forward, swayed, righted himself, and put his hands onto the coal wagon. It was a more powerful and terrible answer than any words could have been.

Monk followed after him, scrambling up onto the rough lumps of coal and feeling the wind batter him and the wagon's bucket around like a ship at sea.

The stoker turned, shovel in his hand. His mouth fell open at the sight. Baltimore, his fair hair streaming back, his face fixed in a grimace of terror, was clambering over the coal toward the engine. A yard behind him, Monk followed, more agile.

The stoker threw down his shovel and lunged toward Baltimore.

Baltimore screamed something at him, but the sound was torn from his lips.

The stoker came forward, hands outstretched.

The train was going ever faster as the incline steepened.

Monk made a desperate effort to claw himself forward and catch up with Baltimore. The coal rolled underneath him. A large lump unsettled and fell sideways, and he slid after it, narrowly missing injuring his shoulder against the mound above.

He heaved himself up, disregarding his torn hands, and threw his weight forward.

Baltimore was almost on top of the stoker.

Monk yelled at him, but his voice was drowned in the roar and crash of steel on steel and the howl of the wind.

Baltimore fell forward and the stoker went down with him.

Monk hauled himself up and swung around to land on his feet.

The brakeman was staring at him, his face streaming sweat as he struggled with the lever and felt it yield. The driver was coming toward them, waving his arms.

Suddenly, Monk knew what to do. He had done it before, hurling his weight and his strength against the brakes, and feeling them rip out just as they were now. He knew exactly what it was, and the memory of it turned him sick with terror. Only then he had been in the rear wagon of the train, and the impact had thrown him off, to roll over and over, bruised and bleeding down the slope but alive—while the others died. That was the guilt that stabbed through his mind with pain—

he had survived, and they had not—not one of them. They had all been crushed in that inferno of flame and steel.

"Stoke!" he yelled with all the power of his lungs. He swung his arms. He understood now what they must do, the only chance. "The brakes are gone! They're no use! Go faster!"

Behind him, Baltimore and the stoker were struggling to their feet. He swiveled around. "Stoke!" he mouthed to Baltimore. "Faster!" He swung his arms.

Baltimore looked terrified. The stoker made to move forward and catch Monk and restrain him physically. Baltimore charged at him. The two of them rocked and swayed as the train roared through the gathering dusk, pitching like a ship in a storm.

Monk picked up the fallen shovel and started to heave more coal into the boiler. It was already yellow hot at the heart, and the blast from it scorched his face, but he threw in more, and then more. They had to pass over the viaduct before the other train came; it was the only chance. Nothing on earth could slow them now.

Baltimore was shouting behind him, waving his arms like a windmill. The stoker was stupefied. Suddenly his kingdom was invaded by madmen, his train was screaming through the twilight like a rocket on fire, and the single-track viaduct lay ahead with another train due on it in minutes.

Then at last the brakeman understood. He had felt the brakes tear out and knew how useless it was to hurl his weight or strength against them anymore. He picked up the other shovel and worked beside Monk.

They were going faster, ever faster. The sound was deafening, like a solid thing against the head; the heat seared the skin, burned the eyelashes; and still they threw the coal on, until the stoker grabbed Monk by the arm and pulled him back. He shook his head. He held his arms across his chest, then flung them wide.

Monk understood. Any more and the boiler would explode. There was nothing to do now but wait, and perhaps pray. They were going as fast as any engine on earth could take them. Sparks were flying in the air, steam like clouds tore from the stack and shredded in the wind. The wheels on the track were one continuous roar.

The viaduct was in sight, and the next moment they were on it.

Monk looked at Baltimore and saw the terror in his face, and a kind of jubilation. There was nothing now but to wait. Either they would make the end of the single track in time, or there would be a crash that would explode and send the wreckage a thousand yards in every direction until there was nothing human left to find on the rocks below.

The breath was torn from their lips; the wind burned and stung with ash, smuts, red sparks like hornets. Their clothes were torn and singed.

The noise was like an avalanche falling.

But Monk had been right: Dundas was innocent, the brakes were as he had said. He had paid a terrible price for it, but knowing it, willing it, to save a young man he had loved profoundly, selflessly, and without limit—love greater than Katrina's hate, to be held in the heart forever.

And now his name would be vindicated!

There was a darkness, an even greater noise, and something rushed by them so quickly it was gone before Monk even realized they were on double tracks again. It had been the train in the other direction. They were safe.

Around them, the other men let off a cheer, but he could hear nothing of it, only see in the furnace light their upraised arms and the triumph in their blackened faces. The driver staggered back against the wall, the controls barely in his grasp. The stoker and the brakeman clasped each other.

Jarvis Baltimore held out his hand and Monk took it.

"Thank you!" Baltimore mouthed. "Thank you, Monk! For the past, and the present!"

Monk found himself grinning idiotically, and could think of nothing at all to say. Anyway he could not have spoken; his voice was choked with tears.

A note from
Anne Perry
introducing her new novel

NO GRAVES AS YET

*Now available in hardcover
from Ballantine Books*

Dear Reader,

First, I would like to thank you for your unwavering support over the last twenty-five years for my two Victorian series—the suspense novels featuring Thomas and Charlotte Pitt and, more recently, William Monk and Hester Latterly. The enthusiasm and loyalty you have brought to my books is genuinely appreciated.

Now I would like to introduce you to *No Graves As Yet*, the first novel in a new series I am very excited about. The idea came to me as I learned more about my maternal grandfather, who studied at Cambridge University before serving as a chaplain in the trenches during World War I. He is the inspiration for my hero, whom I have named Joseph Reavley. Joseph, his brother, and two sisters are the characters through whose eyes I plan to write this new series—with each novel addressing the issues of war, ethical decisions, loss and heroism.

Joseph, the oldest child in the Reavley family, is a Bible languages professor at Cambridge before becoming a chaplain on the front line; Matthew is in the Secret Intelligence Service; Hannah stays in England and experiences the shattering social changes on the home front; and Judith drives an ambulance in France and Belgium. Hers is the great love story of the five books.

Each novel is separate and complete unto itself, but there is one story of supreme ambition and betrayal that spans throughout all five, and it is not resolved until the very last pages of the final book, set in 1918. I hope you will find these novels a passionate and human look at the Great War—which was the end of the old order and the beginning of modern times.

As a preamble, I give you the opening pages of *No Graves As Yet*. . . .

Sincerely

It was a golden afternoon in late June, a perfect day for cricket. The sun burned in a cloudless sky, and the breeze was barely sufficient to stir the slender, pale skirts of the women as they stood on the grass at Fenner's Field, parasols in hand. The men, in white flannels, were relaxed and smiling.

St. John's were batting and Gonville and Caius were fielding. The bowler pounded up to the crease and sent the ball down fast, but a bit short and wide. Elwyn Allard leaned forward, and with an elegant cover drive, dispatched the ball to the boundary for four runs.

Joseph Reavley joined in the applause. Elwyn was one of his students, rather more graceful with the bat than with the pen. He had little of the scholastic brilliance of his brother, Sebastian, but he had a manner that was easy to like, and a sense of honor that drove him like a spur.

St. John's still had four more batsmen to play, young men from all over England who had come to Cambridge and, for one reason or another, remained at college through the long summer vacation.

Elwyn hit a modest two. The heat was stirred by a faint breath of wind from across the fenlands with their dykes and marshes, flat under the vast skies stretching eastward to the sea. It was old land, quiet, cut by secret waterways, Saxon churches marking each village. It had been the last stronghold of resistance against the Norman invasion eight and a half centuries ago.

On the field one of the boys just missed a catch. There was a gasp and then a letting out of breath. All this mattered. Such things could win or lose a match, and they would be playing against Oxford again soon. To be beaten would be catastrophic.

Across the town behind them, the clock on the north tower at Trinity struck three, each chime on the large A-flat bell, then followed the instant after on the smaller E-flat. Joseph thought how out of place it seemed, to think of time on an eternal afternoon like this. A few feet away, Harry Beecher caught his eye and smiled. Beecher had been a Trinity man in his own years as a student, and it was a long-standing joke that the Trinity clock struck once for itself and once for St. John's.

A cheer went up as the ball hit the stumps and Elwyn was bowled out with a very respectable score of eighty-three. He walked off with a little wave of acknowledgment and was replaced at the crease by Lucian Foubister, who was a little too bony, but Joseph knew his awkwardness was deceiving. He was more tenacious than many gave him credit for, and he had flashes of extraordinary grace.

Play resumed with the sharp crack of a strike and the momentary cheers under the burning blue of the sky.

Aidan Thyer, master of St. John's, stood motionless a few yards from Joseph, his hair flaxen in the sun, his thoughts apparently far away. His wife Connie, standing next to him, glanced across and gave a little shrug. Her dress was white broderie anglaise, falling loosely in a flare below the hip, and the fashionable slender skirt reached to the ground. She looked as elegant and feminine as a spray of daisies, even though it was the hottest summer in England for years.

At the far end of the pitch Foubister struck an awkward shot, elbows in all the wrong places, and sent the ball right to the boundary. There was a shout of approval, and everyone clapped.

Joseph was aware of a movement somewhere behind him and half turned, expecting a grounds official, perhaps to say it was time for lemonade and cucumber sandwiches. But it was his own brother, Matthew, who was walking toward him, his shoulders tight, no grace in his movement. He was wearing a light gray city suit, as if he had newly arrived from London.

Joseph started across the green, anxiety rising quickly. Why was his brother here in Cambridge, interrupting a match on a Sunday afternoon?

"Matthew! What is it?" he said as he reached him.

Matthew stopped. His face was so pale it seemed almost bloodless. He was twenty-eight, seven years the younger, broader-shouldered, and fair where Joseph was dark. He was steadying himself with difficulty, and he gulped before he found his voice. "It's . . ." He cleared his throat. There was a kind of desperation in his eyes. "It's Mother and Father," he said hoarsely. "There's been an accident."

Joseph refused to grasp what he had said. "An accident?"

Matthew nodded, struggling to govern his ragged breathing. "In the car. They are both . . . dead."

For a moment the words had no meaning for Joseph. Instantly his father's face came to his mind, lean and gentle, blue eyes steady. It was impossible that he could be dead.

"The car went off the road," Matthew was saying. "Just before the Hauxton Mill Bridge." His voice sounded strange and far away.

Behind Joseph they were still playing cricket. He heard the sound of the ball and another burst of applause.

"Joseph . . ." Matthew's hand was on his arm, the grip tight.

Joseph nodded and tried to speak, but his throat was dry.

"I'm sorry," Matthew said quietly. "I wish I hadn't had to tell you like this. I . . ."

"It's all right, Matthew. I'm . . ." He changed his mind, still trying to grasp the reality. "The Hauxton Road? Where were they going?"

Matthew's fingers tightened on his arm. They began to walk slowly, close together, over the sun-baked grass. There was a curious dizziness in the heat. The sweat trickled down Joseph's skin, and inside he was cold.

Matthew stopped again.

"Father telephoned me late yesterday evening," he replied huskily, as if the words were almost unbearable for him. "He said someone had given him a document outlining a conspiracy so hideous it would change the world we know—that it would ruin England and everything we stand for. Forever." He sounded defiant now, the muscles of his neck and jaw clenched as if he barely had mastery of himself.

Joseph's mind whirled. What should he do? The words hardly made sense. John Reavley had been a member of Parliament until 1912, two years ago. He had resigned for reasons he had not discussed, but he had never lost his interest in political affairs, nor his care for honesty in government. Perhaps he had simply been ready to spend more time reading, indulging his love of philosophy, poking around in antique and secondhand shops looking for a bargain. More often he was just talking with people, listening to stories, swapping eccentric jokes, and adding to his collection of limericks.

"A conspiracy to ruin England and everything we stand for?" Joseph repeated incredulously.

"No," Matthew corrected him with precision. "A conspiracy that *would* ruin it. That was not the main purpose, simply a side effect."

"What conspiracy? By whom?" Joseph demanded.

Matthew's skin was so white it was almost gray. "I don't know. He was bringing it to me . . . today."

Joseph started to ask why, and then stopped. The answer was the one thing that made sense. Suddenly at least two facts cohered. John Reavley had wanted Joseph to study medicine, and when his firstborn son had left it for the church, he had then wanted Matthew to become a doctor. But Matthew had read modern history and languages here at Cambridge, and then he joined the Secret Intelligence Service. If there was such a plot, John would understandably have notified his younger son. Not his elder.

Joseph swallowed, the air catching in his throat. "I see."

Matthew's grip eased on him slightly. He had known the news longer and had more time to grasp its truth. He was searching Joseph's face with anxiety, evidently trying to formulate something to say to help him through the pain.

Joseph made an immense effort. "I see," he repeated. "We must go to them. Where . . . are they?"

"At the police station in Great Shelford," Matthew answered. He made a slight movement with his head. "I've got my car."

"Does Judith know?"

Matthew's face tightened. "Yes. They didn't know where to find you or me, so they called her."

That was reasonable—obvious, really. Judith was their younger sister, still living at home. Hannah, between Joseph and Matthew, was married to a naval officer and lived in Portsmouth. It would be the house in Selborne St. Giles that the police would have called. He thought how Judith would be feeling, alone except for the servants, knowing neither her father nor mother would come home again, not tonight, not any night.

His thoughts were interrupted by someone at his elbow. He had not even heard footsteps on the grass. He half turned and saw Harry Beecher standing beside him, his wry, sensitive face puzzled.

"Is everything . . . ?" he began. Then, seeing Joseph's eyes, he stopped. "Can I help?" he said simply.

Joseph shook his head a little. "No . . . no, there isn't anything." He made an effort to pull his thoughts together. "My parents have had an accident." He took a deep breath. "They've been killed." How odd and flat the words sounded. They still carried no reality with them.

Beecher was appalled. "Oh, God! I'm so sorry!"

"Please—" Joseph started.

"Of course," Beecher interrupted. "I'll tell people. Just go." He touched Joseph lightly on the arm. "Let me know if I can do anything."

"Yes, of course. Thank you." Joseph shook his head and started to walk away as Matthew acknowledged Beecher, then turned to cross the wide expanse of grass. Joseph followed him without looking back at the players in their white flannels, bright in the sunlight. They had been the only reality a few moments ago; now there seemed an unbridgeable space between them.

Outside the cricket ground Matthew's Sunbeam Talbot was parked in Gonville Place. In one fluid motion Joseph climbed over the side and into the passenger seat. The car was facing north, as if Matthew had been to St. John's first and then come all the way through town to the cricket ground looking for Joseph. Now he turned southwest again, back along Gonville Place and finally onto the Trumpington Road.

There was nothing to say now; each was cocooned in his own pain, waiting for the moment when they would have to face the physical proof of death. The familiar winding road with its harvest fields shining gold in the heat, the hedgerows, and the motionless trees were like things painted on the other side of a wall that encased the mind. Joseph was aware of them only as a bright blur.

Matthew drove as if it demanded his entire concentration, clutching the steering wheel with hands he had to loosen deliberately now and then.

South of the village they turned left through St. Giles, skirted the side of the hill over the railway bridge into Great Shelford, and pulled up outside the police station. A somber sergeant met them, his face tired, his body hunched, as if he had had to steel himself for the task.

"Oi'm terrible sorry, sir." He looked from one to the other of them, biting his lower lip. "Wouldn't ask it if Oi din't 'ave to."

"I know," Joseph said quickly. He did not want a conversation. Now that they were here, he needed to proceed as quickly as possible, while his self-control lasted.

Matthew made a small gesture forward, and the sergeant turned and led the way the short distance through the streets to the hospital mortuary. It was all very formal, a routine the sergeant must have been through scores of times: sudden death, shocked families moving as if in a dream, murmuring polite words, hardly aware of what they were saying, trying to understand what had happened and at the same time deny it.

They stepped out of the sunlight into the sudden darkness of the building. Joseph went ahead. The windows were open to try to keep the air cool and the closeness less oppressive. The corridors were narrow, echoing, and they smelled of stone and carbolic.

The sergeant opened the door to a side room and ushered Joseph and Matthew in. There were two bodies laid out on trolleys, covered decently in white sheets.

Joseph felt his heart lurch. In a moment it would be real, irreversible, a part of his own life ended. He clung to the second of disbelief, the last, precious instant of *now*, before it all changed.